About the Authors

Melanie Milburne read her first Mills & Boon at age seventeen in between studying for her final exams. After completing a Masters Degree in Education she decided to write a novel, and thus her career as a romance author was born. Melanie is an ambassador for the Australian Childhood Foundation, a keen dog lover and trainer, and enjoys long walks in the Tasmanian bush. In 2015 Melanie won the HOLT Medallion, a prestigious award honouring outstanding literary talent.

USA TODAY bestselling author **Kat Cantrell** read her first Mills & Boon novel in third grade and has been scribbling in notebooks since she learned to spell. She's a So You Think You Can Write winner and a Romance Writers of America Golden Heart® Award finalist. Kat, her husband, and their two boys live in north Texas.

Lindsay Armstrong was born in South Africa. She grew up with three ambitions: to become a writer, to travel the world, and to be a game ranger. She managed two out of three! When Lindsay went to work it was in travel and this started her on the road to seeing the world. It wasn't until her youngest child started school that Lindsay sat down at the kitchen table determined to tackle her other ambition — to stop dreaming about writing and do it! She hasn't stopped since.

One Night...

One Night...
of Convenience

MELANIE MILBURNE

KAT CANTRELL

LINDSAY ARMSTRONG

MILLS & BOON

First Published in Great Britain 2023
By Mills & Boon, an imprint of HarperCollins*Publishers,* Ltd
1 London Bridge Street, London, SE1 9GF

www.harpercollins.co.uk

HarperCollins*Publishers*
Macken House, 39/40 Mayor Street Upper,
Dublin 1, D01 C9W8, Ireland

ISBN: 978-0-263-31862-3

MIX
Paper | Supporting
responsible forestry
FSC™ C007454

BOUND BY A
ONE-NIGHT VOW

MELANIE MILBURNE

To my three writing doggy companions,
Polly, Lily and Gonzo, who through the writing
of this particular novel pulled me through the
rough patches with their funny antics
and adorable ways. xxx

CHAPTER ONE

ISABELLA BYRNE PUT down her coffee cup in the crowded café with a sigh. Husband-hunting would be so much easier if she actually wanted to get married. She. Did. Not. The thought of marrying someone was enough to bring her out in hives. Anaphylactic shock. A stroke. She wasn't the girl who'd been planning her wedding day since the age of five. She wasn't a hankering-after-the-fairy-tale fanatic like most of her friends. And now that she'd put her 'wild child' days behind her, even the thought of dating made her want to vomit.

She was Over Men.

Izzy looked at all the couples sitting at the other tables. Was no one single any more in London? Everyone had a partner. She was the only person sitting by herself.

She could have tried online dating in her find-a-husband quest, but the thought of asking a stranger was too daunting. And the small handful of friends she might have considered asking to do the job were already in committed relationships.

Izzy folded her copy of her father's will and stuffed

it back in her tote bag. No matter how many times she read it, the words were exactly the same. She must be married in order to claim her inheritance. The inheritance would go to a distant relative if she didn't claim it. To a relative who had a significant gambling problem.

How could she let all that money be frittered away down the greedy gobbling mouth of a slot machine?

Izzy needed that money to buy back her late mother's ancestral home. If she failed to claim her inheritance, then the house would be lost for ever. The gorgeous Wiltshire house, where she had spent a precious few but wonderful holidays with her grandparents and her older brother before he got sick and passed away, would be sold to someone else. She couldn't bear the thought of losing the one place where she had been happy. Where she and Hamish and her mother had been happy. Truly happy. She owed it to her mother and brother's memory to get that house back.

There was twenty-four hours left before the deadline. One day to find a man willing to marry her and stay married for six months. *One flipping day.* Why hadn't she looked a little harder this month? Last month? The month before? She'd had three months to fulfil the terms of her father's will, but the thought of marrying anyone had made her procrastinate. As usual. She might have failed at school but she had First Class Honours in Procrastination.

Izzy was about to push back her chair to leave when a tall shadow fell over her. Her heart gave an extra beat…or maybe that was the double macchiato she'd had. She should never mix caffeine with despair.

'Is this seat taken?' The deep baritone with its rich and cultured Italian accent made her scalp prickle and a tingling pool of heat simmer at the base of her spine.

Izzy raised her eyes to meet the espresso-black gaze of hotel magnate, Andrea Vaccaro. Something shifted in her belly—a tumble, a tingle, a tightening.

It was impossible to look at his handsome features without her heart fluttering like rapidly shuffled cards.

Eyes that didn't just look at you—they penetrated. Seeing things they had no business seeing.

His strong, don't-mess-with-me jaw, with just the right amount of stubble, always made her think of the potent male hormones pushing those spikes of black hair out through his skin. A mouth that was firm but had a tendency to curve over a cynical smile. A mouth that made her think of long, sensual kisses and the sexy tangling of tongues…

Izzy had taught herself over the years not to show how he affected her. But while her expression was cool and composed on the outside, on the inside she was fighting a storm of unbidden, forbidden attraction. 'I'm just leaving so—'

His broad tanned hand came down on the back of the chair opposite hers. She couldn't stop staring at the ink-black hairs that ran from the back of his hand and over his strong wrist to disappear under the crisp white cuff of his shirt. How many times had she fantasised about those hands on her body? Stroking her. Caressing her. Making her feel things she shouldn't be feeling. Not for him.

Never for him.

'No time for a quick coffee with a friend?' His mouth curved over the words, showing a flash of white, perfectly aligned teeth. An I've-got-you-where-I-want-you smile that made the fine hairs on the back of her neck stand up and pirouette in panic.

Izzy suppressed a shiver and forced herself to hold his gaze. 'Friend?' She injected a double shot of scorn into her tone. 'I don't think so.'

He pulled the chair out and settled his lean athletic form into it, his long legs bumping hers under the table. She jerked her legs back as far as they would go but it wasn't fast enough to avoid the electrifying zap of contact.

Hard. Virile. Male flesh.

Izzy began to push back her chair in order to leave but one of his hands came down on hers, anchoring her to the table. Anchoring her to *him*. She snatched in a breath, the warm tensile strength of his hand making every female hormone in her body get all giggly and excited. Every cell of her body vibrated like the plucked string of a cello. She looked at his hand trapping hers and disguised a swallow. Heat travelled from her hand, along her arm and all the way to her core like a racing river of fire.

She gave him a glare so cold it could have frozen the glass of water on the table. 'Is this how you usually ask a woman to have coffee with you? By brute force?'

His thumb began a lazy stroking of the back of her hand that sent little shockwaves through her body as if a tiny firecracker had entered her bloodstream. *Pippity pop. Pippity pop. Pippity pop.* 'There was a time when you wanted more than a quick coffee with me. Remember?' The glint in his eyes intensified the searing heat travelling through her body.

Izzy wished she could forget. She wished she had temporary amnesia. Permanent amnesia. It would be worth acquiring a brain injury if she could eradicate the memory of her seduction attempt of Andrea seven years ago at one of her father's legendary boozy Christmas parties. She had been eighteen and tipsy—deliberately, dangerously, defiantly tipsy. Just like she had been at every other party of her father's. It had been the only way she could get through the nauseating performance he gave of Devoted Dad. She'd been intent on embarrassing her father because of all the behind-closed-doors torment he put her through. All the insults, the put-downs, the biting criticisms that made her feel so utterly worthless and useless.

So unloved.

So unwanted.

She'd foolishly thought: How better to embarrass her overbearing father than to sleep with his favourite protégé?

Izzy pulled her hand out from under Andrea's and rose from her seat with a screech of her chair along the floorboards. 'I have to get back to work.'

'I heard about your new job. How's that going for you?'

Izzy searched his expression for any sign of mockery. Was he teasing her about her job? Or was he just showing mild interest? There was no note of cynicism in his tone, no curl of his top lip and no mocking glint in his eyes, but even so she wondered if he, like every-one else, thought she couldn't get through a week in a new job without being fired.

But, whatever he was thinking behind that unfath-omable expression, Izzy was determined not to lose her temper with Andrea in a crowded café. In the past she'd created more scenes than a Hollywood screenplay writer. But how she wanted to shove the table against his rock-hard chest. She wanted to throw the dregs of her coffee cup in his too-handsome, too-confident face. She wanted to grab the front of his snow-white busi-ness shirt until every button popped off.

How like him to doubt her when she was trying so hard to make her way in the world. To her shame, it was one of many jobs she had won and lost over the years. Her reputation always got in the way. Always. Everyone expected her to fail and so what did she do?

She failed.

She had found it hard to settle on a career because of her lack of academic qualifications. She had bombed out during her exams, unable to cope with the pres-sure of trying to measure up to the academic standard of her older brother, Hamish. She hadn't been one of those people who always knew what they wanted to be when they grew up. Instead she'd drifted and dreamed and dawdled.

But now she was clawing her way back, studying for a degree in Social Work online and with her job at the antiques store. Which made her all the more furi-ous at Andrea for assuming she was lazy and lacking in motivation.

Izzy kept her chin high and her eyes hard. 'I'm surprised you haven't come in to the shop by now and bought some hideously expensive relic to prove what a filthy-rich man you are.'

His lazy smile tilted a little further. 'I have my eye on something far more priceless.'

She snatched up her tote bag from the floor and hoisted it over her shoulder, sending him another glare that threatened to wilt the single red rose on the table. 'Nice seeing you, Andrea.' Sarcasm was her second language and she was fluent in it.

Izzy wove her way through the sea of chairs to pay for her coffee at the counter but, before she could take out her purse, Andrea came up behind her and handed the assistant a note. 'Keep the change.'

Izzy mentally rolled her eyes at the way the young female assistant was practically swooning behind the counter. Not at the size of Andrea's tip—although it had been more than generous—but from the mega-charming smile he gave the young woman.

Was there a woman on the planet who could resist that bone-melting smile?

Izzy was conscious of him standing just behind her. He was so close she could feel the warmth of his body. Too close. So close she could feel electric energy fizzing along every knob of her backbone.

His energy.

His *sexual* energy.

She could smell his aftershave—a subtle blend of lemon and lime and something fresh and woodsy that made her think of a sun-warmed citrus orchard fringed by a dark, dangerously dense forest. She allowed herself a little moment of wondering what it would be like to lean back against him. To feel his muscled arms go around her, to feel his pelvis brush against the cheeks of her bottom. She imagined how it would feel to have his large hands settle on her hips and draw her nearer... to feel the surge of his hard, virile male flesh between her legs...

Oh, God. She had to stop this fantasy stuff or she would be doing a *When Harry Met Sally* scene right here and now. Meg Ryan would have nothing on her.

Andrea took Izzy by the elbow and ushered her out of the café into the watery spring sunshine. She decided to go with him without a fuss because people were already starting to point and stare. She didn't want to be photographed with him. Associated with him. Linked to him. To be seen as yet another of his sexual conquests.

Andrea Vaccaro wasn't just a press magnet—he was press superglue. Triple-strength superglue. He was an international playboy with a turnstile on his penthouse instead of a door—the protégé of the late high-flying businessman Benedict Byrne. An Italian kid from the wrong side of the tracks who had made good due to the largesse of his well-to-do English benefactor.

Izzy wasn't so much a press magnet but a press target with a big red circle on her back marked Spoilt Trust Fund Kid. But while there was a time when she had deliberately courted their attention, and even found perverse enjoyment in its negativity, these days she preferred to be left alone. Gone were the days of stumbling out of nightclubs pretending to be drunk in order to shame her father. But unfortunately the paparazzi hadn't got that particular memo. She was still seen as a wild child whose main goal in life was to party. She only had to walk past a balloon or a streamer these days and someone would post a shot with a crude caption about her.

Andrea slid his hand down from her elbow to brush his fingers against her ringless left hand. 'Found yourself a husband yet?'

Izzy knew he was aware of every word and punctuation mark on her father's will. He had probably helped her father write it. It galled her to think of Andrea being party to such personal information. He didn't know the true context of her relationship with her father. Benedict Byrne had been too clever to reveal the darker side of his personality to those he championed or wanted to impress. Only Izzy's mother knew and she was long dead, finally resting in peace beside Izzy's older brother, Hamish. The adored son. The perfect son Izzy had been expected to emulate—but she had never quite managed to meet her father's expectations. 'I have no intention of discussing my personal life with you. Now, if you'll excuse me, I have to—'

'I have a proposition for you.' His expression was as inscrutable as a blank computer screen but she could sense the secret operating system of his thoughts. Wicked thoughts. Dangerous thoughts. *Gulp*. Sexual thoughts.

Izzy opened and closed her hand, trying to rid herself of the sensual energy he had evoked in her flesh.

She tightened her stomach muscles, hoping it would quell the restless feeling deep in her pelvis, but all it did was make her even more aware of how he made her feel. 'The answer is an emphatic I'm-only-going-to say-this-once no.'

He gave her a sleepy-eyed smile as if he found her refusal motivating. A stimulating challenge he couldn't wait to overcome. 'Don't you want to know what I'm proposing before you say no?'

Izzy gritted her teeth, mentally apologising to her orthodontist. 'I have no interest in anything you might say to me.' *Especially if it involves the word marriage.* But would he offer to marry her? For what possible reason?

He held her gaze in a silent lock that made her heart skip a beat. Two beats. The air seemed to be tightening as if all the oxygen was being sucked out of the atmosphere, atom by atom. He was looking good. More than good. But then, he always did. Tanned and toned, with the sort of classic features you mostly only saw in men's expensive aftershave ads. The bad boy made good. His not long, not short wavy black hair was styled in a casual manner that highlighted his intelligent forehead and the strong blade of his nose. The dark slash of his eyebrows—one of them interrupted by a zigzag scar—over eyes so dense and deep a brown it was hard to tell what was pupil and what was iris. Knowing, assessing eyes fringed by thick lashes that every now and again would lower just enough for her to think…

No. No. No.

She must not think about sex and Andrea in the same sentence.

Izzy could outstare most men. She could put them in their place with a cutting look or a sharp word.

But not Andrea Vaccaro.

He was her nemesis. And, damn him to hell, he knew it.

'Have dinner with me.' It wasn't an invitation. It was a command.

Izzy raised her eyebrows like a haughty school-marm. 'I'd rather eat a fistful of fur balls.'

His gaze moved over every inch of her face, from her eyes to her mouth, lingering there for so long she became aware of her lips in a way she had never been before. They started tingling as if his mouth had brushed them. Heated them. Tempted them. Whenever he looked at her she thought of sex. Hot bed-wrecking, pulse-racing sex. The sort of sex she hadn't been having.

Had never had.

Izzy wasn't a virgin but neither had she had as much sex as the press had made out. She didn't even like sex. She was hopeless at it. Embarrassingly, patheti-cally hopeless. And the only way she could tolerate it was to get tipsy so she didn't have to think about how much she wasn't enjoying it.

Andrea's obsidian-black gaze came back to hers. 'We can discuss this out here on the street where any-one can hear or we can do it in private.'

Do it in private.

The double entendre of his words sent a shiver rolling down her spine. Images popped into her head of him *doing it* with her. His hands on her breasts, his mouth on hers, his body pumping and rocking and—

Izzy pulled away from her thoughts like someone springing back from a sudden flame. She hoped she wasn't showing any sign of how flustered she felt, but she suspected there was little Andrea Vaccaro missed. It was why he was so successful in business. He could read people. He could read situations. He was clever and calculating and tactical.

She hated how he made her feel. Hated how easily he could trigger anger or desire in her. Or both. She had no interest in repeating her foolish behaviour of the past. She was no longer that brash attention-seeking flirt. She was no longer the spoilt little rich girl acting out her inner pain and shame.

She had reinvented herself.

'I'm not doing anything with you in private, Andrea.' Izzy only realised her vocal slip when she saw the way his dark eyes gleamed. *Got you.*

'Scared of what I might say?'

Scared of what I might do. Izzy raised her chin and eyeballed him. 'Nothing you say is of the remotest interest to me.'

Something moved at the back of his eyes. A camera shutter movement before the screen came back up. 'Just dinner, Isabella.' His Italian accent caressed the four syllables of her name. He was the only person who called her by her full name. She wasn't sure if she liked it or not.

Just dinner. Could she go and see what he had to

say? He had intrigued her interest, and with the clock ticking like a nuclear bomb on the deadline she would be crazy not to hear him out. But being anywhere near him unsettled her. His energy collided with hers and created something in her she wasn't sure she could control.

Wasn't sure she *wanted* to control, which was even more disturbing.

Izzy folded her arms and sent him one of her trademark bored teenager looks. 'Tell me the time and the place and I'll meet you there.'

He gave a sudden laugh that made something at the back of her knees fizz. 'Nice try.'

'I mean it, Andrea. I will only have dinner with you if I come by myself.'

The satirical gleam was back in his eyes. 'Do you usually prefer to come by yourself?'

Izzy could feel her cheeks pulsating with heat. But they weren't the only part of her body pulsating. Her feminine core gave off little pulses of lust that reverberated through her entire body. She put on her game face—the face she'd perfected during her wilful teens, the wild child seductress face. The I-don't-give-a-fig-what-you-think-about-me face. Driven by an urge she couldn't quite explain, she moistened her lips with a slow sweep of her tongue, secretly delighted by the way his eyes followed the movement.

He wasn't immune to her.

The realisation was strangely thrilling. He might not like her. He might not respect her. But he sure as hell wanted her. He had resisted her seven years ago.

Resisted her easily. Made her feel foolish for trying to seduce him. He'd called her a silly spoilt child playing at grown-ups.

But *now* he wanted her.

Izzy tucked that knowledge away and gave herself a mental high five. It gave her an edge, a bit of power in a relationship that had always been tipped in his favour in the power stakes. She gave him a look through her half-lowered lashes. 'Wouldn't you like to know?'

His eyes darkened until they were black bottomless pools of male mystery. 'I'll make it my business to find out.' His voice was smooth with a base note so deep every nerve in her body trembled like a shivering leaf.

Izzy knew she was being reckless in flirting with him. Reckless and foolish. But something about the way he interacted with her always made her feel like challenging him. Pushing him. Needling him. Peeling back the carefully constructed layers of civilised man-about-town to reveal the primal man she sensed was simmering just under the surface. 'Where shall we have dinner?'

'I've booked a table at Henri's. Eight thirty tonight.'

Izzy was annoyed she hadn't put up more of a fight. She didn't like thinking of herself as predictable. She had made a lifetime's work of being anything but. How had he known she would give in? Had he been *so* sure of her?

Maybe because there's less than twenty-four hours left on the deadline?

Argh. Don't remind me.

'Your arrogance never ceases to amaze me,' Izzy said. 'Does anyone ever say no to you and mean it?'

A smile flirted with the edges of his mouth. 'Not often.'

Izzy could well believe it. She had to get her will-power back into shape. Send it to boot camp. Pump it full of steroids or something. She couldn't allow him to manipulate her into doing what he wanted. She had to stand up to him. To show him she wasn't like the droves of women who paraded in and out of his life. She might have slipped once, but she was older and wiser now. Older and wiser and wary of allowing him any hold over her. Of allowing *any* man any hold over her. She adjusted the strap of her tote bag over her shoulder and turned to leave. 'See you later, then.'

'Isabella?'

Izzy turned back to face him, carefully keeping her features in neutral. 'Yes?'

His gaze drifted to her mouth and back to her eyes, holding them like a steely vice. 'Don't even think about not showing up.'

Izzy wondered how he could read her mind. She'd planned to leave him waiting in that restaurant to show him she wasn't going to play whatever game he had in mind. He had probably never been stood up before. It was time he was taught a lesson and she would enjoy every second of teaching him it.

But now she had to think of another plan. She couldn't show up at that restaurant and meekly agree to his 'proposal'. Couldn't. Couldn't. Couldn't. He was the last man she would ever consider marrying. For it was marriage he wanted, of that she was sure. She could see the ruthless determination in his eyes.

She was desperate, but not *that* desperate.

'Oh, I'll show up.' She gave him a smile so sugar-sweet it would have made any decent dentist reach for fluoride. 'I quite fancy a free dinner. You did say just dinner, right?'

His eyes smouldered with incendiary heat, making her insides coil and twist and tighten with need. A need she didn't want to feel. A need she had strictly forbidden herself to feel. 'Just dinner.'

Izzy turned and walked back along the street towards the antiques shop where she worked. She was conscious of Andrea's gaze following her but didn't turn back to look at him. She was quite proud of her willpower—it had made a remarkable recovery, although it had been touch and go there for a minute. But when she got to the front door of her workplace and glanced back, Andrea's tall figure had disappeared into the crowd. Why she should be feeling disappointed she didn't know. And nor should she care.

But somehow—*annoyingly*—she did.

CHAPTER TWO

'GOSH. DO YOU need a bodyguard with you when you're
wearing that dress?' Izzy's flatmate, Jess, asked later
that evening when she poked her head around Izzy's
bedroom door.

Izzy smoothed her hands down the front of her
shimmery silver mini dress that sparkled like Christmas tinsel. 'How do I look?'

'Seriously, Izzy, you have amazing legs. You should
give up your job selling those dusty old antiques and
be a model instead.' Jess tilted her head to one side.
'So who's your date? Anyone I know?'

'Just an acquaintance.'

Jess's eyebrows rose. 'That's a pretty impressive
show of thigh for a mere acquaintance.'

Izzy picked up a tube of blood-red lipstick and
smeared it over her lips and pressed them together to
set it in place. She knew she would be risking press
attention by being seen with Andrea dressed in such a
way but this time she didn't care. It would be worth it
to show him she wasn't playing by his rules. He was
known for dating elegant and sophisticated women.

She would be the antithesis of elegant and sophisticated dressed in this get-up. This outfit screamed *party girl out for a wild time.* 'I'm teaching my…date a lesson.'

'A lesson in what? How to look but not touch?'

Izzy recalled the firm press of Andrea's hand with a delicate shiver. She was still trying not to think about him pinning her to a bed with his body doing all sorts of wicked things to her. 'I'm teaching him not to be so arrogant.' She pulled out the large Velcro rollers she'd put in her hair to give it extra volume, and finger-combed it into a cloud of curling tresses around her shoulders.

Jess sat on the edge of Izzy's bed. 'So, who is this guy?'

Izzy glanced at her flatmate in her dressing table mirror. She had only known Jess a few months and didn't want to go into the details of her complicated relationship with Andrea. She picked up a pair of cheap dangly earrings and inserted them into her earlobes, then adjusted the front of her dress to boost her cleavage. 'Just someone my father used to know.'

Jess got off the bed and came to stand next to the dressing table mirror so she could face her. 'But isn't this the last day before the deadline on your father's will?'

Izzy wished she hadn't let slip about the will in an unguarded moment a couple of nights ago over a take-out curry and a bottle of wine. It was a little lowering to admit to her friend and flatmate that her father had wanted to punish her from the grave. Her father had known how against the institution of marriage she was.

She had witnessed him over-controlling her mother like a bullying tyrant until her mother hadn't been able to decide what clothes to wear without asking him first. No way was Izzy going to allow any man that sort of power over her and especially not Andrea Vaccaro. 'Yes, but he's not a candidate.'

'Are you going to forfeit your inheritance, then?'

Izzy slipped on a collection of jangling bracelets. 'I don't want to, but what else can I do? I can't just walk out on the street and pick up someone to be my husband.'

Jess's gaze drifted over Izzy's outfit again. 'You probably could wearing that get-up.' She frowned again. 'But this guy you're meeting tonight. Why isn't he a candidate? Has he actually said no?'

Izzy picked up a slimline evening purse and popped the lipstick tube inside and snapped it shut. 'I haven't asked him. And I never will. I know what I'm doing, Jess. I know how to handle men like Andrea Vaccaro.'

Jess's eyes went as wide as the make-up compact on the dressing table. 'You're going on a date with Andrea Vaccaro? *The* hotel king Andrea Vaccaro? And you think he's not a candidate? Are you out of your mind? That man is the world's most eligible bachelor.'

Izzy scooped up a leather biker jacket from the bed and fed her arms through the sleeves, pulling her hair out of the back of the collar and settling it back around her shoulders. 'He might be considered a prize catch but I don't want him. I would rather rummage through rubbish bins and sleep under cardboard for the rest of my life than marry that arrogant, up-himself jerk.'

Jess's brows disappeared under her fringe. 'Wow. I've never seen so you…so worked up. Did something happen between you two in the past?'

Izzy did a final adjustment of her outfit. 'He thinks he can have anyone he wants but he can't have me.' She smiled a confident smile. 'Don't worry. I know *exactly* how to handle him.'

Andrea hadn't planned on being late for his dinner date with Isabella but he got caught up in traffic after a minor accident in central London. He'd sent her a text to tell her he would be a few minutes late but she hadn't replied. Her attitude towards him was exactly the reason he was going to offer her a temporary marriage. He needed a wife. A temporary wife who wouldn't make a fuss when he called it quits. No love-you-for-ever promises. No happy-ever-after. What he wanted was a six-month contract that would conveniently solve two problems with one brief, impersonal ceremony.

The teenage stepdaughter of an important business colleague was making things difficult for him by making no secret of her crush on him. The hotel merger he was working on would be jeopardised if he didn't take preventative action. And because Andrea had been asked to be best man at the businessman's upcoming wedding in a few weeks, he had to do something, and do it fast.

If it had been any other business deal he would have walked away without a qualm. There were plenty of other hotels he could buy. But this one was the one he wanted the most. Buying the hotel he'd once hung outside of as a homeless teenager looking for scraps of food made it too important to walk away. Buying that hotel in Florence—more than any other he'd bought or would buy in the future—would signify he had moved on from his difficult past.

Moved on and triumphed.

A convenient wife was what he needed and Isabella Byrne was the perfect candidate.

He figured he could help Isabella with her little dilemma while sorting out his own. Marriage was not something he had ever considered for himself. He had personally witnessed the human destruction when a match made in heaven turned into a hell on earth. He admired those who made it work and felt sorry for those for whom it failed. He enjoyed his freedom. He enjoyed the flexibility of moving from relationship to relationship without any lasting ties or responsibilities.

But he was prepared to sacrifice six months of his freedom because he wanted to nail that deal. And, more importantly, to prove he could still resist Isabella Byrne. He didn't want to want her. It annoyed him she still had that effect on him. It was a persistent ache he'd always tried his best to ignore. He had always kept his distance out of respect to his relationship with her father. Benedict Byrne had had his faults, but Andrea would never forget how Benedict's early help had launched him in the hotel business, allowing him to put his disadvantaged past well and truly behind him. He had worked hard to build an empire even bigger than Benedict's. An empire that more than made up for the miserable months he'd spent living as a street kid. No one looking at him now would ever associate him with that starving and shivering youth who had fought so hard to survive a childhood of poverty and neglect.

But now his mentor was dead, Andrea figured a short-term marriage to settle the terms of Isabella's father's will would also give him the chance to prove once and for all he no longer suffered from the Isabella itch. The itch that had been driving him mad for the last seven years.

For as long as he'd known her she'd been acting out, bringing shame to her long-suffering father. She'd been the typical trust fund kid—spoilt, overindulged, lazy and irresponsible. Not much had changed now she was an adult. She was still wilful and defiant, with a body made for sin.

He couldn't be in the same country as her without going hard. It irritated the hell out of him that she had that effect on him. He was no stranger to lust—he enjoyed a satisfying and active sex life. But something about the attraction he felt for Isabella unnerved him. Her feminine power over him was unlike any he'd felt before. He prided himself on his ability to control his primal urges. He had boundaries he skirted around but never crossed. It would be dangerous to compromise those boundaries by marrying her, but just this once he was prepared to risk it. He would insist on a paper marriage. A hands-off affair that would give them both what they wanted.

She had less than twenty-four hours left to find a husband. He'd spent the last three months bracing him-

self for the announcement of her engagement to some
man she'd somehow managed to convince to marry her.

But she hadn't found anyone.

Or maybe she hadn't wanted to.

Not because she didn't want the money. Andrea
knew she wanted that money more than anything.
How else was she going to fund her lifestyle? She had
an appalling employment record. The longest she'd
held down a job was a month. But as much as she
wanted that money, she wanted him as her husband
even less. Or so she said. She would have no choice
but to marry him and she knew it, which was why
he'd already sorted out the paperwork. They would be
married by morning or she would lose every penny of
her inheritance.

And once his ring was on her finger, and hers on his,
he would be off the market, so to speak, so his business deal would be safe.

Andrea saw her as soon as he walked into the restaurant. His body had sensed her three blocks away.
She was sitting in the bar area, looking like a teenage
boy's fantasy in a skin-tight silver lamé mini dress
that showed the creamy length of her slim legs. She
had big hair and more make-up and flashy jewellery
than a drag queen. He couldn't help a secret smile. She
knew she would have to accept his proposal, but she
was making it as uncomfortable as possible for him.
Did she think her wild child party girl outfit was going
to put him off?

She was twirling the little colourful umbrella in her

cocktail but she turned on her stool as if she had sensed his arrival. Or his arousal. Or both.

Her eyes sparkled with her usual defiance. 'You're late.'

He perched on the stool next to her, fighting the urge to stroke a hand down the slim curve of her thigh. 'I sent you a text.'

Her chin came up and something about the tight set of her mouth made him want to loosen it with a slow, sensual stroke of his tongue. 'I don't like to be kept waiting.' The words came out as cold and hard as ice cubes.

'Understandable since you've so little time left in which to find yourself a husband.' He hooked one eyebrow upwards. 'Unless you've been lucky enough to find one in the last couple of hours?'

Her glare was as arctic as her voice, making him wonder if he was going to get out of this without serious frostbite. 'Not yet, but I haven't given up hope.'

Andrea picked up a loose curl of her hair and twirled it around his finger, holding her gaze with his. She didn't pull away but her throat moved up and down over a small swallow and her pupils widened like spreading pools of ink. He could smell the exotic notes of her perfume—frangipani and musk and something that was unique to her. He carefully tucked the tendril of hair behind her ear and smiled. 'So, here we are on our first date.'

Her eyes flashed as if something exploded behind her irises. 'First and last.' She turned on her stool and picked up her cocktail glass and took a large sip. She put it down on the bar with a little clatter. 'You'd better say what you came here to say and be done with it.'

'I like your outfit.' Andrea dipped his gaze to the delicious shadow of her cleavage. 'I haven't seen this much of you in years.'

Her cheeks darkened into twin pools of pink and her mouth tightened until her full lips all but disappeared. 'I thought it'd be appropriate, given what I suspect you're going to say to me.'

He stroked a finger along the back of her hand, the base of his spine tingling when he saw his darker skin against her creamy whiteness. He could resist her. Sure he could. But he couldn't stop imagining her silky-smooth legs wrapped around his, her soft mouth beneath his own. His aching need driving into her warm, wet womanhood and taking them both to oblivion. 'You need me, Isabella. Go on. Admit it. You need me so bad.'

She snatched her hand away and used her index finger to poke him in the chest, each word like a heavy punctuation mark. 'I. Do. Not. Need. You.'

Andrea captured her hand and brought it up close to his mouth, pressing a kiss to the back of her knuckles. 'Marry me.'

Green and blue chips of ice glittered in her gaze and the muscles in her hand contracted as if his touch burned. 'Go fry in hell.'

He tightened his hold on her hand. 'You'll lose everything if you don't find a husband by morning. Think about it, Isabella. That's a heck of a lot of money to forfeit for the sake of six months living as my wife.'

He could see the indecision on her face—the doubts, the fears, the calculations. She had grown up surrounded by wealth. She had wanted for nothing but seemingly had been grateful for nothing. She had wasted the education her father had paid for by getting expelled numerous times for rebellious behaviour and poor academic performance. She had frittered away or sabotaged all the opportunities her father had provided. She acted like a selfish and sulky spoilt brat who had expected to inherit her father's entire estate without doing anything to earn it. It was no wonder she hadn't been able to find a husband willing to marry her. Her reputation was of a hell-raiser who deliberately drew negative attention to herself.

But lately Andrea had often wondered if there was more to Izzy than met the press's eye. It was like she *wanted* people to think the worst of her. She took no steps to counter the negative opinions written about her in the media. It was like she was playing a role, just as she had done this evening, dressing in an eye-popping outfit that made her look like a wild child out on the town. But in spite of her garish look-at-me clothes and make-up, he could see tiny glimpses of insecurity in the way she carried herself when she thought he wasn't looking.

Andrea knew most people wouldn't consider her ideal wife material, but he figured any wife would be better than no wife given the urgency of his situation with his business merger and the man's upcoming wedding. Besides, he was confident he could cope with

Izzy. She was like a flighty thoroughbred in need of skilful handling.

And when it came to handling women, no one could say he wasn't skilful.

Her eyes suddenly hardened as if her resolve had shown back up for duty. Her hand pulled out of his and she began rubbing it as if it was tingling. 'I can think of no worse torture than to be tied to you in marriage.'

'It will be a paper marriage.'

Her eyes widened and her mouth dropped open. 'A…a paper marriage?'

'That's what I said.'

She blinked and then blinked again, slowly, as if her eyelids were weighted. 'Do I have your word on that?'

He held her look. 'Do I have yours?'

Her mouth thinned again to a flat white line. 'You're assuming I'm going to say yes to your proposal.'

Andrea picked up her left hand and stroked her empty ring finger. Her body trembled as if his touch triggered a tiny earthquake in her flesh. Touching her triggered the same in his. He could feel himself tightening, swelling, his blood heating with want and need. A need he would continue to ignore because when he said it was to be a paper marriage, that was exactly what it would be. Even if he had to put his desire for her in chains. And a straitjacket. 'You don't have any choice but to accept and you know it.' He let her hand go and reached into the inside pocket of his jacket. He handed her a velvet ring box. 'If you don't like it you can change it.'

Her eyes flew from the ring box to his, narrowing

to slits so only her hatred shone through. 'You were so *sure* I was going to accept?'

'I'm your only chance to get your hands on that money. Even if, by some chance, you found someone at this late stage, you wouldn't be able to marry without the necessary paperwork. I've seen to it. I have a lawyer and a marriage celebrant on standby. Marry me or lose everything.'

She opened the ring box and took out the diamond and sapphire ring. She spent time eyeing it, turning it this way and that. Her gaze came back to his and she gave him a tight little smile that didn't quite reach her eyes. 'You want me to wear this?'

'That's the general idea.'

She slipped off the stool, standing so close to him he could smell the fresh flowery fragrance of her hair. Her mouth was still set and her eyes as hard and blue as the diamonds and sapphires glittering in the ring. She picked up the tail of his silk tie and tugged him even closer, posting the ring down the loosened collar of his shirt. It bumped and tumbled down his chest until it lodged coldly and sharply against his stomach.

'Thanks, but no thanks.' She gave his stomach a little pat as if to emphasise her point.

Andrea captured her hand and held it against his abdomen, every one of his muscles contracting under her touch. 'I'll give you two minutes to make up your mind and then the deal is off the table. Permanently. Understood?'

CHAPTER THREE

TWO MINUTES? IZZY could feel that clock ticking in her chest like a pin pulled on a grenade. She wanted to walk away. Wanted to slap that confident smile off his face. Wanted to poke him in the eyes and kick him in the shins and stomp on his size twelve Italian leather–clad feet.

But another part of her wanted to fish that gorgeous ring out from underneath his shirt and put it on her finger before her inheritance slipped out of her reach. For ever.

He was offering her a paper marriage but his eyes and his body were promising something else. She could feel that erotic promise thrumming in her own body. If she married him she would never have to worry about money again. She could pursue her dream of buying back her mother's childhood home and turning it into a happy place for other people, a place where families could go on holiday together during tough times, just as she and Hamish had done before he'd got cancer.

She could set herself up for life. She would no longer have to work in underpaid jobs just because she hadn't focused enough in school. Once the six months was up she would be totally free. At no one's mercy. Under no one's command.

But if she married Andrea she would be thrown into his company. Sharing his life. And yes, in spite of what he said to the contrary, sharing his bed. She could see the desire in his eyes. She could sense it in his body. She could feel it in the air when he was near her.

Could she agree to such a plan? Six months married to a man she hated and wanted in equal measure? His touch had evoked a fire in her blood that sizzled even now. He only had to look at her with those pitch-black eyes and her insides contracted and coiled and cried out loud with lust.

Izzy met his gaze and knew she couldn't possibly say no. She would have to trust him. More to the point…she would have to trust herself. He had her cornered. Trapped. She could not refuse him at this late hour and he knew it. He had it all organised. He had been so sure of her. So damn sure of her.

Why hadn't she tried harder to find someone? Why had she let it get to this? Why had she wasted her one last chance to get away from him?

Maybe you didn't want to.

Izzy refused to listen to the prod of her conscience. She *had* wanted to get away from him. She hated him. She hated that he had received her father's love and attention, not her. He was a rich self-made man who thought he could have anyone he wanted.

Well, he was in for a big surprise because she would hold him to this paper marriage. She blew out a long breath and sat back on the stool and held out her hand. 'Okay. Give me the ring.'

His eyes held hers in a steely tussle. 'Come and get it.'

A shiver coursed down her spine at the thought of touching him again. His abs had felt like coils of concrete. And she didn't want to think about the hardness that lay just beneath them.

It was always this way between them—this tug of war of wills. She hated letting him win. It went against everything in her to allow him that much power over her. But the only way to handle him was to stand up to his challenges. Show him she was immune to him even if she wasn't and never had been. She had acted her way out of situations in the past, especially with men. Pretending to feel things she didn't. Faking it. She was an expert at fooling those she wanted to fool.

Izzy decided to brazen it out. She would prove she wasn't his for the asking. She would marry him but it would be a hands-off affair… Well, it would be once she got that wretched ring out of his shirt. She took a steadying breath and stepped between his thighs, every cell of her body intensely aware of his arrant maleness. She took the end of his tie and flipped it over his left shoulder. She undid the middle button of his shirt just above his belly button, revealing tanned muscled flesh sprinkled with jet-black hair that tickled the backs of her fingers. She undid another two buttons, breathing in the warm musky scent of him, her senses reeling like stoned bees in an opium field.

She chanced a glance at his face, her breath locking

in her throat when she saw the dark satirical gleam in his eyes. His lean jaw was liberally dusted with stubble, making her want to trail her fingertips across its sexy prickliness. His hands settled on her waist and something in her stomach fell from a shelf and landed with a soft little thud that sent a shivering shockwave to her core.

'You're getting warm.' His voice was husky and low. 'Warmer.'

Izzy had to remind herself to breathe. His thighs moved closer together, brushing against the outside of hers like the slowly closing doors of a cage. She undid another button on his shirt and dipped her hand into the opening to search for the ring. He sucked in a breath and gave a slight shiver as if her touch electrified him. She knew the feeling. The feel of his hard warm body against her hand was enough to send her ovaries into spasm. The press of his hands on her hips were melting her bones. Sending tongues of fire to her secret places. She located the ring and drew it out of his shirt and stepped back but his powerful thighs gripped her tighter.

'What are you doing?' Her voice was breathless. Too breathless. I'm-not-immune-to-you breathless.

He held out his hand for the ring, his eyes tethering hers. 'I believe it's the man's job to put the ring on his future bride's finger.'

Izzy dropped the ring into his palm before she dropped it on the floor. He slid it over her ring finger, gently but firmly pushing it into place, and gave her a smile that made something dark and dangerous glint at the back of his eyes. 'Will you marry me, Isabella?'

Izzy had never hated him more than at that moment. He was making a mockery of one of the most important questions a man could ever ask a woman. He was grinding her pride to powder. Pummelling it. Pulverising it. Relishing in the chance to overpower her.

To *control* her.

'Yes. I will marry you.' The words tasted like bile and Izzy wanted to wash her mouth out with soap. Buckets and buckets of soap.

He relaxed his thighs and she was suddenly free. Well, apart from his ring on her finger. The ring was as effective as a noose. He had her where he wanted her and there wasn't a thing she could do to stop it.

He rose from the bar stool and offered her his hand. 'We have a date with a lawyer and a marriage celebrant in fifteen minutes. Once that's done we can come back and have dinner to celebrate our marriage.'

Izzy glanced towards the restaurant, desperate to stall the inevitable for as long as she could. 'Don't you have to let the maître d' know to hold the table?'

Andrea's smile made something prickle across her scalp like millions of miniature marching feet. 'I've already told him.'

Izzy stood like an ice sculpture beside Andrea as the female marriage celebrant took them through the short ceremony. Five minutes before she had signed a prenuptial agreement in front of Andrea's lawyer. She hadn't minded signing...not really. Did he really think she would come after his money once their marriage was over?

She didn't want his money. She wanted hers.

Izzy tried not to think of the importance of the words they were saying to each other—the vows that were meant to be sacred and meaningful. And the fact she was dressed like a party girl while saying them. Why had she been so headstrong and stupid? She should've known he wouldn't let a silly look-at-me outfit get in the way of his plans. Anyway, why should she care she was mouthing words she didn't mean? Andrea didn't mean them either.

She tried to think of the money instead. Heaps of money that would help her finally buy back her grandparents' house and turn it into something special, something healing and special so that her mother's and Hamish's death weren't in vain. Izzy's grandparents' house had been sold after their death in a car crash not long after Hamish had died, because her father insisted on using the money to prop up his business, even though he knew Izzy's mother didn't want to sell it. Even when they were first married, her father had used her mother's wealth to build his empire and then told everyone he had done it on his own. Her mother hadn't had the strength to stand up to him. She had handed over everything—her money, her pride and her self-esteem.

But Izzy was not going to be that sort of wife— the sort of wife who said yes when she meant no. She would not bend to Andrea's will the way her mother had to her father.

She would remain strong and defiant to the bitter, inevitable end.

Andrea slipped the white-gold wedding band on her ring finger. His dark gaze seeming to say, *Mission accomplished.*

Izzy was surprised he'd been prepared to wear one himself. She placed it over his finger as instructed by the celebrant and repeated the vows in a voice that didn't sound like hers. It was too husky and whispery so she made sure her gaze counteracted it.

'I now pronounce you man and wife.' The celebrant smiled at Andrea. 'You may kiss the bride.'

Andrea dropped his hold of Izzy's hands. 'That won't be necessary.'

Izzy stared at him, desperately trying to conceal her shock. Or was it relief? No. It wasn't relief—it was rage. Red-hot rage. Why wasn't he going to kiss her? They might not have meant the vows, but surely for the sake of appearances he would have kissed her? She glanced at the celebrant but the older woman seemed unsurprised. Perhaps the celebrant had witnessed dozens of impersonal marriages and thought nothing untoward of a groom who refused to kiss his bride.

Anger curdled cold and hard and heavy in Izzy's belly—a festering, simmering stew of wrath. How dare he make a fool of her in front of the celebrant and witnesses? Damn it. She would *make* him kiss her. She softened her expression to that of a dewy-eyed bride. 'But, darling, I was so looking forward to that part of the ceremony. I know you're stuffy and uptight about public displays of affection, but surely just this once will be okay? You don't want everyone to think you don't love me, do you?'

His gaze held hers for a beat then went to her mouth and his eyes darkened to coal. His hands took hers, bringing her closer so their bodies were touching from chest to thigh. His fingers interlocked with hers in a way that contained a hint of spine-tingling eroticism. She tried to ignore the reaction in her body—the contraction of her core, the increase of her heart rate, the wings flapping sensation in her stomach. His eyes became hooded, his head bending down so his mouth was within reach of hers. She felt the warm breeze of his mint-scented breath against her lips, every nerve in her lips tingling in anticipation of his touchdown. She suddenly felt as if she would die if he didn't kiss her. Not from any sense of loss of pride, but because she needed to feel his mouth like she needed air to breathe.

His mouth connected with hers with a brush as soft as a floating feather. He lifted off but his lips were dry against her lipstick and clung to hers for an infinitesimal moment. He came back down and pressed a little harder, sealing her mouth and drawing her closer with a hand at the small of her back, the other moving up to cradle the side of her face.

Izzy had enjoyed and, yes, even endured many kisses. But nothing had ever felt like Andrea's mouth. It was electric. Exhilarating. Erotic. His lips moved against hers in a soft, exploratory way, as if he were testing and tasting the surface of her lips, storing the feel and texture of them deep in his muscle memory. She breathed in his clean male scent, her senses overloaded with sun-warmed citrus and dark, cool wood. She could feel the graze of his stubble against her face, the sexy rasp of hard male against soft female that sent a tumultuous wave of longing through her body. Even the spread of his fingers where they cradled her face made her aware of every whorl of his skin, every muscle and tendon and finger pad like her skin was reading his code.

He opened his mouth over her lower lip, stroking his tongue along its contours with such slowness, such exquisite, almost torturous slowness her legs threatened to give way. She had to cling to the front of his jacket to keep upright, pressing her body even closer. But that only made her want him more, the hungry need clawing at her, making her aware of her breasts where they were crushed so intimately against his chest, the nipples hard and tight, sensitive, aching for his touch.

She told herself she was only reacting this way because it had been so long since she'd had a lover. But she had a feeling making love with Andrea would be completely different from making love with another man. Her body recognised his touch. Reacted to it. Revelled in it. Rejoiced in it. She couldn't bear the thought of him ending the kiss. She wanted it to go on and on and on, giving her time to explore the secrets of his mouth and body, the delicious ridges and contours she could feel jutting against her body.

He sucked on her lower lip and then gently nipped at it in little tugs and releases that made her senses sing like an opera star. His tongue moved against hers in teasing little stabs that were so shockingly sexual she could feel her lower body intimately preparing itself.

Izzy heard herself whimper, those most betraying of sounds that showed she was not as immune to him as she'd wanted him to think. Her only consolation was he seemed just as undone by their kiss. She could feel the tension of his lower body, the surge of his male flesh against her, ramping up her need to an unbearable level. His breathing rate changed, so did the way he was holding her. His hand at her back pressed her more firmly against him as if he couldn't bear to let her go.

But then suddenly it was over.

He dropped his hands from her and stepped back, his expression shuttered. 'We'll lose that table if we don't get going.' His words were a slap down to her ego, making her wonder if she had imagined what had just transpired between their mouths. But then she noticed the way he ran his tongue over his lips when he thought she wasn't looking as if he was still savouring the taste of her.

Izzy followed him out of the room with her senses still spinning like circus plates on sticks. She felt dazed, drugged, disordered. Her mouth felt swollen. She could taste him on her lips. Inside her mouth. Her body was tingling from head to foot, her insides twisted and tight with unrelieved lust. For years she had wondered what it would be like to be kissed by him.

Now she knew.

But even more mortifying…she wanted him to do it again.

* * *

Izzy waited until they were inside a cab on their way back to the restaurant before she turned to look at Andrea. 'What was all that about?'

He was scrolling through his messages on his phone and didn't even glance up. 'What was all what about?' His tone sounded bored, disinterested, as if he'd been forced to share a cab with a stranger and couldn't be bothered making small talk.

She snatched his phone out of his hands and glared at him. 'Will you at least look at me when I'm talking to you?'

His expression showed no tension but she could sense it all the same. He was a master at cloaking his feelings, but something about the way he was holding his body suggested he wasn't quite as in control as he would like. 'The kiss, you mean?' His eyes drifted to her mouth as if he were remembering every pulse-racing second of when it had been crushed beneath his. His eyes came back to hers but they now had a hard sheen as if an internal screen had come up. His top lip curled over a slow but cynical smile. 'I thought we agreed our marriage was a paper one. Or are you keen to shift the goalposts?'

Izzy affected a laugh but even to her ears it didn't sound convincing—kind of like a mortician trying to be a clown. She handed him back his phone, careful not to touch him in the process. 'In your dreams, Vaccaro.'

'You will address me by my Christian name or a term of endearment when we're in public.' His voice had a note of stern authority that made her bristle like a cornered cat. 'I will not have you imply to anyone that our relationship is not a normal one. Do you understand?'

Izzy glanced at the driver, who was behind a glass soundproof screen. She turned back to look at Andrea, anger a bubbling, blistering brew in her belly. 'You think you can make me do what *you* want? Think again. You didn't marry a doormat.'

'No. I married a spoilt brat who doesn't know how to behave like a grown woman of twenty-five.' His smile had gone and in its place was a white line of tension. 'We can fight all we like in private, but in public we will behave as any other married couple who love and are committed to each other.'

Izzy folded her arms to stop herself from slapping that stern schoolmasterly expression off his face. 'And what if I don't?'

He held her gaze for a long beat. 'If either of us walks out of this marriage before the six months is up, you will be the one to lose. It's in your interests to keep me invested in this. I have much less at stake.'

Izzy frowned so hard she would have frightened off a dose of Botox. 'What exactly do you get out of this marriage? You've never actually told me your motivations.' It shamed her that she hadn't asked before now. Not that there had been much time to do so, but still. It made her look foolish and naïve. And the last thing she wanted to appear in front of him was foolish and naïve.

He slipped his phone into the inside pocket of his jacket. 'My reasons are quite simple. It suits my ends to be married for a few months.' He gave her a tight no-teeth smile that wasn't quite a smile. 'Your situation was timely. We both needed to be temporarily married and here we are.'

'But…but why me?'

He shrugged one broad shoulder. 'Better the devil you know.'

You don't know me. Izzy swallowed back the words. She didn't want him to know her… Did she? She shook off the thought and refocused. 'What do you think people are going to think of us being married? The press and so on? It's not like we've been seen together other than at some of my father's functions. And his funeral hardly counts. You barely spoke a word to me.'

'I've already informed the press.' He patted his phone in his pocket. 'They'll be waiting for us when we get back to the restaurant.'

Izzy's mouth dropped open, panic gouging a hole in her chest. 'But I can't face them dressed like this! What will everyone think?'

His smile had a hint of malice. 'You should have thought of that before.'

She sat forward on her seat and tapped at the glass separating the driver from the back. 'Pull over, please.'

The uniformed driver looked to Andrea for verification. 'Sir?'

'Drive on,' Andrea said, leaning forward to close the panel.

'No. You will not drive on.' Izzy reached for the panel again but Andrea caught her arm. 'Let go of me. I want to get out. This is kidnap. This is abduction. This is—'

'This is the bed you made and now you'll lie on it.' His fingers were like a steel bracelet around her wrist, but his thumb found her pulse and moved over it in mesmerising little circles that made it hard for her to think. His eyes were dark—impossibly, impenetrably dark.

Izzy wet her bone-dry lips, her heart thumping as if she were having some sort of medical event. Even her legs felt woolly and useless. She couldn't do this. She couldn't allow him to make a fool of her. She would have to try another tactic. She pulled out of his hold and put a hand to her head, rubbing at her tight temples. 'Please, Andrea. Could I go home and change first? Henri's is such an upmarket restaurant. I didn't realise tonight would end like this. It's all happened so quickly and I—'

'You've had three months to find yourself a husband.'

She steepled her hands against her nose and mouth, taking a deep calming breath. She didn't want to disgrace herself in front of him. To show how vulnerable she really was. She had to be strong. Strong and invincible, otherwise she would break and she wouldn't be able to put herself together again.

She had skated too close to the abyss before.

Terrifyingly close.

She had worked hard to get herself strong again.

Must not cry. Must not cry. Must not cry.

'I know…but I kept putting it off,' Izzy said. 'I was frightened of making a mistake…marrying the wrong man or something, one who wouldn't agree to the six-month time limit and make things even more impossible than they already are.' She lowered her hands and looked at him again. 'I mean, it's not exactly a normal situation, is it? How many fathers would do this to their only daughter? Their only remaining child?'

He studied her for a moment. 'Your father loved you but you constantly disappointed him. It grieved him terribly that you didn't make more of an effort with all the opportunities he gave you.'

Izzy closed her eyes in a slow blink and sat back heavily against her seat. 'That's me all right. One big disgusting disappointment.' She released a shuddering sigh. 'Go me.'

There was a long silence.

Andrea leaned forward again and slid open the glass panel. 'Driver. Change of plans.'

CHAPTER FOUR

ANDREA WAITED IN Izzy's sitting room while she changed her outfit. He tried not to think about their kiss at the ceremony—the kiss that had almost got out of his control. For years he'd thought about kissing her and he hadn't been one bit disappointed. Her mouth was as soft and yielding and as passionate as he'd dreamed. More so. It had been like tasting delicious nectar, finding his tastes so attuned to its sweetness he couldn't stop the desperate craving for more.

Even now he could still taste her. He could still recall the pillowy softness of her lips moving under his. Could still feel the darting flickers of her tongue and her beautiful breasts crushed against his chest. His body was aching with need—a need she had stirred in his flesh, making him feel like a horny teenager. He'd prided himself on his control and yet one press of those soft lips against his and he'd been tempted to change the terms of their agreement.

Sorely tempted.

Dangerously tempted.

Why was it Izzy who made him feel so close to the

edge of his control? During that kiss he'd all but forgotten they were in a registry office in front of witnesses. His senses had been so tuned in to her, every thought had flown from his head other than how much he'd wanted her. His blood had pounded with it.

Damn it, it was still pounding.

He needed more than a cold shower. He needed an ice bath. He needed to stay in control. He wanted her, wanted her desperately, but it didn't mean he would act on it. Acting on it would complicate things. Make their relationship even trickier than it already was.

Andrea swept his gaze around the room, wondering how a young woman from such a wealthy background could live in such a cramped space. The furniture looked second-hand and, while it was shabby chic, it seemed strange she hadn't decorated in the manner to which she had been born. She had stubbornly refused to live in the Hampstead flat her father bought her for her twenty-first birthday. It was now part of her inheritance, having been rented out for the last four years.

Had this been her way to snub her father? To live like an impoverished student? But then his gaze went to a stack of textbooks on a table next to the sofa. A laptop was perched nearby. He looked at the social work titles and frowned. Did the books belong to her flatmate or was Izzy studying online? Perhaps the impoverished student atmosphere of the flat was a reality. But she'd enrolled in courses before and spectacularly failed.

Andrea had always struggled to understand her attitude to her father. While he had never considered Benedict Byrne to be a perfect father, he still didn't think Benedict had deserved how Izzy had behaved towards him. Her rebellious streak had caused her father so much shame and heartache. Her behaviour throughout her teens and early adulthood had been outrageous at times. Underage drinking, hard partying, mixing with the wrong people—all of it orchestrated to draw as much negative attention to herself as possible. Andrea found it hard to have any sympathy for her because the only father figure he'd known had been a cruel sadistic bastard of a stepfather who had beaten his mother, and when Andrea had tried to defend her he'd been kicked out on the streets.

He'd been fourteen years old.

Andrea hated thinking about his past. He was no longer that terrified boy who had no roof over his head. The boy who had been sick-to-his-guts worried about his mother, but when he came back the next day to help her escape, to his shock and despair, she had asked him to go away. Told him she didn't want him any more. His mother had chosen to stay with her violent partner rather than have Andrea help her get away. He had bled for days from the wound on his face from the backhand from his stepfather and to this day carried the scar. It was a permanent reminder of how ugly relationships could get, and how even people who you thought loved you most in the world could still turn against you when you least expected it.

If it hadn't been for Izzy's father crossing paths with Andrea a few months later, who knew what would have become of him? He had gone from begging for food outside hotels and restaurants to owning some of the most luxurious hotels in Europe. With Benedict's help he had chosen a different path, a different life, a different future.

And for the next six months that future included Izzy as his temporary wife.

Izzy came out dressed in a navy blue knee-length dress with three-quarter sleeves with velvet-covered heels to match. The colour of her outfit intensified the blue of her eyes, but a shutter had come up in her gaze, reminding him of unreachable galaxies in a midnight sky. Her mouth was shiny with lip gloss and he couldn't stop thinking about how it felt beneath his own. How she tasted. How she responded. The fire in her had struck a match to the simmering coals of his desire.

Her gaze moved out of reach of his. 'I'm ready.'

He pointed to the books and the laptop. 'Are these yours?'

Her chin came up. 'Yes. What of it?'

'You're studying for a degree?'

Her eyes moved away from his. 'What if I am?'

'Isabella.' Andrea touched the back of her hand and she raised her gaze to meet his. He knew he should try not to touch her so much but the temptation, the need was *always* there. She was like a potent drug he couldn't summon the willpower to resist. And now he'd fed the desire to touch her by kissing her and holding her in his arms, he was going to have to work a lot harder to keep his desire under control.

She pulled her hand away as if his touch disturbed her. 'Yes?' Her voice had a coating of frost around the edges.

'It's great that you're studying. Really great.' He opened and closed his fingers to stop them from tingling from her touch. 'You're doing a Social Work degree?'

'I had to do some extra night classes to get in but I'm scraping through so far.'

'I'm sure you're doing much more than scraping through,' Andrea said, wondering if she had failed in the past by choice rather than lack of academic ability. 'We need to talk about our living arrangements. Or, more to the point, yours.'

Her eyes widened to pools of startled blue ink. 'Pardon?'

'We will be expected to live under the same roof now that we're—'

'I'm not living with you.' She flung away to the other side of the room, spinning back around to glare at him. 'You planned this, didn't you? You tricked me into marrying you and now you're insisting on ridiculous living arrangements. I won't do it. I won't live with you.'

'I said under the same roof, not in the same bed,' Andrea said with measured cool. 'But if you change your mind I'm more than willing to see to your needs.' *What are you doing?* But he didn't want to listen to the voice of his conscience. His conscience could get the hell out of his head. He wanted Izzy and she wanted him. He could feel her desire for him like a current in the air. The same current that was moving through his body in ripples and tingles that left no part of him unaffected.

Her cheeks were fire-engine red, her hands in tight fists by her sides. 'I will not change my mind. I loathe you. You disgust me.'

'That wasn't the message I was getting when you were kissing me back at the celebrant's office.'

Her eyes flashed with vivid blue venom. '*You* kissed me.'

'You asked for it, remember? You practically begged me to—'

She picked up a scatter cushion and threw it at him but it missed and knocked over a photo frame instead. Andrea bent down to pick up the cushion and the frame, setting the frame on the lamp table and then placing the cushion back on the sofa with measured calm. 'Rule number one. No violence. Ever. Not under any circumstances.'

Her expression was a road map of resentment. 'You provoked me.'

'Doesn't matter. No amount of provocation makes it acceptable to throw something at someone, even if it's just a cushion. You have the same assurance from me. You're entitled to feel safe at all times with me. I give you that promise.'

She began to chew at her lower lip, glancing at him from beneath lowered lashes. 'Okay…but I still don't want to live with you.'

'That is not negotiable, I'm afraid,' Andrea said. 'I'll send packers to collect your things in the morning. We will spend the night in my hotel in Mayfair. Tomorrow we will fly to my villa in Positano in Italy.'

'But what about my lease here?' Her brow was troubled with a frown. 'I'll have to pay the rent even if I'm not here because my flatmate—'

'I'll settle it with your landlord and your flatmate.'

'What about my job?'

'You can hand in your notice tomorrow and concentrate on your studies instead. You'll have no need to work unless you particularly want to. Your full inheritance won't be available until the six months is up but, along with the sum your father stipulated you receive upon your marriage, I'll pay you an allowance in the meantime, a generous one, so you'll want for nothing.'

Her eyes flashed another round of fire at him. 'Except my freedom.'

'Isabella.' Andrea released a long-suffering sigh. 'Your future freedom depends on you abiding by the terms of your father's will. I'm making that possible for you so the least you can do is be grateful.'

Her plump lips thinned to a sneer. 'Would you like me to drop to my knees in front of you and demonstrate my gratitude right now?'

Andrea's groin twitched at the sultry challenge in her eyes. He considered calling her bluff. He could think of nothing he wanted more than to have his lust for her satisfied by her lush mouth and hot little tongue. Had he ever wanted a woman more than this one? She stirred in him the most primal urges—urges he could only just control when he was around her. His desire for her was growing, swelling, expanding in his blood and rocketing through his body like a virulent virus. He was hot for her. There wasn't a part of his body that didn't want her to crawl all over it and suck and lick and stroke and, yes, even to bite.

'Pack an overnight bag,' he said, doing everything in his power to keep his gaze away from her mouth. 'I'll wait in the cab.'

Izzy stuffed a few things in a bag with such anger barrelling through her system she thought the top of her head would explode. How had she allowed herself to be so blindsided by Andrea? She'd foolishly assumed they would marry and that would be it. He would go one way and she would go the other.

But no.

He wanted a wife. It *suited* him to have a wife. But why her? She was the most unsuitable wife in London. You didn't have to look too far back online to see some of the things that had been reported about her. Not all of them true, but 'once a tart, always a tart' as far as the press and the public were concerned.

Izzy hadn't done herself any favours in that regard. Deliberately inciting negative press, making her nights out clubbing look far more incriminating than they were. She had relished the shame it had brought to her father's door. She had enjoyed every cringeworthy second of her payback for all the disappointment and hurt and despair he'd inflicted.

But she hadn't been mature enough back then to realise the shame would stick like mud on her door far longer than it would on his. She couldn't apply for a job these days without someone finding an oftentimes ambiguous but no less damning shot of her on social media.

Once that stuff was online it was always online.

Why had Andrea waited until now to force her hand? Why not approach her three months ago? Why leave it until the midnight hour when all her other options were gone?

Not that she'd had any other options. And, truth be told, she hadn't looked as hard as she should have to find a husband. She'd only just enrolled in her course and juggling work and study had been more than enough to handle. She'd been so angry at the way her father had engineered things that she'd wasted two months seething. And then the sick, sinking feeling every time she thought about finding a man to marry her had made it impossible to do much other than search through the list of contacts on her phone and break out into a prickly sweat because no one was suitable or, even if they had been, they would never have been agreeable.

But, strangely, Andrea Vaccaro was agreeable. More than agreeable. He'd made it all but impossible for her to say no. He'd made sure she wouldn't be *able* to say no. He'd covered all the bases, tied up all the loose ends, ensnaring her so cleverly in his web like a spider did an unsuspecting fly. That self-congratulatory glint in his eyes at the ceremony proved how much he was enjoying having her in his power. *Grrr*. Under his command.

Izzy had never considered him as a temporary husband. Never. She'd skipped past his name in her phone as if she were avoiding contamination. Just seeing his name there had been enough to make her heart stutter and her breath stick in the walls of her throat.

But now she was wearing his ring on her finger and the only way she would be free of him was when the six-month period was up. *Six months!* Six months living with Andrea, pretending to be his wife in public.

How would she survive the torture?

Even more worrying…how would she survive the temptation?

Izzy remained silent in the cab until it pulled into the forecourt of Andrea's luxury hotel in Mayfair. The paparazzi had gathered and were waiting under the crimson and gold awning that sheltered the drive-through area in front of the grand old building. Had he given the press the heads-up? Or had they automatically assumed he would bring her here for their…*gulp*…wedding night? It was, after all, his home when he came to London. He mostly lived between his two homes in Positano and Florence. She glanced at Andrea with a frown. 'I thought we were going back to Henri's for dinner?'

'It's been a big day.' That self-satisfied gleam was back in his eyes. 'We both need an early night, *si*?'

Izzy couldn't control the shimmery little tremor that went through her body. It was as if champagne had been injected into her bloodstream—little bubbles of forbidden excitement that made her breath hitch and her heart hammer. She couldn't be alone with him until she got herself back under control. She had no defence against the pull of attraction. It was like trying to fight a bloody battle with a paper sword. 'But I was looking forward to eating at Henri's. It's one of my favourite places. I'm hungry and—'

'I'm sure I'll find something in my hotel to satisfy that appetite of yours.' Something about his tone made her suspect he might not be talking about food. 'I'll handle the press,' he added. 'And remember, we're madly in love and are now on our honeymoon.'

A hotel porter came to collect Izzy's overnight bag from the cab. Andrea led Izzy past the paparazzi, stopping long enough to say they would like some privacy to celebrate their marriage. The congratulations were hearty and enthusiastic, and some of the comments he made back to the press made it sound like Izzy had been waiting for this moment for most of her life. Sickening. Just sickening. She had never felt more furious. How dare he tell the world she'd had a crush on him since she was a teenager?

She hadn't.

She didn't.

She *never* would.

The cameras continued to flash and click like rapid gunfire, the recording devices thrust in front of their faces to such a degree Andrea put his arm up to shield Izzy's from them. 'Thank you, everyone,' he said. 'It's time for us to be left alone now to enjoy our first night together.'

Their first night together...

How those words made her insides shiver and her pulse race. His arm around her waist was a steel cord of strength but, strangely, she felt protected by it. She hadn't felt as threatened as she normally would when the press surged at her. He had made sure no one bumped her or came too close. It was nothing but an act—a charade of Loving Husband for the cameras. But, even so, it made her solid dislike of him soften a little around the edges.

Andrea took her to a private elevator that only senior hotel staff used, the doors closing off the rest of the world with a gentle swish. Izzy immediately sprang to the other side of the elevator and folded her arms across her body, shooting him a glare that was multiplied by the mirrored walls.

He leaned with indolent grace against the side wall. 'It seems we have created quite a storm of interest, *cara*.' His lazy smile came at her from every wall of the elevator. 'The heiress *enfant terrible* and the billionaire hotelier has quite a ring to it, does it not?'

Izzy ground her teeth until her molars threatened mutiny. 'Did you have to make up such absolute rubbish about me? I have not, did not and will not ever have a crush on you.'

His gaze swept over her body as if he was removing every stitch of her clothing. Heat flared between her thighs when his gaze came back to hers. Smouldering eyes. Eyes that burned holes into her resolve like laser pointers. 'You have always wanted me, *cara*. I feel it every time you look at me.'

'Right back at you, buddy.' Izzy raised her chin. 'I've seen the way you look at me. And for God's sake stop calling me *cara*.'

He pressed the emergency stop button on the elevator and it came to a gliding halt. So did Izzy's breathing. 'W-what are you doing?'

He came to where she was standing against the back wall of the elevator, stopping so close to her she felt his muscled thighs brush hers. He put one hand on either side of her head, caging her between his arms. His chocolate-brown eyes meshed with hers in a lock that made the floor of her belly shiver like tinsel in a breeze. 'I'm not denying I want you, *tesoro mio*. I want you very much. But I think you want me more, *sì*?' One of his thighs gently nudged her legs apart and she gasped when the hard ridge of his muscle-packed leg came in contact with her mound.

Izzy couldn't breathe. Her heart was beating so fast and so erratically she thought it might pop right out of her chest. Every pore of her body was aware of him—acutely, thrillingly aware. She couldn't stop staring at his mouth—the sexy masculine contours that had felt so magical against her own. She moistened her lips and he followed every millimetre of its journey with his hooded gaze. 'Other people might need to use the elevator.' Her voice was so croaky it sounded like she'd been hanging around a frog pond and got too friendly with the natives.

His smile tilted a little further, making his eyes darken even further. 'It's my hotel. My elevator. And you are my wife.'

Izzy intended to push him away but somehow her hands fisted in his shirt instead. The toned muscles of his chest were like plates of steel against her knuckles, the citrus and woodsy fragrance of him making her dizzy with longing. 'In name only.'

'So far.' He lowered his head to brush his stubbly jaw against the side of her face, sending her senses into frenzy. 'But how long will that last?'

Desire flooded her being. Giant, thumping, pumping waves of it moving through her with such force she had trouble standing. Had she ever felt lust so powerful? So overwhelming? It was like a fever in her blood, a racing, raging red-hot fever that made it impossible for her to think of anything but how he made her feel. 'I'm not going to sleep with you, Andrea.' *But I want to. I want to so badly.*

He moved his mouth to just an inch above hers, his warm breath mingling intimately with hers. His thigh moved against her, teasing the heart of her with slow rubs and nudges that made her knees wobble and her spine melt like honey in a heatwave. 'We'll be good together, *cara*. Better than good.'

Izzy's fingers gripped his shirt even tighter but still she didn't push him away. *Why aren't you pushing him away?* The alarm bell of her conscience was too faint for her to take notice. It was like trying to hear someone's whisper at a heavy metal concert. Her need of him was too strong, too powerful. She closed the distance between their mouths, pressing her lips to his, delighting in the tantalising feel of him responding.

He took control of the kiss with a bold stroke of his tongue across her lips, entering her mouth and calling her tongue into a sexy tango that made every knob of her vertebrae tingle like fairy dust was being trickled down her spine. She pressed herself closer, linking her arms around his neck, her fingers delving into the thickness of his hair. She stretched up on tiptoe so she could feel every delicious hard ridge of him against her body, the friction revving up her desire like bellows in front of a fire. Her breasts were crushed against his chest and she was suddenly aware of their sensitivity, as if they were already anticipating the stroke of his hands, the glide of his tongue, the gentle scrape of his teeth.

She whimpered against his mouth, wanting more, needing more, aching for more. His mouth was still crushed to hers, his tongue playing with hers in a kiss that mimicked the erotic caress of his thigh against her. Sensations sparked and fizzed like fireworks in her body. Sensations she had not felt with a partner before. She could do this alone but never with a partner. She'd always had to fake it rather than admit her failure.

But Andrea had unlocked her sensuality in a way no other man had. The tension in her core grew and grew, the sensitive nerves tight and tingling. Her legs, her thighs, deep in her body the tingles ran up and down and around and around until she was unable to process thought. He increased the friction of his thigh as if he was reading every nuance of her body. She couldn't possibly be feeling like this…how could it happen so easily? How could he have so much sensual power over her to reduce her to a quivering, whimpering wanton? She gasped as the wave rose and rose inside her, the little ripples growing, swelling, burgeoning until they broke over her in a massive rush, shattering her senses into thousands of pieces like confetti fluttering through her blood.

Izzy opened her eyes and then closed them, squeezing them tight against the smug expression on Andrea's face. Oh, God, why had she allowed him to reduce her to this? To a reckless, shameless wanton who hadn't enough self-control to withstand the temptation of his touch. Why hadn't she resisted him? Where was her willpower? Damn it. Where was her pride? Why had she allowed him to prove his point with such embarrassing, devastating accuracy?

He wasn't the one who couldn't control himself.

She was. And he had proven it.

Izzy hadn't thought it possible to hate someone so much for bringing her such amazing pleasure. If this was what his hard thigh could do to her, what on earth would making love with him be like?

Andrea lifted her chin, his eyes gleaming with triumph. 'What did I tell you? Dynamite.'

Izzy summoned what was left of her pride. She pushed him away and schooled her features into a mask of cool indifference. 'How do you know I wasn't faking it?'

He studied her for a beat or two. 'You don't have to feel ashamed of how you respond to me. It will make our marriage much more satisfying.' He pressed the button to get the elevator going again. 'For both of us.'

The doors opened on his floor and he ushered her out of the elevator with a hand at her elbow. Izzy knew she should move away from the warm, gentle cup of his hand but somehow couldn't bring herself to do it.

He opened his penthouse suite with his key card and turned to her. 'Shall I carry you over the threshold?'

Izzy shot him a glare so lethal it could have blacked out the lights. 'Don't even think about it.'

CHAPTER FIVE

Izzy STEPPED INTO the suite, the sound of the door clicking shut as Andrea came in behind her making her heart give a little stumble and her legs tremble.

She was his wife.

He was her husband.

They were alone.

Inside his hotel suite.

Her body was still tingling from the shocking intimacy he had subjected her to. Intimacy she should have put a stop to but somehow hadn't. Why not? Why had she allowed him to prove how much more she needed him than he needed her? The power balance was all out of kilter.

Izzy drew in a shaky breath and glanced around the suite. The décor of the suite was stunning but not in an over-the-top way. The crystal chandeliers, ankle-deep dove-grey carpet and grey-blue velvet-covered sofas with stylish scatter cushions gave the room a welcoming, restful feel. Lamps were turned down low to give a muted glow that highlighted the private, sanctuary-like atmosphere of the suite. It was a masculine suite and yet it had softer touches such as vases of fresh flowers and cashmere throw rugs draped elegantly on each of the sofas. The curtains were the same blue-grey as the sofas and were drawn back from the windows to showcase the view.

Izzy moved through the suite, stopping to look at the artwork on the walls—originals, not prints, of course. There was a dining area off the main sitting room and the master bedroom and en suite bathroom through another door. She peered inside the master bedroom, her eyes going straight to her overnight bag positioned on the velvet-covered luggage rest. No doubt it had been delivered while she and Andrea were in the elevator. She closed the door and turned and looked at him. 'Where's the other bedroom?'

'There isn't one.' He shrugged off his jacket and laid it across the back of one of the sofas. 'You'll be sharing mine.'

Izzy's stomach dropped so far it bounced and knocked her heart into her throat. 'What? What sort of penthouse is this if it only has one bedroom?'

His expression was inscrutable. 'Is that going to be a problem for you?'

'Of course it's a problem.' She stalked as far away from him as she could get, sending him a glare so blistering she was surprised the paint didn't peel off the walls. 'I told you I'm not sleeping with you. I want my own room.' She folded her arms and planted her feet. 'I want my own suite.'

Andrea casually loosened his tie, his gaze still meshed with hers. 'Not possible, I'm afraid.'

'But you own the flipping hotel!' Izzy's voice was so shrill she thought it might shatter the chandeliers. She knew her outraged virgin reaction could be considered a little inconsistent given her reputation, but she couldn't possibly share a bedroom with him. Sharing a bedroom meant sharing a bed. She'd shared an elevator with him and look how *that* turned out.

Andrea's tie landed alongside his jacket and he reached up to undo a couple of the buttons of his shirt. His calm demeanour and his slow and methodical movements as he released the buttons were in stark contrast to how she was feeling, which made her even more furious with him. 'Precisely,' he said, his eyes so dark her insides gave a little flutter. 'Which is why you're sharing this suite with me. I will not have my domestic staff think this is not a genuine marriage.'

Izzy began pacing the floor in case she was tempted to undo the rest of those buttons for him. She forced her gaze away from his tanned and toned chest with its dusting of crisp masculine hair. She had to get a hold on herself. She was meant to be standing up to him, resisting him, not gawking at him like some kind of sex-starved spinster.

He was enjoying every second of her panic. He was so cool. So enviably, damnably cool. He reminded her of a cat who had cleverly cornered a mouse. He was biding his time, waiting for the perfect moment when one of his velvet-covered paws would strike his hapless prey.

There was going to be no such moment.

Izzy straightened her spine as if she were the star

student at deportment school. 'If you think I'm going to get in that bed with you and allow you to touch me, think again. If you so much as lay one finger on me I will scream so loud your staff will have to replace all the chandeliers. And the windows. In the entire hotel.'

Andrea gave a low deep chuckle. 'I have no problem with a little screaming coming from my bedroom. The louder the better.'

Izzy spun away to stand stiffly in front of one of the windows. She couldn't allow him to do this to her—reduce her to a tantrum-throwing termagant. She had to act cool and unmoved by his attempt to unsettle her. She had to call his bluff. He was doing this to needle her. He knew how much she hated him. He was trying to get the upper hand in their relationship. And she was handing him free points every time she reacted like a spoilt child.

She had to think of another tactic—another way to outsmart him. *Think. Think. Think.*

Izzy took a calming breath and turned around to face him. 'All right. You win. We share the bed. But I should warn you I'm a terribly restless sleeper.'

His expression showed no apparent satisfaction that she'd changed her mind, but she couldn't help wondering what was going on behind the screen of his impenetrable gaze. 'Perhaps I can find a way to relax you, *si*?'

Izzy turned away before he saw the longing she was trying to suppress. Why was he the only man who could do this to her? Make her angry and aroused in equal measure. 'I'm going to have a shower.' She turned for the master bedroom and its en suite bathroom.

'What about dinner?'

'I'm not hungry.'

'You might change your mind after your shower,' Andrea said. 'I'll order something for you.'

Izzy closed the bedroom door by way of answer. She leaned back against it with a heavy sigh, wondering how she was going to get through a whole night sleeping beside Andrea. It was like asking a chocolate addict to spend the night in a chocolate factory. How would she stop herself from touching him? And what if he touched her? He only had to look at her to get her hot and bothered.

What had happened to her defences?

To her resolve?

She moved away from the bedroom door and went to the luxurious en suite. The bathroom was decked out in marble with the same blue-grey tones of the bedroom, teamed with a white freestanding bath and twin basins with stunning ornate silver-trimmed mirrors. Soft fluffy towels as big as blankets were on the silver towel rails and more were rolled stylishly on a glass shelf. The shower was so big it could have housed an entire football team, and it had a large square rainwater showerhead. The bathroom smelt of exotic essential oils and there were bottles of the Vaccaro signature toiletries positioned on the marble counter near the basin and more in the shower and next to the bath. Two blue-grey bathrobes hung on silver hooks on the back of the door, and Izzy couldn't help wondering who had been the last woman to spend the night with Andrea here.

Izzy stripped off her clothes and stepped under the

shower, tilting her head back so the water could wash
over her as if she were standing in a waterfall in a rain-
forest. She was no stranger to luxury. While she was
growing up, her father had always insisted on staying
at the best hotels because he believed a businessman
of his status deserved the best. But something about
Andrea's hotel had more than just over-the-top luxury.
It had class. Sophistication. Understated glamour. The
simplicity of design and detail hinted at a man who
liked and appreciated the good things in life but was
not one to flash his wealth around in a status-seeking
manner.

Once she'd finished showering, Izzy dried off and
dressed in her nightgown and slipped on one of the
bathrobes. She roughly dried her hair using the hair-
dryer she found in one of the bathroom drawers and
then scooped it loosely on top of her head in a make-
shift ponytail. She looked at her make-up-free face and
wondered if she should put on some cosmetic armour,
but then decided against it. She wasn't out to impress
him. What did it matter if she didn't look anything like
his gorgeous and sophisticated bed buddies?

She. Did. Not. Care.

Izzy came out of the bathroom to find the suite
empty apart from a dinner trolley that was set up next
to the dining table off the sitting room. She did a quick
search of the rest of the suite but there was no sign of
Andrea. She went back to the dinner trolley and lifted
the silver domes off to see if he had eaten anything
but the delicious-looking food was untouched. There
wasn't a note left anywhere and when she checked her

phone there was no text message either. If he was so keen to keep up appearances, then why wasn't he in the suite with her?

Izzy leaned down to smell the food and momentarily closed her eyes in bliss. There was a bottle of champagne in an ice bucket, desserts under another lid, fresh fruit and a cheese plate under another. There were little savoury pastries and tartlets and some crab cakes and fresh oysters. A seafood dish that was fragrant with lemongrass and lime and chilli and coconut milk was in another dish with a bowl of fluffy jasmine rice flecked with coriander. It was a feast of her fantasies and she was suddenly so hungry she felt faint. She looked at her phone, wondering if she should call or text Andrea to see where he was but decided against it. She didn't want to start acting like a suspicious wife, checking up on his whereabouts.

Why should she care where he was?

There was a message on her phone from her flatmate, Jess, who had apparently seen something on Twitter about Izzy and Andrea's surprise marriage. It was a little shocking to realise how quickly the news had travelled. Izzy texted back to say she would be moving out but not to worry about the rent because Andrea had promised to pay out the lease. Even as she typed the words, she realised how much control she had handed to him. He was paying her bills, sorting out everything for her like she had no mind of her own.

Izzy put down her phone and sighed. She would have to suck it up because the only way she could get her grandparents' house back was to abide by the terms

of her father's will. The allowance Andrea had offered
to pay her would help, so too would the money her father had stipulated would be paid to her upfront upon
her marriage, but the full balance would not be in her
hands until the six months was up. She had already
spoken to the current owners and they had graciously
agreed to hold back from putting the house on the market until December. She'd had to make them an offer
they couldn't refuse to get them to hold off selling but
she didn't care how much it cost her.

Buying back her grandparents' house was a way
to right the wrongs of the past—a way to honour her
mother and her brother by bringing back what should
never have been taken away.

Andrea sat in his office on the first floor of the hotel
and sorted out a couple of issues his manager had
brought to his attention. He knew he could have just
as easily seen to them in the morning, but he felt the
need to clear his head. Izzy's response to him in the
elevator had made him realise the electric heat that
fired between them. He became like a horny teenager
when he was with her. She excited him like no other
woman. There was a dangerous element to what he
felt about her. The raw desire that pumped in his blood
pushed him into a place he had never allowed himself
to go before now.

He wanted her so badly it was all he could think
about. How much he wanted to drive himself into her
moist heat. How he wanted to hear her scream his name.
How he wanted to feel her come apart around him.

He'd contained his lust for her for years. For years he'd thrown himself into work, pummelled the forbidden desire out of him by long punishing hours, driven himself to achieve what others only dreamed about. He had everything money could buy. He had achieved more than he had set out to achieve.

He wasn't after the happy-ever-after package. And Izzy was certainly not the woman to give it to him. Her negative attitude to marriage was his safety hatch—the escape route so that when the six months was up he could walk away without a qualm. It was a means-to-an-end marriage. A mutually satisfying arrangement that would give them both what they wanted. He'd been rethinking his paper marriage stance. Why shouldn't he indulge his desire for her and hers for him? It was clear they wanted each other. The way she'd responded to him in the elevator proved that she wasn't immune to him any more than he was to her.

She would get her inheritance and he would get her.

But Andrea was prepared to take his time about it. He wanted her to be the one to come to him. And her coming apart on his thigh in the elevator was an indicator of how close she was to capitulating. She was only resisting him because he had rejected her advances seven years ago. He knew she had only targeted him back then because she knew it would jeopardise his relationship with her father. He'd been tempted. Sure he had. Every cell in his body had felt the strain of resisting her come-and-get-me eyes. For years he'd worked hard not to show it. Whenever he came into contact with her at one of her father's parties or events he would screen his desire behind a mask of cynicism. But inside he was simmering, smouldering with lust.

It was different now. She wanted him, not as a rebellious teenager out to make mischief. This time she wanted him as a fully grown passionate woman.

He closed down his computer and smiled. Yes. It was only a matter of time before she would be finally his.

Izzy had eaten so much she had to lie down, but she refused to lie on Andrea's bed. That seemed way too intimate, too…anticipatory, as if she was waiting for him to come and make love to her. She wasn't… But she had thought about it. A lot. It was all she seemed to think about. Her body felt agitated, restless, needy. The response he had evoked in her in the elevator had made her hungry for more. She wanted to feel his arms around her, his body within her, his mouth locked on hers.

She had a reputation as a sleep-around slut but she'd only had a handful of lovers and none of them had been satisfying. She'd always been uncomfortable with physical intimacy and had made herself tipsy in order to get through it. None of her partners had taken the time to get to know her needs or preferences but carried on regardless. She figured it was easier to pretend she was having a good time rather than speak up and risk being called a freak or frigid.

Not that she felt frigid when she was around Andrea. Far from it. He only had to put his knee between her thighs and she'd shattered into a million pieces of bliss. What would happen if he made love to her in every sense of the word?

Izzy curled up on one of the sofas in the sitting room and wrapped herself in one of the cashmere throw rugs. She had to stop thinking about Andrea making love to her. She had to stop craving his touch. She had to stop imagining his hands and lips and tongue on her flesh. *Had. To. Stop.* She turned on the television to watch one of her favourite shows but it didn't capture her interest as it normally would. She closed her eyes and promised herself she would keep an ear out for when Andrea came back in…

Andrea entered the suite and found Izzy fast asleep on one of the sofas. She was wearing one of his hotel's bathrobes but it had fallen open, revealing the slender length of her legs. Her feet were bare and her toenails were painted in an electric blue. Her hair was tied up in a ponytail but some strands had loosened and now fell about her face. Her skin was make-up free and as pure and unblemished as a cream-coloured rose, her eyelashes and eyebrows so dark in contrast she looked like a modern version of Sleeping Beauty. He had always considered her beautiful, but without the adornment of make-up and proper hair styling she looked almost ethereal, like an angel in a Renaissance painting. Serene and untouchable.

He approached the sofa but she didn't stir. He gently straightened the throw rug so it covered her legs, then he brushed back her hair, tucking it behind the shell of her ear. She smelt of the essential oils he had selected as the signature scent of his hotel chain. She gave a little murmur and burrowed her head further against the scatter cushion she was leaning on.

He felt a jab of disappointment she hadn't woken at the sound of him entering the suite. He hadn't realised how much he'd been looking forward to sparring with her. He enjoyed the way she not only locked horns with him but threatened to rip his off and stab him with them. The way she stared him down and threw insults at him like darts. He enjoyed baiting her, watching her colour rise and her eyes flash. She hated him but she wanted him, and to him that was a sexy combination.

He began to move away when she suddenly jerked upright, pushing her hair out of her face and looking at him through narrowed eyes. 'What are you doing?'

'I was covering your legs with the throw rug.'

She got up from the sofa and tied the edges of her bathrobe more securely, her cheeks stained a light pink. 'Have you eaten?' She glanced at the dinner trolley and her cheeks darkened a notch. 'I was kind of hungry so you might need to order up some more.'

Andrea picked up the bottle of champagne out of the ice bucket. 'Fancy some?'

'It might seem strange to you but I don't actually feel like celebrating.' Her tone was so sour it would have curdled milk.

He uncorked the bottle and poured two glasses. 'You should celebrate. You're now a very wealthy young woman.' He handed her a glass of champagne. 'A very wealthy *married* young woman.'

Her eyes flashed and her mouth thinned. She took

the champagne and for a moment he wondered if she was going to throw it in his face. Then she touched her glass against his. 'That is if we last the distance.' She gave a small frown. 'How can I be sure you won't sabotage this by walking out before the six months is up? As you so kindly pointed out, I have the most to lose.'

Andrea stroked a finger down the curve of her cheek. 'You'll have to trust me, won't you, *cara*?'

Something hardened in her eyes and she brushed his hand away from her face as if she were shooing away a fly, almost spilling her champagne in the process. 'Stop touching me. I can't think when you do that. And I thought I told you not to keep calling me that. No one's here but us. It's totally unnecessary and it's damn annoying.'

'What you find annoying is how much you like it when I call you that,' Andrea said. 'You like lots of the things I do to you but you're too proud to admit it.'

She plonked her glass down on the nearest surface. 'I'm going to bed.' She threw him another glare. 'And no, that is not an invitation for you to join me.'

Andrea put his glass down and came to her, taking her by the hands before she could step away. 'I will not take advantage of you, Isabella. We'll only make love if or when you give me the go-ahead. You have my absolute word on that.'

She didn't try to pull away from his hold and her expression softened slightly, the tight muscles of her jaw eased and her eyes lost their sheen of don't-mess-with-me brittleness. 'I still don't understand why you're doing this… Why you wanted to marry me in the first place. It doesn't make sense.'

He massaged the backs of her hands with his thumbs, holding her gaze with his. 'Remember I told you it was convenient for me to get married just now? I have a hotel merger I've been negotiating for a while. The owner has a teenage stepdaughter who has developed a rather embarrassing crush on me. I figured if I had a wife then that little problem will be taken care of until I get the merger completed. A temporary marriage between us seemed a perfect solution to both of our problems.'

Izzy's expression looked like she had eaten something that had disagreed with her. 'What a pity you didn't think to pull a convenient wife out of a hat seven years ago when I made that pass at you.'

'I knew what you were up to back then. You wanted to embarrass your father.' He gave her hands another slow stroke with his thumbs. 'It would have been wrong for me to get involved with you, not just because of my relationship with your father but because you were too young and headstrong to be in a proper adult relationship.'

Her teeth pulled at her lower lip, her eyes lowered. 'He always made me feel so inadequate…so stupid and useless.' Her voice held a note of bitterness that underlined each word.

Andrea frowned. Was she talking about the man he had known and admired for his business acumen and charitable work? 'Your father?'

She pulled out of his hold, her eyes glittering with

the bitterness he'd heard in her voice. 'I don't want to talk about it. Not to you.'

'Why not to me?'

Her gaze shifted. 'You wouldn't believe me, that's why.'

Andrea had always been aware that there were facets to Benedict Byrne that were less honourable than others. It was why he had distanced himself from Benedict over the last couple of years. He knew Benedict had found being the father of a wilful daughter a complex and emotionally draining experience. But he realised he had only ever heard Benedict's side. He had never asked Izzy directly what it was like for her being her father's daughter. 'I'd like you to tell me, Isabella,' he said. 'It's important to me to know why you felt he didn't value you.'

Her gaze was wary. Guarded. 'Important to you, why? So you can tell me what a screwed-up, selfish and spoilt brat I am for not appreciating all the sacrifices my father made? No, thanks. I'll go and find a brick wall to talk to instead. I bet I'd feel more listened to.'

Andrea could see it was going to take some time for Izzy to learn to trust him. Their relationship had always been a combative one so changing it would take time and careful handling on his part. But it concerned him he might have been too quick to judge her in the past, too quick to believe the things her father told him about her without speaking to her himself. He'd been so intent on avoiding her, of being alone with her, he had let himself be swayed by her father's version of her behaviour.

'I'm sorry you think I wouldn't listen to you about something this important,' he said. 'Your father wasn't perfect. I had to set limits with him at times because he could be a little overpowering in his enthusiasm for a project. I always felt a little sorry for him for the loss of your brother and your mother. I may have let that colour my judgement of him and, of course, you.'

Izzy's expression lost some of its wariness, her mouth softening from a tight white line of bitterness to release a jagged sigh. 'He acted like Father of the Year when he was around everyone else, but when we were alone he was always berating me. Putting me down, telling me I wasn't as smart as my brother, Hamish, or I was too fat or too thin or not confident enough—the list went on and on. I was never able to please him. Never.'

Andrea knew Benedict Byrne had been a difficult man at times. He hadn't suffered fools gladly and he had exacting standards that hadn't always won him lasting friendships. Andrea tried to recall all the times he'd seen Izzy and her father together. All he could remember was Izzy acting out, being rude or belligerent, deliberately defying curfews and blatantly disregarding her father's wishes. Benedict had always seemed so patient with her—far more patient than one would expect any parent to be. Andrea had always seen Izzy as a typical overindulged and ungrateful teenager who didn't understand the sacrifices her father had made for her.

But what if he had misread things?

What if he had wanted to see her that way? What if *Benedict* had wanted him to see her that way?

What if the man he'd admired and owed so much was not the decent and hardworking man Benedict Byrne wanted everyone to think he was? Andrea had personal experience of chameleon-like men. His stepfather could be utterly charming in company but could turn into an anger-crazed demon when no one was looking.

'Isabella…' Andrea said, not sure where to begin with an apology that was too little, too late. 'You're describing someone I barely recognise—'

'So you'll believe what my father wanted you to believe other than accept what I'm telling you.' She didn't say it as a question but as a given, as if it was a reality she had heard many times before.

'No. I want to listen to your side. I want to understand why you found him so difficult to love.'

Her eyes suddenly brimmed with unshed tears and he realised he had never seen her cry before. Not even at her father's funeral. 'He didn't love me so why would I love him?' Her tone was defiant but underneath there was a deep chord of sadness.

He blotted one of her tears with his thumb. 'But you did love him, *si*?'

She swallowed and blinked a few times, the tears drying up as if she regretted losing control. Her expression tightened as if all of her facial muscles were holding in her emotions and only just managing to contain them. 'You knew him as Benedict Byrne the successful business developer. As your friend and mentor. The philanthropic businessman who gave generously to others. You didn't know him as a father.'

Andrea thought again of the times he'd seen Izzy and her father together. But this time it was like putting on a different pair of reading glasses, the images developing a startling new clarity. Images of Benedict's calm expression when Izzy had made a cutting comment— he had almost been *too* calm.

Deadly calm.

Revenge-will-come-later calm.

Images of Benedict's arm around Izzy's waist and her rigid body posture, which Andrea had always put down to her surly and intractable nature. But what if Benedict's hold had a touch of cruelty about it? Benedict had spoken at length to Andrea about his hurt and disappointment over Izzy's behaviour, but what if those cosy little man-to-man confessions had been nothing but a cover-up? An emotional alibi to hide the ugly truth?

'You're right,' Andrea said. 'And no father is the same for every child within a family. I know the loss of Hamish devastated him, as it would any parent.'

'I'm not saying he didn't love my brother,' Izzy said. 'He did. But that was part of the problem. He didn't have enough love left over for me. I was just a girl and I didn't have the skills and abilities Hamish had. I was a failure in my father's eyes. A big, fat disappointing failure.'

Andrea gently placed his hands on her shoulders. 'Did he say that to you?'

Her lips pulled tight as if she wasn't sure if she should say any more. Then she let out a long breath. 'Many times. But never within anyone's hearing. My only chance to get back at him was to act out in public. I know it was stupid of me. It only made him look all the more wonderful because he was always so long-suffering and patient when anyone was watching.'

Andrea's scalp began to prickle, his stomach pinching, his conscience grimacing in shame. *He had been fooled by Benedict.* Shockingly, shamefully fooled. It was even more painful for him to admit it, given he had suffered under his stepfather's tyrannical rule, while everyone thought it was Izzy's fault for being defiant. 'What happened when everyone left?'

'He was too smart to shout at me because of the household staff who might overhear. He would tell me what he thought of me behind closed doors in this really hushed and angry voice and his eyes would get all bulgy and mad-looking.' Pain flickered over her face. 'He'd tell me how he wished I'd been the one to die instead of Hamish.'

Izzy was painting a picture Andrea didn't want to look at in too close detail but he knew he must. He couldn't allow himself to be blinded by his own personal bias. He had always prided himself on being a good judge of character but now he felt as if he had been duped. Duped by someone he had admired. He had benefited so much from her father. He would not be the success he was today without the older man's help. But he knew even the best men could have bad sides.

But how bad had Benedict Byrne's been?

'Was he ever…violent?' He stumbled over the word and all its ugliness.

'Only once.' Her eyes flashed with bitterness. 'He

slapped me across the face when I was fourteen, soon after my mother died of cancer. The irony is that I told him much the same he told me. I told him I wished he'd been the one to die instead of my mother. He never hit me after that but the threat he might do so again was always there.'

Andrea was shocked and ashamed he hadn't picked up earlier on the Byrne family dynamics. He'd met her father in Italy twenty years ago, not long after the tragedy of Hamish's diagnosis of terminal bone cancer. When Benedict found Andrea begging for food on the streets, he'd been exactly the same age as the son and heir Benedict had just buried. Fourteen. There was a part of Andrea that had always wondered if Benedict would have given him the leg up he had if it hadn't been for the loss of his son. But he had been so grateful for the help he never questioned the motives behind it.

'I'm sorry you went through such treatment at the hands of someone who was supposed to love and protect you,' Andrea said. 'I only knew your father as a generous man who liked making a difference in people's lives. But I realise all people have shadow sides. But he kept his hidden far better than most.'

'So you...believe me?' The note of uncertainty in her voice made him realise what little hope she must have held that he would believe the version she had shared of her father. Had she tried to tell others and not been believed? Or hadn't she even bothered trying, knowing how hard it would be to dispel the good father image Benedict had exhibited so convincingly?

Andrea slid his hands down from her shoulders to

take her hands again. 'I believe you. I thought I knew your father pretty well. But I once lived with a man who had two faces, the one he showed in public and the one he revealed in private. No one would have believed him capable of the things he did in private. I'm sorry I didn't cotton on to Benedict earlier. I would have spoken to him. Called him out on his behaviour.'

She looked down at their joined hands, releasing a little shuddery breath. Then her gaze climbed back to his. 'He was awful to Mum as well. She had no hope of standing up to him. She'd bought into the belief that wives should always obey their husbands. She took all his insults and put-downs, which made me so angry and all the more determined to stand up to him to show him he couldn't push me around the same way. But I'm not sure it worked the way I intended. I ended up wrecking my own life…'

Andrea could see why Izzy had railed against his insistence they marry. He'd hardly given her a choice. He'd acted like an overbearing army sergeant issuing commands and orders. No wonder she'd pushed back and fought him at every opportunity. 'Isabella… I don't know what to say, other than I'm sorry things have turned out like this. Your father had no right to treat you and your mother like that. I'm shocked and deeply ashamed I didn't suspect it earlier. I guess the only consolation is he's left you well provided for, even if the conditions attached to his will are not what you would have chosen.'

Her expression became brooding and resentful. 'But that's the point—he didn't expect me to fulfil the conditions of his will. He knew how much I hated the thought of marriage, of giving up my freedom. He made his feelings for me perfectly clear. He would rather give all of his wealth—a large proportion of which originally belonged to my mother—to a distant relative with a gambling problem than give it outright to me, his only remaining heir.'

Andrea could see so clearly now there were things about Izzy's father he had ignored the whole time he'd known him. Ignored or dismissed or excused. Why hadn't he taken the time to look a little more closely? He'd made allowances for Izzy's father because he felt sorry for all Benedict had suffered in losing a son and having to deal with a difficult daughter and a grief-stricken wife, and then the subsequent loss of his wife to liver cancer. Andrea had been too ready to lay the blame at Izzy's door, believing her to be the problem. He'd taken the view that Benedict was doing all he could to keep what was left of his family together, throwing himself into work and charitable causes to compensate for his terrible loss. Izzy's mother had struggled both physically and mentally since Hamish's death, as any mother would, but Benedict had always given Andrea the impression he was a loving husband and father, endlessly, tirelessly patient and hardwork-ing.

Andrea felt sick to his gut he hadn't realised the truth earlier. Shame ran through his body like a fetid tide. He'd married Izzy with the intention of 'taming' her. He'd been intent on schooling her like a flighty filly, but how crass and boorish that seemed now.

It made one thing clear to him, though. How could he consummate the marriage now he knew the history of her relationship with her father? How could he cross that boundary, knowing what he knew now? But it wasn't the physical boundary he was most worried about. Getting close to her would mean crossing an emotional boundary he never crossed with anyone. Although it would just about kill him to keep his hands off her he would do the right thing by her—see the six months out so she received her inheritance—but it would be a paper marriage.

He let out a long breath. 'I wasn't comfortable with the way your father wrote his will, but I didn't consider it my place to interfere with his wishes.'

A frown pulled at her smooth brow. 'Why weren't you comfortable?'

'I was concerned you might marry someone in haste who would do the wrong thing by you.'

'So you volunteered your…erm, services?'

Andrea released her and put a little distance between them. He had to get himself out of the habit of touching her. *Hands off. Hands off. Hands off.* It was a mantra inside his head but the rest of his body wasn't listening.

If he were truly honest with himself, he wasn't exactly sure why he'd stepped into the breach and offered to marry her. *Forced, not offered.* He cringed at how he'd made it virtually impossible for her to refuse. But a part of his reasoning had been that he hadn't liked the thought of her marrying some creep who would take half her inheritance in a subsequent divorce. He hadn't liked the thought of her marrying anyone…other than him. 'Here's the thing. I'd been rethinking our paper marriage deal, offering you a six-month affair that would suit both our ends. But, knowing what I know now, well, that's not going to happen.'

Shock flashed over her features. 'You're not thinking of walking out on our—?'

'No. Of course not.' He gave her a reassuring smile. 'We will stay in the marriage for six months, as the will states, but, as agreed, it will be a marriage in name only.'

CHAPTER SIX

IN NAME ONLY... Izzy was shocked at how disappointed she felt at those three little words. A crushing, stomach-hollowing disappointment. She should be feeling relieved...but ever since that interlude in the elevator, privately all she had wanted was to have Andrea make love to her.

Properly. Naked. Skin to skin.

But in the midst of her shock and disappointment was relief that he had listened to her and believed her about her father's behaviour. She'd expected him to shut her down or to say there was no way her father could have been so unkind.

But he hadn't.

He'd listened and soothed and comforted her when her emotions had threatened to overspill. It softened some—*not all*—of the antagonism she felt towards Andrea. He was still her arch-enemy; she had seen him as such for too long for that to change in a hurry. But that didn't mean they couldn't make the most of the time they had together, did it?

But now he was refusing to consummate their marriage. What was she supposed to feel about that? Why wasn't she happy? She should be happy. She should be ecstatic. She would get her inheritance and her freedom when the six months was up.

But she wouldn't get Andrea.

She wouldn't experience the passion and fire of his lovemaking, the searing possession of his kisses and caresses. She would never know what it was like to spend the night in his arms. Never know what it was like to feel his body move within hers. Never know what her body was capable of when being pleasured by his.

Izzy drew the edges of her bathrobe around her body, unsure of what to do with her hands. She wanted to reach for him. To tell him not to be so silly, not to be so damn honourable. To beg him to make love to her. But she had already shown too much vulnerability this evening, far more than she'd ever shown to anyone. 'It sounds like you've given this some thought...' She couldn't remove the note of disappointment from her voice.

'I have and I believe it's the best way forward. The *only* way forward.' His tone had an edge of finality that precluded further discussion on the topic.

Izzy picked up her abandoned champagne glass and took a sip. 'If I'd told you earlier about my father would you still have married me?'

Andrea took his glass as if he too needed something to do with his hands. He swirled the contents for a moment, watching as the bubbles danced in a little whirlpool. 'I considered offering three months ago but decided it was better to wait.'

'Until I was desperate.' Izzy didn't ask it as a question, more as a wry statement of fact.

He gave a brief smile. 'I can't imagine what is wrong with all the young men in London. You should have been snatched up years ago.'

Izzy made a grimace. 'Don't you read the gossip pages? I'm not exactly ideal wife material. I'm the girl men have flings with before they settle down with someone far more suitable.'

Something flickered over his face. 'Women are entitled to have just as many sexual encounters as men if that's what they want to do.'

Izzy frowned. 'So you're not judging me for my past? Is that what you're saying?'

His gaze became direct, like a detective examining important evidence. 'How much of your past is fact and how much is fiction?'

She gave an offhand shrug to cover how exposed she suddenly felt. Why had she got herself into this conversation? She wasn't interested in getting his good opinion… Well, maybe that wasn't quite true. There was a part of her that did want his approval. She wanted it far more than she should. 'Make a guess.'

'If what they write about me is any indication, I would say not much is true.' He kept his gaze trained on hers. 'Am I correct?'

Izzy toyed with her champagne glass. 'In the early days I would deliberately court negative attention from the press. I wanted to embarrass my father and I didn't care how I achieved it. Pictures of me stumbling out of nightclubs in the early hours of the morning were my modus operandi. It was so easy. All I had to do was look a little wasted and they would take the money shot. I soon got a reputation for wild partying but the truth was much more boring.'

His expression was shadowed with a combination of confusion and concern. 'Were you drunk at your father's Christmas party when you were eighteen or just pretending?'

Izzy gave a regretful sigh. 'Not drunk, tipsy—just as I was every year. It was the only way I could get through my father's Devoted Dad act. Silly, now that I think about it. The only person I ended up hurting was myself.'

Andrea touched her on the arm. 'Reputations can be repaired in time. But it's important *you* feel good about yourself. What other people think isn't something you can control.'

Did she feel good about herself? Izzy wasn't sure she could answer that with any certainty. A childhood of being told she wasn't good enough wasn't an easy thing to dismiss. She felt those negatives messages in the fabric of her soul. They were like bruises that would throb whenever self-doubt bumped against them. She forced a smile. 'I think I'll have to work on that.'

He lifted her chin with his finger, his eyes holding hers for a long, intense moment. His gaze flicked to her mouth and his throat tightened over a swallow. His hand fell away from her face and he stepped back. 'You have the bed. I'll take the sofa.'

Izzy could still feel the tingle from his touch and the ache of disappointment that he hadn't kissed her. The air seemed charged with energy—a sexual energy that made her skin prickle and tighten. 'Andrea?' Her voice came out soft and husky.

The muscles of his face tensed as if he was garnering his resolve. 'We need to be sensible about this, Isabella.' The stern drill sergeant note was back in his voice as if he were speaking to an insubordinate refusing an exercise.

'What is sensible about a six-foot-four man trying to sleep on a sofa?' Izzy said. 'We can share the bed without touching, surely? It's certainly big enough.'

'Believe me. It's not big enough.' His tone was dry.

Izzy frowned. 'But what about the housekeeping staff? Didn't you say you wanted everyone to think our marriage was genuine?'

He let out a slowly rationed breath. 'We will fly to Positano tomorrow. There's more privacy at my villa as I keep staff down to a minimum. My housekeeper is the soul of discretion. You can have your own room and she won't say a word.'

'But what about my job? And my studies? I have to call my boss and—'

'I've already seen to it,' Andrea said. 'He wishes you well. And you can study anywhere these days as long as you've got access to Wi-Fi.'

'You've thought of everything.' Izzy hadn't meant to sound so cynical but everything was spinning out of her control. Had been from the moment she'd accepted his offer of marriage. She wasn't used to it. But another part of her—a secret part—was enjoying having someone take care of her.

Andrea turned away and poured himself a small measure of the champagne they'd had earlier. She suspected it had more to do with him needing to do something with his hands than any desire for more alcohol. She had never seen him drink to excess. It was another thing she had, albeit reluctantly, admired about him. 'Go to bed, Isabella.'

'Why do you always call me by my full name instead of Izzy?'

He took a sip of his drink and then lowered the glass to look at her, his thumb moving on the side of the glass in a circular motion. 'It's a beautiful name. Elegant and regal. Sophisticated.'

Izzy gave a little snort. 'I'm hardly what anyone would describe as sophisticated.'

'You're too hard on yourself.' His voice had a softer note that glided along her skin like a caress.

Izzy forced a smile. 'I'll leave you to it, then. I'm feeling pretty tired. It's been a big day.'

She was almost at the door of the bedroom when his voice stalled her. 'Were you disappointed we didn't have a more formal church wedding?'

Izzy turned to look at him but there was nothing in his expression she could read, other than mild interest. 'I never intended getting married in a church or otherwise so how could I be disappointed?'

He gave a slight nod as if her answer made perfect sense, but there was a shadow in the back of his gaze that made her wonder if he would ever take what she said at face value again. It unnerved her to think she had revealed so much to him in so short a time. Impersonal or not, their wedding ceremony had shifted something in their relationship. It was not the same as before. She was finding it harder and harder to see him as the enemy, especially when his touch made her feel so alive. She needed to keep him at a distance—an emotional distance—if she were to get out of this six-month marriage without getting hurt.

Izzy somehow managed to sleep in spite of her worries about the new shape of her relationship with Andrea. But it appeared the same couldn't be said of him when she came out of the suite the next morning. He looked like he'd been awake all night. Dark stubble peppered his jaw and his eyes were drawn and his hair looked like it had suffered the repeated shove of his fingers. He unfolded himself from the sofa and rubbed the back of his neck. 'How did you sleep?' he asked, wincing against the sunlight when she drew back the curtains.

'Clearly a whole lot better than you,' Izzy said, picking up the throw rug that had fallen to the floor and folding it neatly into a square. She hugged it against her body. 'Shall I make you some coffee?'

'You don't have to wait on me, Isabella.' The gruff note in his voice nicked at her fraught nerves.

She placed the throw rug over the end of the sofa and straightened. 'Are you usually this grumpy in the mornings?'

'Grumpier.'

She raised her brows. 'Even after a night of hot sex?' *You should not have asked that.*

Something darkened in his gaze. 'There's not usually someone around in the morning to witness my mood.'

Izzy frowned. 'You mean you don't allow sleepovers?'

'No.' There was an emphatic tone to the word that made her wonder what made him insist on such a rule.

'Is that in the playboy's rulebook? No emotional entanglements, no cosy pillow talk?'

His mouth moved in a wry smile that didn't quite reach his eyes. 'I don't like giving mixed signals. Sex is sex. It's not a promise of forever.'

'But what if you see the same person for a few weeks or even months? You've had such relationships, surely?'

'Occasionally.'

'And?'

'I don't like morning-after-the-night-before scenes,' he said. 'It's much simpler to make sure they don't happen in the first place. Then no expectations get raised. No one gets hurt.'

Izzy studied him for a moment. 'It kind of makes me wonder what sort of women you've dated. I wouldn't be too keen on a man who didn't want to see me wake up beside him the next morning. I'd find it insulting if he asked me to leave once the deed was done.'

'I make sure they're more than adequately compensated.'

'What with? Flowers, chocolates or designer jewellery delivered to their door the next day?'

'No jewellery.'

'Why?'

'It's too…personal.'

Izzy moved across to the tea and coffee making area in the suite, busying herself with the task of making herself a cup of tea. She didn't want to think about the women he'd dated. Or the fact that he'd bought her a gorgeous diamond and sapphire ring and wedding ring. *What did that mean?* But the voice of reason came down hard on her silly romantic musing. It meant he wanted everyone to think this was a real marriage and not a six months sham. She turned to glance at him over her shoulder. 'Are you sure about that cup of coffee?'

'Quite sure.'

Izzy reached for a luxury muslin teabag and dropped it into her cup. 'I guess I should congratulate myself on being the first woman you've bought jewellery for.' She turned and looked at him again. 'Or do you want me to give the rings back when we annul this marriage?'

His eyes went to her mouth, lingering there for a heart-stopping moment as if wondering if their marriage was ever going to stay unconsummated. His gaze returned to hers but a screen had come up. 'They're nothing but props. You can keep them or give them away or sell them. It doesn't matter to me.' He turned and strode to the suite she had not long vacated.

After a few minutes she heard the shower running and she sat and quietly sipped her tea, trying not to picture him naked under that hot stream of water where she had showered not half an hour ago.

* * *

Andrea stood under the punishing spray of the shower, trying to wash away his unruly desire. He'd made a promise to keep their marriage unconsummated but every time he was within touching distance of Izzy his body went on high alert. Every cell in his body wanted her. He ached with the need to hold her, to feel her body pressed against his, to feel her response to him. A response he knew would be as passionate and heady as her kiss had been. Knowing what he did now about her father made him even more determined to keep his promise. But Izzy seemed determined to poke at his resolve to see if it was as firm as he claimed.

He closed his eyes under the shower spray but he could still picture her mouth. Could still feel it moving beneath his. How many times had he wanted to forget about his damn principles and stride into that bedroom last night and join her in that bed? Desire had throbbed in him all night in fierce combat with his resolve to resist the temptation. It had made it impossible for him to sleep. All he could think about was Izzy lying on his sheets next door, her hair splayed out over his pillow, her slim sexy limbs stretched out and her gorgeous breasts on show. The breasts he fantasised about touching, caressing, kissing until she whimpered with the same longing he could feel thrumming in his blood.

How would he survive six months of this torture?

He would go mad in the process. He wondered now if it was a mistake to whisk her with him to Italy, but the London paparazzi were unbearable. At his private villa in Positano he could at least keep such intrusions to a minimum. And his long-term housekeeper, Gianna, was the soul of discretion. Gianna was the only person he would trust with the secret of his marriage to Izzy.

No one else must know it wasn't the real deal.

Andrea stepped out of the shower and roughly dried himself, trying not to think of how Izzy had stood in this very spot earlier. Her used towel was hung neatly back on the rail, her cosmetics tidily put back into her toiletries bag. There was a trace of her flowery perfume lingering in the air.

When he came out of the bathroom with a towel slung around his hips, Izzy was sitting on the end of the king-sized bed scrolling through her phone. She looked up and her eyes darted to the towel and then back to his gaze. She sprang up from the bed, her cheeks staining a soft pink. 'I'll leave you to get dressed.'

Andrea shouldn't have reached for her. His mind said, *Don't do it*, but his body had other ideas. Wicked, forbidden ideas over which he had no control. His fingers encircled her slim wrist and he felt the flutter of her pulse under the pad of his thumb. 'Don't run away.' His voice was so husky it sounded like he'd swallowed a handful of gravel.

Her eyes rounded and her throat moved up and down over a swallow. 'I thought you said we were going to be sensible about this…?'

Andrea lifted her hand to his face, pressing a kiss to her bent knuckles. 'I said no sleeping together. But

I didn't say no touching. We'll be expected to touch in public. It would look strange if we didn't.' Even he could hear how he was rationalising his behaviour, but he didn't much care. He felt like he would die if he didn't touch her.

Doubt flickered in her gaze. 'What sort of touching?'

He slid his hand along the side of her face until his fingers were enmeshed in her fragrant hair, the silky strands tickling his fingers. Her eyes shone with anticipation, the same anticipation he could feel rolling through his body with unstoppable force.

'This,' he said, bringing his mouth to within a breath of hers. He didn't touch down, but nudged her soft lips with his, once, twice, three times.

Her lips quivered as if she was fighting her own battle to resist the temptation he had laid before her. Her breath mingled with his, sweet and fresh with a hint of vanilla. Her tongue crept out and left a layer of moisture on her lips. He moved that little bit closer to her, his thighs coming into contact with hers. He could feel the quake of awareness that shot through her like aftershocks. Her breasts bumped into his chest. He placed a hand at the small of her back and pressed her closer, his body erupting into flames when he felt her softness against his hardness. He was intoxicated with her closeness. The smell of her. Her womanly heat igniting him like a match to tinder.

His mouth covered hers and he swallowed her sigh of pleasure. Her arms came up to link around his neck, her body pressed so tightly against him he could feel every soft pliable contour. Her mouth opened under his, her tongue tangling with his in a sexy duel that made his blood head south in a throbbing gush. He took control of the kiss, holding her face in his hands to get better access, his tongue stabbing and flicking against hers in a mimic of what his body wanted more than anything. He finally lifted his mouth off hers, resting his forehead against hers as he fought for control. 'Maybe this wasn't such a great idea.'

Izzy's hands began to toy with his hair, sending hot darting tingles down his spine and deeper into his groin. 'It's just a kiss…' Her eyes met his. 'Isn't it?'

Andrea wasn't sure if he had the self-control to just kiss her. What had he been thinking? He was pushing himself beyond his limits. Torturing himself with what he wanted but couldn't—*shouldn't*—have. He traced her mouth with a lazy finger, watching as she quivered again against his touch. 'You have such a beautiful mouth.' He couldn't seem to keep the gravel out of his tone.

Her eyes went to his mouth, the tip of her tongue sneaking out to moisten her lips once more. 'Yours isn't so bad either.' She brought one of her hands down from around his neck to trace over his bottom lip. 'It's a lot softer than it looks.'

He captured her hand and pressed a kiss to the tip of her finger, holding her gaze with his. 'There isn't a whole lot of me that's soft right now.'

Her cheeks were delicately tinged with pink. 'So I can feel.' She moved against him; a subtle shift that sent an earthquake of lust through his body. His self-control strained at the leash like a rabid dog. Blood pounded and pulsed through his veins, driven by raw primal need. Had he ever wanted someone as much as he wanted her? Or was it because he had made a promise to himself not to have her? There was a war inside him. A raging battle he wasn't sure he could win.

But he would have to win it.

He couldn't allow things to get any more complicated than they already were. But a kiss or two was fine. That wasn't going to do any harm...was it?

He gripped her by the hips, holding her to him, not caring how much it was torturing him. He wanted. Wanted. Wanted her with a need so great it blasted every other thought out of his head. He brought his mouth back down to hers, crushing her to him, his tongue tangling with the moist heat of hers. He slid his hands down the sides of her body and then up again, slipping underneath her top and travelling up her smooth skin, stopping just below the satin curve of her breasts. He stepped back from her with a willpower he hadn't known he possessed, his body thrumming, humming, aching with need.

Disappointment flared in her eyes. But then her expression became masked and she stepped away from him and straightened her clothes. 'What time is our flight?'

Andrea tried not to look at her kiss-swollen mouth and the little patch of stubble rash on her chin. Seeing that intimate marking on her soft creamy skin made something in his stomach slip sideways. He tight-

ened the towel around his hips and moved across to
the wardrobe to dress. 'We leave at eleven a.m. Your
things will be sent on from your flat. If you need anything else we can buy it in Italy.' He closed the wardrobe and turned back around but she had gone.

CHAPTER SEVEN

A FEW HOURS later they arrived via chauffeur-driven car at Andrea's private villa high on the slopes above the seaside village of Positano. Izzy hadn't been to the Amalfi coast for years and yet it was as magical and picturesque as she remembered it. The startling blue of the ocean below, the wincingly bright sunshine from a perfectly clear sky and the scent of fragrant blossom from the luxurious garden at the villa made her senses sing with joy. Scarlet bougainvillea cascaded from a stone wall, standing pots and hanging baskets of red and white geraniums provided more eye-popping colour. Birds twittered in the shrubs and hedges behind, and in front of the villa was an infinity pool that overlooked the view of the coast below. It was picture post-card perfect and Izzy couldn't imagine a nicer place to hide away from the penetrating eyes of the public and the press.

Andrea led her to the front door of the villa but, before he could unlock it, an older woman dressed all in black opened it. Her sun-weathered face was wreathed in smiles and her black button eyes twinkled like the sun-dappled ocean below. A torrent of Italian came pouring out of her mouth but Izzy could only understand a couple of words, which she took to be an enthusiastic welcome. Such a welcome seemed a little surprising given the circumstances of her marriage to Andrea, but then she didn't know what he'd told his housekeeper.

'English please, Gianna,' Andrea said.

The housekeeper beamed brighter than a searchlight. '*Mi dispiace.* Sorry. I am so excited to welcome Signor's new bride to Villa Vaccaro. You have had a good journey, *sì*?'

'Lovely, thank you,' Izzy said, warming to the older woman's friendly nature.

'I have prepared the master bedroom for you,' Gianna said, sweeping her hand in front of the entrance. 'You must carry your bride over the threshold, *sì*?'

Andrea frowned. 'Gianna. I thought I'd told you not to make a fuss. Isabella requires her own room.'

Gianna rolled her eyes like marbles. 'You bring a beautiful bride home and you expect me to make up the spare room for her? Pah! What sort of marriage is that?'

'A marriage of convenience sort, that's what.' Andrea's voice had a thread of impatience running through it. 'Isabella and I don't intend for this arrangement to last longer than the six months required to fulfil the terms of her father's will. I explained all this when I called you last night.'

The housekeeper was clearly not intimidated by her employer's stern expression. She stood her ground with her arms folded and her dark gaze fixed on Andrea's frowning one. 'Marriage of convenience or not, you should still carry her over the threshold. It's bad luck not to.'

Andrea let out an exasperated breath and turned to Izzy. 'Do you mind?'

'Not at all,' Izzy said, trying not to laugh. She wasn't used to seeing Andrea backed into a tight corner. It showed a softer side to him she hadn't seen before. He clearly cared for and respected his housekeeper and was prepared to indulge her even if it was inconvenient to him.

Andrea scooped Izzy up in his strong arms and she linked her arms around his neck. The iron bands of his arm along her back and beneath her knees sent her senses spinning. His jaw was set in a tight line and his mouth pressed flat, but even so she could feel the way his body responded to her closeness. The way his nostrils flared as if he were taking in her scent, the way his hooded gaze went to her mouth. The contraction of his abdomen muscles where her body brushed against him. She couldn't help wondering what it would be like if she really was his bride of choice. What if their on-paper arrangement was torn up and they gave in to the passion and heat that simmered and smouldered and sizzled between them? How wonderful it would be for him to whisk her upstairs to the master suite and make earth-rocking love to her.

He set her down in front of him inside the villa but he kept hold of one of her hands. 'You'll have to excuse my housekeeper,' he said once Gianna was out of earshot. 'She's a hopeless romantic.'

'I like her,' Izzy said. 'How long has she worked for you?'

'Clearly too long since she's ignoring my instructions.' His tone had a dry edge. 'I'll get her to show you around. I have some things to see to in my office. Gianna?' he called out to the housekeeper, who had moved further inside the villa. 'Please show Isabella to the guest room.'

Izzy followed Gianna up the sweeping staircase, wondering if Andrea had pressing business to see to or whether he was putting distance between them because of the reaction of his housekeeper to his marriage.

Gianna led the way to a lovely suite on the first floor of the four-storey villa with a breathtaking view over the coast. 'Signor Vaccaro's suite is next door. See? There is a connecting door here.' She pointed out the door with a twinkling smile. 'Not that I think you'll need the key, *si*? I see the way he looks at you.'

Izzy could feel a blush stealing over her cheeks. 'It really is a marriage of convenience. Neither of us really want to be married and certainly not to each other.' Hadn't the housekeeper heard about Izzy's reputation? It seemed a little odd Gianna was so enthusiastic about their union given all that had been reported about Izzy in the past.

Gianna made another one of her *'pah'* noises and started fussing over the pillows on the bed. 'He has known you for a long time, *si*?'

'Yes, but we're hardly what you'd call best friends.'

Gianna straightened and turned to look at her. 'Your father was very good to him. He helped him get started in the hotel business. He is not a man to forget those who have helped him.'

'Did you ever meet my father?'

Gianna turned to a vase of fresh flowers on the table near the window but not before Izzy saw her expression sour slightly. 'He was a guest here once or twice. He was keen to tell me about all the charity causes he supports.' Gianna picked up a fallen pale pink rose petal and popped it in her apron pocket. She turned and looked at Izzy again. 'I was sorry to hear of his passing for the sake of those charities if nothing else. I'm sorry. I'm speaking out of turn. You must miss him, *sì*?'

Izzy gave a lip shrug. 'Yes and no.'

Gianna's gaze narrowed in query. 'You were not close?'

'Not particularly.'

The housekeeper shifted her lips from side to side in a musing manner. 'Yes, well, I wondered about that when Andrea told me about your father's will. It was a strange thing to do to his only heir, was it not?'

'Not strange if you knew my father,' Izzy said with a sigh. 'We had a complicated relationship.'

Gianna tut-tutted. 'But all is well now you are married to Andrea. He will take good care of you. He will make sure you get your inheritance. He is an honourable man, not that he boasts about all the good he does for others. No one would ever know about the many charities he supports. He insists on anonymity. I only know because I dust his office and came across the paperwork. You are a little bit in love with him, *si*?'

Izzy didn't like to burst the housekeeper's romantic bubble but her feelings towards Andrea were complex enough to her, never mind explaining them to someone else, especially to someone she'd only just met. 'Let's say I'm starting to see him in a different light.'

Gianna smiled. 'I will leave you to settle in. Would you like tea or coffee, a cool drink?'

'Tea would be lovely, but I'll come downstairs. You don't have to wait on me.'

'It is no trouble,' Gianna said. 'After all, you are the first woman Andrea has brought here to stay. That must count for something, no?'

The first woman he'd brought here to stay... It was hard not to feel a twinge of delight to think Andrea's private sanctuary had never been shared with one of his casual lovers. Why did he keep himself so separate from others? Surely it was a little unusual to spend so much time alone? No wonder the housekeeper was in such raptures about Izzy's arrival as his 'bride'. But it didn't mean he cared about her. Yes, he was honourable and had stepped up to help her claim her inheritance by marrying her according to the terms of her father's will. And he had made a promise to keep their marriage on paper so there would be a less complicated cessation of it when the time was up.

Why then was Izzy wondering if their marriage could be more than that? Had the housekeeper's romantic fantasy nonsense brushed off on her?

She looked at the adjoining door and suppressed a shiver. She moved across the room and touched the brass key sticking out of the lock. Her fingers curled around it and she gave it a single turn but, instead of locking the door, it unlocked with an audible click.

She held her breath for a moment and watched her hand going to the doorknob as if it belonged to someone else. She turned the doorknob and the door opened into a large suite that overlooked the coast below as well as a sweep of the wooded hills and rocky outcrops on the other side. The suite smelt faintly masculine—the hint of warm citrus and cool cedar she couldn't help associating with Andrea. The décor was cream and white with black and gold trimmings that gave the room a regal air.

Izzy's eyes strayed to the king-sized bed and her head swam with images of his tanned naked body lying against the pristine white of the sheets. She went over to the bed and trailed her fingers across the nearest pillow. No one else had shared this bed with him. No one. What did that mean? That he valued his privacy. That he came here to get away from the prying eyes of the press. It didn't mean that Izzy held any special significance in his life. She was a temporary wife to solve his problem as well as her own.

The main door of the master suite opened and Andrea came in. He closed the door behind him, his eyes locking on hers with dark lustrous intensity. 'I hope you're not letting Gianna's happy-ever-after fantasy mess with your head.'

It wasn't just her head that was getting messed

with—her whole body was full of restless longing. 'I was just checking the lock.' Izzy waved her hand back towards the connecting door.

'I told Gianna to put you in a suite further down the corridor.'

'Was that for my benefit or yours?'

His eyes darkened to black ink. 'Both.'

Izzy's tummy tingled at the thought of him trying to keep his distance. It was thrilling to think he was as tempted as she was to put aside their on-paper marriage and indulge in a red-hot affair. 'Gianna told me I'm the first woman you've ever brought here to stay.'

He gave a rough-sounding laugh. 'It would look odd if I didn't bring you here since we're married, would it not?'

'I think Gianna thinks you're secretly in love with me and me with you.'

His gaze became even more direct. 'And are you?'

It was Izzy's turn to laugh but she didn't quite pull it off with the same convincing ease. 'Of course not.'

He gave a stiff on-off smile. 'Better keep it that way.'

Izzy tossed her hair back behind her shoulders. 'Don't worry. I have no intention of falling in love with you.'

'But you want me.' His gaze went to her mouth and back to her eyes in a heartbeat. 'Don't you, *cara*?'

Izzy swallowed, her heart kicking up its pace the longer he held her gaze with the searing probe of his. Desire throbbed in the air like an electrical current. She felt it zinging along her flesh, up and down her spine, pooling in a cave of molten heat between her thighs. 'We agreed this was going to be a hands-off arrangement.' Why had her voice betrayed her by coming out so breathy and husky?

Andrea came to stand in front of her—every pore of her body was acutely, desperately aware of him. His eyes dipped to her mouth and a wave of longing swept through her at the thought of his hard possessive mouth taking hers captive. His hand came up and cradled the side of her face. It was such a tender caress, a disarming resolve-melting touch that made her desire for him escalate even further. His thumb moved across her cheek in a slow-moving stroke that made her skin tingle and her heart skip a beat. 'You shouldn't have come in here.' His voice was a deep bass with a grace note of gravel.

Izzy licked her suddenly bone-dry lips, her gaze flicking to the lazy curve of his mouth. 'You should have locked and bolted the door on your side.'

He inched up her chin, meshing his gaze with hers in a sensually charged lock that made her stomach swoop. 'I'm trying to do the right thing by you, but you keep making it so damn difficult.' His thumb brushed over her lower lip, sending hot little pulses of delight through her sensitive skin. 'A sexual relationship between us will only complicate things.'

Izzy sent her tongue over where his thumb had just been and tasted his saltiness on her lip. 'I'm not asking you to sleep with me.'

A glint of cynicism lit his eyes. 'Are you not?'

She lowered her gaze from the probe of his, but

looking at his mouth made her desire for him all the more intense. 'I'm not sure what I'm asking...' It was a lie. She knew exactly what she was asking. What she wanted. What she craved. Him.

He brought up her chin and meshed his gaze with hers. 'If we slept together it would only be for the duration of our marriage. You do understand that, don't you?'

Izzy placed her hands on the hard flat plane of his chest, her fingers curling into the fabric of his shirt. 'It's not like we can sleep with anyone else while we're married. So why not make the most of being tied together for six months?' She could barely believe she had been so brazen about her desire to sleep with him when for all this time she had vehemently denied wanting him. But it seemed pointless to deny it when he only had to look at her to see how much he affected her. Hadn't he always?

Andrea framed her face in his broad hands, his thumbs moving back and forth across her cheeks in a mesmerising caress that made her skin sing with delight. 'Something about this feels wrong and yet so damn right.' He brought his mouth down to hers and brushed his lips against hers. It was a soft experimental touchdown but, as if the warmth from her lips ignited a flare in his, the kiss became suddenly passionate, a bruising press of hungry lips fuelled by primitive carnal need.

Izzy was swept away by the thrilling heart-stopping force of it, the glide and thrust of his tongue against hers making her legs feel like the ligaments had been

severed. It was all she could do to stay upright. Her
lips clung to his, her tongue dancing and darting in intimate play, the erotic sensations travelling from her
mouth to her core as if her entire network of nerves
were on fire. Her heart raced with the sheer excitement
of arousal. An arousal she had never felt like this before. Her whole body was tuned in to his every movement, every touch, every stroke or glide or pressure
of his flesh against hers. His lips were firm and then
achingly, disarmingly soft. His tongue spine-tinglingly
bold and commanding. His hands moved from her face
to hold her by the hips, his fingers firm and possessive
and yet respectful. She didn't feel rushed or pushed or
shoved. She didn't feel that this was all about him and
less about her. This was a mutual exploration of need,
a discovery tour of their chemistry—the chemistry
that had snapped and crackled between them for years.

He brought her closer to his body, hip-to-hip,
arousal-to-arousal. The hard ridge of his erection making her inner core contract, the band of his chest against
her breasts making her feel more feminine than she
had ever felt before. Their bodies seemed to fit together like a complicated puzzle, no awkward pieces
or edges left over.

Izzy slid her hands up from his chest to tangle her
fingers in his hair, tugging and releasing the thick dark
strands, her mouth still fused to the magical pressure
of his. His hands moved from her hips to skate up the
sides of her body to settle just below her breasts. To
feel them there, so close and yet not touching where
she longed to be touched, was an exquisite torture. She

made a whimpering sound and he moved his right hand to gently cup her breast, his thumb moving over the pointed tip of her nipple that, even through her clothes, made her snatch in a sharp breath of delight. His other hand slipped beneath her top and glided along her bare skin, the graze of his masculine fingers making her stomach free-fall. He unhooked her bra and took her breasts into his hands, cradling them, caressing them, worshipping them. He bent his head to her right breast, his tongue sending a slow lick across the upper curve before encircling her areola, leaving the nub of her nipple until last. The moist lave of his tongue made the hairs on her scalp stand up and stretch and twirl like thousands of tiny music box ballerinas. She was breathless with desire, the excitement building like a tumultuous storm inside her body.

Andrea moved to her other breast, exploring it in the same intimate detail, leaving her senses spinning with every stroke and lick of his tongue and every nudge and nibble and suckle of his lips.

Every time he caressed her another stitch came undone in her chest—the tight stitches she'd placed around her carefully guarded heart.

He led her to the bed, bringing her down with him, his mouth coming back to hers in a long drugging kiss that made her wonder why she had resisted him for so long. How could she have denied herself this magic? The thrill of his touch. The excitement of being in his arms. The dizzying pleasure she could feel building in her body, triggered by him and only him.

Andrea pushed back her hair from her face to look down into her eyes. 'Still sure about this?'

Izzy touched the stubble along his jaw, her fingers catching like silk on sandpaper. 'I'm sure.'

He planted another soft kiss to her lips, then moved his mouth in a hot trail of fire down her neck and to her décolletage. His tongue traced over each curve of her breasts, his mouth closing over each nipple in turn in a gentle suckle that made her back arch off the bed. He moved his hand down the flank of her thigh, peeling away her clothes to leave smouldering kisses in their wake. Every movement of his was slow and languorous, not rushed and threatening in any way.

Izzy worked on his shirt buttons, uncovering the muscled planes of his chest and trailing her fingers through the dusting of hair sprinkled across his chest and abdomen, arrowing down to a V to disappear below the waistband of his trousers. He drew in a breath when her fingers brushed against his taut lower abdomen and, with a boldness she would not have thought possible even hours ago, she brushed her fingers over the tented fabric of his trousers.

His dark eyes locked on hers and her belly quivered at the blatant desire gleaming there. 'I want you. Damn it, but I want you.' His tone was gruff with a side note of resentment.

Izzy coiled her finger around a lock of his hair. 'You make it sound like it's some sort of affliction.'

He pressed a firm kiss to her mouth. 'It is. It's plagued me for years.'

She pushed his head back up by placing her hand against his forehead. 'How many years?'

He gave a lopsided smile that made something in her chest ping. 'Seven.'

Izzy outlined his mouth with her fingertip. 'So you really did want me back then.'

'Madly.' He captured her finger and closed his mouth over it, drawing on it like he had done on her nipple earlier. It was the most erotic feeling to have his tongue flickering against her finger, and her inner core reacted in anticipation.

'You told me to go away and grow up.'

'Which you have done.' His eyes glinted as they glanced at her naked breasts. 'It's been all I could do to keep my hands off you.'

Izzy took his hands and placed them on her breasts. 'I want your hands on me. I want you inside me.'

Something flickered across his gaze. 'Are you on the Pill?'

'Yes.'

'Good, because having sex is one thing, having a baby is another.'

'I'm not going to get pregnant, Andrea.' Izzy hadn't intended to snap at him but the way he was carrying on made her feel he suspected her of trying to trap him with a surprise pregnancy.

'It can happen even when precautions are taken.'

'It hasn't happened so far.'

'But if it did, what would you do?' he asked.

Izzy had never thought of having a baby. It was something other people did—they got married to someone they fancied themselves in love with and then had a child or two together. She had taught herself *not* to want such things. Watching the way her mother had suffered under the over-controlling behaviour of her father had made her wary of allowing any man to have such a hold over her. And even though she had only been five when her brother, Hamish, had died, watching the over-whelming grief her parents had gone through, particularly her mother, had further entrenched her decision to stay single and childless. Falling in love with someone would make her too vulnerable and needy. Having a child with them would only increase that vulnerability. It had always seemed far more sensible, not to mention safer, to keep men at an emotional distance.

Thinking about a baby and Andrea in the same sentence was dangerous. It opened a door inside her head that until now had always been firmly locked. Images flooded her brain of him cradling a newborn baby, its downy head covered in ink-black hair, making something tighten around her heart like the slow closing grip of an invisible fist.

Izzy let out a measured breath to bring herself back under control. 'You really know how to kill a mood, don't you?' Her attempt at humour didn't quite hit the mark.

Andrea took one of her hands and pressed it to his mouth, his eyes still holding hers. 'It's an important conversation to have because this is only for six months. A child would change everything.'

'Rest easy, Andrea. I don't want to have kids. Do

you have this conversation with every woman you sleep with?'

'I always use condoms. No exceptions.' A small frown pulled at his forehead. 'My relationships don't normally last longer than a few weeks, if that.'

'Why's that?'

He twirled a strand of her hair around one of his fingers, his gaze dropping to her mouth. 'I don't like giving my partners false hope. I'm not the settling down type. I bore too easily.'

'So you end things before they get too clingy?'

'Works for me.'

Izzy wondered why he had got to the age of thirty-four without wanting more than a few weeks of passion with yet another lover he would then let go without a backward glance. Didn't he want more than that?

Didn't she?

Izzy blocked the thought like slamming the door on an unwelcome guest. What she wanted was to buy back her grandparents' house to honour her mother's wishes. That was her goal and she was not going to rest until she achieved it. She touched his jaw again, moving beneath his weight, her body still on fire. 'Are we done talking now?'

His lips curved up at one corner, a glint in his eyes. 'What else did you have in mind?'

Izzy pulled his head down so his mouth was just above hers. 'Figure it out.'

His mouth covered hers in a kiss that triggered a wave of longing deep in her body. His hands moved over her in barely touching strokes that heightened her skin's awareness, ramping up her need to feel him crush her to him. He took his time pleasuring each erotic zone on her body—her breasts, the underside of her wrists, her thighs. He moved down her body, leaving kisses on her electrified flesh, teasing her into a frenzy of want that made her writhe and whimper. Clothes were removed and discarded, both his and hers, and for once she didn't feel naked and exposed and embarrassed.

He parted her thighs and stroked her with his fingers, making her snatch in a breath as the sensations tingled through her most tender private flesh. She had never allowed a partner to be so intimate with her. Not that her less than a handful of lovers had even tried. But Andrea's touch was so gentle, so respectful and giving she was swept away on the sheer eroticism of it, her inhibitions fading as tingles of pleasure shot through her in tiny little fizzes. His lips and tongue caressed her, opening her to a new world of feeling, a world of cataclysmic pleasure that left no part of her body untouched. Ripples of delight ran from her core to her extremities, even to her fingertips and toes. A shiver ran over her scalp, coursed down her spine and back up again as every muscle and tendon in her body shook and shuddered with a release so exquisite it blew every thought out of her mind.

Andrea stroked the side of her thigh as she came back to her senses. Izzy couldn't speak. Didn't want to speak in case she ruined the atmosphere by saying the wrong thing—an unsophisticated, self-conscious comment that would make him realise how disparate their lives were when it came to sex. She was in no doubt of his experience. Hadn't he just proven it? He had played her body like a maestro played a temperamental instrument. He had made her senses sing with such harmony and balance that she couldn't imagine ever allowing any other man to touch her now she had experienced his caresses.

Andrea brushed back her hair from her face, his gaze hooded but with a light of intensity—a probing light of contemplation. 'You've gone very quiet, *cara*.'

Izzy forced a smile. 'Don't you want to…?' She waved a hand to their where their bodies were pressed together. 'Finish off?'

He took her hand and pressed a kiss to the middle of her palm, his eyes still holding hers. 'There's no hurry. I want to savour every minute.'

Izzy chewed the side of her mouth, her gaze slipping out of reach of his. With her free hand she traced the carved contour of his left pectoral muscle with her finger. 'I've never slept with someone so…so not in a hurry…'

He brought her chin up with the end of his finger, locking his gaze on hers. There was a soft concerned look in his eyes that made her wonder if her enmity towards him had been misplaced, misguided, mishandled. 'Your pleasure is important to me. I want our first time together to be mutually satisfying, not a fast and furious fumble that leaves you frustrated.' His thumb brushed over her lower lip for a moment, his brow furrowing. 'Are you telling me you haven't always enjoyed sex?'

Izzy lost herself in the dark warmth of his gaze. How could he so easily read her mind? Her body? Her emotions? 'I'm not as experienced as I've made it appear or sound in the press.' She sighed and continued. 'I've never been all that comfortable with physical intimacy. I couldn't bear the thought of being intimate with anyone without numbing myself first with alcohol. None of my partners seemed all that interested in whether I was having a good time or not. Everyone assumed I was the up-for-it party girl, but in reality... Well, this is the first time I've had an orgasm with a partner. I used to fake it to get sex over with.'

He touched her face with a slow-moving finger from her cheek to her chin and back again. 'Oh, Isabella.' His voice had a soft note of compassion that derailed her even further. 'Sex is supposed to be a mutual thing, not a one-way street. Your partners should have checked to see if you were comfortable with what they were doing. You shouldn't have to endure sex but enjoy it.'

Izzy gave him a self-deprecating smile, so touched by his understanding she was worried she might get emotional. 'Speaking of one-way streets... Are you going to finish making love to me?'

The shadow of concern was back in his gaze. 'Is that what you want? What you *really* want?'

Izzy stroked his face from ear to stubbly jaw. 'I want you to make love to me. I want to experience your pleasure as well as my own.' Her voice was nothing more than a breathy whisper but it contained all the longing she felt for him, the longing she could feel throbbing, deep and heavy, in her blood.

He brought his mouth down to just above hers. 'Are you sure?' His warm breath caressed her lips and his hesitancy melted her heart.

'I'm sure,' she said and closed the gap between their mouths.

CHAPTER EIGHT

Izzy's mouth was on fire as soon as Andrea's met hers. His tongue a flame of need that echoed her own. The mutual exchange of passion thrilled her, ramping up her excitement because with every sensuous touch and caress it erased the bad memories of the past. It was an awakening of her flesh, of her desire, of her ability to give and receive pleasure and she gloried in it.

Andrea was slow and thorough in attending to all her pleasure spots, leaving no secret place undiscovered. He kissed and stroked her breasts, nibbled and nudged and gently grazed them with his teeth so that every hair on her head was tingling at the roots.

But she was just as keen to explore him and ran her hands over his taut muscles and his steely flanks and his flat abdomen. She took him in her hands and learnt his likes and dislikes, reading him as he had read her and enjoying the way he responded to her touch. Feeling powerful in a way she had never felt before.

Andrea sourced a condom and positioned himself at her entrance. The final moment of physical connection was so strongly erotic and yet surprisingly tender, it took her breath clean away. Her body welcomed him, accepting him and wrapping around him with no fear, no reluctance and no pretence. The slow movement of him within her drew from her a fevered response as her nerves began to sing at the friction. She was climbing to a far off summit, each of her muscles becoming taut with built-up tension. She was not quite there and yet so close it was like hovering on the edge of a precipitous cliff.

Andrea brought his hands between their rocking bodies and caressed her intimately, his fingers cleverly stroking her over the edge into a free fall into the abyss. Her senses were reeling, spinning her away from conscious thought, her body a blissful array of sensations that rippled through every pore of her flesh. It was like her nerves were on the outside of her skin, every movement, every touch of his hands and body making her hum and throb with pleasure.

Izzy felt his release follow soon after. There was none of the huffing and grunting and crushing, almost suffocating weight of her previous partners. Andrea held her close and gave himself up to the moment of completion with a deep guttural groan that reverberated through her body as if his pleasure was intimately tied to hers. She felt every one of his spasms as if they were her own, making her feel closer to him than she had ever felt to anyone. Emotion suddenly clogged her throat, her eyes stinging with unshed tears. She lamented her lack of sophistication for feeling so exposed and vulnerable and hid her face against his

neck, hoping he would put her silence down to her sa-
tiated senses.

After a minute or two of silence, Andrea propped
himself up on his elbows and turned her head so she
was facing him. His brows came together when he saw
the glimmer of tears in her eyes. 'Did I hurt you?' His
tone had a ragged edge that made the stitches around
her heart loosen even more.

Izzy gave a lopsided smile. 'No, of course not. You
were wonderfully gentle. It's just I… I didn't realise
it could be that good. That satisfying and…not sleazy
or rushed or shameful in any way.'

He mopped a couple of tears that had escaped from
beneath her eyes, the look in his gaze so tender it made
her want to cry all over again. She was used to partners
rolling away and leaving. Job done. End of story. Andrea's approach was so different…so touchingly different it was like he had made love with not just her
body but with her mind and soul.

'You were wonderful too,' he said. 'I always knew
we would be good together.'

Izzy trailed her fingers down the hairy roughness of
his forearm, her eyes avoiding his. 'Why wait so long
to act on it?' She slowly brought her gaze up to his.
'I mean, for all this time we could have been making
love instead of war.'

His smile was rueful and he captured a strand of
her hair and tucked it back behind her ear. 'It's one
of the reasons I've always kept my distance. I didn't
trust myself around you. But my housekeeper, Gianna,

knew I was beaten the minute she met you. Even before she met you.'

'Because I'm the first woman you've brought here?'

'Because you're the first woman I've married.'

Izzy glanced at the rings on her left hand. They looked so real and yet... An invisible hand fisted around her heart. This was for six months and six months only. He didn't want a wife any more than she wanted a husband. They weren't doing *for ever*. They were doing *for now*. For money. For mutual advantage. She brought her gaze back to his. 'But Gianna knows this is a marriage of convenience. We've both told her that none of this is real.'

He moved away to dispose of the condom. 'I told you—she's a die-hard romantic. A marriage of convenience to her means an opportunity to fall in love. She married her late husband to settle family debts and they had thirty-odd happy years together before he died a couple of years ago.' He glanced back at her but his expression was now masked. 'Don't let her get to you. We'll do it our way and when it's time to end it, we'll do so without tears. Agreed?'

Izzy didn't care for the slightly clinical tone he used. Surely this wasn't like any old business deal? This was about two lives intersecting, two bodies giving and sharing pleasure. She screened her own expression, hiding her niggling doubts behind a smile she wasn't sure made the distance to her eyes. 'Agreed.'

He leaned down to brush her mouth with a brief kiss, and then he straightened and reached for his trousers. 'I have to see to a couple of things in my office

to do with my business merger. Will you be okay to
entertain yourself for an hour or two? We'll have dinner out on the terrace. Maybe have a moonlight swim
afterwards. I'll give Gianna the night off so we won't
be disturbed.'

'Sounds like fun,' Izzy said, already tingling at the
thought of sharing a moonlit swim with him.

An hour and a half later and Andrea still hadn't worked
his way through the pile of paperwork sitting on his
desk. His mind kept drifting back to making love
with Izzy. He still couldn't believe he had crossed the
boundary he'd been so adamant not to cross. But the
things she had shared about her past and her insecuri-
ties had made it virtually impossible for him to resist
her. A barrier had been removed between them and it
had opened up a world of sensuality that until now he
had been avoiding. Their lovemaking had been both
tender and passionate and his body was still tingling
from her touch. He knew it was dangerous to tweak
the terms of their arrangement but he assured himself
it was only for six months. Yes, a bit longer than his
usual relationships, but they both stood to gain from
the deal. His colleague's wedding was only a couple
of weeks away and he figured now he was sleeping
with Izzy it would make their marriage look all the
more authentic.

It sure felt damn authentic, which was a thought he
shouldn't be allowing inside his head. But he reassured
himself that Izzy didn't want a long-term marriage any
more than he did. They had both been clear from the

outset on what they wanted out of this arrangement. She had far more to lose than he and he was counting on her abiding by the rules so she got what she wanted. Her inheritance. Which she *deserved*, for he firmly believed now she had been badly treated by her father. It angered Andrea that he had held her father in such high esteem when all the time Benedict had been manipulative and cruel towards Izzy. Andrea knew enough about her to know she was a lot more sensitive and soft-hearted than she let on. The brash don't-mess-with-me exterior was an act, a ruse to put people off so they wouldn't see how easily she could be hurt.

But making love with her had made Andrea realise how careful he would have to be not to end up hurting her himself. They had made an agreement. Six months. He wasn't interested in prolonging their relationship or indeed any relationship in the future. He had no desire to lay himself open to rejection again. To be shunted aside when feelings died. To be kicked out of someone's life as if he were nothing more than useless trash.

No. He would stick to the plan. Keep his emotions out of the arrangement and enjoy the physical chemistry he had going on with Izzy.

Stick to the plan.

That was all he had to do.

Izzy showered and came downstairs in time to receive instructions from Gianna about the heat and serve dinner she had prepared. A candlelit table with a crisp white tablecloth was set up on the terrace overlooking the pool and the Positano coastline below. Two cushioned chairs were positioned either side of the table and a gorgeous arrangement of fresh flowers was elegantly draped either side of the scented candles. It was the most romantic setting Izzy had ever seen and yet she couldn't help feeling a little conflicted. Making love with Andrea had changed something in their relationship. She didn't hate him. Her hatred had been her armour and now she was fighting a battle without a weapon. What defences could she use if not her dislike of him?

But how could she dislike someone who made her feel such magical things?

Her body was still alive with the sensations he'd evoked. She had only to think of his powerful body entering her and her stomach would flip over and a hot rush of longing course through her. It was dangerous to let her guard down but how could she not? They were tied together for six months and now they had this new intimacy she couldn't turn things back to the way they had been. A switch had been flicked. A force had been activated. A desire had been fed and fuelled and fostered.

Andrea came out to the terrace carrying a bottle of champagne. He too had recently showered, for his hair was still damp and curling around the collar of his casual shirt. Izzy hadn't seen him since they had made love but his office door had remained closed every time she'd walked past as she'd helped Gianna set up dinner before the housekeeper left for the evening.

Andrea's eyes ran over Izzy's oyster silk dress, the

only decent thing she'd had time to slip into her overnight bag. 'You look beautiful. The rest of your things should be here by tomorrow. But we can shop for anything else you need.'

'Thanks.' Never good with compliments, Izzy feasted her eyes on him instead. The way his muscles bunched on his tanned forearms when he popped the champagne cork, the way his olive skin contrasted with the white of his shirt. Her gaze drifted to his mouth, remembering how it had felt on her own, how his tongue had mated with hers in such an erotic way. Something shivered deep and low in her belly when his eyes met hers. Was he remembering how it felt to be inside her? Was he thinking of how it had felt to be consumed by passion and want until nothing else mattered? She licked her suddenly dry lips and made a business out of straightening the perfectly straight tablecloth. 'It's a gorgeous night. So lovely and warm. I can't remember the last time I ate al fresco.'

He placed a warm hand on her bare shoulder, his touch sending a wave of longing through her body. 'You're nervous.' He said it with a note of surprise rather than as a question.

Izzy could feel her cheeks betraying her. 'I'm just not used to relating to you like this…you know, without biting your head off. It's kind of…weird. Weird but…nice.'

He gave a slow smile and leaned down to press a kiss to the sensitive flesh just below her ear. She could smell the fresh citrus of his aftershave, her senses intoxicated by lemon and lime and cleanly showered man. Even though he'd recently shaved she could still feel the slight prickle of his sexy stubble. His breath caressed her skin, then his tongue glided in a blistering pathway following the line of her jaw until he finally came to her mouth. His kiss was slow and sensual, lighting fires in her flesh that sent hot flames licking along her veins. Her mouth opened under the commanding pressure of his, her arms slipping around his neck, bringing her closer to the heat and hardness of his body. Her breasts were bare under her shoe-string-strap dress and never had they felt more sensual than with the cool silk stretched over them as they were crushed against his muscular chest. His hands skimmed her from her shoulders to her hips, his hands settling there to bring her even closer against his pulsing need. She could feel her body preparing itself, excitement kicking up her heartbeat, making her intensely aware of every inch of her body where it was pressed against his.

His mouth continued its sensual exploration of hers, their tongues tangling in a sexy dance of one-upmanship that stirred her desire even more. His hands came back up to cradle her face as he changed position, his mouth softening against hers, his tongue no longer combative but cajoling.

Izzy had had no idea a kiss could be so mind-blowing, so thrilling that her whole body would be involved. Every nerve and cell throbbing with growing need—a need he activated and nurtured with each mesmerising movement of his mouth on hers. His hands splayed into her hair, electrifying her scalp with his touch.

He lifted his mouth off hers to look at her through sexily hooded eyes. 'This is a much better way to relate to each other, *si*?'

Izzy smiled against his mouth. 'Much better.'

He kissed her again, deeply, holding her against his aroused body while the scent of the flickering candle and the flowers and the sea air worked their magic on her senses.

Izzy felt like she had stepped into a fairy tale, one she had never realised she'd wanted until now: a romantic setting, a warm fragrant night, champagne and delicious food and a man who had eyes only for her.

What more could she want?

Andrea pulled back from her with a smile. 'We won't do the dinner Gianna has prepared for us service if we get distracted. Some champagne, *cara*? To celebrate our truce.'

'Yes, please.' Izzy held out her hand for the glass of sparkling bubbles he poured. He held out her chair and she sat and gazed at the view below. 'This is the most beautiful place. How long have you had it?'

He took his seat opposite. 'I bought it five years ago. I got sick of living in my hotels. I wanted a base, a place to separate me from work.' His lips moved in a rueful movement. 'Not that it always works that way. Gianna is always telling me off for spending way too much time in my office here.'

Izzy sipped her champagne and studied him for a moment over the rim of her glass. He looked far more relaxed than she had ever seen him. His shirt was undone to midway down his chest and the sleeves rolled up past his forearms. She wondered now why she'd found him so intimidating and gruff in the past. 'How did you get into hotels? Why not some other business?'

He handed her a crisp bread roll from the basket on the table between them. 'When I left home when I was fourteen—'

'Fourteen?' Izzy looked at him in alarm. 'You were fourteen when you left home?'

He gave her a grim smile that wasn't really a smile. 'Not by choice, although it was proving to be impossible to live with my stepfather.'

Izzy glanced at the scar on his left eyebrow, her stomach feeling queasy at what he might have been exposed to as a young boy. 'Is that how you got that scar? From your stepfather?'

He touched the scar as if to see if it was still there, a shadow passing over his expression as if the memories of that time in his life were unpleasant. 'He was a bastard of a man—a coward who used his fists instead of his intellect. Not that he had much of an intellect.' His tone was flat and bitter, the line of his mouth tight.

Izzy swallowed, remembering all too well how terrifying it was to live with a man with a hair trigger temper. 'Was he violent towards your mother?'

Andrea's dark eyes glittered and his jaw clenched. 'He was clever how he went about it. He didn't leave her with bruises you could see. I intervened whenever I could but in the end she chose to stay with him.' His mouth thinned into a white line. 'That's what hurt me the most. I came back the next day after he kicked me out and begged her to leave with me. I promised I'd keep her safe—find a shelter or something for us. But she told me she never wanted to see me again. She wanted to stay with my stepfather. Go figure.'

Izzy frowned, her heart squeezing at the thought of Andrea as a young teenager, thrown out of home and rejected by his mother. 'Oh, Andrea. How awful that must have been. You must have been so distraught. What did you do? Where did you go?'

He took a sip of his champagne, and then another sip, each time swallowing deeply. 'I lived on the streets for a couple of months until I met your father. He found me looking for food at the back of a hotel in Florence. The kitchen hand used to watch out for me and give me some leftovers.' Andrea's smile became crooked. 'Your father might not have been an angel, but if it hadn't been for him taking a chance on me, who knows where I might have ended up?'

It was certainly a side to her father Izzy had been aware of but the various charities and people he'd championed didn't make up for how he'd made her feel. 'How did he help you?'

'He found a place for me to stay and then offered me a job. It was menial work at first, just cleaning and stuff, but he said later my work ethic had impressed him.' He reached across and refilled her glass but she noticed he didn't refill his own. 'I went back to school and studied for a business degree after that. When I was living on the streets I made a promise to myself that one day I would own a hotel where the homeless would be welcome to find shelter and food.' He put the bottle back in the ice bucket and sat back in his chair.

'Enough about me. Tell me about Hamish. What was he like?'

Izzy wondered if anyone else knew the darker secrets of his past and felt touched he'd shared as much as he had with her. She could tell from his expression that he was not used to talking about his background at length. There was a shuttered look in his eyes as if he had cordoned off the memories and would not be revisiting them any time soon. 'Hamish was a lot older than me, as you know—my mother had a few miscarriages in between having him and me. But he was wonderful. Funny and smart—all the things a big brother should be. I idolised him and he spoilt me rotten. But then he got sarcoma and everything in our family changed. The much-adored son and heir couldn't be saved, no matter how much the doctors and my parents tried.' She let out a ragged sigh. 'It was a terrible time. As the years went on, my father expected me to step up and do all the things Hamish would have done if he'd lived. But I wasn't strong academically. I wasn't able to cope with the pressure and I rebelled.' She frowned at the memory of that difficult period in her life. 'I wish I'd had someone to talk to about it, but the sad irony was Hamish was the only person I would have shared something like that with but he was gone and so I floundered.'

'What about your mother? Were you close to her?'

Izzy always felt sad when she thought of her mother. Talking about her made her realise how much she still missed her. Missed what they'd once had before tragedy struck. 'I was close to her before Hamish got sick.

We had a happy family until then, or so it felt from my young, childish perspective. It was happiest when my father wasn't around, though. That's why I loved going to my grandparents' house so much because Dad never came with us. He didn't get on with his in-laws. But then Hamish got sick and Mum was understandably devastated. She felt she'd failed as a mother, as a wife. Then my grandparents got killed in a car crash a couple of years later and Mum retreated further into herself and soon after she got liver cancer. It was like our family was cursed.'

Andrea's expression was full of concern and compassion. 'How did your father handle it all?'

Izzy puffed out her cheeks on another sigh. 'He worked. He went away a lot, which suited me because we only ever argued when he was around. He couldn't see me without making some cutting comment about how I was dressed or how badly I'd done in my latest test or how much I disappointed him with my behaviour. I used to dread him coming home, and yet often I would deliberately set him off because it was a way to get his attention. Immature, now that I think about it.'

'So you were never close to him? Even as a younger child?'

Izzy gave him a pained movement of her lips that was not quite a smile. 'He wasn't comfortable around little kids. He didn't understand their needs, or perhaps didn't want to. Mum let slip once that he was the same with Hamish until Hamish grew up a bit. But then, even when I got a bit older, I realised I would never be good enough because I wasn't a boy. It was all my father had ever wanted. A son to carry on the family line. I was close to my mother's parents, though. They were lovely to me and, of course, to Hamish.' She met his gaze. 'That's why I want my inheritance. I want to buy back their home. My father insisted it be sold after they were killed. My mother didn't want to sell it but he talked her into it.'

'Where is it?'

'In Wiltshire,' Izzy said. 'A few kilometres out from a quaint tiny village no one's ever heard of but to me it's like paradise. Some of my earliest and best memories are of being at my grandparents' house with Hamish and Mum. It was the happiest time of our lives. I won't rest until I get it back. The current owner has promised me they won't sell for another six months.'

'What will you do with it once you buy it? Will you live there?'

'That's the plan,' Izzy said. 'I have to iron out a few more details but I'd like to open it up as a short-term holiday place for families going through difficult times. Maybe even kids with cancer. There's a lovely little gardener's cottage that could be done up to house guests as well as the main house.' She picked up her bread roll and tore off a piece. 'I suppose it all sounds a little hare-brained to a hotshot hotel owner like you. It's not like I've got a business plan or anything. I haven't even been down to see the place in years.'

He reached for her hand and gave it a gentle squeeze. 'I started small and built up gradually. You've got passion about the project, which is far more important than anything else.'

Izzy glanced at their joined hands, her wedding and engagement rings winking up at her as if to remind her of the terms of their marriage. She pulled her hand away and went back to buttering her bread roll. 'Do you ever see your mother?' He was silent for so long she looked back up at him. 'Andrea?'

He blinked as if bringing himself back to the present. 'No.'

'Have you ever tried to make contact?'

'What would be the point?' There was a line of hardness around his mouth that hinted at the bitterness he still carried about his childhood.

Izzy chewed her lip, wondering if she'd strayed into dangerous territory. 'I don't know… I just thought it might help you understand why she did what she did.'

'She made her choice. That's the end of it as far as I'm concerned.'

'But what if it hadn't been her choice?' Izzy met his black-as-pitch gaze. 'What if she was frightened of your stepfather? Of what he would do to her, to both of you, if she left with you? Maybe he forced her to tell you to go away and never come back.'

Something flickered over his face like ice cracking on the surface of a frozen lake. 'She's had plenty of time to find me if she was so inclined. I've not exactly been hiding under a rock.'

'But would you agree to see her if she did come looking?'

A cynical glint appeared in his eyes. 'And what do you think she'd want from me all these years on? Money?'

'I can understand why you'd feel so cynical about her motives but surely—'

'Isabella. Please, can we change the subject?' His matter-of-fact tone brooked no resistance. 'You have your father issues. I have my mother ones. Let's leave it at that.'

'But your mother might still be alive,' Izzy said, trying to ignore the jab of pain just below her heart. The pain of guilt and regret that it was now too late for her to make her peace with her father.

Andrea's eyes lost their glaze of hardness and he reached for her hand again. *'Cara...'* His voice was softer now, almost tender, his touch a soothing press of fingers against her hand that made her feel understood and supported. 'Forgive me. My stuff happened a long time ago. So long ago it feels like it happened to someone else, not me. But your grief is still fresh. Raw. Your father was wrong to make you jump through hoops. But he had his own issues. Unhappy people hurt others because it's a way of controlling them.'

Izzy forced a stiff little smile. 'I wonder what he'd think of you marrying me. Do you think he envisaged it might happen?'

He stroked his thumb over the back of her hand. 'Who knows? But the main thing is you get your inheritance once the six months is up.' He gave her hand a little Mexican wave-like tap with his fingers and withdrew his hand. 'Which reminds me—I have my business colleague's wedding coming up in two weeks. It's being held in Venice. It will be a glamorous affair so let me know if you'd like help choosing an outfit. I'll pay, of course.'

'You don't have to buy me clothes.'

He shrugged and reached for his champagne. 'Think of it as one of the perks of the deal. Any amount of money is worth spending when it gets you what you want.'

'Why do you want this business merger so much?' Izzy asked. 'You have lots of hotels now. What's so special about the one you're trying to buy?'

'The hotel in Florence is the one where your father found me begging for food. For years I've wanted that hotel and when I set my sights on something I don't give up until I achieve it.' The determined set to his mouth reminded her of his iron will and take-no-prisoners attitude. 'Patrizio Montelli's hotel is small by industry standards but I won't rest until I own it. But first I have to solve the issue of his stepdaughter.'

'I hope his stepdaughter buys our marriage as the real deal and not a sham,' Izzy said. 'I mean, for a man of your wealth and position, you did marry me rather quickly and with little or no fanfare.'

His eyes smouldered like coal as they held hers. 'Alexis will only have to take one look at us together to know what we have is real. You can't fake chemistry like ours.'

Izzy picked up her glass in case she was tempted to give in to that crackling chemistry right here and now. 'Are we going to do justice to this dinner Gianna made for us? It's probably getting cold.'

He gave a lazy smile. 'Dinner first and then a swim.'

'I haven't got a swimming costume with me.'

His eyes glinted. 'Trust me. You won't need one.'

CHAPTER NINE

AFTER THEY CLEARED away the remains of dinner Izzy
followed Andrea back out to the pool. He turned off
most of the garden lights for added privacy and the pool
became bathed in moonlight, the surface perfectly still
in the balmy evening air.

Andrea unbuttoned his shirt, giving her a smouldering look that made her insides quiver with longing.
'Have you ever skinny-dipped before?'

'No.' Izzy slipped one shoulder strap down. 'I seem
to be having a few firsts with you.'

He removed the rest of his clothes and came to help
her with hers. His hands were warm and sensual as
they slid the other strap off her shoulder, the dress
falling into a silken pool at her feet, leaving her with
nothing but her knickers. His eyes devoured her naked
breasts, his hands cupping them so gently it made every
pore of her skin react. His thumbs brushed over her
nipples, teasing them into tight buds, the flesh aching
and tingling with a torturous longing. He brought his
mouth down and stroked his tongue over the upper
curve of each breast, his teeth taking each nipple in a

soft bite that made her spine shiver. His tongue swirled around her nipple, a warm soothing stroke that sent a shockwave straight to her core. He peeled her knickers away and they too fell to her feet and she stepped out of them, desperate to press her body as close to his as possible.

The contact of his hard male body against hers made her womb contract with need—a tight, aching need that begged to be assuaged. It moved through every part of her body in a rolling tide, making her heart race and her breathing quicken. No one had ever made her feel desire like this. So powerful. So consuming. So enthralling.

Andrea bent down in front of her, bringing his mouth to her most intimate place. She placed her hands on his head to anchor herself, preparing for the tumultuous storm his lips and tongue promised. Izzy gave herself up to the sensations as his mouth continued its erotic exploration, the tension building in her body until finally it could take no more. She shattered around his tongue, gasping and shuddering as the ripples of pleasure coursed through her in cascading waves.

Andrea rose to gather her close, his hands warm on her hips, his eyes backlit with desire. 'I love how you come apart when I do that. You're so responsive.'

Izzy reached up to touch his mouth with her finger. 'I never thought I'd ever feel comfortable enough to let anyone pleasure me like that.' She touched his lower lip and sighed. 'I can't imagine doing it with anyone else...'

Something flickered in his gaze as quick as a jab of

pain. But then his gaze relaxed but somehow his smile didn't match. 'I promised you a swim. Let's do it.' He stepped away from her and dived into the deep end of the pool, his lean athletic body slicing through the water, sending rippling waves to the edges, not unlike the ones he had sent through her body moments earlier.

Izzy stood on the edge of the pool, hesitant to dive because there was no way she could do it as expertly as Andrea. She watched him swim up and down, privately envying the way he executed deft tumble turns at each end as if he were at an Olympic training session. He reminded her of her brother, Hamish, who had been an excellent swimmer. But the swimming gene hadn't come her way, which was another thing her father had berated her for, to such a degree she hadn't swum in years.

Andrea surfaced and flicked his wet hair back with one of his hands. 'Come on. It's not cold.'

Izzy went to the shallow end where the steps were and cautiously entered the water, only going waist-deep. The water was like warm silk against her naked skin, making her aware of every inch of her body. 'I'll just have a paddle up this end,' she said.

He joined her at the shallow end, his gaze searching hers. 'What's wrong? Don't you like swimming?'

Izzy gave a self-conscious grimace. 'I'm not a great swimmer. Hamish was but I didn't share his natural talent.'

Andrea frowned. 'Did your father make unhelpful comparisons?'

She marvelled at his ability to read between the lines

whenever she spoke of her childhood. 'It took all the enjoyment out of it to have my father standing by the side of the pool telling me what I was doing wrong.'

His hands took hers, his expression gentle with concern. 'He was a hard taskmaster. He expected perfection and got frustrated when people didn't measure up. But he should never have treated you like that. No one should be treated like that and especially not a child.'

Izzy moved closer to him, her arms going around his waist, her pelvis in intimate contact with his. 'Thank you for understanding. I know it must be hard to see my father with new eyes. I know he was good to you. He was good to a lot of people. He just wasn't able to be the sort of father I needed.'

He brushed her forehead with his lips. 'I'm grateful for what he did for me. But I wasn't as close to him as he made out. I wasn't close to anyone.' He let out a brief sigh and added, 'I'm still not.'

What about me? Her unspoken question seemed to hover in the air between them. Didn't he feel close to her? She had told him stuff she had told no one. He had shared things about his past she was sure he had not revealed to anyone else. They had shared their bodies with such breathtaking intimacy. What would it take for him to lower his guard enough to feel close to her?

Izzy stroked her hands over the small of his back, feeling his tense muscles relax at her touch. 'I guess it would be hard to be close to anyone after being deserted by your mother,' she said. 'How could you trust anyone after that?'

His lips moved in the semblance of a smile and his

gaze went to her mouth. 'Hey. I thought we came down here to swim?'

Izzy gave him a sultry smile. 'Do you really want to swim?'

His eyes darkened with desire and he brought his mouth closer to hers. 'Not right now.'

The next two weeks passed in a sensual haze that Izzy never wanted to come out of even though she knew at some point she must. It was always lurking at the back of her mind that none of this was going to last—that this dream of living with Andrea at his gorgeous villa on the Amalfi coast was temporary. No amount of Izzy's words to the contrary could convince his house-keeper, Gianna, to believe Izzy's marriage to Andrea wouldn't magically turn into the real thing. Gianna smiled knowingly every time she saw Izzy coming out of the master bedroom and Izzy had to remind herself that, no matter how passionate his lovemaking, Andrea was not in love with her and didn't want their marriage to last any longer than it needed to in order to fulfil the terms of her father's will.

As for her feelings about him… Izzy sighed and tried not to think about how much she enjoyed being with him. Thinking too much made her want too much. Want things she hadn't even realised she wanted. Had never wanted until now.

But for now she tried to be content about being in a relationship that was mutually satisfying, not just physically but intellectually. He never made her feel she was a high school dropout. He engaged in debates and discussions with her about current affairs and, while he didn't always agree with her on every topic, he never made her feel embarrassed or foolishly naïve for holding a different view.

Andrea somehow juggled his demanding work while leaving enough time available to spend time with her. He took her shopping for clothes and took her to wonderful local restaurants where the food was as divine as his company. On Gianna's days off Izzy took over the cooking and, again mentally apologising to her feminist self, actually relished every moment of preparing meals for him as if she were channelling a nineteen-fifties housewife.

The day before they were to leave for Andrea's business colleague's wedding in Venice, Izzy woke during the night to the familiar twinge of period pain. Not wanting to wake Andrea, she quietly slipped out of bed and into the en suite bathroom, where she'd left some tampons in her toiletries bag. There was no paracetamol in her toiletries or her tote bag, so she went downstairs to the kitchen to a first aid cupboard where she had seen Gianna take out a Band-Aid a couple of days ago. She found the tablets and poured herself a glass of water and swallowed the pills, hoping it wouldn't be too long before they kicked in.

But as she stood looking out at the moonlit view over the coast she felt a strange twinge of disappointment. She placed a hand on her cramping abdomen and allowed a thought to slip under the locked door in her brain. The thought of carrying Andrea's child—a child conceived in love, not just in lust. A child they would raise as a married couple, invested in their relationship, not for material gain or to fulfil the terms of a will but because they truly loved each other and wanted to bring up a family together.

Izzy's hand fell away from her stomach. She was being silly allowing such a thought to take a foothold. What on earth would she do with a baby? She had never even held one. She didn't know the first thing about being a mother. She had watched her mother struggle all through her childhood to stand up for herself let alone her children. Who was to say Izzy would be any better at motherhood than she had been at anything else? She hadn't even completed school. What sort of mother would she make?

'*Cara?*' Andrea's deep voice shocked her out of her reverie. 'What are you doing down here at this time of night?' His gaze went to the paracetamol packet still lying on the kitchen bench. 'Are you unwell?' He came up close and placed a gentle hand on her forehead. 'You do look a little flushed but I don't think you've got a temperature.'

Izzy dipped away from the press of his hand and crossed her arms over her stomach. 'It's nothing. I just needed some paracetamol.'

He was still frowning. 'Do you have a headache?'

'No.' She let out a tight breath. 'Period cramps.'

He placed his hands on the tops of her shoulders. 'What can I do for you?'

Fall in love with me...

Izzy was terrified he would see the longing in her

eyes so kept hers averted. 'Nothing. I've taken the pain-killers so it'll ease soon enough.'

He brought up her chin with his finger. 'You should have woken me, *mio piccolo*. Do you often have painful periods?'

Izzy was aware of a thickness building in her throat—emotion that threatened to spill over the sand-bags of her self-control. His tender care reminded her of all she would be missing out on once their marriage was over. Who had ever held and comforted her while she had period pain? Who had ever comforted her and looked at her with such concern? She blinked a couple of times and swallowed. 'Now and again.' She forced her lips into a stoical smile. 'I'll be fine, Andrea. You can go back to bed. I'll come up in a minute.'

He cradled her cheek with one of his hands, his eyes dark and intense as they held hers. 'Can I get you a hot pack? I'm sure Gianna has one somewhere.'

'Please don't fuss.' Izzy pulled out of his hold and put some distance between them.

'Stop pushing me away, Isabella. I'm concerned about you.' His tone was still gentle but underpinned with a hint of frustration.

Izzy turned to the sink and poured herself another glass of water, chancing a sideways glance at his frowning features. 'You should be feeling relieved.'

'Why's that?'

She turned and waved a hand in front of her belly. 'I'm not pregnant.'

Something flickered over his face. 'Were you concerned you might be?'

Izzy shrugged. 'Not really.'

There was a loaded silence, as if he was thinking through an alternative scenario—the one she had been thinking about moments earlier. Was he imagining her belly growing round and heavy with their child? Was he picturing a dark-haired, dark-eyed baby with chubby limbs and tiny dimpled fingers?

Andrea cleared his throat and sent his fingers through his bed-tousled hair. 'I'll get you that heat pack.' He turned and went to a drawer at the other end of the kitchen and took out a microwavable pack and placed it in the microwave. 'Go up to bed. I'll be up with it in a couple of minutes.'

Izzy turned to leave the room, but when she glanced back from the doorway he was standing staring fixedly at the heat pack as he turned on the turntable.

Andrea took the heat pack out of the microwave and frowned. Izzy was right. He should be feeling relieved. Damn it. He *was* relieved. Incredibly relieved. The last thing he wanted to do was get her pregnant. A pregnancy would change everything. He didn't want that. Too many things had already been changed and he was only just keeping control. He was happy with how things were going. They were enjoying their relationship. But that didn't mean he wanted it to last any longer than the time they'd agreed on. He was keeping his emotions out of this. Wasn't he? Of course he was. He wasn't in any danger of blurring the boundaries.

Was Izzy relieved at not being pregnant? He had scrutinised her features but she was good at hiding her feelings. Better than he was at times. She was twenty-five years old. Was she hearing the tick-tock of her biological clock? She had told him she didn't want kids, but would she change her mind? It was a big issue. A life-changing issue that had to be thought about carefully. It was an issue he had thought about years ago and never revisited. Why would he? He had no knowledge of what a happy family looked like. His 'family' had been a disaster from the get-go. His biological father hadn't stayed around long enough to welcome Andrea into the world. His stepfather—one of a few over the years—had shown no interest in him other than as a punching bag. In theory, Andrea quite liked the idea of a loving and happy family but it was so rarely what happened in practice. He had decided it was easier, less painful, to move through life without the emotional encumbrances of a wife and children.

He refused to think of how lonely it might be once Izzy and he moved on with their lives.

He was used to being alone.

He'd been alone for most of his life.

Andrea took the heat pack upstairs to the master bedroom. Izzy was lying on her side with her head resting on one hand, her other hand pressed against her abdomen. There was an almost wistful cast to her features but when he approached she blinked and gave him a twisted smile. 'Sorry to have ruined your beauty sleep.'

He sat beside her on the bed and placed the heat pack against her belly. He used his other hand to brush her hair back from her forehead. 'Have those painkillers kicked in yet?'

'A little...'

Andrea traced his finger down the curve of her cheek. 'Will you be okay to come to Venice with me tomorrow for Patrizio Montelli's wedding?'

She turned over so she was lying on her back and held the heat pack against her stomach. 'Of course. It's just a period, Andrea. I've been having them every month since I was thirteen.'

He gave a wry smile. 'And here I was thinking shaving every day was a pain.'

She reached up and touched his jaw with her fingertips, her gaze going to his mouth. The tingle of her touch made every nerve in his body stand to attention. Her fingers were so soft, as light as a dove's feather brushing his skin, and yet they created a storm of fervent longing in his flesh. He captured her hand and brought it to his mouth, kissing each fingertip as he held her gaze. 'You should try and get some sleep.' His voice came out so husky it was as if his vocal cords had been rasped with a steel file.

Her eyes met his, her teeth snagging her lower lip. 'Andrea?'

He gave her hand a soft squeeze. 'Yes, *cara*?'

She opened her mouth to speak but then closed it again, her eyes slipping away from his. 'Never mind...'

He inched up her chin and locked his gaze on hers. 'Is something troubling you, *mio piccolo*? The wedding tomorrow? There might be press there but I'll try and—'

'No, it's not about that.'

'What, then?'

She let out a gust of breath and her mouth moved in a vestige of a smile that looked sad rather than anything else. 'Nothing... I'm just feeling a little emotional, I guess. Hormones.' She lowered her gaze and began to pluck at the sleeve of his bathrobe as if she needed something to do with her hands.

Andrea bent down and pressed a soft kiss to the middle of her forehead. 'I can sleep in one of the spare rooms if you'd like? It might help you sleep better.'

Her hand gripped his arm. 'No. Please don't do that. I...' She moistened her lips with the tip of her tongue, her gaze shimmering. 'Would you just...hold me?'

Andrea slipped into bed beside her and gathered her close, his head resting on the top of hers as she nestled into his chest. Her silky hair tickled his chest and her body curled up so close made him feverishly aware of every place where it touched his. Her breathing slowly settled and he stroked the back of her head as if he were soothing a child. He couldn't remember a time when he had held someone in such an intimate embrace. Not sexually intimate, but with an emotional honesty he found strangely moving.

A faint alarm bell sounded in his head but he disregarded it. He wasn't getting *too* close to Izzy. They were both clear on the rules of their marriage. She was just feeling a little emotional due to hormones and he was comforting her. That was what any decent man would do, right? He wasn't falling in love with her. That was a line he was never going to cross.

Not with Izzy.

Not with anyone.

Izzy sighed and made a sleepy murmur and then turned over so her back was towards him, her legs in a sexy tangle with his and her neat bottom pushed up against his groin. Andrea wrapped his arms around her, enjoying the feel of her spooning against him. His hand held the heat pack to her stomach, and then, when it lost its warmth, he replaced it with his hand. Her stomach was flat but a thought crept into his head—of her belly slowly expanding as it accommodated a baby. *His* baby. He pushed away the thought but it kept coming back like smoke curling under a locked door. He had never pictured himself as a husband, much less a father. Having children was what other people did. Whenever he walked past families he thought, *Not for me*. It was an automatic response and he had never questioned it.

But now, holding Izzy in his arms with his hand pressed against her abdomen, he wondered why he was feeling this vague sense of emptiness. Like something was missing from his life but he wasn't sure what it was. Maybe it was the merger still hanging over him. Once that was sorted he would feel more balanced.

More in control.

And right now a little more control was exactly what he needed.

CHAPTER TEN

WHEN IZZY WOKE the next morning Andrea was already up and showered. He brought her a cup of tea and some toast on a tray and sat on the edge of the bed as he set it across her lap. 'How are you feeling this morning, *cara*?'

'Much better, thanks.' She took the cup of tea and cradled it in her hands. 'Thanks for taking such good care of me. It's a long time since I was cosseted like that.'

He gave her leg a little pat. 'You deserve to be cosseted. I was worried about you.'

'It would have been far more worrying if I hadn't got my period.' Izzy brought the cup to her mouth to take a sip of her tea.

'True.' He gave an on-off smile but a frown flickered across his brow.

There was a silence.

Izzy put her cup back on the tray. 'What time do we leave for Venice?'

He rose from the bed. 'Our flight leaves in about an hour or so. It's a late afternoon wedding so there'll be plenty of time to dress at the hotel before the service.'

'Will it be a big wedding?'

'Big enough.'

Izzy tilted her head at him. 'You're not looking forward to it, are you?'

He gave her another brief smile. 'Let's put it this way: I'll be glad when today is over.'

They arrived at their hotel in Venice—one of Andrea's smaller ones, but for all that no less gorgeous. Izzy freshened up her make-up and hair and then dressed in one of the outfits Andrea had bought her when they'd gone shopping a few days ago. It was navy blue satin that clung to her figure like a glove and she teamed it with a matching satin wrap and high heels.

Just as she was about to put on some costume jewellery, Andrea came over to her carrying a jewellery box. 'These are for you,' he said.

Izzy opened the box to find a stunningly beautiful sapphire and diamond pendant and matching droplet earrings nestled in a bed of luxurious velvet. 'Oh, my goodness…they're gorgeous.' She glanced up at him but his expression was difficult to read. 'You really shouldn't have spent so much money.'

He shrugged as if spending thousands and thousands of euros on designer jewellery was no big deal. 'You need to look the part at Patrizio and Elena's wedding.'

Izzy felt a sharp pang of disappointment like a needle stab to her heart. He hadn't bought the jewellery specifically for her but as a stage prop to convince everyone their marriage was not the sham it really was.

She looked back down at the earrings and pendant, touching the shimmering diamonds with one of her fingers. 'You have excellent taste in jewellery...' Then she frowned and looked up at him again. 'But I thought you said you never bought your lovers jewellery?'

He took the box from her and removed the pendant. 'I don't. But this is different. Turn around and I'll put it on for you.'

Different? In what way? Did it mean he was beginning to care for her? To really care for her?

To feel *close* to her?

Izzy turned and lifted the back of her hair out of the way so he could fasten the pendant around her neck. The brush of his fingers against her skin made her shiver as if he had sent a current of electricity through her body. Once the pendant was in place she turned back around to face him. 'Why is it different?'

His gaze drifted to her mouth and back to her eyes but his expression was still as inscrutable as ever. 'You're my wife. People will expect you to be wearing nice jewellery.'

Izzy touched the pendant hanging around her neck. 'But I'm only a temporary wife. Spending heaps of money seems a little over-the-top, given the circumstances.'

His mouth tightened for the briefest moment as if her comment had landed like a punch. 'No one knows this is temporary but us.'

'And Gianna.'

He gave a grunt that could have been agreement or scorn or both. 'I'm starting to wonder if I should have let her in on the secret.' He picked up his jacket and shrugged it on. 'You look beautiful, by the way. That colour suits you.'

Izzy smoothed down the front of her dress, ridiculously thrilled by his compliment. 'Thank you.' She picked up the earrings and inserted them into her ears. 'Will I do?'

His dark gaze ran over her like a minesweeper and he gave her a bone-melting smile. 'You'll more than do.'

The Montelli wedding service was conducted at St Mark's Basilica in Venice and Izzy took her assigned seat near the front on the groom's side while Andrea went forward to stand with Patrizio at the altar as his best man. The front of the church was beautifully adorned with flowers and each pew draped with white ribbons and bows and more garlands of flowers. A boy soprano choir sang with such exquisite scalp-tingling perfection, Izzy had tears sprouting in her eyes and a thickness developing in her throat. If she had been the type to imagine a dream wedding, then this would have been close to it. It was a painful reminder of how cold and impersonal her wedding ceremony to Andrea had been. It had been little more than a business transaction and, while their relationship had improved over the last couple of weeks, it didn't erase the fact that their marriage was not for ever.

The organist began playing the Wedding March and the congregation audibly drew in a collective breath when the bridesmaids—led by Patrizio's stepdaughter

Alexis—came up the aisle. Dressed in the softest shade of rose, each bridesmaid carried a posy of tea roses and the cute little flower girl, who was only about three years old, carried a little basket of rose petals, but she proved too shy to do much other than hold her head down and clutch the hand of the nearest bridesmaid.

And then it was time for the bride to enter the church. Izzy turned and watched Patrizio's bride Elena walk up the aisle in a wedding dress that was like something out of a fairy tale. With a lace bodice and long sleeves and a full skirt with a partial train and a voluminous veil, Elena glowed with beauty and happiness.

Izzy tried to suppress the pangs of envy but the closer the bride got to her beaming-with-pride groom, the worse she felt. It was as if someone was crushing her heart inside her chest when she thought of her own wedding day. Her travesty of a wedding ceremony with its impersonal witnesses and cynical seen-it-all-before marriage celebrant. The ceremony where no feelings were involved, no future planned, no promises of forever.

Just words without meaning, without conviction and commitment.

She glanced at Andrea but he was concentrating on his role as best man, although Izzy noticed Alexis casting him covert glances and blushing. The teenager reminded Izzy of herself at that age—awkward, not quite an adult and yet not really a child. Caught in a weird limbo with hormones and urgings but without the maturity to deal with them.

It was a painful reminder of all the mistakes Izzy had made in trying to get her father's attention.

So many mistakes. Mistakes she was still paying for now.

The service began and the bride and groom exchanged heartfelt vows. Izzy swallowed a lump in her throat as the bride and groom kissed. Andrea's eyes met hers and Izzy gave him a smile that was so tight it felt like her mouth would crack.

By the time the bridal procession left the church and the official photos were taken it was over an hour before Izzy got anywhere near Andrea. She felt like an extra on a film set. Not important enough to be in the main cast, just a walk-on figure.

But that was exactly what she was in Andrea's life. A walk-on part. A temporary bride who had no hope of a more permanent role. How could she have agreed to such an arrangement when she could have had what Patrizio and Elena had? No one looking at the new bride and groom could be in any doubt of their feelings for each other. Real feelings. Genuine feelings, not pretend.

Why couldn't Andrea look at *her* like that?

Izzy met his gaze during the reception and tried to fool herself he *was* looking at her like that, but then she realised he was acting the role of devoted husband. It was a jarring echo of what her father used to do. Pretending. Playing to an audience. There was nothing genuine about her relationship with Andrea, apart from the desire they shared. But how soon would that burn out for him? He was known for only staying with a lover for a month or so. She had been with him a little over two weeks. Would she be able to hold his interest for another five and a half months? How could she live with him, pretending she was happy with how things were?

She wasn't happy.

How could she be when all she had ever wanted was to be loved for who she was? Accepted and valued, not expected to be someone she could never be. Could she really pretend she was fine with how things were for another few months and then smile and wave goodbye when it was over? Didn't Andrea want more than a six-month affair? Especially after all they had shared both physically and emotionally? She had fooled herself he was getting close to her. He had shared his painful past, as she had shared hers.

Didn't that mean he felt something for her that he hadn't felt for anyone else?

The reception was being held at a private villa along the canals. The bridal party were transported in gondolas, but again Izzy felt on the outside, arriving on foot and having to sit with people she didn't know because Andrea was on the top table.

During the reception Andrea introduced her to Patrizio and Elena and Alexis, holding Izzy close to his side and smiling down at her with every appearance of being madly in love, but Izzy felt even more conflicted. More of a fraud. More of a misfit. More miserable. Every smile he sent her way made her heart contract. Every touch of his made something in her stomach plummet in despair because she knew the truth even if the wedding party and guests did not.

Andrea didn't love her. If he did wouldn't he have said so? Wouldn't he have taken the time limit off their relationship? Wouldn't he have at least hinted that things had changed for him? That his feelings had changed?

'Is everything all right, *cara*?' Andrea asked, drawing Izzy to one side during the last stages of the reception.

'We need to talk.' Izzy kept her frozen smile in place in case any wedding guests were watching.

He cupped her face, his brown eyes dark with concern. 'Tired? Sorry it's been such a long day for you. We can't leave until the bride and groom go, but it won't be long now.'

Izzy couldn't bear for another minute to go past without telling him how she felt. She looked up into his eyes and tried to keep hers from tearing up. 'I can't do this, Andrea. I just can't.'

His hands took her gently by the upper arms. 'Are you still unwell? I'm sorry, I should have asked earlier.'

Izzy moved out of his hold and stepped further into the quiet alcove they were in. She crossed her arms over her body, suddenly chilled although the night was warm. 'I'm not sick. I'm just sick of pretending. I can't do it. It feels wrong to be fooling everyone our relationship is something it's not and never will be.'

A flicker of annoyance passed over his features. 'Can't this wait until we get back to our hotel?'

Izzy stood her ground, facing him with what was left of her pride. 'Did you feel *anything* during that wedding ceremony today? Anything at all?'

His expression tightened into a mask of steel. 'Isabella. This is not the time or place for this discussion.'

'I asked you a simple question.'

'And I told you I am not going to discuss this here.' His tone was so cold she felt another shiver pass over her flesh.

'I'll tell you how I felt. I felt guilty,' Izzy said. 'Guilty and disappointed and ashamed because I agreed to marry you for all the wrong reasons. I looked at Elena and Patrizio at the ceremony and saw two people who love each other. I want that. I want what they have.'

He frowned. 'You want us to have a formal ceremony? Is that what you're saying? You want a big fancy church wedding even though we've only got a few more months to the—'

'You don't get it, do you?' Izzy's heart felt as if it were being pulverised, along with her pride. 'It's not about having a big flashy wedding, Andrea. I want a genuine marriage, one where there isn't a clock ticking. One where there isn't pretence and lying and acting but real feelings. Feelings that last a lifetime.'

'No one can guarantee that.' His lips barely moved over the clipped words. 'You can't. I can't.'

'Maybe not, but I'd still like to try.'

The silence was so thick it was like a suffocating fog.

Andrea let out a long slow breath but there was no reduction of tension in his expression. 'You're asking for something I can't give. We agreed on six months. I've told you what I'm prepared to give and a long-term commitment isn't part of it.'

She searched his gaze, desperately hoping to see a flicker of warm emotion instead of clinical indifference. 'But why isn't it? Why is committing to someone so difficult for you?'

He opened and closed his mouth as if carefully monitoring his choice of words before he spoke. 'I'm not prepared to discuss this now. We agreed on the terms and—'

'I should never have agreed,' Izzy said. 'But I wanted my grandparents' house so much it was all I could think about. But I realise now I want something else so much more. I can't spend another minute of my life trying to be what other people want or expect me to be. I have to be me. I have to be true to myself. For most of my life I thought I never wanted to be married. I can't believe I told myself such lies and for so long. But what I realise now is what I didn't want was my parents' marriage. My father didn't love my mother. If he'd loved her he wouldn't have tried to control her and squash her spirit.'

'I have no interest in trying to control you or squash your spirit, so please don't insult me by comparing me to your father,' Andrea said through tight lips.

'But you don't love me, do you?' Izzy felt as if she were stepping off a tall building into mid-air by asking such a question.

Every muscle on his face looked like it was having a spasm. Tension rippled along his jaw, his gaze as shuttered as a boarded-up window. 'That wasn't part of the bargain,' he said in a voice so devoid of emotion he could have been a robot.

Izzy knew she had been asking for the impossible but still she had clung to hope. But that fragile hope was now in the final throes of survival, gasping for air even as death crept inexorably closer. 'I don't want a business contract for a relationship. I don't want a bargain drawn up with terms and conditions and rules. I just want what most people want. Love. Commitment.'

'Look, we'll go back to our hotel and once you've had a good night's sleep you'll see this differently in the morning,' he said in a more conciliatory tone. 'You're tired and emotional.'

Izzy knew if she went back to the hotel with him she would end up in bed with him. She would end up going back to Positano with him and would spend the next five months hoping he would change his mind. She had spent too much of her life hoping for things she couldn't have. She had to be strong. She had to stand up for what she wanted. She owed it to herself. She couldn't live by someone else's agenda any longer. 'I'm not going back with you, Andrea. Not to your hotel. Not to your villa. It's over. We are over because we were never together in the first place.'

His eyes flinched as if too bright a light had struck him in the face. But then his expression turned to stone. 'Are you doing this deliberately?' He waved his hand towards the reception they could hear in the other room. 'Is this what you planned? To jeopardise everything I've worked so damn hard for?'

Izzy let out a sigh. 'That you would even think that proves how little you know me. I'm sorry if this ruins your merger but I consider my needs just as important as a business deal. I can't pretend to be happy with what we agreed on. I'm not happy. I could never be happy with someone who is unable to love me.'

'Are you saying you love me?' His frown was so heavy it made him look angry rather than confused.

Izzy considered telling him of her feelings for him but knew it wouldn't change anything. She had to keep some measure of pride. To offer her heart to him, only to have him hand it back with a *Thanks, but no thanks* would be too painful. 'I'm saying I want more than you can give me.'

'If you loved me, then you'd accept whatever I offered you,' he said. 'You'd accept it and be grateful because without me you're going to lose every penny of your inheritance.'

Izzy wondered how she could have ever thought that money would have been enough. Twice or thrice the amount wouldn't be enough in exchange for a loveless life. She only had to think of her mother to be reminded of how empty such a life could be. Even her dream of buying back her grandparents' estate seemed a pointless mission. What she had been trying to buy back was her happiness—the happiness she had once felt and longed to feel again.

But she wouldn't do it—*couldn't* do it—if it compromised her sense of self. Her sense of worth.

'I won't live with you under those terms, Andrea,' Izzy said. 'I'd be little more than a paid mistress, waiting for you to call time on our affair. I want to be an equal partner in a relationship. Not a pawn on a chessboard.'

'Your father was the one who put you on the chessboard, not me.' His lips were so flat they turned white. 'You should be grateful I was prepared to step in to help you. No one else was going to.'

'Is that what I'm supposed to feel? Grateful?' Izzy threw him an embittered glare. 'For what, exactly? That you fancied me? But how long is it going to last? Another week or two? A month? You don't stay with a lover longer than a few weeks. I can't live like that. I *won't* live like that.'

'Go, then.' He jerked his head towards the exit. 'Leave, and see how far it gets you. You'll be crawling back to me, begging me to take you back, before a day goes past.'

'I don't think you're listening to me, Andrea.' Izzy underscored her tone with a thread of steel. 'I'm not going to change my mind. I've finally grown up, like you told me to do all those years ago. I know what I want and I won't settle for anything less.' She forced herself to hold his unfathomable gaze. 'I'm going to collect my wrap and my purse from the reception and unless you want to create a scene that will be splashed over every newspaper and turn your friend's wedding into more of a farce than ours, then I suggest you let me leave without a fuss.'

One side of his mouth tipped up in a cynical curl. 'Blackmail, *cara*?'

Izzy raised her chin. 'You'd better believe it.'

CHAPTER ELEVEN

ANDREA DIDN'T BELIEVE IT. *Refused* to believe it. How could she walk away from her inheritance? How could she walk away from more money than most people saw in ten lifetimes?

How could she walk away from him?

His feelings were as raw as when he'd been a kid of fourteen, kicked to the kerb as if he was worth nothing. It freaked him out how similar the feelings were. Feelings he had spent a lifetime avoiding. He'd taught himself not to need people because he didn't want to feel like this.

Empty.

Blindsided.

Gutted.

He'd barely been able to speak to Izzy without betraying how shocked and disappointed he felt. He hadn't seen it coming. She couldn't have picked a worse time to drop that on him. He hadn't been prepared for her sudden bombshell. He'd fooled himself she wouldn't jeopardise her inheritance. Fooled himself that what they had together was…was what? More lasting?

No.

He didn't do forever. It wasn't on his radar. *Short-term and simple* was his credo. He had made no promises. He had made it clear right from the start he didn't want the complication of a long-term relationship. He accepted that it worked for other people but he didn't want it for himself. How could he when he had seen first-hand—*felt* first-hand—the blunt blow of rejection?

What was Izzy thinking? She had too much at stake to pull out now. They were only two weeks into their marriage. They had months left. Months and months he'd been looking forward to far more than he should. He'd known it was dangerous to get close to her. Known it and done it anyway, and now she had walked away. Thrown him over for what? She couldn't inherit without him.

She was calling his bluff—that was what this was. How could it be anything else? It was an attention-seeking tantrum to make him confess something he hadn't confessed to anyone and never would. The wedding had got to her. It was a grand and romantic affair that would have got to anyone. Even he'd felt a twinge or two of envy over Patrizio and Elena's commitment to each other.

But that didn't mean he wanted it for himself. He was happy with how things were. He and Izzy had been getting on so well. Their relationship was working the way he'd hoped it would—mutually satisfying, exciting and passionate.

And close...

Yes, well, that was the problem right there, wasn't

it? He'd allowed her too close. Way too close. He'd been blinded by the intimacies they'd shared, not just the physical but the emotional. He had got to know her, the real Izzy, not the wild child façade she put on as a form of armour. Getting close to her, knowing her more deeply, had brought out the protector in him. She was the first woman he'd allowed close enough to stir that in him. Close enough to see his pain and shame over his troubled past.

But would she go through with her threat to walk away? There was no way she would walk out on him in the middle of his colleague's wedding. She knew how much was at stake, and not just for him but also for her. Was this her way of exacting revenge? Was that what she was doing? Making him pay for forcing her into marriage? But that didn't fit well with his new under-standing of her. She wasn't a brash pay-you-back type. She was impulsive and feisty and, yes, a little sensitive and emotional, but those were the things he'd come to admire about her.

He'd thought they were getting on just fine. He'd thought their relationship was going exactly the way he'd wanted it to. They enjoyed each other's company. They were good together. Better than good—amaz-ing. They'd shared the best sex he'd ever had and he'd looked forward to it continuing for another few months.

Anger coiled in his belly, tight and terrible anger mixed up in a toxic stew of disappointment and an even more disquieting sense of dismay. He was not the sort of man to feel dismayed or distraught. He hadn't felt like that since he was a teenager without a home, without a family.

Without anyone.

He never allowed anyone the opportunity to hurt him the way he'd been hurt back then. Izzy was probably still feeling a little hormonal. She would cool off in an hour or so and realise what was at stake for her and rethink her decision. By the time he got back to their hotel tonight she would be tucked up in bed and waiting for him.

He was counting on it.

Izzy only stayed at Andrea's hotel long enough to collect her passport and her overnight bag. She booked an early-morning flight back to London and moved into another hotel so she wouldn't encounter Andrea. How could she spend another night with him, knowing he didn't love her? Would never love her? Refused to love her? As much as she wanted him, it would be emotional suicide to continue to sleep with him. Even if he came back now and said he loved her, how could she be sure he wasn't pretending? Hadn't she heard her father say it numerous times without once meaning it?

Izzy barely slept that night and got to the airport early and boarded her flight with her heart so heavy she wondered if she would be charged an excess baggage fee. London greeted her with rain and dismal skies and when she called her flatmate, Jess, she found her room had been rented out to someone else.

'I'm so sorry, Izzy, but I thought you weren't coming back,' Jess said. 'What's happened? Where's Andrea?'

'We're not together any more,' Izzy said. 'I made a mistake. I shouldn't have married him. He doesn't love me.'

'Do you love him?' Jess's voice was soft with concern.

Izzy bit her lip to stop it from trembling. 'I'm an idiot for falling for someone like him. I don't know how it happened. One minute I hated him and the next...'

'But what will you do now? Doesn't this mean you lose your inheritance if you break up before the six months?'

'I don't care about the money,' Izzy said. 'Well, only a little bit.'

'Where will you live? I could put you up on the sofa for a night or two but—'

'It's all right. I'll find my own place. I'm not exactly destitute.' *Yet.*

Andrea arrived at his villa in Positano the following day with the expectation Izzy would be there once she'd had time to cool off. His hotel staff had told him she had left the hotel late but they had no idea of where she had gone. He'd done a quick ring around but hotel security was tight on giving out guest details, which was something he totally supported. But it was frustrating to spend the night pacing the floor with a host of ghastly scenarios flooding his brain. He'd tried calling her but her phone was switched off. He didn't leave a message because he wasn't sure what to say. *Come back, I need you* were not phrases he used. To anyone.

Gianna greeted him with her usual cheery smile

but her expression faded when she saw he was alone. 'Where's Izzy?'

'I was hoping she'd be here.' Andrea's stomach curdled anew with disappointment. A dark and bitter disappointment that yet again she had failed to do as he'd expected. As he'd hoped.

Gianna's dark brown eyes almost popped out of her head. 'Why didn't she come back with you? What's going on?'

'I'd rather not talk about it.'

'But where is she?'

Andrea strode past the housekeeper to go to his office. 'I don't want to be disturbed. Take the week off. Take a month off.'

He sat at his desk and stared at his computer screen. How had it come to this? He had been hoping Izzy would be back by now. He had given her twenty-four hours. How much longer did she need to see what a stupid thing she was doing? She was sabotaging her future. She was throwing away her chance of financial freedom. It was a ludicrous thing to do. No one in their right mind would walk away from that amount of money.

But money wasn't everything...

Andrea clenched his jaw until his teeth ached. Yes, it damn well was. Money might not buy happiness but it got you off the street. It got you out of the gutter and into a lifestyle that was the envy of others. It fed you and clothed you and transported you to places you'd only ever dreamed of as a child living in abject poverty.

He pushed back his chair and paced the floor until

he was sure he would bald the carpet. He might have plenty of money but he had never felt so powerless. He was used to being in the driving seat of his life. He was the one who started and ended his relationships. He wasn't used to being left hanging, hoping for what he couldn't quite say. His pride had taken a hit. That was why he was feeling so out of sorts. What else could it be? He had been so sure Izzy wouldn't compromise her chance to inherit. She wanted her grandparents' house more than anything. He knew what it felt like to want something so badly nothing else mattered. Was she disappointed? Crushed that her dream of buying back that property was now out of her reach?

He went over to the window to look at the view from his office. The ocean sparkled below, the sun shone with brilliance and warmth but inside he felt cold and empty. He was like a king confined to his castle, surrounded by wealth and possessions that failed to deliver the contentment they had before.

Andrea rubbed a hand over his face and sighed. He needed to do something. Anything. Work was his panacea, wasn't it? The least he could do was buy the wretched property for her. Call him a sentimental fool but he couldn't stand by and let her miss out on that house. He sat back at his desk and searched online for the property details. Within an hour he had made an offer—way too generous, of course, and it would take a few days for a building inspection to be completed and a legal contract drawn up, but he wanted that property for Izzy and what he wanted he made it his business to get.

Well…mostly.

Work was what he needed to get back on form. Hard, relentless work. He had to stop thinking about Izzy and focus on something else. He needed to pour his frustrations into ticking off tasks. He was not going to let Izzy's desertion undo him. He hated to think what the press would make of their break-up once they heard about it.

But he was determined they wouldn't hear it via him.

Izzy found a temporary bedsit and a few days later hired a car and travelled down to take one last look at her grandparents' house. The day before she'd received a call from the owners to say a buyer had approached them and, due to the generosity of the offer, they'd felt compelled to sell rather than wait another few months. They were apologetic but pragmatic and Izzy could hardly blame them. She had been expecting such a call ever since she'd first hoped to buy the property. It was always going to be risky without having drawn up a legal agreement, but she hadn't been in the position to draw up anything.

She had just hoped. Vainly, foolishly, naïvely hoped.

But going down now to the house was her way of saying goodbye to the dream she'd had of reclaiming it. She'd heard nothing from Andrea since she'd arrived in London, although she had noticed a couple of missed calls the night she'd left Venice, but he hadn't left a message. She'd been bracing herself for the press to report on their failed relationship but so far there had been nothing. It was ironic to think of all the times in the past where she had courted scandal and now the sudden break-up of her marriage to Italy's most eligible bachelor had failed to rate a mention.

The country lane lined by hedgerows on the way to her grandparents' house brought a prickly lump to Izzy's throat. How many times had she been down this lane with Hamish by her side? Not enough. Nowhere near enough but those few precious memories were all she had left to treasure. Every field, every tree and wildflower were like old friends greeting her. There was the old oak she had stood under and watched in wonder as Hamish had built a tree house specially for her. There was the little bridge over the babbling stream that she and Hamish had walked over on their way to his favourite fishing spot. There was the copse of trees where they'd had a picnic and he'd played hide and seek with her. She could almost smell the fragrance of her grandmother's home-baked treats, could almost hear the sound of her grandfather mowing the lawns on his ride-on mower because he enjoyed the task so much even though there had been a gardener.

This was where Izzy had felt closest to her mother and she had hoped by reclaiming the house she would somehow feel her mum would be proud of her.

The Georgian house finally came into view and her heart stuttered when she saw the 'SOLD' notice on an estate agent's sign by the entrance gates.

Izzy's shoulders slumped in defeat. So it really was over. Even after the phone call from the owners she had still hoped it wasn't true. But it was true. Her dream was destroyed. But strangely it didn't feel as devastating as she'd thought. The house looked tired and in need of some urgent attention. The garden was overgrown and the paintwork on the house faded and even peeling in places. But even if the house were beautifully restored, would she have been happy without someone to share her vision of it with her? The only someone she wanted to share it with was Andrea and he didn't want to share his life with anyone, much less her.

It was just a house that had once been a happy place but the people who had made it happy were no longer there. But in a way they lived on in Izzy's heart. It was up to her now to honour her mother's and brother's and grandparents' memories by living a fully authentic life, not settling for second best or half measures.

Izzy turned the car around and drove back along the lane, leaving her childhood memories—and a little part of herself that would always belong there—behind.

A couple of days later Andrea received a package delivery by courier from Izzy containing the wedding and engagement rings and the jewellery he'd bought her. He sat in his office in Positano and stared at the diamonds and sapphires and wondered why she'd sent them back when she could have sold them. At least then she could have raised some funds to compensate for what she'd lost by bailing on their marriage. He searched through the packaging and found a handwritten note.

Dear Andrea,
I didn't feel comfortable keeping these any longer. I'll leave it to you to make the divorce ar-

*rangements. Please say hello to Gianna for me
and apologise for how I left without saying goodbye. I hope she understands.*

*By the way, my grandparents' house was sold
but I'm okay about it. It needs a lot of work and I
would never have been able to afford it.*
Izzy

Andrea stared at the note for a long moment. Why
was she leaving the divorce arrangements to him? He
picked up her wedding ring and suddenly realised he
was still wearing his. Why hadn't he taken it off? He
let out a sigh that scraped at his throat like a crab claw.
He knew exactly why. It was the same reason he'd gone
to such trouble to buy her grandparents' property even
though it would need hundreds of thousands of pounds
thrown at it to restore it. As white elephants went it
was a big one. It had gone against every business prin-
ciple he prided himself on but he'd felt compelled to at
least make sure she had something she wanted, even
if it wasn't all she'd hoped for. He'd been waiting for
all the legal work to be cleared up before he sent the
deeds to her. Maybe he should have contacted her before now but he didn't want her to think he was black-
mailing her into coming back to him. The house was
a gift. Wasn't it? Why else had he bought such a run-
down sad excuse for a place?

But she didn't want possessions. She wanted love.
Wasn't that what everyone wanted?

And yes, even him.

He'd been such a fool to let her go without a fight.

He'd let her walk away because he hadn't had the guts to ask her to stay. He hadn't had the courage to admit to how he felt about her. He hadn't even recognised his feelings because for most of his life he'd been shut down emotionally. He had done the same thing to his mother. She had rejected him and he'd walked away without trying to understand what was going on for her. But he had already taken steps to fix things with his mother. He had Izzy to thank for showing him how blind he had been to his mother's point of view. It shamed him to think he had wasted all those years resenting his mother when he could have been helping her, protecting her.

But for now Izzy was his top priority—his only priority.

He had locked away his heart for fear of getting hurt and yet he had hurt Izzy. She hadn't told him she loved him but the signs were all there. He had to see her to tell her how he felt. He had to prove he was worthy of a second chance because he couldn't bear to live his life without her at the centre of it.

Izzy was in her bedsit, mindlessly watching a movie on her phone, when the doorbell rang. She used the term 'doorbell' loosely for it sounded more like a cat being slowly strangled than anything else. She clicked off her phone and answered the door, to find Andrea standing there carrying a package and a business-sized envelope. A sinkhole formed in her stomach. *The divorce papers.* He was bringing her the divorce papers to sign to activate proceedings. 'Hi,' she said, surprised her voice got past the lump in her throat. 'Won't you come in?'

He stepped through the doorway and closed the door behind him. 'How are you?' His voice had a gruff sound to it as if he'd swallowed something rough.

Izzy tried to smile but it didn't quite work. 'I'm fine. You?' Oh, God, how polite they both sounded. Like strangers. She glanced at the envelope in his hand and swallowed. 'Are those what I think they are?'

'What do you think they are?' Something about his expression made her wonder if he was smiling behind the screen of his shuttered gaze. How cruel of him to be amused at the end of their relationship. But then, why wouldn't he be amused? He wasn't the one who would lose everything once they divorced.

'The divorce papers.' How it hurt for her to actually say those words out loud.

He passed the envelope to her. 'Why don't you open it and see if you're right?'

Izzy took the envelope with fingers that trembled. She broke the seal and pulled out the document, but it took her a moment to work out what it was. It was a legal document but it had nothing to do with a divorce. It was a property deed. The deed to her grandparents' property. She looked up at Andrea in puzzlement. 'I don't understand... Why are you giving me these?'

'It's yours, Izzy. The property is yours. I bought it for you.'

Izzy wasn't sure what had surprised her more—the fact he'd called her Izzy or his purchase of the property. 'I don't know what to say... I'm completely gob-smacked as to why you would do something like that.'

'Do you have no idea?' His eyes began to twinkle. 'No idea at all, *cara*?'

Izzy moistened her lips, which were suddenly drier than the document she was holding. She put the document down and looked at the other package he was carrying. 'W-what's in there?' Her voice stumbled over a budding hope.

He handed her the jewellery she'd sent back to him only a few days ago. 'I want you to put those rings back on, *cara*. I love you and I can't spend another day without you.'

Izzy opened and closed her mouth, her heart beating so fast she could almost hear it. 'You love me?'

He took her by the upper arms, his smile so tender it made her heart beat all the faster. 'I've been such a fool, *tesoro mio*. I can't believe I let you walk out of my life like that. I was so angry that you'd ended things that it took me a while to realise how I really felt. I love you so much. My life is so empty without you. All I do is work and mope around the place. Gianna is sick of me. She's threatening to resign. You have to put me out of my misery—and hers—and come back to me. Please? Forgive me for being a heartless brute in not telling you how I feel before now. I love you desperately.'

Izzy threw her arms around him and hugged him so tightly he grunted in pain. 'Oh, Andrea, I love you so much too. I can't believe how lonely and miserable I've been.'

He lifted her face so his gaze meshed with hers. 'You are the best thing that's ever happened to me. You make me feel alive in a way I've never felt before. I'm sorry we fought so much over the years. What were we thinking, wasting so much time?'

Relief at knowing he loved her as she loved him flooded Izzy like a powerful drug. A calming, healing drug that took away all the pain and sadness of the past. 'We'll make up for it in the future. No more fighting, only loving.'

He stroked his fingers across her cheek. 'The last few days have been torture, coming home to an empty house. Not seeing you. Not hearing your voice. Not sleeping beside you. I've missed you so much.'

Izzy smiled up at him, her gaze misty with happy tears. 'I've missed you so much too. I only realised how much I loved you at Patrizio and Elena's wedding. It made me feel so sad that our marriage hadn't been genuine. I hated our ceremony. It made me feel so cheap and disposable. I never want to feel like that again. Promise me we won't do that to each other.'

'We'll get married again,' Andrea said, holding her close. 'We'll have all the bells and whistles you like as long as you'll agree to be my wife for ever.'

Izzy gave him a teasing smile and linked her arms around his neck. 'I thought you didn't believe in forever love?'

He pressed a kiss to her mouth. 'I didn't until I fell in love with you. I want to grow old with you. I want to have babies with you. We can be a family, the sort of family both of us missed out on. You've taught me so much about love, my gorgeous girl. For all these years I've been blaming my mother, kicking me out on the street, but you got me thinking about her circumstances. I've managed to track her down and you were right. She sent me away because she was frightened my stepfather would kill me if I came back. She was terrified of him. I can't thank you enough for making me see how blind I was. It's still early days in rebuilding our relationship, but I want to buy her a nice house in a safe suburb. I also want to buy a house and turn it into a women's shelter. I'm hoping she'll let me name it after her to make up for my ignorance of her situation in the past.'

'Oh, darling, I'm so thrilled for you that you've got her back in your life,' Izzy said. 'You're such a good man. She must be so proud of who you've become. I was so against marriage before I met you because I was frightened I would end up with a marriage like my parents'. But you're nothing like my father. You make me feel like I'm worth something. You make me feel like a princess.' She couldn't stop some tears from falling from her eyes. 'You bought me that house not even knowing if I'd come back to you.'

Andrea took out a handkerchief and gently mopped her tears, his own eyes looking suspiciously moist. 'You are my world, Izzy. No amount of wealth I've accumulated over the years compares to you. When I thought I'd lost you I realised how little I care for possessions and status. I care only about you. You are my world and you are worth everything to me.'

'No one has ever said anything so wonderful to me before,' Izzy said, sniffing. 'I'm so happy I can't stop crying.'

He smiled and gathered her close. 'I hope I don't

make you cry too often. I can't promise our life together will be perfect but I can promise I will be by
your side no matter what. And this time, when we get
married in church, do you know what I'm going to do
when the priest says, "You may kiss the bride"?'

Izzy smiled back. 'What?'

His eyes glinted and his mouth came down to hers.
'I'm going to do this.' And then he kissed her.

* * * * *

ONE NIGHT STAND BRIDE

KAT CANTRELL

One

The Las Vegas tourism department needed to change their slogan because what happened in Vegas did *not* stay there. In fact, what had happened in Vegas followed Hendrix Harris home to North Carolina and landed above the fold on every media outlet known to man.

He wanted his money refunded, a spell to wipe the memories of an entire city and an aspirin.

Though even he had to admit the photographer had perfectly captured the faces of Hendrix and Rosalind Carpenter. The picture was erotic without being pornographic—a trick and a half since it was abundantly clear they were both buck naked, yet somehow, all the naughty bits were strategically covered. A miracle that had allowed the picture to be print-worthy. It was a one-in-a-million shot. You could even see the steam rising from the hot tub.

And thanks to that photographer being in the right place at the wrong time, Hendrix's luck had run out.

He'd fully expected his mother to have a heart attack when she saw her son naked with the daughter of the wealthiest man in North Carolina. Especially since Hendrix's mother had warned him to keep his clothes on once she launched her gubernatorial campaign.

Joke was on Hendrix. No heart attacks. Instead, his mother was thrilled. *Thrilled* that he'd gotten chummy with Paul Carpenter's daughter. So thrilled that somehow she'd gotten Hendrix to agree that marrying Rosalind would fix everything.

Really, this whole scandal was his fault, and it was on him to make amends, or so he'd been told. The Carpenter family had old money and lots of influence, which provided a nice balance to the Harris new money.

Grumbling in his head because he loved and respected his mother too much to do it out loud, Hendrix threw himself into the task of figuring out how to contact Roz. Their naked Vegas romp had been most definitely of the one-night stand variety. Now he would have to convince her that she loved his mother's plan.

Hendrix didn't hate the idea of marriage, per se, not when it solved more than one problem. So it was now his goal to make sure a big fat yes was Roz's response to the question *Will you marry me?*

The only problem being that he hadn't actually spoken to her since that night and they'd expressly agreed they wouldn't see each other again. Minor detail. When he put his mind to something, rare was the obstacle that didn't get the hell out of his way.

Luck crept back onto his side. Roz hadn't blocked

all the web crawlers that posted her address to one of those seamy "find anyone for a price" sites. Hendrix had no qualms about throwing money at this problem.

Hendrix drove himself to the building Rosalind Carpenter lived in on Fayetteville Street instead of taking a car. Arriving with fanfare before he'd gotten this done didn't fit his idea of a good plan. After she said yes, of course there'd be lots of sanctioned pictures of the happy couple. And they'd be dressed.

His mother hadn't properly appreciated just how hard her son had worked to get his abs to look so centerfold-worthy. It was a shame that such a great shot of what had been a truly spectacular night with the hottest woman he'd ever met had done so much damage to Ms. Harris's family values campaign.

He charmed his way past the security desk because everyone liked him instantly, a fact of life he traded on frequently. Then he waited patiently until someone with the right access to Roz's floor who was also willing to listen to his tale of woe got on the elevator. Within fifteen minutes, he knocked on Ms. Carpenter's door.

To her credit, when she answered, she didn't even blink.

He did.

Holy hell. How could he have forgotten what she did to him?

Her sensuality leaped from her like a tidal wave, crashing over him until he scarcely knew which way was up, but he didn't care because surfacing was the last thing on his mind. He gasped for air in the wake of so much sensation as she tucked a lock of dark hair behind her ear. She pursed those lush lips and surveyed him with cool amusement.

"You don't follow instructions well," she fairly purred, leaning on the door, kicking one foot to the side and drawing attention to the sexy slice of leg peeking out from her long flowy skirt.

"Your memory is faulty," he returned easily, a smile sliding across his face in spite of the reason for his visit. "I recall being an instant slave to your instructions. 'Faster, harder, take me from behind.' I can't think of a single thing you told me to do that I didn't follow to the letter."

One dark brow rose. "Other than the one where I said Vegas was a onetime thing?" she reminded him with a wry twist of her lips. "That there were reasons we shouldn't hook up at home and you agreed."

Hendrix waved that off with a grin. "Well, if you're going to get into specifics. Sure. That was the only one, though."

"Then I guess the only thing left to do is ask to what do I owe the pleasure?" That's when she blinked. "Perhaps I should rephrase the question since I have the distinct impression this is not a social call."

No point in dragging it out when they were both to blame for the scandal and they both had a vested interest in fixing the problem. But he did take a moment to appreciate how savvy she was. Contrary to what the majority of women in the Raleigh-Durham-Cary area would argue, Hendrix did notice when a woman had assets outside of the obvious ones.

Roz's brain turned him on. She saw things—layers—that normal people took at face value. It was captivating. He still wasn't sure why it had taken a trip to

Vegas for them to hook up when they'd known each other peripherally for years.

"You saw the picture," he said.

"Along with half of the eastern seaboard. But it's been circulating for a week." She slid a once-over down his body, lingering along the way like she'd found something worth noting. "Not sure why that would suddenly cause you to seek me out now."

The region under her hot gaze woke up in a hurry, galvanized into action by the quick, sharp memories of this woman under his mouth as he'd kissed, licked and tasted his way over every inch of her luscious body.

"We're definitely going to have to do something about your defective memory," he growled as he returned her heat with a pointed glance of his own. "If you can look at that photograph and not want to immediately repeat the experience."

She crossed her arms over her filmy top that did little to curb his appetite. "Nothing wrong with my memory and I have no problem admitting that your reputation is well-founded. What's not going to happen is a repeat. Vegas was my last hurrah. I told you that."

Yeah, she had. Repeatedly. While they'd been naked in her bed. And maybe once in the shower. It had been an all-night romp that had nearly caused him to miss his friend Jonas's wedding the next morning. But Hendrix had left behind his delectable companion and made it to the chapel on time, assuming he'd never see her again, as instructed.

His mother, Helene Harris, presumptive future Governor of North Carolina, had reset his thinking. It had taken a week to work through the ramifications and about that long to get him on board with the idea of a wedding as the antidote. But he was all in at this point. And he needed Roz to be all in, too.

"Here's the thing. The picture never should have happened. But it did. So we need to mitigate the damage. My mother's people think that's best accomplished by the two of us getting married. Just until the election. Then her people have agreed that we can get a quiet divorce."

Roz laughed and the silky sound tightened all the places that she'd affected so easily by sheer virtue of standing there looking lush and gorgeous.

"Your mom's people, Hendrix? That's so precious."

"Like your dad doesn't have people?" Carpenter Furniture ranked as one of the top-grossing businesses in the world. Her father had been the CEO since its inception thirty years ago. He had people.

The mirth left her face in a snap. "My dad's people aren't spewing nonsense like a *marriage* to fix a nonexistent problem. This conversation is boring me and I have things to do, so if you'll excuse me."

"Not so fast." Hendrix stuck a foot in the door before Roz could slam it in his face. Time to change tactics. "Let me buy you a drink so we can discuss this like rational adults."

"Yeah. You and alcohol creates a rational atmosphere."

Sarcasm dripped from her tone and it was so cute, he couldn't help but grin.

"Aww. That was very nearly an admission of how crazy I can make you."

"And I'm done with this." She nearly took off his foot with the force of the door closing but he didn't yank it free, despite the pinch in his arch.

"Wait, Roz." He dropped his tone into the *you can't resist me even if you try* realm. "Please give me five minutes. Then you can sever my toes all you want."

"Is the word marriage going to come out of your mouth again?"

He hesitated. Without that, there was no reason for him to be here. But he needed her more than she needed him. The trick was to make sure she never realized that.

"Is it really so much of a stretch to contemplate a merger between our families that could benefit us all? Especially in light of the photograph."

Her face didn't relax, but he could tell he had her attention. Pushing on their mutual attraction wasn't the ticket, then. Noted. So he went with logic.

"Can you honestly say you've had no fallout from our…liaison?" he asked. "Because I have or I wouldn't be standing on your doorstep. I know we agreed no contact. I know the reasons why. Things changed."

But not the reasons why. The reasons for no contact were for pure self-preservation.

He and Roz were like kindling dropped into a forest fire together. They'd gone up in flames and frankly, he'd done more dirty things in one night with Rosalind Carpenter than with the last ten women he'd dated. But by the time the sun rose, they were done. He had a strict one-time-only rule that he never broke and not just because of the pact he'd made his senior year at Duke. He'd vowed to never fall in love—because he'd been rejected enough in life and the best way to avoid all that noise was to avoid intimacy.

Sex he liked. Sex worked for him. But intimacy was off the table. He guaranteed it with no repeats.

Only at his mother's insistence would he consider making Roz his onetime exception.

"So this marriage idea. That's supposed to fix the fallout? From where I'm sitting, you're the reason for the scandal. Where's the plus for me?"

Like she hadn't been the one to come on to him on the dance floor of the Calypso Room, with her smoky eyes undressing him, the conclusion of their evening foregone the second their bodies touched.

At least she hadn't denied that the photograph had caused her some difficulty. If she had, he'd remind her that somewhere around 2:00 a.m. that night, she'd confessed that she was looking to change her reputation as the scandalous Carpenter daughter. The photograph couldn't have helped. A respectable marriage would.

That fact was still part of his strategy. "Helene's your plus. You'll be the daughter-in-law of the next governor of North Carolina. I'm confused why you're struggling with this."

"You would be." She jerked her head toward him. "I'm morbidly curious. What's in this for you?"

Legitimacy. Something hard to come by in his world. His family's chain of tobacco shops wasn't a respected industry and he was the bastard son of a man who had never claimed him.

But what he said was, "Sex."

She rolled her eyes. "You're such a liar. The last thing you need to bargain for is a woman willing to get naked with you."

"That sounded like a compliment." He waggled his brows to hide how his insides suddenly felt wobbly and precarious. How had she seen through that flippant answer?

That was what he got with a smart woman, apparently.

"It wasn't. Seduction is less of an art when you're already starting out with the deck stacked."

He had to laugh, though he wasn't quite sure if he was supposed to say thank you for the backhanded nod to his skill set. "I'm not leaving here without an answer. Marry me and the scandal goes away."

She shook her head, a sly smile spreading over her face. "Over my dead body."

And with that, she pushed his foot from the gap and shut the door with a quiet click.

Dumbfounded, Hendrix stared at the fine-grain wood. Rosalind Carpenter had just rejected his proposal. For deliberately not putting anything emotional on the line, the rejection sure stung.

Roz leaned on the shut door and closed her eyes.

Marriage. To Hendrix Harris. If she hadn't understood perfectly why he'd come up with such a ridiculous idea, she'd call the cops to come cart away the crazy man on her doorstep.

But he wasn't crazy. Just desperate to fix a problem. She was, too.

The big difference was that her father wasn't working with his "people" to help her. Instead, he was sitting up in his ivory tower continuing to be disappointed in her. Well, sometimes she screwed up. Vegas had been one of those times. Fixing it lay solely at her feet and she planned to. Just not by marrying the person who had caused the scandal in the first place.

Like marriage was the solution to anything, especially marriage to Hendrix Harris, who indeed had a reputation when it came to his exploits with the opposite sex. Hell, half of her interest back on that wild night had been insatiable curiosity about whether he could be as much trouble as everyone said.

She should have run the moment she recognized him. But no. She'd bought him a drink. She was nothing if not skilled at getting into trouble.

And what trouble she'd found.

He was of the hot, wicked and oh-so-sinful variety—the kind she had a weakness for, the kind she couldn't resist. The real question was how she'd shut the door in his face a moment ago instead of inviting him in for a repeat.

That would be a bad idea. Vegas had marked the end of an era for her.

She'd jetted off with her friend Lora to let loose in a place famed for allowing such behavior without ramifications. One last hurrah, as Roz had informed him. Make it memorable, she'd insisted. *Help me go out with a bang*, had been her exact words. Upon her return to the real world, she'd planned to make her father proud for once.

Instead, she'd found exactly the trouble she'd been looking for and then some.

It was a problem she needed to fix. She'd needed to fix it before she'd ever let Hendrix put his beautiful, talented mouth on her. And now memories of his special brand of trouble put a slow burn in her core that she couldn't shake. Even now, five minutes after telling him to shove off. Still burning. She cursed her weakness for gorgeous bad boys and went to change clothes so she could dig into her "make Dad proud" plan on her terms.

Marriage. Rosalind Carpenter. These two things did not go together under any circumstances, especially not as a way to make her father proud of her.

After watching her father cope with Roz's mother's extended bout with cancer, no thank you. That kind of pain didn't appeal to her. Till death do you part wasn't a joke, nor did she take a vow like that lightly. Best way to avoid testing it was to never make a vow like that in the first place.

Roz shed the flirty, fun outfit she'd worn to brunch with Lora and donned a severe black pencil skirt coupled with a pale blue long-sleeved blouse that screamed "serious banker." She twisted her long hair into a chignon, fought with the few escaped strands and finally left them because Hendrix had already put her behind for the day. Her afternoon was booked solid with the endless tasks associated with the new charity she'd founded.

She arrived at the small storefront her father's admin had helped her rent, evaluating the layout for the fourteenth time. There was no sign yet. That was one of the many details she needed to work through this week as she got Clown-Around off the ground. It was an endeavor of the heart. And maybe a form of therapy.

Clowns still scared her, not that she'd admit to having formed a phobia during the long hours she'd sat at her mother's hospital bedside, and honestly, she didn't have to explain herself to anyone, so she didn't. The curious only needed to know that Rosalind Carpenter had started a charity that trained clowns to work in children's hospitals. Period.

The desk she'd had delivered dwarfed her, but she'd taken a page from her father's book and procured the largest piece she could find in the Carpenter warehouse near the airport. He'd always said to buy furniture for the circumstances you want, not the ones you have. Buy quality so it will last until you make your dreams a reality. It was a philosophy that had served Carpenter Furniture well and she liked the sentiment. So she'd bought a desk that made her feel like the head of a successful charity.

She attacked the mountain of paperwork with gusto, cheerfully filling out forms and ordering supplies. There was an enormous amount of overhead that went along with running a charity and when you had zero income to use in hiring help, there was only one person to do the work—the founder.

Before she'd barely dug into the task, the lady from the first hospital Roz had called her back.

"Ms. Smith, so happy to speak with you," Roz began smoothly. "I'd like to see what your requirements are for getting Clown-Around on the approved list of organizations available to work with the children at your hospital."

"I could have saved you some time, Ms. Carpenter," the liaison replied and her tone could only be described as frosty. "We already have an approved group we work with. No need for any additional ones."

That threw Roz for a loop. "Oh. Well, we'd be happy to go on the backup list. You know, in case the other group cancels unexpectedly."

"That's okay," she cut in quickly. "That almost never happens and it's not like we have scheduled times. The clowns come in on a pretty casual basis."

This was not a good conversation. Unease prickled at the back of Roz's neck and she did not like the feeling. "I'm having a hard time believing that you can't use extra cheer in the children's ward. We're talking about sick kids who don't want to be in the hospital. Surely if your current clowns come and go at will, you can add some of mine to the rotation. A clown is a clown, right?"

The long pause boded badly. Roz braced for the next part.

"To be frank, Ms. Carpenter, the hospital board would not appreciate any association with a charity you helm," Ms. Smith stated bluntly. "We are required to disclose any contact a patient has with outside parties, particularly when the patients are minors. The clowns must have accreditation and thorough vetting to ensure we're not exposing patients to…unseemly influences."

Roz went hot and then cold as the woman's meaning flashed through her. The reputation of the charity's founder preceded her apparently. "I take it I qualify as an unseemly influence. Then may I be as frank and ask why you bothered to call me back?"

"Strictly in deference to your father. One of his vice presidents is on the board, if you're not aware," she replied tightly. "If we've reached an understanding…"

"We have. Thank you for your candor." Roz stabbed the end call button and let her cell phone drop to the desk of a successful charity head. Too bad that wasn't who was sitting at it.

Wow. Her hands were shaking.

And because her day hadn't been crappy enough, the door she'd forgotten to lock behind her opened to the street and Hendrix Harris walked into her nightmare.

"What are you doing here?" she snapped, too off-kilter to find some manners when she'd already told him to step off once today. "This is private property. How did you find me?"

Not one perfect brown hair out of place, the man waltzed right in and glanced around her bare-bones operation with unabashed curiosity. "I followed you, naturally. But I didn't want to interrupt your phone call, so I waited."

"Bless your heart," she shot back and snatched up her phone to call the cops. "You have two seconds to vacate or I'm going to lodge a trespassing complaint."

Instead of hightailing it out the door—which was what he should have done—Hendrix didn't hesitate to round the desk, crowd into her space without even a cursory nod to boundaries and pluck the phone from her hand. "Now, why would you do a thing like that? We're all friends here."

Something that felt perilously close to tears pricked beneath her lashes. "We're not friends."

Tears. In front of Hendrix. It was inexcusable.

"We could be friends," he announced quietly, without an ounce of flirt. Somehow that was exactly the right tone to burn off the moisture. "Friends who help each other. You didn't give me much of a chance to tell you how earlier."

Help. That was something she needed. Not that *he* needed to know that, or how grateful she was that he'd found a way to put her back on even footing. She didn't for an instant believe he'd missed her brief flash of vulnerability and his deft handling of it made all the difference.

The attitude of the hospital lady still chilled her. But she wasn't in danger of falling apart any longer, thank God.

"Because I have a zone of crazy around me." She nodded to the floor, near his feet. "There's the perimeter and you're four feet over the line."

Problem being that she liked him where he was—one lean hip cocked against her desk and all his good stuff at eye level. Naked, the man rivaled mythical gods in the perfection department. She could stare at his bare body for hours and never get tired of finding new ways to appreciate his deliciousness.

And dang it, he must have clued in on the direction of her thoughts. He didn't move. But the temperature of the room rose a few sweat-inducing degrees. Or maybe that was just her body catching fire as he treated her to the full force of his lethal appeal.

His hot perusal did not help matters when it came to the temperature. What was it about his pale hazel eyes that dug into her so deeply? All he had to do was look at her and sharp little tugs danced through her core.

It pissed her off. Why couldn't he be ugly, with a hunchback and gnarled feet?

Which was a stupid thing to wish for because if that was the case, she wouldn't be in this position. She'd never have hooked up with him in Vegas because yes, she was that shallow and a naked romp with a man built like Hendrix had righted her world—for a night.

Now she'd pay the price for that moment of hedonism. The final cost had yet to be determined, though.

Hendrix set her phone down on the desk, correctly guessing he had her attention and the threat of expulsion had waned. For now. She could easily send him packing if the need struck. Or she could roll the chair back a few inches and move the man into a better position to negotiate something of the more carnal variety. This was a solid desk. Would be a shame not to fully test its strength.

No. She shook her head. This was the danger of putting herself in the same room with him. She forgot common sense and propriety.

"Since I'm already in the zone of crazy," he commented in his North Carolina–textured twang, "you should definitely hear me out. For real this time. I don't know what you think I'm proposing, but odds are good you didn't get that it starts and ends with a partnership."

That had *not* come across. Whatever he had in mind, she'd envisioned a lot of sex taking center stage. And that she'd have to do without because she'd turned over a new leaf.

A partnership, on the other hand, had interesting possibilities.

As coolly as she could under the circumstances, she crossed her arms. Mostly as a way to keep her hands to herself. "Talk fast. You've got my attention for about another five minutes."

Two

Hendrix had been right to follow Rosalind. This bare storefront had a story behind it and he had every intention of learning her secrets. Whatever leverage he could dig up might come in handy, especially since he'd botched the first round of this negotiation.

And the hard cross of Roz's arms told him it was indeed a negotiation, one he shouldn't expect to win easily. That had been his mistake on the first go-round. He'd thought their chemistry would be good trading currency, but she'd divested him of that notion quickly. So round two would need a completely different approach.

"What is this place?" he asked and his genuine curiosity leaked through. He had a vision in his head of Rosalind Carpenter as a party girl, one who posed for men's magazines and danced like a fantasy come to life. Instead of tracking her down during an afternoon shopping spree, he'd stumbled over her *working*.

It didn't fit his perception of her and he'd like to get the right one before charging ahead.

"I started a charity," she informed him with a slight catch in her voice that struck him strangely.

She expected him to laugh. Or say something flippant. So he didn't. "That's fantastic. And hard. Good for you."

That bobbled her composure and he wouldn't apologize for enjoying it. This marriage plan should have been a lot easier to sell and he couldn't put his finger on why he'd faltered so badly thus far. She'd been easy in Vegas—likable, open, adventurous. All things he'd assumed he'd work with today, but none of those qualities seemed to be a part of her at-home personality. Plus, he wasn't trying to get her into bed. Well, technically, he *was*. But semi-permanently, and he didn't have a lot of experience at persuading a woman to still be there in the morning.

No problem. Winging it was how he did his best work. He hadn't pushed Harris Family Tobacco Lounge so close to the half-billion mark in revenue without taking a few risks.

"What does your charity do?" he asked, envisioning an evening dress resale shop or Save the Kittens. Might as well know what kind of fundraiser he'd have to attend as her husband.

"Clowns," she said so succinctly that he did a double take to be sure he hadn't misheard her. He hadn't. And it wasn't a joke, judging by the hard set of her mouth.

"Like finding new homes for orphan clowns?" he

guessed cautiously, only half kidding. Clown charity was a new one for him.

"You're such a moron." She rolled her eyes, but they had a determined glint now that he liked a lot better than the raw vulnerability she'd let slip a few minutes ago. "My charity trains clowns to work with children at hospitals. Sick kids need to be cheered up, you know?"

"That's admirable." And he wasn't even blowing smoke. It sounded like it meant something to her and thus it meant something to him—as leverage. He glanced around, taking in the bare walls, the massive and oddly masculine dark-stained desk and the rolling leather chair under her very fine backside. Not much to her operation yet, which worked heavily in his favor. "How can I help?"

Suspicion tightened her lush mouth, which only made him want to kiss it away. They were going to have to fix this attraction or he'd spend all his time adjusting her attitude in a very physical way.

On second thought, he couldn't figure out a downside to that approach.

"I thought you were trying to talk me into marrying you," she said with a fair amount of sarcasm.

"One and the same, sweetheart." He gave it a second and the instant his meaning registered, her lips curved into a crafty smile.

"I'm starting to see the light."

Oh yes, *now* they were ready to throw down. Juices flowing, he slid a little closer to her and she didn't roll away, just coolly stared up at him without an ounce of give. What was wrong with him that he was suddenly more turned on in that instant than he had been at any point today?

"Talk to me. What can I do in exchange for your name on a marriage certificate?"

Her smile gained a lot of teeth. "Tell me why it's so important to you."

He bit back the curse. Should have seen that one coming. As a testament to her skill in maneuvering him into giving up personal information, he opted to throw her a bone. "I told you. I've had some fallout. My mother is pretty unhappy with me and I don't like her to be unhappy."

"Mama's boy?"

"Absolutely." He grinned. Who didn't see the value in a man who loved and respected his mama? "There's no shame in that. We grew up together. I'm sure you've heard the story. She was an unwed teenage mother, yadda, yadda?"

"I've heard. So this is all one hundred percent about keeping your mom happy, is it?"

Something clued him in that she wasn't buying it, which called for some serious deflection. The last thing he wanted to have a conversation about was his own reasons for pursuing Roz for the first and only Mrs. Hendrix Harris.

He liked being reminded of his own vulnerabilities even less than he liked being exposed to hers. The less intimate this thing grew, the better. "Yeah. If she wasn't in the middle of an election cycle, we wouldn't be having this conversation. But she is and I messed up. I'm willing to do whatever it takes to get this deal done. Name your price."

"Get your mom to agree to be a clown for me and I'll consider it."

That was what she wanted? His gaze narrowed as

they stared at each other. "That's easy. Too easy. You must not want me to figure out that you're really panting to get back into my bed."

Her long silky laugh lodged in his chest and spread south. She could turn that sentiment back on him with no trouble at all.

Which was precisely what she did. "Sounds like a guilty conscience talking to me. Sure you're not the one using this ploy to get me naked without being forced to let on how bad you want it?"

"I'm offended." But he let a smile contradict the statement. "I'll tell you all day long how much I want you if that floats your boat. But this is a business proposition. Strictly for nonsexual benefits."

Any that came along with this marriage could be considered a bonus.

She snorted. "Are you trying to tell me you'd give up other women while we're married? I don't think you're actually capable of that."

Now, that was just insulting. What kind of a philanderer did she take him for? He'd never slept with more than one woman at a time and never calling one again made that a hundred percent easier.

"Make no mistake, Roz. I am perfectly capable of forgoing other women as long as you're the one I'm coming home to at the end of the day."

All at once, a vision of her greeting him at the door wearing sexy lingerie slammed through his mind and his body reacted with near violent approval. Holy hell. He had no problem going off other women cold turkey if Roz was on offer instead, never mind his stupid rules about never banging the same woman twice. This situation was totally different, with its own set of rules. Or

at least it would be as soon as he got his head out of her
perfect cleavage and back on how to close this deal.

"Let me get this straight. You're such a dog that the
only way you can stay out of another woman's bed is if
I'm servicing you regularly?" She wrinkled her nose.
"Stop me when I get to the part where I'm benefiting
from this arrangement."

Strictly to cover the slight hitch in his lungs that her
pointed comment had caused, he slid over until he was
perched on the desk directly in front of her. Barely a
foot of space separated them and an enormous amount
of heat and electricity arced through his groin, draining
more of his sense than he would have preferred. All he
could think about was yanking her into his arms and
reminding her how hot he could get her with nothing
more than a well-placed stroke of his tongue.

He let all of that sizzle course through his body as
he swept her with a heated once-over. "Sweetheart,
you'll benefit, or have you forgotten how well I know
your body?"

"Can you even go without sex?" she mused with a
lilt, as if she already knew the answer. "Because I bet
you can't."

What the hell did that have to do with anything?

"I can do whatever I put my mind to," he growled.
"But to do something as insane as go without sex, I'd
need a fair bit of incentive. Which I have none of."

Her gaze snapped with challenge. "Other than getting my name on a marriage license you mean?"

The recoil jerked through his shoulders before he
could catch it, tipping her off that she'd just knocked
him for a loop. That was uncool. Both that she'd realized it and that she'd done it. "What are you propos-

ing, that I go celibate for a period of time in some kind of test?"

"Oh, I hadn't thought of it like that." She pursed her lips into a provocative pout that told him she was flat-out lying because she'd intended it to be exactly that. "That's a great deal. You keep it zipped and I'll show up at the appointed time to say 'I do.'"

His throat went dry. "Really? That's what it's going to take?"

"Yep. Well, that and Helene Harris for Governor in a clown suit. Can't forget the children."

Her smug tone raked at something inside him. "That's ridiculous. I mean, my mom would be happy to do the clown thing. It's great publicity for her, too. But no sex? Not even with you? There is literally no reason for you to lay down such a thing except as cruel and unusual punishment."

"Careful, Hendrix," she crooned. "It's starting to sound like you might have a problem keeping it in your pants. I mean, how long are we talking? A couple of months?"

A couple of *months*? He'd been slightly panicked at the thought of a week or two. It wasn't that he was some kind of pervert like she was making it sound. Sex was a necessary avoidance tactic in his arsenal. A shield against the intimacy that happened in the small moments, when you weren't guarded against it. He kept himself out of such situations on purpose.

If he wasn't having sex with Roz, what would they *do* with each other?

"I think the better question is whether *you* can do it," he countered smoothly. "You're the same woman who was all in for every wicked, dirty escapade I could dream up in Vegas. You're buckling yourself into that chastity belt too, honey."

"Yeah, for a reason." Her eyes glittered with conviction. "The whole point of this is to fix the problems the photograph caused. Do you really think you and I can keep ourselves out of Scandalville if we're sleeping together?" His face must have registered his opinion on that because she nodded. "Exactly. It's a failsafe. No sex—with *anyone*. No scandals. Or no 'I do.'"

The firm press of a rock and a hard place nearly stole his breath. If no sex was important to her, how could he refuse?

"Six weeks," he said hoarsely. "We'll be engaged for six weeks. Once we're married, all bets are off."

"We'll see. I might keep the no sex moratorium. You and I don't make sense together, Hendrix, so don't pretend that we do."

She swallowed that sentence with a squeak as he hauled her out of that chair and into his arms for a lesson on exactly how wrong she was. God, she fit the contours of his body like the ocean against the sand, seeping into him with a rush and shush, dragging pieces of him into her as her lips crashed against his.

Her taste exploded under his mouth as he kissed her senseless. But then it was his own senses sliding through the soles of his feet as Roz sucked him dry with her own sensual onslaught. For a woman who'd just told him they didn't work, she jumped into the kiss with enthusiasm that had him groaning.

The hot, slick slide of her tongue against his dissolved his knees. Only the firm press of that heavy desk against his backside kept him upright. The woman was a wicked kisser, not that he'd forgotten. But just as he slid his hand south to fill his palms with her luscious rear, she wrenched away, taking his composure with her.

"Where are you going?" he growled.

"The other side of the room." Her chest rose and fell as if she'd run a marathon as she backed away. Frankly, his own lungs heaved with the effort to fill with air. "What the hell was that for?"

"You wanted that kiss as much as I did."

"So it was strictly to throw it back in my face that I can't resist you?"

Well, now. That was a tasty admission that she looked like she wished to take back. He surveyed her with renewed interest. Her kiss-reddened lips beckoned him but he didn't chase her down. He wanted to understand this new dynamic before he pressed on. "You said we didn't work. I was simply helping you see the error in that statement."

"I said no such thing. I said we don't make sense together. And that's why. Because we *work* far too well."

"I'm struggling to see the problem with that." They'd definitely worked in Vegas, that was for sure. Now that he'd gotten a second taste, he was not satisfied with having it cut short.

"Because I need to stay off the front page," she reminded him with that funny hitch in her voice that shouldn't be more affecting than her heated once-overs. "There are people walking by the window as we speak, Hendrix. You make me forget all of that. No more kissing until the wedding. Consider it an act of good faith."

The point was painfully clear. She wanted him to prove he could do it.

"So we're doing this. Getting married," he clarified.

"As a partnership. When it stops being beneficial, we get a divorce. No ifs, ands or buts." She caught him in her hot gaze that still screamed her desire. "Right? Do we need to spell it out legally?"

"You can trust me," he grumbled. She was the one who'd thrown down the no-sex rule. What did she think he was going to do, force her to stay married so he could keep being celibate for the rest of his life? "As long as I can trust you."

"I'm good."

He thought about shaking on it but the slightly panicked flair to her expression made him think twice. It didn't matter. The deal was done, as painful as it would ultimately end up being.

It was worth it. He had to make it up to his mom for causing her grief, and this was what she'd asked him to do. And if deep inside, he craved the idea of belonging to such an old-guard, old-money family as the Carpenters, no one would be the wiser.

All he had to do was figure out how to be engaged to Roz without trying to seduce her again and without getting too chummy. Should be a walk in the park.

Being engaged was nothing like Roz imagined. Of course she'd spent zero time daydreaming about such a thing happening to her. But her friend Lora had been engaged for about six months, which had been a whirlwind of invitations and dress fittings. Until the day she'd walked in on her fiancé and a naked barista who was foaming the jackass's latte in Lora's bed. Roz and Lora still didn't hit a coffee place within four blocks of the one where the wedding-wrecker worked.

Roz's own engagement had a lot fewer highs and

lows in the emotion department and a lot less chaos. For about three days. The morning of the fourth day, Hendrix texted her that he was coming by, and since there'd been no question in that statement, she sighed and put on clothes, wishing in vain for a do-over that included not flying to Vegas in the first place. Or maybe she should wish that she and Lora had gone to any other club besides the Calypso Room that night.

Oh, better yet, she could pretend Hendrix didn't do it for her in a hundred scandalous ways.

That was the real reason this engagement/marriage/ partnership shouldn't have happened. But how could she turn down Helene Harris in a clown outfit? No hospital would bar the woman from the door and thus Clown-Around would get a much-needed lift, Roz's reputation notwithstanding. It was instant publicity for the gubernatorial candidate and the fledgling charity in one shot, which was a huge win. And she didn't have to actually ask her father to use his influence, which he probably wouldn't do anyway.

Plus, and she'd die before she'd admit this to Hendrix, there had to be something about being in the sphere of Helene Harris that Roz's father would find satisfactory. He was so disappointed about the photographs. If nothing else, marrying the man in them lent a bit of respectability to the situation, right? Now Roz just had to tell her father about the getting married part. But first she had to admit to herself that she'd actually agreed to this insanity.

Thus far it had been easy to stick her head in the sand. But when Hendrix buzzed her to gain access to the elevator, she couldn't play ostrich any longer.

"Well, if it isn't my beloved," he drawled when she opened the door.

God, could the man look like a slouch in *something*? He wore the hell out of a suit regardless of the color or cut. But today he'd opted for a pair of worn jeans that hugged his hips and a soft T-shirt that brazenly advertised the drool-worthy build underneath. He might as well be naked for all that ensemble left to the imagination.

"Your beloved doesn't sit around and wait for you to show up on a Saturday," she informed him grumpily. "What if I had plans?"

"You do have plans," he returned, his grin far too easy. "With me. All of your plans are with me for the next six weeks, because weddings do not magically throw themselves together."

She crossed her arms and leaned against the doorjamb in a blatant message—*you're not coming in and I'm not budging, so...* "They do if you hire a wedding planner. Which you should. I have absolutely no opinion about flowers or venues."

That was no lie. But she wanted to spend time with Hendrix even less than she wanted to pick out flowers. She could literally feel her will dissolving as she stood there soaking in the carnal vibe wafting from him like an invisible aphrodisiac.

"Oh, come on. It'll be fun."

The way his hazel eyes lit up as he coaxed her should be illegal. Or maybe her reaction should be. How did he put such a warm little curl in her core with nothing more than a glance? It was ridiculous. "Your idea of fun and mine are worlds apart."

A slow, lethal smile joined his vibrant gaze and it

pretty much reduced her to a quivering mess of girl parts inside. All the more reason to stay far away from him until the wedding.

"Seems like we had a pretty similar idea of fun one night not too long ago."

Memories crashed through her mind, her body, her soul. The way he'd made her feel, the wicked press of his mouth against every intimate hollow an unprecedented experience. It was too much for a Saturday morning after she'd signed up to become Mrs. Hendrix Harris.

"I asked you not to kiss me again," she reminded him primly but it probably sounded as desperate to him as it did to her.

She could *not* get sucked into his orbit. As it was, she fantasized about that kiss against her desk at odd times—while in the shower, brushing her teeth, eating breakfast, watching TV, walking, breathing. Sure it was prudent to avoid any more scandals but that was just window dressing. This was a partnership she needed to take seriously, and she had no good defenses against Hendrix Harris.

He was temporary. Like all things. She couldn't get invested, emotionally or physically, and one would surely lead to the other. The pain of losing someone she cared about was too much and she would never let that happen again—which was the sole reason she liked sex of the one-night stand variety. What she'd do when that wasn't an option, like after she said I do, she had no clue.

"Wow. Who said anything about kissing?" He waggled his brows. "We were talking about the definition of fun. That kiss must have gotten you going something fierce if you're still hung up on it."

She rolled her eyes to hide the guilt that might or might not be shuffling through her expression. "Why are you here?"

"We're engaged. Engaged people hang out, or didn't you get the memo?"

"We're not people. Nor is our engagement typical. No memos required to get us to the…insert whatever venue we're using to get hitched here. Until then, I don't really feel the need to spend time together." She accompanied that pitiful excuse of his with crooked fingers in air quotes.

"Well, I beg to differ," he drawled, the North Carolina in his voice sliding through her veins like fine brandy. "This partnership needs publicity or there's no point to it. We need to be seen together. A lot. When people think of you, they need to think of me. We're like the peanut butter and jelly of the Raleigh social scene."

"That's a nice analogy," she said with a snort so she didn't laugh or smile. That would only encourage him to keep being adorable. "Which one am I?"

"You choose," he suggested magnanimously and that's when she realized she was having fun. How dare he charm her out of her bad mood?

But it was too late, dang it. That was the problem. She genuinely liked Hendrix or she wouldn't have left the Calypso Room with him.

"I suppose you want to come in." She jerked her head toward the interior of her loft that had been two condos until she bought both and hired a crew of hard hats to meld the space into one. They should probably discuss living arrangements at some point because she was *not* giving up this condo under any circumstances.

"I want you to come out," he countered and caught her hand, tugging on it until she cleared the threshold on the wrong side of the door. "We can't be seen together in your condo and besides, there are no people walking past the window. No photographers in the bushes. I could slip a couple of buttons free on this shirt of yours and explore what I uncover with my tongue and no one would know."

He accompanied that suggestion with a slow slide of his fingertip along the ridge of buttons in question, oh so casually, as if the skin under it hadn't just exploded with goose bumps.

"But you won't," she said breathlessly, cursing her body's reaction even as she cursed him for knowing exactly how to get her hot and ready to burst with so little effort. "Because you promised."

"I did." He nodded with a wink. "And I'm a man of my word."

She'd only reminded him of his promise as a shield against her own weaknesses, but he'd taken it as an affirmation. He would keep his promise because it meant something to him. And his sense of honor was doing funny things to her insides that had nothing to do with desire. Hendrix Harris was a bad boy hedonist of the highest order. Nothing but wicked through and through. Or at least that was the box she'd put him in and she did not like the way he'd just climbed out of it.

She shook her head, but it didn't clear her sudden confusion. Definitely they should not go into her condo and shut the door. Not now or any day. But at that moment, she couldn't recall what bad things might happen as a result. She could only think of many, many very good things that could and would occur if she invited him in for a private rendezvous.

"I think we should visit a florist," he commented casually, completely oblivious to the direction of her thoughts, thank God.

"Yes. We should." That was exactly what she needed. A distraction in the form of flowers.

"Grab your handbag." The instruction made her blink for a second until he laughed. "Or is it a purse? I have no clue what to call the thing you women put your lives into."

Gah, she should have her head examined if a simple conversation with a man had her so flipped upside down. Nodding, she ducked back into the condo, snagged her Marc Jacobs bag from the counter in the kitchen and rejoined Hendrix in the hall before he got any bright ideas about testing his will behind closed doors. Hers sucked. The longer she kept that fact from him, the better.

He ushered her to a low-slung Aston Martin that shouldn't have been as sexy as it was. At best, it should have screamed *I'm trying too hard to be cool*. But when Hendrix slid behind the wheel, he owned the beast under the hood and it purred beneath his masterful hands.

She could watch him drive for hours. Which worked out well since she'd apparently just volunteered to spend the day planning flowers for her wedding with her fiancé. Bizarre. But there it was.

Even she had heard of the florist he drove to. Expensive, exclusive and very visible, Maestro of the Bloom lay in the Roundtree shopping district near downtown.

Hendrix drove around the block two times, apparently searching for a parking place, and she opened her mouth to remind him of the lot across the street when he braked at the front row to wait for a mother and daughter to get into their car. Of course he wanted the parking place directly in front of the door, where everyone could see them emerge from his noteworthy car.

It was a testament to his strategic mind that she appreciated. As was the gallant way he sped around to her side of the car to open the door, then extended his hand to help her from the bucket seat that was so low it nearly scraped the ground. But he didn't let go of her hand, instead lacing their fingers together in a way that shouldn't have felt so natural. Hands nested to his satisfaction, he led her to the door and ushered her inside.

A low hum of conversation cut off abruptly and something like a dozen pairs of eyes swung toward them with varying degrees of recognition—some of which held distaste. These were the people whose approval they both sought. The society who had deemed their Vegas tryst shocking, inappropriate, scandalous, and here the two of them were daring to tread among more decent company.

Roz's fingers tightened involuntarily and dang it, Hendrix squeezed back in a surprising show of solidarity. That shouldn't have felt as natural as it did either, like the two of them were a unit already. Peanut butter and jelly against the world.

Her knees got a little wobbly. She'd never had anything like that. Never wanted to feel like a duo with a man. Why did it mean so much as they braved the social scene together? Especially given that she'd only just realized that turning over a new leaf meant more than fixing her relationship with her father. It was about shifting the tide of public opinion too, or her charity wouldn't benefit much from Helene's participation. Roz would go back to being shunned in polite society the moment she signed the divorce papers.

Against all odds, he'd transformed Roz into a righteous convert to the idea of marriage with one small step inside the florist. What else would he succeed in convincing her of?

With that sobering thought, Roz glanced at Hendrix and murmured, "Let's do this."

Three

As practice for the bigger, splashier engagement party to come, Hendrix talked Roz into an intimate gathering at his house. Just family and close friends. It would be an opportunity to gauge how this marriage would fly. And it was a chance to spend time together as a couple with low pressure.

The scene at the florist had shaken Roz, with the murmurs and dirty looks she'd collected from the patrons. That was not okay. Academically, he knew this marriage deal was important to his mother and her campaign. In reality, he didn't personally have a lot of societal fallout from that photo. No one's gaze cut away from him on the street, but he was a guy. Roz wasn't. It was a double standard that shouldn't exist but it did.

Who would have ever thought he'd be hot to ease Roz's discomfort in social situations? It had not been on his list of considerations, but it was now. If this party helped, great. If it didn't, he'd find something else. The fragile glint in her eye while they'd worked with the florist to pick out some outrageously priced flowers had hooked something inside and he'd spent a considerable amount of time trying to unpierce his tender flesh, to no avail. So he did what he always did. Rolled with it.

The catering company had done a great job getting his house in order to host a shindig of this magnitude. While the party had been floated as casual, Hendrix had never entertained before. Unless you counted a handful of buddies sprawled around his dining room table with beer and poker chips.

Roz arrived in the car he'd sent for her and he ignored the little voice inside taunting him for hovering at the front window to watch for her. But it was a sight to see. Roz spilled from the back of the car, sky-high stilettos first, then miles of legs and finally the woman herself in a figure-hugging black cocktail dress designed to drive a man insane.

She'd even swept up her wavy dark hair into a chignon that let a few strands drip down around her face. It was the sexiest hairstyle he'd ever seen on a woman, bar none.

He opened the door before she could knock and his tongue might have gone numb because he couldn't even speak as she coolly surveyed him from under thick black eyelashes.

"Thanks for the car. Hard to drive in heels," she commented, apparently not afflicted by the stupid that was going around.

He shouldn't be, either. He cleared his throat. "You look delicious."

Amazing might have been a better term. It would make it seem more like he'd seen a beautiful woman before and it was no big thing. But she was *his* beautiful woman. For as long as they both deemed it beneficial.

That seemed like a pretty cold agreement all at once for two people who'd burned so very hot not so long ago.

She smiled with a long slow lift of her pink-stained lips. "I'll take that as a compliment, as weird as it is."

"Really? It's weird to tell my beautiful fiancée that she looks good enough to eat?" he questioned with a heated once-over that she didn't miss.

"You can't say stuff like that," she murmured and glanced away from the sizzling electricity that had just arced between them right there on his doorstep.

"The hell I can't. You said no kissing. At no point did I agree to keep my carnal thoughts to myself, nor will I ever agree to that. If I want to tell you that I'm salivating to slide that dress off your shoulders and watch it fall to the ground as it bares your naked body, I will. I might even tell you that I taste you in my sleep sometimes and I wake up with a boner that I can't get rid of until I fantasize about you in the shower." Her cheeks flushed. From embarrassment at his dirty talk or guilt because she liked it? He couldn't tell. He leaned closer and whispered, "Believe it or not, I can tell you what I want to do to you without acting on it."

A car door slammed behind her and she recoiled as if it had been a gunshot to her torso.

"Invite me in," she muttered with a glance over her shoulder. "This is a party, isn't it?"

Should have been a party for two with a strict dress code—birthday suits only. Why had he agreed to her insane stipulation that they abstain from any kind of physical contact until the wedding? It was a dumb rule that made no sense and if Jonas and his wife, Viv, weren't waltzing up the front walk at that precise moment, Hendrix would be having a completely different conversation about it with his fiancée.

He stepped back and allowed Roz to enter, slipping an arm around her waist as she tried to flounce past him into the living room. "Oh, no you don't, sweetheart. Flip around and greet the guests. We're a couple."

Her smile grew pained as he drew her close. "How could I forget?"

Jonas and Viv hit the welcome mat holding hands. Funny how things worked. Jonas and Viv had gotten married in Vegas during the same trip where Hendrix had hooked up with Roz.

"Hey, guys. This is Roz," Hendrix announced unnecessarily, as he was pretty sure both Jonas and Viv knew who she was. If not from the photo flying around the internet, strictly by virtue of the fact that she was glued to his side.

Viv, bless her, smiled at Roz and shook her hand. "I'm Viv Kim. It's nice to meet you, and not just because I love any opportunity to use my new name."

With an intrigued expression, Roz glanced at the male half of the couple. "Are you newly married?"

Jonas stuck his hand out. "Brand-new. I'm Jonas Kim. My name is still the same."

Hendrix nearly rolled his eyes but checked it in deference to one of his oldest friends. "Thanks for coming.

Roz and I are glad you're here to celebrate our engagement. Come in, please."

He guided them all to the cavernous living area that had been designed with this type of gathering in mind. The ten-thousand-square-foot house in Oakwood had been a purchase born out of a desire to stake his claim. There was a pride in ownership that this house delivered. It was a monument of a previous age, restored lovingly by someone with an eye for detail, and he appreciated the history wafting from its bones.

The house was a legitimate home and it was his.

Curiously, Viv's gaze cut between the two of them as she took a seat next to Jonas on the couch. "Have you set a wedding date?"

"Not yet," Roz answered and at the same time, Hendrix said, "Five weeks."

She shot him a withering look. "We're waiting until we pick a venue, which might dictate the date."

The doorbell rang and his mother arrived with Paul Carpenter right on her heels. Introductions all around went smoothly as nearly everyone knew each other. As the CEO of Kim Electronics, Jonas had met Mr. Carpenter several times at trade shows and various retail functions. Helene frequented Viv's cupcake shop on Jones Street apparently and exclaimed over the baker's wares at length. It was Paul and Helene's first meeting, however.

Hendrix raised a brow at the extra beat included in their hand shake, but forgot about it as Roz's friend Lora showed up with a date. Hendrix's other best friend, Warren Garinger, was flying solo tonight, which was lately his default. He arrived a pointed thirty minutes late.

It wasn't until later that evening that Hendrix had a chance to corner his friend on his tardiness.

"Just the man I was looking for," he said easily as he found Warren in the study examining one of the many watercolors the decorator had insisted went with the spirit of the house.

Warren pocketed his phone, which should have melted from overuse a long time ago. He worked ninety hours a week running the energy drink company his family had founded, but Hendrix didn't think that was what had put the frown on his friend's face. "I had to take a call. Sorry."

"The CEO never gets a day off," Hendrix acknowledged with a nod. "It's cool. I was just making sure you weren't hiding out in protest."

"I'm here, aren't I?" Warren smoothed out his expression before it turned into a full-bore scowl. "You've obviously made your decision to get married despite the pact."

Hendrix bit back a sigh. They'd been over this. Looked like they were going over it again. "The pact means something to me. And to Jonas. We're still tight, no matter what."

Jonas, Warren and Hendrix had met at Duke University, forming a friendship during a group project along with a fourth student, Marcus Powell. They'd had a lot of fun, raised a lot of hell together in the quintessential college experience—until Marcus had gotten his heart tangled up over a woman who didn't deserve his devotion. She'd been a traitorous witch of a cheerleader who liked toying with a man's affections more than she'd liked Marcus. Everyone had seen she was trouble. Except their friend.

He'd grown paler and more wasted away the longer she didn't give him the time of day and eventually, his broken heart had overruled his brain and somehow suicide had become his answer. Shell-shocked and embittered, the three surviving friends had vowed to never let a woman drive them to such lows. They'd formed a pact, refusing to fall in love under any circumstances.

Hell, that had been a given for Hendrix, pact or not. Love wasn't something he even thought much about because he never got close enough to a woman to develop any kind of tender feelings, let alone anything deeper.

But the pact—that was sacred. He'd had little in his life that made him feel like he belonged and his friendship with Jonas and Warren meant everything to him. He'd die before violating the terms of their agreement.

"If the pact is so important, then I don't understand why you'd risk breaking it with marriage," Warren countered and the bitterness lacing his tone sliced at Hendrix far more severely than he'd have expected.

They both glanced up as Jonas joined them, beers in hand. "Thought I'd find you two going at it if I looked hard enough. I'm the one you want to yell at, Warren. Not this joker."

Hendrix took the longneck from his friend's hand and gave Warren a pointed look until the other man sighed, accepting his own beer. No one was confused about the significance. It was a peace offering because Jonas had already broken the pact by falling in love with Viv. Warren had not taken it well. The three of them were still figuring out how to not be bachelor pals any longer, and how to not be at odds over what Warren viewed as Jonas's betrayal.

Hendrix just wanted everything to be on an even keel again so he didn't get a panicky feeling at the back of his throat when he thought of losing the one place where he felt fully accepted no matter what—inside the circle of his friends.

"If it makes you feel better," Hendrix said after a long swallow of his brew, "the odds of me falling in love with Roz are zero. We're not even sleeping together."

Jonas choked on his own beer. "Please. Is this April Fools' Day and I missed it?"

"No, really." Hendrix scowled as both his friends started laughing. "Why is that funny?"

"You've finally met the one woman you can't seduce and you're *marrying* her?" Warren clapped Hendrix on the back, still snickering.

"Shut up," he growled. Why did that have to be the one thing that got his buddy out of his snit? "Besides, I can go without sex."

"Right." Jonas drew the word out to about fourteen syllables, every one of them laden with sarcasm. "And I can pass as Norwegian."

Since Jonas was half-Korean, his point was clear. And Hendrix didn't appreciate his friend's doubt, never mind that he'd been angling for a way to kibosh the no-sex part of his agreement with Roz. "I don't have to explain myself to you guys."

Jonas sipped his beer thoughtfully. "Well, I guess it's a fair point that this is a fake marriage, so maybe you're pretty smart to skip sex in order to avoid confusion. I of all people can understand that."

"This marriage is not fake," Hendrix corrected. "*Your* marriage was fake because you're a moron who thought it was better to live together and just pretend you're hot and heavy. I'm not a moron. Roz and I will have a real marriage, with plenty of unfake hot and heavy."

Especially the honeymoon part. He was already glancing at travel websites for ideas on places he could take his bride where they'd have no interruptions during a weeklong smorgasbord where Roz was the only thing on the menu.

Jonas raised his eyebrows. "You're trying to tell me you're waiting until marriage before you sleep together? That's highly unconventional for anyone, let alone you."

It was on the tip of his tongue to remind Jonas how late Hendrix had been to his wedding. Roz had been the reason, and these yokels were lucky he'd showed up at all. It had been sheer hell to peel himself out of Roz's bed to make it to the chapel before the nuptials were over.

But something held him back from flinging his escapades in his friends' faces. Maybe it had something to do with their assumption that he was a horndog who couldn't keep it in his pants, which had frankly been Roz's assumption, too. Was that all there was to him in everyone's mind? Always on the lookout for the next woman to nail? There was a lot more complexity to his personality than that and he was suddenly not thrilled to learn he'd overshadowed his better qualities with his well-deserved reputation.

"That's me. Unconventional," he agreed easily.

And now he had an ironclad reason to stick to his agreement…to prove to himself that he could stay out of a woman's bed.

* * *

Roz's father had smiled at her tonight more times than he had in the past five years. As much as she'd craved his approval, all this cheer made her nervous. Paul Carpenter ran a billion-dollar furniture enterprise, with manufacturing outlets and retail stores under his command as far away as the Philippines and as close as within walking distance. He rarely smiled, especially not at Roz.

"I've always liked this house," her father commented to her out of the blue as they found themselves at the small minibar at the same time.

"I think Hendrix mentioned it's on the Raleigh Historical Society's list as one of the oldest homes in Oakwood. It's really beautiful."

Small talk with her father about her fiancé's house. It was nearly surreal. They didn't chat often, though that could be because she rarely gave him a chance. After years of conversations laden with her father's heavy sighs and pointed suggestions, she preferred their communication to be on a need-only basis.

Maybe that tide had turned. Hendrix, Jonas and Warren had disappeared, likely having a private no-girls-allowed toast somewhere away from the crowd, so there was no one to interrupt this nice moment.

"You haven't mentioned it, but I'd really like it if you allowed me to walk you down the aisle," her father suggested casually.

Something bright and beautiful bloomed in her chest as she stared at his aged but still handsome face. She'd never even considered having the kind of wedding where such a thing happened, largely because it had never occurred to her that he'd be open to the idea.

They'd never been close, not even after her mother died. The experience of witnessing someone they both loved being eaten alive by cancer should have bonded them. For a long time, she let herself be angry that it hadn't. Then she'd started to wonder if he'd gotten so lost in his grief that he'd forgotten he had a daughter dealing with her own painful sense of loss.

Eventually, she sought to cauterize her grief in other ways, which had led to even further estrangement. Was it possible that she'd erased years of disappointment with the one simple act of agreeing to Hendrix's outrageous proposal?

"Of course." She swallowed a brief and unexpected tide of emotion. "That would be lovely."

Thankfully, her fiancé was already on board with planning an honest-to-God wedding with all the trimmings. She'd have to talk him into a longer engagement if they were going to have the type of wedding with an aisle, because she'd envisioned showing up at the justice of the peace in a Betsey Johnson dress that could support a corsage. The simpler the better.

But that was out the window. She had another agenda to achieve with her wedding now, and it included walking down an aisle on her father's arm. Dare she hope this could be a new beginning to their relationship?

"I wasn't sure you'd like the idea of me marrying Hendrix Harris," she said cautiously, trying to gauge how this new dynamic was supposed to work. She'd left a message to tell him about the party and its purpose, effectively announcing her engagement to her father via voice mail so he couldn't express yet more disappointment in her choices.

"I think it's great," he said with enthusiasm she'd rarely heard in his voice. "I'm happy that you're settling down. It will be good for you."

Keep her out of trouble, more like. It was in the undertone of his words and she chose not to let it sour the moment. She did have some questionable decisions in her rearview mirror or she wouldn't have needed to marry Hendrix in the first place. The fact that her dad liked the move was a plus she hadn't dared put on the list of pros, especially given that she was marrying a man her father and everyone else had seen in the buff.

"I think it will be good for me, too," she said, though her reasons were different than his.

"I did wonder if this wedding wasn't designed to eliminate the negative effects of that unfortunate photograph on Helene Harris's campaign." Her father sipped the scotch in a highball, deliberately creating a pregnant pause that prickled across the back of Roz's neck. "If so, that's a good move. Additionally, there are a lot of benefits to being the governor's daughter-in-law, and I like the idea of being tied to the Harris family through marriage."

That had not been a chance statement. "What, like maybe I could put in a good word for you?"

He nodded thoughtfully, oblivious to her sarcasm. "Something like that. I've had some thoughts about going into politics. This is an interesting development. Lots of opportunities unfolding as we speak."

She shouldn't be so shocked. But her stomach still managed to turn over as she absorbed the idea that her father only liked that she was marrying Hendrix because of how it benefited *him*. Did it not occur to her father that she didn't have any sort of in with Helene Harris yet? Geez. She'd only met the woman for the first time tonight. And Roz might only have a certain number of favor chips to cash in. The first item on her list was Ms. Harris in white face paint with big floppy shoes.

What was going to happen if she couldn't create the opportunity her father was looking for?

Everyone was expecting something from this union. Why that created such a bleak sense of disillusionment, she had no idea. It wasn't like she'd ever done anything else her father liked. It was just that for once, she'd thought they were finally forming a relationship.

Of course that wasn't the case. Fine. She was used to losing things, used to the temporary nature of everything good that had ever happened to her. It was just one more reason to keep everyone at arm's length.

But Hendrix made that vow harder to keep almost immediately, cornering her in the kitchen where she'd gone to lick her wounds.

"Studying up on my pots and pans so you can cook me a proper dinner once you're the little woman?" he asked as he sauntered into the room and skirted the wide marble-topped island that separated the sink from the 12-burner Viking range to join her on the far side.

"Unless you like your balls in your throat, I would refrain from ever referring to me as the little woman again," she informed him frostily, not budging an inch even as the big, solid wall of Hendrix's masculinity overwhelmed her. "Also, this is a private party. See yourself out."

He had some nerve, waltzing into her space without invitation. All it would take was one slight flex of her hips and they'd be touching. Hell, that might even happen if she breathed deeper.

Instead of getting huffy about her command, he just watched her, his eyes darkening. He was too close, smelled too much like a memory of sin and sex.

"What?" she asked testily as a long, sensual thread pulled at her center.

She swallowed a yelp as he snagged a lock of hair, tucking it behind her ear. But the touch was just an excuse to get even closer, of course, because once he had his hand on her, he didn't stop there. His thumb cruised down her jaw, sensitizing her entire face.

In some alternate dimension, there was a Rosalind Carpenter with the will to slap this man's hand away when he took liberties she hadn't invited. In this dimension, her stilettos had been cemented to the floor and she couldn't do anything but stand frozen as he tipped up her chin.

She braced for the crush of his lips on hers. Anticipated it. Leaned into it ever so slightly.

But then he shocked the hell out of her by tilting her head to the side and grazing her cheek as he murmured in her ear, "Wanna tell me what's got you so upset?"

Oh, no he didn't. How dare he make this about something other than sex and be dead on target about her reasons for hiding out at the same time?

"I'm not upset." Her pulse tripped all over itself, scrambling to sort his dominating presence from his uncanny ability to read her. "Maybe I like the kitchen."

And sure enough—with each breathy catch of her lungs—their bodies brushed and the contact sang through her.

"You can't snow the master of winter," he advised

her so softly that she had to lean in a little closer to hear. Or at least that was her excuse and she'd cling to it as long as she could. "So lie to your friends, your dad. Anyone other than me. We're in this together and I need you."

Her knees went a little mushy. *Mushy.* The one person she had zero intention of letting under her skin had just demonstrated a remarkable ability to blaze right past every barrier she'd ever constructed. And it didn't even seem to matter that he hadn't meant those words the way they'd sounded, like he cared about her and had her back.

No. He wanted her to stick to the deal and stop being such a big baby about the fact that her father expected favors from this union. Weren't favors the whole purpose of this marriage? For God knew what reason, the fact that Hendrix had figured out all the subtle nuances of her mood hooked something inside her.

That pissed her off. He wasn't supposed to be good at handling her. He wasn't supposed to be anything but a means to an end.

"Yes," she purred and let her hips roll forward just a touch until she hit the thick, hard length she'd been seeking. "I can feel how much you need me."

"Careful." His lips feathered against her ear, sending shafts of need deep inside *her.* "Or I might think you're trying to entice me into breaking my promise. The Roz I know wouldn't play so dirty. So I'm going to assume it's a distraction from what's really going on with you and roll with it."

Before she could blink, his arm snaked around her waist, shoving her firmly into the cradle of his body, exactly where she wanted to be.

What did it say that he knew that about her too without being told?

"Put some of that sass where it belongs," he said into her ear as their embrace got a whole lot more intimate. He pressed her back against the counter, one leg teasing her thighs like he might push between them but he'd give her a minute to think about it. "Don't let a stray comment cramp your style. Be the life of the party because no one else's opinion matters."

Her eyes burned all at once. Oh, God, he was going to make her cry. What was wrong with her that a couple of compassionate phrases from a player like Hendrix could yank loose *tears*?

Except he wasn't just a creep looking to score. They were engaged, as unbelievable as that was to reconcile, and he needed her to *pull it together*.

"You're right," she admitted. "I'm letting crap that doesn't matter get me down."

What was she doing skulking around in the kitchen when there was a party going on? More importantly, he'd given her the perfect excuse to step out of his arms as everything settled inside.

She didn't move.

"Of course I am," he told her and she could hear the smile in his voice even as she absorbed his heat through her little black dress. "Roz, this is practice for the wider swath of society that we have to wade through an exhausting number of times over the next few weeks. They're not going to be any more forgiving. But I'm here. I'm not going anywhere and I'll be holding your hand the whole time."

"PB&J for the win," she murmured and dang it, her arms fit so well around his waist that she couldn't do anything but leave them there. "Although I have to ask why we couldn't have had this conversation without you wrapping yourself around me like an octopus."

"Oh, we could have." He nuzzled her ear. "This was strictly for me. You're driving me insane in that dress and all I can think about is that I don't get to take it off at the end of the night. I deserve something for my suffering."

That shouldn't have made her laugh. Especially since the whole of his body pressed into hers felt more like the opening act than the finale.

"Also," he continued, "I didn't think you were in the mood for an audience. If anyone came through that door right now, they'd exit pretty quickly for fear of intruding on a moment between lovers."

Did the man ever miss an angle? She did not want to appreciate any of his qualities, let alone the non-sexual variety.

Neither should she be recalling with perfect clarity what he'd said to her on his front porch. He'd never been shy about using his mouth in whatever inventive way came to mind, and he had a really great imagination, especially when it came to talking dirty.

That was enough to jump-start her brain. This wasn't the start of a seduction, never mind how easily it could be. It was a Come to Jesus at the hands of her partner and she was the one who'd taken sex off the table. For a reason. The man made her forget her own name and she needed to keep her wits about her, or she'd never survive this. She had to get Clown-Around off the ground and Hendrix was nothing to her except a ticket to achieving her goals.

"The moment is over," she informed him through sheer force of will.

"I disagree." But he stepped back immediately, taking all his delicious heat with him.

Even in that, he'd read her expertly, extracting himself as soon as he sensed her consent had changed. His gaze burned hot and she had no doubt he'd sweep her back into his arms if she gave the word.

And that put the steel in her spine that had been missing. She had equal power in this partnership. He wasn't going to slip through her fingers when she wasn't looking because they weren't a couple basing their relationship on fleeting feelings. They both had goals, none of which would be accomplished when one of them moped around poking at old bruises.

Hendrix was a smart choice. Obviously. He got her in ways no one ever had and she refused to examine how much she liked that.

"We're a power couple." She held out her hand to him. "Let's go act like one."

Four

Hendrix nursed a Jack Daniel's on the rocks as he hung out near the fireplace on the east end of the house and wished like hell he could blame the whiskey for the burn in his throat. But that pain was pure Roz.

And maybe some leftover crap from the discussion with Jonas and Warren, where his so-called friends had made it known in no uncertain terms how weak they thought he was when it came to women.

He could go without sex. He could. Hadn't he walked away from Roz when she'd said walk? If that wasn't a stellar test of his iron will, he didn't know what was. And he'd passed.

So why was he still so pissed? His skin felt like a hundred ants were crawling over it as he failed yet again at keeping his eyes off his fiancée. She lit up the room as she talked to his mother. So what if anyone caught him staring? He and Roz were engaged and he was allowed to look at her. In fact, he'd say it was expected.

The unexpected part was how…fierce the whole encounter in the kitchen had made him. Someone had upset Roz and he didn't like it. Didn't like how fragile she'd felt in his arms as he did his best to beat back whatever was going on with her internally. But she'd snapped out of it like the champ she was and he'd had a hard time letting her go when what he really wanted to do was explore that lush mouth of hers. That wasn't what she'd needed. Wasn't what he needed, either.

Okay, it was what he *needed* all right. But he also needed to prove to everyone—and maybe to himself—that he had what it took to reel back his sex-soaked lifestyle. If he'd learned to do that when his mother had asked him to, Vegas wouldn't have happened and there'd be no photograph of Hendrix's bare butt plastered all over the internet.

Paul Carpenter loomed in Hendrix's peripheral vision and then the man parked near him with a lift of his glass. "Haven't had a chance to speak to you one-on-one yet."

"No, sir."

Hendrix eyed the older man whose wealth and power in the retail industry eclipsed almost everyone in the world. Certainly a smaller chain like Harris Tobacco Lounge had nothing on Carpenter Furniture, nor did people get vaguely distasteful looks on their faces when talking about the business Roz's father had founded. Tobacco wasn't in vogue any longer, not the way it had been in the late eighties when Helene had partnered with her brother to build a string of shops from the ground up. Hendrix had joined the company almost a year after Uncle Peter died and then worked ninety hours a week to pull miracle after miracle from thin air to increase revenue over the past decade as he gradually took over the reins from his mom.

But Hendrix didn't assume for a moment that a man like Paul Carpenter respected one thin dime of Harris tobacco money, regardless of how hard he and his mom had worked for their fortune.

Mr. Carpenter eyed Hendrix as he swished his own amber liquid around the ice in his highball. "I suppose soon enough you'll be my son-in-law."

"Yes, sir." Why did it feel like he'd been called to the principal's office? He'd bet every last dollar of Harris money that Carpenter didn't think Hendrix was good enough for his daughter. "Roz is pretty important to me."

Uncomfortable didn't begin to describe this conversation. Hendrix shifted his stance. Didn't help.

"She's important to me, too," Paul said with a small smile. "It's just been the two of us since she was eight, you know."

"Yes, she mentioned that her mother had passed away." It was something they had in common—a missing parent. But Carpenter hadn't thrown that tidbit in for anything close to the same reason as Roz had. At the time, they'd been playing truth or dare and doing Jell-O shots off each other's bare stomachs. "I'm sorry for your loss, sir."

The memory of Roz's hot body decked out on the bed with the little circle of raspberry gelatin covering her navel slammed through his senses with far more potency than he'd have expected given that he'd just had the woman in his arms less than fifteen minutes ago.

Problem was that she'd been dressed. And off-limits. And probably even if he'd had permission to boost her up on the counter so he could get underneath that black dress, he'd still want her with a bone-deep ache. That had happened in Vegas, too. He couldn't get enough of her skin, her abandon, the way she was always game for whatever he did next.

And that was a conviction of his crimes as much as anything else. He had few memories of Roz that didn't involve her naked. That was the way he liked it…and lent entirely too much credence to everyone's certainty that he was a walking boner, panting after the next piece of tail he could get his hands on.

God, what was wrong with him? He was having a conversation with his future father-in-law and all he could think about was casting the man's daughter in the dirtiest sex scenario imaginable.

Something that might have been a blush if he'd been a girl prickled across his cheeks. But embarrassment wasn't something he did. Ever. He had nothing to be ashamed of. Except for the handful of scandals he'd managed to fall into over the past few years—Roz had certainly not been the first. She was just the one that had been the most worth it.

He sighed as Paul nodded his thanks over Hendrix's condolences. Maybe if he thought about something else, like cars, he could pretend the hard-on he'd been carrying around since Roz walked through his front door would eventually go away.

"I'm not one to pry," Paul said in that tone people used when they meant the exact opposite of what they'd just claimed. "And it's none of my business. But I wanted you to know that if you're marrying Roz to eliminate the scandal, I approve."

"You, um…what?" Hendrix swallowed. It didn't work. Throat still burned. He gulped enough whiskey to choke a horse, coughed and then had to wipe his watering eyes.

Paul Carpenter *approved* of Hendrix's marriage to Roz. As if Hendrix was someone he might have picked out for his daughter. It was as shocking as it was un-believable.

For the first time in his life, he'd been automatically accepted by a male of note, one he wasn't related to, whom he admired, one whose approval he would have never sought, save this specific situation. And he'd *never* expected to get it.

"It's high time that Roz take responsibility for the questionable decisions she makes, especially the one that led to so much trouble for you and your mother's campaign. I appreciate that you've been a willing party to the *fix*." Paul accompanied that word with two fingered air quotes.

The elation that had accompanied the man's initial statement fizzled. Fast.

A willing party? As if Roz had somehow seduced him into indulging a one night stand and then orches-trated the photograph? As if Hendrix had been an in-nocent victim of her stupidity?

Agape and unable to actually close his mouth around the sour taste coating his tongue, Hendrix let Paul's meaning filter through his brain for a good long while. At least until he felt like he could respond without punching Paul in the mouth.

"It takes two to tango. Sir." Hendrix lifted his chin. "Roz and I are partners. I'm making all my own decisions and rest assured, one of them is to treat her like the amazing, wonderful woman that she is."

He stopped short of telling Paul that he should take a lesson.

Figured the one time he'd had a few moments of approval from a man who could have been a father figure would end in the realization that Roz hadn't had a relationship with her surviving parent the way Hendrix had. Hendrix's mother loved him and while his exploits exasperated her, she never judged. Not the way this sanctimonious jerk had just judged Roz.

Roz was Paul's daughter and he should be on her side. If anything, Hendrix had been expecting a talking-to about corrupting the Carpenter daughter with his evil ways, which would have been well-deserved and easy to pretend didn't affect him. Instead, he felt like he needed to take a shower and then tuck Roz away where this man couldn't touch her.

"Well, be that as it may, I for one am quite happy with the development. Marriage will be good for Roz and with any luck, she'll stop the naked romps in hot tubs."

"Sir, I mean this with all due respect, but I sincerely hope not."

Hendrix whirled and left Paul standing by the fireplace with a bemused look on his face. Having an in with Carpenter Furniture wasn't going to pave the way to belonging in the upper echelon of North Carolina businessmen then. But what *would* make Hendrix finally feel like he was legitimate?

He found Roz talking to Lora in his study and took only half a second to gauge Roz's mood. Better. She didn't seem fragile any longer. Good. He grabbed his fiancée's hand, threw an apologetic glance at her friend and dragged Roz from the room.

"What are you doing?" she demanded once they hit the hall.

"You and I are going to go do something together. And we'll be dressed."

Then he'd have a memory of her that had nothing to do with sex. They both needed that.

"Darling, we *are* doing something together. Dressed." And Roz's sarcasm wasn't even as thick as it should be. "We're at our engagement party, remember?"

"Of course I do," he grumbled. A lie. He'd forgotten that he couldn't just leave and take Roz on an honest-to-God date.

Soon. It was an oversight that he'd beat himself up for later. He and Roz would—and *should*—go on lots of dates with each other while they weren't having sex. Spend time together. Get to know each other. Then he could stop thinking about her naked forty-seven times a minute.

But one thing he *couldn't* stop thinking about was the fact that he'd never have realized she was upset earlier if he'd been permitted to turn it into a sexual encounter. What else had he already missed because his interactions with his fiancée started and ended with how best to get into her panties? That question put a hollow feeling in his chest that stayed with him the rest of the night.

* * *

Roz took a long shower when she got home from the engagement party, hoping it would wash the evening from her brain. But nothing could dislodge the surprising things she'd learned about Hendrix in the course of a few hours. The man never did what she expected. But she'd already known *that*.

What she hadn't known was how easily he'd figure out how to bend her to his will. She'd naively assumed that as long as they weren't naked, she'd be good. Wrong. Somehow, he'd gotten her to agree to a date.

A date with Hendrix Harris. That was almost more unbelievable than the fact that she was marrying him. Yeah, their "date" was a public spectacle that he'd dreamed up as a way to push their agenda. Couldn't get society used to the idea that they were a respectable couple if they hid at home. She got that.

But for the love of God… What were they going to talk about? She didn't date. She had a lot of sex with men who knew their way around a woman's body but conversation by candlelight in an intimate booth at a swanky restaurant wasn't in her repertoire—by design. One she could handle; the other she could not. Intimacy born of conversation and dating led to feelings she had no intention of developing, so she avoided all of the above like the plague.

One surefire way to ensure a man never called you again? Sleep with him. Worked every time. Unless his name was Hendrix Harris, apparently. That guy she couldn't figure out how to shake, mentally or physically.

At least the concept of going on a date with her fiancé had pushed the unpleasantness of the encounter with her father to the background. Actually, Hendrix had almost single-handedly done that with his comfort-slash-seduction scene in the kitchen, which she'd appreciated more than she'd ever let on.

The less the man guessed how much he affected her, the better.

The next morning, she rifled through her closet for something appropriate for a date with the man who'd blown through half the female population of Raleigh. All eyes would be on her and not for the normal reasons.

Nothing. How was it possible not to have a thing to wear in an entire eight-hundred-square-foot closet? She'd have to go shopping after she got some work done.

Donning a severe suit that she secretly called her Grown-up Outfit, she twisted her hair into a sleek up-do that made her feel professional and drove to Clown-Around to push some paperwork across her desk.

Her phone rang and she almost didn't answer the call from an unfamiliar number. It was too early and she hadn't had nearly enough coffee to endure more rejection from yet another hospital.

But she was the only one here. There was no one else to do the dirty work. She answered.

"Rosalind?" the female voice said. "This is Helene Harris. How are you?"

Roz nearly dropped the phone but bobbled it just enough to keep it near her face. "Ms. Harris. I'm fine. Thank you. It was lovely to meet you last night."

"Likewise. I hope you don't mind that I asked Hendrix for your number. I'd like to take you to lunch, if you're free."

"I'm free." That had probably come out a little too eagerly. Thank you, Jesus, she'd worn an outfit that even a future mother-in-law would approve of. "And thank you. That would be lovely."

They made plans to meet at a restaurant on Glenwood Avenue, dashing Roz's notion to go shopping for a date dress, but she couldn't think about that because *holy crap*—she was having lunch with her future mother-in-law, who was also running for governor and who had presumably agreed to be a clown. Plus there was a whole mess of other things running through her head and now she was nervous.

By lunchtime, Roz truly thought she might throw up. That would put the cap on her day nicely, wouldn't it? A photo of her yakking all over a gubernatorial candidate would pair well with the one of her *in flagrante delicto* with the woman's son.

Ms. Harris had beaten her to the restaurant and was waiting for Roz near the maître d' stand, looking polished, dignified and every inch a woman who could run a state with one hand tied behind her back. In other words, not someone Roz normally hung around with.

"Am I late?" she asked Ms. Harris by way of greeting. Because that was a great thing to point out if so.

Ms. Harris laughed. "Not at all. I got here early so I didn't have to make you wait."

"Oh. Well, that was nice. Thank you." A little floored, Roz followed the older woman to a table near the window that the maître d' pointed them to.

The murmur of voices went into free fall as the two ladies passed. Heads swiveled. Eyes cut toward them.

But unlike what had happened to Roz the last time she'd braved polite society, the diner's faces didn't then screw up in distaste as they recognized her. Instead, the world kept turning and people went back to eating as if nothing had happened.

Miraculous.

Roz slid into her chair and opened her menu in case she needed something to hide behind. Ms. Harris didn't do the same. She folded her hands on the table and focused on Roz with a sunny smile that reminded her of Hendrix all at once.

"I'm so jealous that you can wear your hair up," Ms. Harris said out of the blue and flicked a hand at her shoulder-length ash-blond hair. "I can't. I look like a Muppet. But you're gorgeous either way."

"Um…thank you," Roz spit out because she had to say something, though it felt like she was repeating herself. "Ms. Harris, if I may be blunt, I need some context for this lunch. Are we here so you can tell me to lie low for the foreseeable future? Because I'm—"

"Helene, please." She held up a hand, palm out in protest, shooting Roz a pained smile. "Ms. Harris is running for governor and I hear that enough all day long. I like to leave her at the office."

"Helene, then." Roz blinked. And now she was all off-kilter. Or rather more so than she'd been since the woman had called earlier that morning. Come to think of it, she'd been upside down and inside out since the moment she'd caught Hendrix's eye at the Calypso Room. Why would lunch with his mother be any different? "I'm sorry. Call me Roz. Rosalind is an old-fashioned name that would be better suited for an eighty-year-old woman who never wears pants and gums her food."

Fortunately, Helene laughed instead of sniffing and finding something fascinating about the tablecloth the way most polished women did when confronted with Roz's offbeat sense of humor. She hadn't grown up going to cotillions and sweet-sixteen balls the way other girls in her class had, and her lack of decorum showed up at the worst times. Her father had been too busy ignoring the fact that he had a daughter to notice that she preferred sneaking out and meeting twenty-year-old boys with motorcycles to dances and finishing school.

"I think it's a beautiful name. But I get that we can't always see our own names objectively. If I had a dime for every person who called me Helen." She made a tsk noise and waved away the waiter who was hovering near her elbow. "And then try to give your own kid an unusual name that no one on the planet can mispronounce and all you get is grief."

In spite of herself, Roz couldn't help but ask. "Hendrix doesn't like his name? Why not?"

Helene shrugged and shook her head, her discreet diamond earrings catching the low light hanging over the table. "He says Hendrix was a hack who would have faded by the time he reached thirty if he hadn't overdosed. Blasphemy. The man was a legend. You'd think your fiancé would appreciate being named after a guitar hero, but no."

"He…he thinks Jimi Hendrix is a *hack*?" Roz clutched her chest, mock-heart-attack style, mostly to play along because she knew who the guitarist was of course, but she had no opinion about his status as a legend. Neither had she been born yesterday. You didn't argue musical taste with the woman who would most likely be sitting in the governor's chair after the election. "I might have to rethink this whole wedding idea."

The other woman grinned wide enough to stick a salad plate in her mouth sideways. "I knew I liked you." Helene evaluated Roz for a moment and then signaled the waiter. "As much as I'd prefer to spend the rest of the afternoon hanging out, duty calls. We should eat."

Since it sounded like a mandate, Roz nodded, trying to relax as Helene ordered a salad and water. This wasn't the Spanish Inquisition that she'd expected, not yet anyway. Maybe that was coming after lunch. She ordered a salad despite loathing them because it was easy to eat and obviously an approved dish since Helene had gotten the same.

And that was the root cause of her nervousness— she wanted Helene to like her but had no clue how to go about that when she had no practice cozying up to a motherly type. Furthermore, the woman had just said she liked her. What more did Roz need in the way of validation, a parade?

She sipped her water and yearned for a glass of wine, which would be highly inappropriate. Wouldn't it?

"Thank you," Helene murmured to her after the waiter disappeared. "For agreeing to this wedding plan that we came up with. It speaks a lot of your character that you'd be willing to do something so unconventional to help me."

"I…" *Have no idea how to respond to that.* Roz sat

back in her chair and resisted the urge to rub at her temples, which would only clue in everybody that she'd fallen completely out of the rhythm of the conversation. "I— You're welcome?"

Smiling, Helene patted Roz's hand, which was currently clenched in a fist on the tablecloth. "Another thing. You're making me nervous, dear. I can't decide if you're about to bolt or dissolve into tears. I asked you to lunch because I want to get to know you. You're the only daughter I've ever had. For as long as I've got you, let's make this a thing, shall we?"

Unexpected tears pricked at Roz's eyelids, dang it. The Harris family shared that gene apparently—Hendrix had that uncanny ability to pull stuff out of her depths, too.

"I don't have a mother," she blurted out. "So this is all new to me."

Helene nodded. "I understand that. I didn't have a good relationship with my mother. Sometimes growing up, I wondered if it would have been easier if she'd disowned me instead of spending every waking second being disappointed in me."

Roz nodded, mortified as she dashed tears away with the white napkin from her lap. This was not the conversation she'd intended to have with her new mother-in-law. She didn't believe for a second that shouting, *I still wonder that about my father!* would be the best way to foster the relationship Helene seemed to be asking for.

But Helene's story so closely mirrored the way Roz felt about her father that it was uncanny. How familiar was she allowed to be on her first one-on-one with Helene? This was uncharted—and so not what she'd expected. If anything, she'd earned an indictment for playing a role in the problems that Helene had just thanked her for helping to solve. There'd been two naked people in that hot tub, after all.

"I'm sorry about the photograph," she said earnestly and only because Helene hadn't called her on the carpet about it. That was why Roz and her father were always at such odds. He always adopted that stern tone when laying out Roz's sins that immediately put her back up.

Accepting the apology with a nod, Helene waited for the server to put their salads on the table and leaned forward. "Trust me when I tell you that we all have questionable exploits in our pasts. You just got lucky enough for yours to be immortalized forever, which frankly wouldn't have happened if you'd been with anyone other than Hendrix."

That was entirely false. Bad luck of the male variety followed her around like a stray dog, waiting to turn its canines on her the moment she tried to feed it. Roz swallowed and ate a tiny bit of salad in order not to seem ungrateful. "I have a tendency to get a little, um, enthusiastic with my exploits unfortunately."

"Which is no one's business but yours. The unfortunate part is that my son forgot that political enemies have long reaches and few scruples. You can only tell the kid so much. He does his own thing." She shrugged good-naturedly, far more so than should have been the case. It was a testament to Helene's grace, which was something Roz had no experience with.

"You're very generous," Roz said with a small frown that she couldn't quite erase. "Most parents aren't so forgiving."

At least that had never been Roz's experience. Parents were harsh, not understanding.

"I'm not most parents. Hendrix is my life and I love him more than I could possibly tell you. He saved me." Helene paused to eat some of her own salad but Roz didn't dare interrupt. "I have a bit of a wild past myself, you know."

Was this the part where Roz was supposed to nod and say, *Why yes, I have heard all the gossip about your rebellious teenage years*? Especially when Roz's own rebellious teenage years had been nothing but practice for her even more defiant twenties, when she'd really tested the limits of her father's patience.

"Getting pregnant at seventeen was a huge wake-up call," Helene recounted in the pause. "Without that baby, I might have continued in a self-destructive cycle that wouldn't have ended well. And now look at me. I created a successful business that Hendrix runs like the maestro of the boardroom that he was born to be and I'm running for governor. *Governor.* Some days, I don't know what I did to earn these blessings."

Roz's own eyes misted in commiseration as Helene dabbed at hers with her napkin. "I honestly wasn't sure what to think when you asked me to lunch. But making each other cry wasn't even on the top ten."

Helene's smile widened. One thing Roz noticed, no matter what, the woman's smile never slipped. It was a trait she'd like to learn because not for one moment did Roz believe that Helene's life was all smooth sailing. No, instead, Helene had some innate quality that allowed her to be happy regardless of the subject or circumstance. Voters must really be drawn to that happiness the same way Roz was.

Of course that apple did not fall far from the tree. Hendrix's bright personality had been a huge turn-on. Still was. He just laced it with pure carnal intentions that he did not mind making her fully aware of, and then followed through like the maestro of the *bedroom* that he was.

Roz shivered and tried like hell to reel back those thoughts because fantasizing about a woman's son while sitting with her in an upscale restaurant felt like bad form.

"I didn't plan to make you cry when I called you," Helene confessed sunnily. "Just happened. But I love that you're a companionable crier. No one wants to cry alone."

No. No one did. But that was some people's lot in life and if they didn't change the subject, there were going to be a lot more tears. The raw place inside was growing a lot bigger the longer she sat here. This wonderful woman had just said she'd be happy having a mother-daughter relationship with Roz for as long as Roz was married to Hendrix. Like that was an invitation Roz got every day and it was no big thing.

It was. And Roz wanted to cling to it, hold it and wrap her arms around it. But like everything—*everything*—in her life, Helene would be gone one day soon. Too soon. Any day was too soon because Roz had just realized that she craved whatever relationship this woman would grant her. Helene could be a…mentor of sorts. A friend. A stand-in mother.

It was overwhelming to contemplate. Overwhelmingly sad to think about having that and then giving it up.

But how could Roz refuse? She didn't *want* to refuse.

Helene was helping her blow away the scandal if nothing else and Roz owed the woman respect and allegiance for that alone.

The rest was all a huge bonus.

Five

Hendrix picked Roz up at the door of her loft for their date because he wanted to and he could. Also? What better way to prove he had all the skill necessary to resist pushing his way inside and having his way with her than not to do it?

But when he knocked on the door, she swung it wide to give him an eyeful of soft, gorgeous skin on display. Being that edible should be a crime. Her cleavage should be framed and hung on the wall of the Louvre.

"What happened to your pants?" he growled hoarsely.

Roz glanced down at the river of bare legs flowing from the hem of the blouse-like thing she had on. "What pants? This is a dress."

"The hell you say." He couldn't take her on a date in that outfit. His will would slide into the toilet in about a microsecond. Surely that would be the easiest dress in the history of time to get his hands under, even if they were someplace normally reserved for hands off, like a high-backed booth in the corner of a dimly lit restaurant.

His will made a nice whooshing sound as it flushed away and all his good intentions crumbled into dust. He might have whimpered.

Do not step over the threshold. Do not. No stepping.

"Let me make this perfectly clear to you," he ground out. "If you wear that dress—and I use that term *very* loosely—I cannot be responsible for what carnal activities may befall you in the course of this evening."

"Please." She waved that off. "You made a promise to keep your hands off me and you will, I have no doubt. What you're really saying is that you'd be embarrassed to be seen with me in this, right? So kiss off. I'm wearing it."

Oh, so it was going to be one of those nights. Not only would he have to contend with the idea that she had absolute faith in him, but she'd also assigned some kind of nefarious intent to his comments.

Her attitude needed to go and fast. "I wasn't embarrassed to be seen with you naked in a photograph. Not embarrassed now. Stop projecting your own crap all over me and get your purse. If you want to wear something that's one stiff breeze away from being illegal, be my guest."

"What's with you?" she called over her shoulder as she did exactly as he'd commanded without seeming to realize it. "You asked me on this date. If you're going to be nasty to me the whole time, then I'd be happy to slam the door in your face and order takeout."

That wasn't happening. He'd been looking forward to this date all day. "Why is it so hard to believe my objection to that dress starts and ends with how spectacular you look in it? You tell me what's with you and I'll tell you what's with me."

She smirked and flounced past him to the building's elevator. "You never had a problem with what I wore in Vegas. What's changed now? Only that we're engaged and you want me to look like a proper Harris bride."

Whatever *that* meant.

"Stop putting words in my mouth." The elevator door closed around them and they were alone in a space that got a whole lot smaller the more of her scent he breathed in. "In Vegas, I didn't care what you wore because I was taking it off you at some point. That's not the situation tonight and if you're really confused about the state of my extreme sexual frustration, the evidence is ready and available for your hands-on examination."

Her gaze flicked to his crotch, which put a little more heat into his already painful erection. Her sweet fingers on it would be legendary indeed but she didn't take him up on the invitation. Shame.

"I— You know what? Never mind." Her lush pink lips clamped together and she looked away.

Not so fast. His beleaguered senses were still working well enough to alert him that there was more here that he didn't know. "Spit it out, sweetheart. Or I'll be forced to kiss it out of you."

"What?" She slid him a sideways glance. "There's no stipulation in the rules that says you're allowed to kiss me to get information."

He shrugged. "How come you get to make all the

rules? If you're not going to be honest with me, I have to make up my own rules."

Her sigh worked its way through his gut and he was a half second away from sweeping her into his arms to show her he always put his money where his mouth was. But then she did as he suggested.

"I am projecting," she admitted.

It was as much of a shock now as it had been in the kitchen during their party—he'd figured out how to make progress with Roz. She was such a mystery, one he'd like to spend many long hours solving. Usually he would do that in bed. But that was off-limits here, so he'd been forced to be more creative. Looked like it was working. "Don't do that. Tell me what's up and then we'll go paint the town."

"Maybe you want a wife more like your mom. Smart and accomplished." She shrugged, her face blank. "That's not who I am. I have to be me, even if I don't look like I'm supposed to be here."

"What does that even mean? Of course you're supposed to be here. What, are you worried how you stack up?" The long, intense silence answered his flippant question in spades. "Are you *kidding* me? That's really something that even crossed your mind?"

Ridiculous. But apparently it wasn't to her. She rolled her shoulders back and her spine went stiff.

"Can we just forget about it?"

That wasn't happening any more than not taking Roz on this date. But first they obviously needed to get a few things straight. The elevator reached the ground floor and he waited until she reached his car.

Instead of opening the door for her, he snagged her by the waist and turned her into his arms, trapping her against the car. Instantly, everything but Roz drained from his mind as her body aligned with his so neatly that he could feel the heat of her core against his leg.

That was some dress.

"I already told you what you wanted to know, Hendrix." She glanced up at him through her lashes and the look was so sexy it put at least an inch on his already impossibly hard erection. "What are you going to do now, kiss me anyway?"

"No need." His hips fit so well into the hollow of her stomach that he swayed into her a little deeper. "This is strictly Exhibit A. B and C will have to wait."

Because he'd given his word. How had that become such a thing? Fine time for something like principles. Before Roz, he'd have said he had none when it came to women. Or rather, women said that on his behalf and he'd never corrected the notion.

"Make no mistake, though. You need kissing," he murmured, ignoring the fact that it was so backward it wasn't even funny. "In the worst way. Anytime you find yourself worried about whether you're the most gorgeous woman in the room, you think about this. Remember what my body feels like against yours and don't you dare question whether you're the woman I want to take home with me."

"I wasn't worried about that," she said and blinked her long sooty lashes coquettishly. "But I do appreciate exhibit A."

Not enough to lift the no-kissing moratorium apparently. She was crushed against his body, wearing a filmy, flirty dress that barely covered her good parts and her lips came together in the sweetest little bow that he wanted to taste so badly he feared for his sanity.

But not enough that he'd lost all decorum. Looked like his will wasn't completely broken because he found the wherewithal to step back. His chest heaved as he met her gaze. It was enigmatic and full of heat.

"Let me know when you're ready for the rest of the exhibit. I can open it up for your viewing pleasure any time."

Why were they torturing themselves like this again?

Due punishment, he reminded himself. His mom deserved to have a campaign free from other people's darts because of her son's actions. He owed it to his mother to fix it, especially after already messing up once because he couldn't resist this woman.

Plus, marrying Roz and introducing something real and legitimate into his life meant something to him, more than he'd ever admit, to her or anyone.

He tucked his fiancée into the car and slid into his own seat. She leaned on the center console instead of settling back against the leather, spilling way too much of her presence into his space.

"This seat has plenty of room for two," he murmured instead of starting the engine like a good boy.

"Don't threaten me unless you plan to follow through," she shot back and tucked her chin into her palm as if she planned to watch him the entire time he drove. "Where are you taking me? Not Randolph Room. That's where your mom took me to lunch."

"You had lunch with my mom?" That was news to him. He frowned.

Had his mother mentioned something about it last night and he'd forgotten in all the hoopla of the engagement party and the disturbing conversation with Paul Carpenter? He distinctly recalled giving Roz's number to his mom, but he'd assumed that was so they could coordinate the clown thing.

His mother usually told him her schedule and it was bothersome that she hadn't given him a heads-up about having lunch with his fiancée. He and Helene were business partners, and Hendrix sometimes offered advice on her campaign. And they were friends, which was often weird to people so he seldom talked about it.

Of course, since the photograph, she'd been a little on edge with him. It stung to find out they weren't totally back to normal.

"Yeah. She called me and asked if I was free. I wasn't going to say no."

"You shouldn't have. What did you talk about?"

"Girl stuff."

That was code for *mind your own business*. Hendrix started the car to give himself something to do that wasn't prying into the social life of his mother and fiancée. Nor did he want to obsess over the reasons why it was bothering him.

At least now he had some context for why Roz had all of a sudden joined the Helene Harris fan club and developed a complex about whether she stacked up against other women.

They drove to the restaurant where he'd made reservations and he cursed the silence that had fallen inside the car. Normally he had no problem finding something to talk about, particularly when it came to Roz, but he didn't want to spend the evening discussing all the ways he planned to have her after the wedding.

Well, he *wanted* to. There was absolutely nothing wrong with a healthy attraction to the woman you were going to marry. But he genuinely didn't think he had it in him to talk dirty to Roz and then not follow through yet again.

"Did you and my mother work out the clown stuff?" That was a safe enough subject.

"No. I mean, she mentioned it, but only to say that she's overcommitted right now and to bug her about it at lunch next week so she can fit it in. She actually said it like that. *Bug* her." Roz laughed. "As if I'd pester Helene like that. 'Mom, Mom, can you be a clown? Pleeeeease?'"

Hendrix did a double take at Roz's cute little girl voice. And the mention of additional lunches. "You're having lunch again?"

"Sure, we decided it was important to have a standing lunch date once a week from now on. Is there a problem with that?"

Yes. A huge problem. He didn't like the idea of his mom getting chummy with Roz. Why? How the hell should he know? He just…didn't. "Of course not. I was making conversation. This is a date. The whole point is to get to know each other, right?"

"That was how you posed it," she reminded him with another laugh that should have had him thinking of all the ways he could get her to do that a lot because it meant she was having fun.

Instead, his back was up and his mood had slid into a place normally reserved for tense board meetings. What was *wrong* with him? Not enough sex lately, most likely.

At the restaurant, they waited in a discreet corner as the maître d' readied their table, both of them ignoring the pointed attention from the other guests. At least Roz hadn't stiffened up like she had at the florist. He'd consider that a win.

Wedding plans. That was a good subject. Surely they could talk about that. He waited until they'd both taken their seats and he'd given the waiter their wine preference.

"So. You're going to hang out with my mom once a week now?"

She lifted a brow. "That's really bothering you, isn't it?"

Apparently. And now it was evident to them both. He bit back a curse.

When was the last time his mom had asked him to lunch? Ages ago. Not since the photograph had hit the news. She'd been really upset. But it had all blown over after he'd agreed to marry Roz—he'd thought.

And look, here he was in a restaurant with Roz. Engaged. That had been a major feat to pull off. People were noticing them together and a waiter had even taken a discreet picture with his phone that would likely make the rounds with some positive press attached. Surely Helene could appreciate all of the steps Hendrix had taken toward legitimizing his relationship with Roz so that his mom's political opponents wouldn't have any fodder to lob at her via the press.

Now would be a great time to stop sulking and get back to the reason he was torturing himself with a stunning companion whom he would not be taking to bed later. They hadn't even scored a dimly lit booth, which was good. And bad.

"This is the part where you're supposed to back me into the kitchen and stick your hands all over my body so I can have something else to focus on besides the stuff in my head," he informed her.

"I would if that would help." She eyed him nonchalantly. "But I'm pretty sure that only works on me. Instead, why don't you tell me why you're so threatened by the idea of me having lunch with your mom?"

Lazily, he sipped his wine to cover the panic that had uncurled in his stomach. The alcohol didn't help. "*Threatened* is a strong word."

And so correct. How dare she be the one to figure that out when he hadn't? The back of his neck flashed hot. That was a big wake-up call.

He'd never in a million years expected that getting married would mean he'd have to share his mother with someone. It had been the two of them for so long, and they'd become even more of a unit as he'd grown into adulthood, made even stronger after Uncle Peter had died. His reaction was pure selfishness and he didn't feel like apologizing for it all at once.

"Then you tell me what would be a better word," she said.

No quarter. If he wasn't already feeling pushed against a wall, her cool insistence would have put him there. "*Curious.*"

Her small smile said she had his number and she'd be perfectly within her rights to call him on his complete lie. *Pissed off* and *tense* would be more applicable. Which was dumb. What, was he actually worried that Roz was going to steal his mother from him?

"Curious about why on earth two women who don't know each other and will soon share the same last name could possibly want to have lunch?" She watched him over the rim of her glass as she sipped her own wine.

"You're changing your name?" This evening was full of revelations.

"Yeah. Why not? That's part of the deal here, right? Marrying you is my get-out-of-jail-free card. Might as well go full throttle. Make sure everyone is clear that I'm tied to the governor's office."

"But you're already a Carpenter—" All at once, the conversation with her father slammed through his consciousness. Was he really that dense? Maybe being a Carpenter wasn't all that great for her. After being treated to a glimpse of the judgment levied in her direction, it wasn't so hard to guess why, if so. Maybe she deserved a name change.

Wow. When had he turned into such an ass?

He picked up her hand to hold it in his. Her touch bled through him, convicting him even further since she didn't pull away. "I shouldn't be jumping down your throat about having lunch with my mom. It's fine. I'm glad you're getting along."

She nodded and the mood lightened. The restaurant he'd selected featured a highly rated chef and the meal reflected that. They ate and conversed about innocuous subjects and he relaxed about halfway through dinner.

It wasn't until he escorted Roz to the valet stand that he realized the tension hadn't completely fled on her side. Her back felt stiff under his fingers. Okay, he'd royally screwed up earlier if she was still uptight over the third degree he'd given her. But why had she dropped it like everything was fine? Just like a woman to nurse a grudge and not bother to say anything about it. That wasn't going to fly.

As he pointed the car in the direction of her loft, he

glanced at her from the corner of his eye. "Silent treatment for my crimes?"

She stared out the window. "Don't be ridiculous. I don't play little-girl games with men."

He let that simmer for a few minutes as he put a tight rein on his temper before he did something like comment on big-girl games. Nothing in his experience had prepared him to do this kind of long-term thing with a woman. And they were *getting married*. For the first time, it occurred to him that maybe he wasn't marriage material, that the reason he'd shied away from relationships wasn't solely because of the pact he'd made with Warren and Jonas, but also because he sucked at navigating emotional land mines.

But like the promise he'd made to keep his hands off her, this conversation was just as much a measure of his character. It was worth it to him to figure this out, if for no other reason than to prove he could.

He pulled over into a shadowy parking lot and killed the engine, then turned to face her. "Talk to me, Roz. You're obviously still upset."

"You asked me on a date so we could get to know each other. But then when you had an opportunity to really lay it all out, you didn't. At least have the courtesy to be honest with me. You don't like me being friendly with your mom because I'm just a good-time girl you had to marry because we got caught up in a scandal. I'm not good enough to be a real wife."

He shut his eyes for a blink, as that barb arrowed through his gut nice and deep. He had no excuse for not having seen that coming. Obviously she was playing back things she'd heard from others, and he'd unwittingly stepped right in the center of the land mines.

Yep. Not marriage material. This was why he stuck to sex, which he was good at, and shied away from anything that smacked of intimacy, which he was not good at.

"Roz, look at me." She did, her eyes barely discernible in the dark as he fumbled his way through. "Don't let your father's pigheadedness color your opinion of yourself. No one here is judging you for your sins. The reason I got testy is solely because I'm a jerk who doesn't like to share. My mom has been mine alone for a long time. We're a unit. I didn't want to lose that, or have that diluted somehow if you... Wow, this sounds really bad out loud."

She smiled with the faintest stirrings of tenderness. "No, it sounds honest. Which I like."

"This is me being honest," he agreed. If that was all she was looking for, maybe he didn't have to botch this too badly. "So you have to believe me when I say earlier was a combination of you in that dress and me being territorial. And maybe a bit of foot-in-mouth disease."

Her laugh washed through him, dissolving a lot of the tension, and he had to fight the muscles in his hand so that he didn't reach for her. The reasons he wanted to were totally mixed up and he didn't fully understand this urge to connect himself with that laugh in a way that had nothing to do with sex.

"Honesty is the best policy. So I'll return the favor. I don't remember my mom from when she was healthy. I just remember her sick and in a hospital bed, dying. Today a woman I admire invited me to lunch for the first time in my adult life. The fact that she's your mother didn't even factor into why it meant so much to me. Are you starting to see why I got a little bent out of shape about you getting bent out of shape?"

Her tone walloped him, dredging through his gut with razor-sharp teeth. He'd behaved like a jackass and stabbed at Roz's wounds at the same time. This wasn't a run-of-the-mill fight, like what normal couples might go through. They were surfacing enormously difficult emotions that he shouldn't want any part of.

But he was still here.

"If I say I'm sorry, will that help?"

Her smile widened. "Maybe."

Hell, why was he fighting this insanely strong urge to touch her? He skimmed his fingertips down her jaw and feathered a thumb across her lips. "I'm sorry."

She didn't even blink, just leaned until her lips hit his, and then treated him to the longest, sweetest kiss of his experience. Everything fell away except her and he froze, letting her drive this to whatever completion she wished because this was about feeling her out, learning who she was besides the woman he'd had hot, dirty sex with in Vegas.

God, he'd needed this, needed her in ways he wouldn't have guessed. The anticipation of getting her into his arms just like this flavored it so heavily that kissing her was nearly mind-altering. And this wasn't even close to the kind of kiss he'd envisioned jumping into all night. This was something else.

She pulled back and tilted her forehead to his until they touched. "I'm sorry, too. For being difficult. But not for kissing you. You needed the reminder that *we're* a unit. Peanut butter and jelly."

Yes. *That's* what it was. A solidifying of their union. No longer was this a marriage favor he was doing for his mother. He and Roz were becoming something. What, he wasn't sure yet, but it was so much more real than what he'd envisioned.

No. That wasn't what was happening here. Something lodged in his chest and he couldn't breathe all at once. He *couldn't* care about Roz, not like they were a couple. Not like there was any possibility of something deeper than a surface connection that started and ended with sex.

She didn't think there was something bigger than a marriage of convenience happening here. Did she? Had he messed up her expectations with all the talk of dates and getting to know each other? Had he screwed up his *own* expectations?

Surely not. Maybe some things had gotten a little out of whack, strictly due to the rules she'd laid down. The solution was to marry her and get to the place where he could block all that out with lots of hot sex, obviously. The lack of it was throwing them both off, that was all. He'd been forced into this pseudo-intimacy because of the scandal and now that he'd proven he wasn't a sex addict, it was time to move on to the next level. Once things were on familiar ground, he could fix all their fights with orgasms and then no one had to apologize for anything.

"We've got to get a wedding date on the calendar and you in a dress," he muttered.

The sooner the better.

Six

Somehow, Hendrix pulled off a miracle and got the wedding planned in record time, even down to the last place-setting. Roz wasn't confused about his motivation. She'd thrown down a gauntlet that they couldn't have sex until the wedding and had unwittingly created an environment that meant they'd be tense and irritable around each other.

Frankly, she was a little tired of it, too. They didn't have anything in common other than blind lust and a desire to fix the scandal. She got that. Their one disastrous attempt at a date had ended with solid reminders that her skill set didn't extend to forming connections with people, especially not with men—because she was good at having sex with them, but nothing else. Hendrix was no exception.

After her patient attempt to work through his unexpected freak-out over what should have been a simple announcement that she'd had lunch with Helene, his response? *Let's get you in a wedding dress so I can finally get what I came for.*

Fine. They weren't a real unit. Not like Hendrix and Helene, and the reminder had been brutal. Maybe she'd started to feel a little mushy about the idea of being part of something, but it had been nothing but a mirage.

They were getting married for reasons that had nothing to do with peanut butter and jelly and she'd agreed to that. It was smart. Not romantic, and that was a good thing. Less painful in the long run.

She liked orgasms as much as the next girl, so there was really no downside. Except for the niggling feeling that she and Hendrix had been on the verge of something special in the car and then it had vanished.

Her life was spiraling out of her control faster than she could grab on to it. She combated that by sticking her fingers in her ears and pretending there was no wedding planning going on. Hendrix handled it all, finally getting the message after his fourth attempt to include her in the decisions. Except for the flowers she'd already picked out, she really didn't care.

None of it mattered. They'd be undoing it all in a matter of months. The wedding music would dwindle from everyone's memory the moment the last note faded. Who cared what the piece was called?

The morning of the wedding dawned clear and beautiful, a rare day in Raleigh when the humidity wasn't oppressive. Figured. It was a perfect scenario to wear her hair down, but the pearl-encrusted bodice of her dress required her hair to be up. She dragged herself out of bed and got started on enjoying her wedding day—likely the only one she'd ever get. If nothing else,

by the end of it, she and Hendrix would be past the
weirdness that had sprung up since their date.

Lora picked her up at nine to take her to the spa,
where they'd planned to spend the morning pampering
themselves, but Roz couldn't get into the spirit. Hell,
what kind of spirit was she supposed to be in on the
day of a wedding that was basically an arranged marriage? She'd moved a few things into Hendrix's mansion in Oakwood yesterday and they planned to live
together for a few months, at least until the election,
at which point they'd agreed to reevaluate. Everything
was on track.

The spa did not relax her. The masseur had ham
hands, the girl who did Roz's bikini wax burned herself—not badly, but she'd had to find someone else to
finish the job—and the facial left Roz's skin feeling
raw and slightly dry, so her makeup wouldn't apply
correctly. Gah, she'd been putting on foundation for
fifteen-plus years. Why did her face suddenly look
like the Grand Canyon in miniature?

Nerves. So much was riding on this marriage. Her
reputation. Clown-Around. Helene's campaign. Her
father's political ambitions. And maybe deep inside,
she hoped that saying *I do* would magically shift things
between her and her father. It wasn't a crime to hope.

But neither was any shifting likely. So far, he'd
stayed on script, expressing nonverbal disapproval in
the usual ways while tossing out backhanded comments about getting chummy with Helene. It had
soured her lunch dates with Hendrix's mom to the point
where she had canceled the last one. It had killed her
to lose that one-on-one time with Helene but Hendrix
had been so weird about it that Roz figured it was bet-

ter not to get too attached. Her response was mostly self-preservation at this point.

As she leaned into the mirror to work on her eyeliner, her hand started to shake.

Lora glanced over from her spot next to the bride. "You okay? You've been jumpy since this morning."

Dang it. If Lora had noticed, Hendrix would, too. Maybe she could sneak a glass of white wine from the reception before walking down the aisle. Just to settle things inside. "Brides are allowed to be jumpy."

Her friend eyed her. "But this isn't a real wedding. You've been so calm and collected this whole time. It's kind of a shock to see you having this strong of a reaction."

"It is a real wedding," she corrected, fielding a little shock of her own that Lora had classified it any other way. "And a real marriage. I'm taking his name. We'll be sleeping in the same bed. Can't get much more real than that."

That started tonight. Holy hell. That was a lot of reality, orgasms notwithstanding. She'd be an honest-to-God wife who could legally sign her name Mrs. Harris. It suddenly felt like a huge gamble with no guarantee of a payoff.

Lora shrugged and tossed her long blond hair over her shoulder, leaning into the mirror to apply her own cosmetics. "But you're not in love. It's not like he swept you off your feet with a romantic proposal that you couldn't resist. I'm kind of surprised you're going through with it, actually. You didn't plan one tiny part of the ceremony. I had to force you to pick a dress."

All of that was true. And sad all at once that such a cold recitation of facts so accurately described her wedding day. She tossed her head. "I never dreamed of my wedding or scrawled my future married name on stray pieces of paper growing up. I'm marrying a man with bedroom skills a gigolo would envy. My life will not suck. And when we get tired of each other, I get a no-fault divorce. It's a business arrangement. It's the perfect marriage for me."

She'd keep telling herself that until *she* believed it too, and ignore the huge gap in her chest that she wished was filled with something special.

Grinning, Lora waved her mascara wand in Roz's direction. "When you put it that way… Does he have a friend?"

"Sure. I'll introduce you to Warren. You'll like him." Doubtful. Lora wouldn't look twice at a man who accessorized with his cell phone 24/7. "Hendrix's other friend is married."

Jonas and Viv had come across as one of those couples who were really in love. You could just tell they both firmly believed they'd found their soul mate. Honestly, Roz thought she'd be exactly like that if she ever fell in love, which was why she hoped she never did. Her parents had been mad for each other and watching her father waste away alongside her dying mother had been a huge wake-up call. Love equaled pain. And then when it was gone, she envisioned being alone for the rest of her life, just like her father. Carpenters weren't good at serial marriage.

The one she'd get with Hendrix Harris *was* perfect for her.

Hendrix sent a limo to pick up the bride and bridesmaid. Roz felt a little silly at the size of the vehicle when she spread out her white pearl-encrusted skirt on the spacious leather seat that could have held four people. But the fact of the matter was that she didn't have a lot of friends that she would have asked to be in her wedding party. She had acquaintances. They'd all been invited to the social event of the season, though she didn't fool herself for a moment that they were coming for any other reason than morbid curiosity.

All at once, the door to the chapel loomed and her feet carried her into the church's vestibule without much conscious effort on her part. Her father waited for her inside as arranged, but she couldn't quite shake the feeling of walking through a surreal dream.

"Roz," her father called as he caught sight of her. "You're looking well."

Geez. Exactly what every bride dreams of hearing on her wedding day. "Thanks, Dad."

He wasn't effusive with his praise, never had been. But was it too much to ask for a little affection on a day when she was doing something that would benefit him?

Crooking his elbow in her direction, he stood where the coordinator directed him to and then it was Roz's turn to get in line behind Lora, who was stunning in a pale pink column dress with a long skirt. It would have been more appropriate for an evening wedding, but that was one thing Roz had cared about picking out. She'd gotten the dress that looked good on Lora, not the one societal convention dictated.

She was still Rosalind Carpenter. For about thirty more minutes. Oh, God.

What if this was a huge mistake?

Music swelled from the interior of the chapel that Hendrix had insisted would lend validity to their union. That seemed be the litmus test for pretty much all of his wedding decisions—how legit the thing was. She'd never have pegged him as that much of a traditionalist but she got more than an eyeful of his idea of what a proper wedding looked like as the coordinator flung open the doors to the chapel, signaling their entrance.

Five hundred guests rose dutifully to their feet, heads craned toward Roz for their first glimpse of the bride. An explosion of color greeted her, from the bouquets at the end of each pew to the multiple stands holding baskets of blooms across the front. Hendrix had chosen pinks to complement Lora's dress, but hadn't seemed too inclined to stick with a flower theme. There were stargazer lilies she'd picked out at the florist, but also roses, baby's breath, tulips, daisies, and something that might be a larkspur, but her father started down the aisle before she could verify.

Wow, was it hot in here. Every eye in the house was trained on her. Her spine stiffened and she let her own vision blur so she didn't have to see whether they were quietly judging her or had a measure of compassion reflected on their faces. No way was it the latter. No one in attendance had a clue how difficult today was for the motherless bride.

Then her gaze drifted past all the flowers and landed on the star of the show. Hendrix. She stared into his pale hazel eyes as her father handed her off in the most traditional of exchanges. Her husband-to-be clasped her fingers and the five hundred people behind her vanished as she let Hendrix soak through her to the marrow.

"You're so beautiful it hurts inside when I look at you," he murmured.

Her knees turned to marshmallow and she tightened her grip on his hand.

That was the proper thing to say to a bride on her wedding day and she didn't even try to squelch the bloom of gratitude that had just unfurled in her chest. "I bet you say that to all your brides."

He grinned and faced the minister, guiding her through the ceremony like a pro when nerves erased her memory of the rehearsal from the night before. The space-time continuum bent double on itself and the ceremony wound to a close before she'd barely blinked once.

"You may kiss the bride," the minister intoned and that's when she realized the complete tactical error she'd made.

She had to kiss Hendrix. For real. And the moratorium on that thus far had guaranteed this would become A Moment. The carnal spike through the gut at the thought did not bode well for how the actual experience would go down.

Neither did the answering heat in his expression. He cupped her jaw on both sides, giving her plenty of time to think about it. No need. Her whole body had just incinerated with the mere suggestion of the imminent follow-through.

And then he leaned in to capture her mouth with his. It was a full-on assault to the senses as their lips connected and she couldn't do anything else but fling her arms around his waist, or she'd have ended up on the ground, a charred shell that was burned beyond recognition.

Oh God, yes. With that one hard press of his mouth, Hendrix consumed her. This kiss was but a shadow of the many, many others they'd shared, but it was enough to slide memories along her skin, through her core.

This was so very right, so perfect between them. Everything else faded—the weirdness, the nerves. This heat she understood, craved. If he was burning her alive from the inside out, she didn't have to think about all the reasons this marriage might not work.

He teased the flame in her belly into a full raging fire with little licks of his tongue against hers. Hell, that blaze hadn't ever really been extinguished from the moment he'd lit that match in Vegas. Masterfully, the man kissed her until she'd been scraped raw, panting for more, nearly weeping with want.

This was why she'd thrown down the no-kissing-no-sex rule. She could not resist him, even in a church full of people. Her body went into some kind of Hendrix-induced altered state where nothing but basic need existed. And he wasn't even in full-on seduction mode. Thank God he'd played by her rules or there was no telling what new and more horrific scandals might have cropped up prior to the wedding.

That was enough to get her brain back in gear. She broke off the kiss to the sound of flutes and strings. The recessional music. They were supposed to walk and smile now. Somehow, that's what happened and then she floated through a million photographs, a limo ride to the reception and about a million well-wishers.

All she really wanted was to dive back into Hendrix and never surface.

The crowd at the reception crushed that hope flat. No less than ten people vied for their attention at any given time and she'd lost count of the number of times Hendrix had introduced her to someone from his business world. The reverse wasn't at all true, a sobering fact that brought home the reasons she was wearing a wedding band.

She'd spent the past few years having what she'd staunchly defend as a "good time" but in reality was a panacea for the pain of losing first her mother to cancer and then her father to indifference and grief. The scandals were just the cherry on top of her messy life and ironically, also the reason she couldn't move forward with something respectable like running a charity.

Her new husband would change all of that. Had already started to.

The pièce de résistance of the event came with the first dance between husband and wife. Hendrix, whom she'd scarcely said two words to since that pantie-melting kiss, whisked her out onto the dance floor. He drew her close and when his arms came around her, the strangest sensation floated through her as they began to move to the classical piece that she'd have never picked out but fitted the occasion.

"Hey," he murmured into her ear. "How is Mrs. Harris doing?"

"I don't know. I haven't spoken to your mother." When he laughed, she realized he hadn't meant Helene. "Ha, ha. I'm out of sorts. It's been a long day."

"I know. That's why I asked. You seem distracted."

She pulled back a touch to look at him. "Ask me again."

The smile in his eyes warmed her, but then it slid away to be replaced by something else as their gazes held in a long moment that built on itself with heavy implications. "How are you, Mrs. Harris?"

A name shouldn't have so much color to it. If anything, it should have sounded foreign to her, but it wasn't strange. It felt…good. She took a deep breath and let that reality expand inside her. *Mrs. Harris*. That was her name. Rosalind Harris. Mrs. Roz Harris.

She liked it. Maybe she *should* have practiced writing it out a bajillion times on a piece of scratch paper. Then the concept wouldn't have been such a shock. There was a huge difference between academically knowing that you were changing your name and actually hearing someone address you that way. Especially when the man doing the addressing had the same name and you were married to him.

"I'm better now," she told him.

Understatement. Hendrix was solid and beautiful and he'd pulled off the wedding event of the season. Why hadn't she participated more in the planning?

Sour grapes. Nothing more complicated than that. She'd started getting a little too touchy-feely with the peanut butter and jelly analogy and he'd set her back on the right path with timely reminders of what they were doing here. For his trouble, she'd frozen him out and then used that as an excuse to pull back from a friendship with his mother.

Well, she was over it. They were married now and both of them knew the score. The no-sex rule wasn't in the way any longer. Thank God. They could spend all their time in bed and never have to talk about mothers, peanut butter or anything difficult.

"This was amazing," she said earnestly. "So much more than I was expecting. Thank you."

Surprise filtered through his expression. "I… You're welcome. I'm glad you liked it. The wedding planner did all the work. I just approved everything."

"I should have done it with you." The fact that she hadn't made her feel petty and childish. If nothing else, it was an effort that benefited her, so she could have done half the work. Then maybe she'd feel more like she'd earned the right to be called Mrs. Harris. "I'm sorry I didn't."

For the first time since their disastrous date, Hendrix smiled at her like he had that night in Vegas. As if he'd found the end of the rainbow and the pot of gold there was more valuable than he'd ever dreamed.

She liked it when he looked at her like that.

"It's okay. It wasn't any trouble." He spun her around as the last notes of the waltz ended and something a little darker and more sensual wafted from the string quartet on the dais in the corner. His arms tightened, drawing her deeper into his embrace. The crowd on the dance floor grew thicker as people filled in around them. "I'm enjoying the benefits of it, so it's all good."

His body pressed against hers deliciously. A slow simmer flared up in her core, bubbling outward until her nerve endings were stretched taut with anticipation. "The benefits?"

"Dancing with my bride, for one," he murmured. His hands drifted along her body with sensual intent, pressing her more firmly against him as he stroked her waist, the curve of her hip, lower still, and there was so much wedding dress in the way that she strained against his touch, yearning for the heat of his hand in places that hadn't been *touched* in so very long.

Dancing was a great excuse to let Hendrix put his hands on her in public. "I'm enjoying that part, too."

"It's been a long time," he said gruffly, "since I had free rein to hold you like this."

Yes, and judging by the oh-so-nice hard length buried in her stomach, he was as affected by their close proximity as she was. "You were a trouper about it."

"Wasn't easy. But it's over now. I can kiss you whenever I feel like it." To prove the point, he nuzzled her neck, setting off fireworks beneath her skin as he nibbled at the flesh.

"That's not kissing," she muttered, biting back a gasp as he cruised to her ear, molding it to his lips as he laved at her lobe.

"I'm getting there."

"Get there faster."

He pulled back and swept her with a glance that was equal parts evaluation and equal parts *I'm a second from throwing you down right here, right now.* "Is that your way of saying you're ready to leave?"

"We can't," she reminded him and tried to ignore how desperately disappointed she sounded.

This was a networking event as much as it was a wedding. Helene had a throng of people around her, and the movers and shakers of Raleigh stood at the bar. If the bride and groom dashed for the door fifteen minutes after the reception started, that wouldn't go over well.

"No," he agreed and bit out a vile curse that perfectly mirrored her thoughts. "We need tongues wagging with positive comments about us, preferably with lots of praise about how respectable we are."

Exactly. Especially if they spouted off at the mouth around her father. He needed a whole lot of reassurance that Roz had turned a corner, that her photo ops with naked men were a thing of the past. From here on out, the only scandal associated with her name should be more along the lines of serving the wrong wine at a party she and Hendrix threw for Harris Tobacco Lounge executive staff.

"So maybe we don't leave," she said as a plausible alternative began to form in her mind. Oh God, did she need that alternative. Fast. Her insides were already tight and slick with need.

His expression turned crafty as he considered her comment. "Maybe not. Maybe there's a…closet in the back?"

"With a door. That locks."

His thumb strayed to the place along her bodice where it met the skin of her back and heat flashed as he caressed the seam, dipping inside just enough to drive her insane and then skimming along until he hit the zipper.

"One tug, and this would be history," he said, the hazel in his eyes mesmerizing her with the promise as he toyed with the hook anchoring the zipper to the bodice. "It feels complicated. Challenging."

"Maybe you don't start there," she suggested and swayed a little to give the couples around them the impression the bride and groom were still dancing when in reality, her attention was on the perimeter of the room where two very promising hallways led to the back of the reception venue. "You might have better luck checking out how easily my skirt lifts up."

"Mrs. Harris, I do like the way you think." In a flash, he grabbed her hand and spun to lead her from the dance floor.

Well then. Looked like the honeymoon was starting early. She had no problem with that and she was nothing if not ready to ignore the fact that the bride and groom were still dashing for the door fifteen minutes after the reception started but with this plan, they'd be back in a few minutes. At least ten. Maybe once wouldn't be enough. Was married sex better than one night stand sex? Oh God, she couldn't wait to find out.

Breathlessly, she followed him, ignoring the multitudes of people who called out to them as they scouted for this hypothetical closet with a door that locked. In a true wedding day miracle, off the kitchen there was a linen closet full of spare tablecloths and empty centerpieces. No one saw them duck through the door, or at least no one who counted. They passed a member of the waitstaff who pretended he hadn't noticed their beeline through the back rooms where guests typically didn't tread. Whether it was a testament to his discretion or the fact that Hendrix and Roz were tied to powerful families, she didn't know. Didn't care.

All that mattered was the door had a lock. She shut it behind her with a click and flipped the dead bolt, plunging the room into semidarkness. Maybe there was a light but before she could reach for it, Hendrix pinned her against the door, his mouth on hers in an urgent, no-holds-barred kiss. No time to search for a light. No time to care.

Her knees gave out as the onslaught liquefied her entire body, but he'd wedged one leg so expertly between hers that she didn't melt to the ground in a big hot puddle. She moaned as his tongue invaded her mouth, heated and insistent against hers. He hefted her deeper into his body as he shifted closer.

Too many clothes. She got to work on his buttons, cursing at the intricacy of his tuxedo. Shame she couldn't just rip the little discs from the fabric but they had to reappear in public. Soon. Giving up, she pulled the fabric from his waistband so she could slide her hands under it.

Oh, yes, he was warm and his body was still drool-worthy with ridges and valleys of muscle along his abs that her fingers remembered well. He pressed closer still, trapping her hands between them, which was not going to work, so she shifted to the back as he gathered up her skirts, bunching the fabric at her waist. Instantly, she regretted not making him take the time to pull the dress off. She wanted his hands everywhere on her body, but then she forgot to care because his fingers slid beneath the white lacy thong she'd donned this morning in deference to her wedding day.

"I want to see this thong later," he rumbled in her ear as he fingered the panties instead of the place she needed him most. "It feels sexy and tiny and so good."

"It feels in the way," she corrected and gasped as he yanked the panties off, letting them fall to her ankles. She toed off the fabric and kicked it aside. She needed him back in place *now*. "Touch me. Hurry."

Fast. Hard. Frenzied. These were the things she wanted, not a speech about her undergarments. This was sex in its rawest form and she knew already that it would be good between them. She hoped it would put them on familiar ground. Eliminate confusion about what they were doing here.

"What's your rush, Mrs. Harris?" He teased her with short little caresses of his fingertips across her shoulder, down her cleavage, which ached for his attention, but had far too many seed pearls in the way for that nonsense.

"Besides the hundreds of people waiting for us?"

Her back arched involuntarily as his fingers found their way beneath the tight bodice of her dress to toy with her breasts. Heavenly heat corkscrewed through her core as he fingered her taut, sensitized nipples.

"Besides that."

"You're my rush," she ground out. "I'm about to come apart and I need your hands on me."

She needed oblivion like only he could give her, where all she could do was feel. Then it didn't matter that he was totally on board with a closet quickie for their first time together as husband and wife. Neither of them did intimacy. It was what made their marriage so perfect.

"Like this?" His hand snaked between them to palm her stomach and she wiggled, hoping to get it lower. He complied inch by maddening inch, creeping toward the finish line with a restraint more suited for a choirboy than the bad boy she knew lurked in his heart.

He'd licked her in places that had never been touched by a man. He'd talked so dirty while doing it that she could practically give herself an orgasm thinking about it. They were having sex in a closet with five hundred oblivious people on the other side of the wall and he had every bit of the skill set necessary to make it intoxicating. She needed *that* man.

"Hendrix, please," she begged. "I'm dying here."

"I've been dying for weeks and weeks," he said and she groaned as he wandered around to the back, wedging his hand between her buttocks and the door to play with flesh that certainly appreciated his attention but wasn't the part that needed him most.

Practically panting, she circled her hips, hoping he'd get the hint that the place he should be focusing on was between her thighs. "So this is my punishment for not letting you have your way with me until now?"

"Oh, no, sweetheart. This is my reward," he murmured. "I've dreamed of having you in my arms again so I could feel your amazing body in a hundred different ways. Like this."

Finally, he let his fingers walk through her center, parting the folds to make way, and one slid deep inside. Mewling because that was the only sound she could make, she widened herself for him, desperate for more instantly, and he obliged with another finger, plunging both into her slickness with his own groan.

"I could stay here for an eternity," he whispered. "But I need to—"

He cursed as she eased her way into his pants, too blind with need to bother with the zipper. Oh, yes, there he was. She palmed his hot, hard length through his underwear and it wasn't enough. "I need, too."

Urgently, she fumbled with his clothes and managed to get the buttons of his shirt partially undone, hissing as he withdrew his magic hands from her body to help. But that was a much better plan because his progress far eclipsed hers and he even had the wherewithal to find a condom from somewhere that she distinctly heard him tear open. That was some amazing foresight that she appreciated.

Then her brain ceased to function as he boosted her up against the door with one arm, notched his hard tip at her entrance and pushed. Stars wheeled across her vision as he filled her with his entire glorious length. Greedily, she took him, desperate for more, desperate for all of it, and he gave it to her, letting her slide down until they were nested so deep that she could feel him in her soul.

No.

No, she could not. That was far too fanciful for what was happening here. This was sex. Only. Her body craved friction, heat, a man's hard thrusts. Not poetry.

Wrapping her legs around him, she gripped his shoulders, letting her fingers sink into the fabric covering them because even if it left marks, who cared? They were married and no one else would see his bare shoulders but her.

He growled his approval and it rumbled through her rib cage. Or maybe that was the avalanche of satisfaction cascading through her chest because Hendrix was hers. No other woman got to see him naked. It shouldn't feel so good, so significant. But there was no escaping the fact that they were a unit now whether he liked it or not.

They shared a name. A house. Mutual goals. If he didn't like peanut butter and jelly, he should have come up with another plan to fix the scandal.

Shifting ever so slightly, he hit a spot inside her that felt so good it tore tears from her eyes. The position sensitized her to the point of madness and she urged him on with her hips as he drove them both into the stratosphere, the door biting into her back as she muffled her cries against his suit jacket, praying she wasn't smearing makeup all over his shoulder.

That would be a dead giveaway to anyone who bothered to notice. And she liked the idea of keeping this encounter secret. Their own little wedding party.

Explosion imminent, she rolled her hips until the angle increased the pressure the way she liked it. Hendrix grabbed one thigh, opening her even wider, and that was it. The orgasm ripped through her and she melted against him, going boneless in his arms until his own cry signaled his release.

He gave them both about five seconds of recovery time and then let her legs drift to the floor so they could hold each other up. Which she gladly did because he'd earned it.

"That was great for starters," she muttered against his shoulder because it felt expected that she should reiterate how hot—and not meaningful—this encounter was. "I can definitely report that took the edge off, but I'm nowhere near done."

There was so much more to explore. Best part? She could. Whenever she felt like it, since they'd be sleeping in the same bed. Married sex had a lot to recommend it.

Someone rattled the doorknob, nearly startling out of her skin.

"You have the key?" a muffled voice from the other side of the wall called.

Oh, God. They were about to be discovered.

Seven

Where was her underwear? It was so dark in here. Had she kicked them to the left? Panic drained Roz's mind and she couldn't think.

The doorknob rattled again. Whoever it was probably had no idea that the bride and groom were in the closet. But they were probably packing a cell phone with a camera. They always were.

Stuffing her fist against her mouth, Roz jumped away from the door and knelt to feel around for her panties, dress impeding her progress like a big white straitjacket for legs. Hendrix fumbled with his own clothes. His zipper shushed, sounding like an explosion in the small room. At least he'd gotten that much covered. Any photographs of this tryst would be of the dressed variety. But still not the commemorative moment they'd like captured digitally for eternity.

The door swung open, spilling light into the closet, and Roz had a very nasty flashback to a similar moment when she was twenty, with the obvious difference this time being that she was wearing a wedding dress and the man tucking in his shirt behind her had recently signed a marriage license.

Two white-coated waiters stared at her and Hendrix and she'd like to say her years of practice at being caught in less-than-stellar circumstances had prepared her for it, but it was never as easy as tossing her hair back and letting the chips fall where they may.

Besides, she refused to be embarrassed. Everything was covered. Married people were allowed to be in a locked closet without fear of judgment—or she wouldn't have bothered to go through with all of this. The wait staff was interrupting *her*, not the other way around.

She shot to her feet and it was a testament to her feigned righteous indignation at being disturbed that she didn't break an ankle as one of her stilettos hit the ground at an awkward angle.

"Um, sorry," the one on the left said, and he might as well have hashtagged it *#notsorry*.

His face beamed his prurient delight, like something naughty was showing, and she had half a moment of pure horror over not actually locating her underwear. She tugged on her skirt to make sure it wasn't caught on itself, but then Hendrix came up behind her, snaking an arm around her waist. Claiming her. They were a unit and he had her back.

She leaned into him, more grateful than she had a right to be.

"Can you give us a minute?" he said smoothly to

the interrupters and actually waited for the one waiter's nod before he shut the door in their face. Brilliant.
Why hadn't she thought of that?

Hendrix flipped on the overhead light, the white
lace scrap on the floor easily identifiable at that point.
But instead of letting her fetch her panties, he tipped
her chin up and laid a kiss on her lips that had nothing
to do with sex. Couldn't. There were people outside
who wanted inside this closet and they'd been busted.

"I wasn't finished, either," he murmured against her
mouth by way of explanation.

She nodded, letting his warmth bleed through her
via their joined lips, mystified why that sweet, unnecessary cap to their closet hookup meant so much. Eventually, he let her go and they got everything situated
well enough to mix in polite company again. Hendrix
reopened the door and they slipped past the waiters
hand in hand.

Her husband's palm burned against hers. She
couldn't recall the last time someone had held her hand,
like they were boyfriend-girlfriend. Or whatever. They
were married. Nothing wrong with holding hands. It
was just…unexpected.

"You okay?" Hendrix said softly, pulling her to the
side of the short hallway that led to the reception area.
His attention was firmly on her, but before she could
answer or figure out why his concern had just squished
at a place inside, more people interrupted them.

Why couldn't everyone leave them alone so she
could spend about a dozen hours exploring why everything with Hendrix felt so different now that she'd
signed a piece of paper?

Hendrix's arm went tense under her fingers and she

turned. Her father. And Helene. They stood at the end of the short hall, varying expressions of dismay and relief spreading across their faces.

Oh, God. The very people they were trying to help with this scandal-fixing marriage. Now it was obvious to everyone that she couldn't resist Hendrix, that she had something wrong with her that made it impossible to wait for more appropriate circumstances before getting naked with the man.

"We got a little concerned when we couldn't find you," Helene said with a smile. "But here you are."

Her father didn't smile. He crossed his arms and even though he could look her in the eye when she wore stilettos, she still felt small and admonished even before he opened his mouth. Marrying Hendrix had been a last-ditch effort to do *something* her father approved of. Looked like that had been a vain effort all the way around.

"Glad to see that you're dressed," her father said and it was clear that he was speaking directly to his daughter.

The *for once* was implied and sure enough, flooded her with the embarrassment she'd managed to fight off earlier, after being discovered by wait staff. Thank God their parents hadn't been the ones to fling open that door.

"That's not really your concern any longer," Hendrix said to her father.

She did a double take. Was he sticking up for her?

"It is my concern," her father corrected. "This marriage isn't guaranteed to remove all of the social shame from the photographs. Additional fodder could still be harmful and Roz is quite good at feeding that fire."

"Still not your concern," Hendrix corrected mildly and his hand tightened around hers.

As a warning to let him handle it? She couldn't speak anyway. The knot in her throat had grown big enough to choke a hippopotamus.

"Roz is my wife," Hendrix continued. "And any bad press that comes her way is my responsibility to mitigate. She has my name now. I'll take care of her."

Okay, there might be crying in her immediate future.

"Hendrix," she murmured because she felt like she had to say something, but that was as much as her brain could manufacture.

With that, her husband nodded to his mother and swept Roz past the inquisition that should have ruined her day. Instead, Hendrix had relegated that confrontation to an insignificant incident in the hall.

How had he done that? She snuck a glance at him. "Thank you. You didn't have to do that."

He shot her an enigmatic smile. "I did so have to do that. Your father should be proud of you, not throwing you to the wolves."

"Um, yeah. He's never really appreciated my ability to keep my balance while having sex against a door."

Hendrix laughed at that, which actually made her relax for what felt like the first time all day.

"I appreciate that skill." He waggled his brows and guided her back into the reception where they were swallowed by the crowd, none of whom seemed to notice they'd been gone.

If it was at all possible to receive an indicator that she'd made the right decision in marrying Hendrix Harris, that moment with her father had been it. Half of her reason for agreeing had to do with gaining approval from a man who had demonstrated time and time again that she could not earn his respect no matter what. That possibility had been completely eliminated…only to be replaced with a completely different reality.

Her husband wasn't going to take any crap from her father.

Maybe she didn't have to, either.

And that's when she actually started enjoying her wedding day.

Despite Paul Carpenter's comments to the contrary, the wedding had apparently gone a long way toward smoothing over the scandal. The snide looks Hendrix had witnessed people shooting at Roz when they'd gone to the florist, and even to some degree during their one date, had dwindled. There were lots of smiles, lots of congrats, lots of schmoozers.

And what kind of crap was that?

It was one thing to have an academic understanding that they were getting married so that Helene Harris for Governor didn't take unnecessary hits, but it was another entirely to see it in action. Especially when he was starting to suspect that some of the issue had to do with what society perceived as his "bad taste" to have mixed it up with the wild Carpenter daughter.

He was fixing it for her. Not the other way around. What was just as crazy? He liked being her go-to guy. The dressing-down he'd given her father had felt good. No one deserved to be judged for a healthy sexual appetite when her partner was a consenting adult.

He needed to get the hell out of here and make some

wedding day memories at home, where his wife could do whatever she so desired without anyone knowing about it.

"Let's go," he growled in Roz's ear. "We've been social for like a million hours already. Everyone here can suck it."

"Including me?" Her gaze grew a hungry edge that had all kinds of appealing implications inside it, especially when she dragged it down his body. "Because coincidentally, that's exactly what I had in mind."

"Really?" His groin tightened so fast it made him light-headed.

"True story," she murmured. "Or didn't you get the memo earlier that I wasn't done?"

Wheeling, he waved at his mother and snagged Roz's hand to lead her to the limo that waited patiently for them at the curb of the North Ridge Country Club. He'd paid the wedding coordinator a hefty sum to manage the logistics of the reception; she could handle whatever came after the departure of the bride and groom.

The limo ride took far too long—a whole ten minutes, during which he kept his hands off Roz like a good boy because this time, he didn't want quick.

Slow would be the theme of his wedding night.

Except his wife smelled divine and she cuddled up next to him on the roomy leather seat, letting her fingers do some serious wandering over his lap. Strands of Roz's dark hair had pulled out of the bun-like thing at her crown, dripping down in sexy little tendrils, and all he could think about was how it had gotten that way—his fingers.

He'd like to tug on a few more strands while deep inside her.

By the time the limo pulled up to the house, which his housekeeper had lit up for their arrival, his hard-on could cut glass and his patience had started to unravel.

"Inside," he growled. "Now."

To help her along, he swept her up in his arms to carry her over the threshold because it seemed like a legit thing that people did on their wedding day. She snuggled down into his embrace, looping her arms around his neck, and then got busy testing out his ability to walk while she nibbled on the flesh near his ear. Her tongue flicked out, sending a shower of sparks down his throat, and he stumbled, catching himself immediately. Wouldn't do to drop his new wife.

"Unless you'd like our wedding night to be memorialized with a trip to the ER, I'd suggest waiting five seconds for any more of that," he advised her, which she pretty much ignored. Now that he was on to her and better able to compensate, he walked faster.

They cleared the double front door, barely, as she'd started exploring his collarbone with her lips. There was no way he was doing stairs in his current fully aroused, highly sensitized state, so he let her slide to the ground and hustled her to the second floor.

Roz beat him to the gargantuan master suite that he'd yet to christen properly. He shut the doors to the bedroom behind him. In Vegas, they'd had a strict rule that no surface would go untouched. His bedroom's decor had been pulled together by a professional and contained solid pieces stained with a shade of espresso that was so dark, it looked black. Not one Carpenter piece in the bunch, not even the woman beckoning him with a hooded, enigmatic expression that portrayed her very naughty thoughts.

Good God she was gorgeous in her white dress. She had the fullest lips that needed nothing extra to be lush and inviting. He could write poetry to her mouth for a decade. And her eyes…they did a thing where they were both transparent and mysterious all at the same time.

Would he ever get tired of her face? What if they were the kind of couple who actually stayed married on purpose, affording him the opportunity to watch her age? One day he might wake up and wonder where her looks had gone. But he didn't think so. She'd still be Roz inside and that was the part he wanted with a burning need he scarcely recognized.

And need was supposed to be his wheelhouse. When he couldn't quantify something related to sex, that was a problem. It felt too much like the intimacy that he religiously avoided.

No, the real problem was that they weren't having sex yet. Sex eliminated all of the weirdness with pure mechanics of pleasure. And while he was busy composing sonnets to his wife's beauty, she was standing there staring at him like he'd lost his mind, likely because he hadn't made a move on her yet.

Clearly, he was slightly insane. What was he waiting for?

Striding forward, he did the one thing he hadn't been able to do thus far. He spun his bride to face away from him, undid the catch on her zipper and yanked it down. The strapless dress peeled from her body, baring her back and oh, yeah, that was nice. Her spine beckoned and he bent to fuse his mouth to the ridges, working his way down until he hit the hollow above her buttocks. Laving at it, he adding some lip action until he earned a sharp little gasp from her.

This was what he'd come for. Blinding, carnal pleasure. All of the other internal noise? Not happening. The faster he got to a place where he couldn't think, the faster all of the stuff inside that shouldn't be there would fade.

That spurred him on enough to want more. Easing the dress down her hips, he pushed her gently, encouraging her to step out of it. That sexy little thong that he'd thus far only felt was indeed amazing in the light. It formed a vee down between her cheeks like an arrow pointing the way to paradise and he groaned as he recalled how much time he'd spent pleasuring her in that exact spot while in Vegas. It was worth a repeat for sure.

Falling to his knees, he slid his tongue beneath the lacy bands, following the dip down and back up again. He accompanied that with a leisurely exploration of the backs of her legs, ending with a nice tour of the covered area between her cheeks. That's when her legs started trembling, whether from excitement or exhaustion he couldn't be sure. He'd have to come back later.

Right now, his bride needed to be more comfortable. He had a lot more where that had come from.

He picked her up in his arms again and without the binding dress, it was so much easier. And more rewarding as her bare breasts were *right there* for his viewing pleasure. That was a much better place to focus his attention.

Laying her on the bed, he looked his fill as he stripped out of his own clothes, impressed that he'd found the stamina to take the time. The last sock hit the floor and the appreciation in Roz's gaze as she watched his show thoroughly stirred him.

The closet gymnastics had done nothing to take the edge off. Roz was dead wrong about that. He wanted her all over again with a fierce urgency that demanded absolute surrender.

Crawling across the mattress and up her body, he took the liberty of kissing his way to the perfect globes of her breasts, licking one bright, hard tip into his mouth. Her flesh rolled across his tongue. Divine. He sucked harder and she arched up off the bed with a tiny gasp. Not enough. Teeth against the tip, he scraped at it while plucking at the other one with his fingertips.

She felt exquisite in his hand. Silky. Excited. She pushed against his mouth, shoving her breast deeper, and he took it all, sucking her nipple against the roof of his mouth. That had driven her wild once before.

It did again. That simple movement got her thrashing under him, driving her hips against his painfully hard erection. The contact lit him up and felt so good, he ground into her stomach with tight circles. *Inside. Now.* His body was screaming for release, shooting instructions to his muscles to tilt her hips and drive to completion.

Not on the agenda. Not yet. He had to slow it down.

Grabbing her hips, he peeled away from her luscious body and kissed down the length of her stomach until he hit her thighs. That lacy thong covered her and as much as he hated to see it go, it went.

He pushed her legs open and kept going. Gorgeous. The faster he sated her, the slower he could go because she was making him insane with hip rolls that pushed her closer to him, obviously seeking relief from the fire that was licking through her veins.

Or maybe that was just him.

Her secrets spread wide, he paused just a moment to enjoy the visual, but she was having none of that.

"Put your mouth on me," she instructed throatily. "I've dreamed about your wicked hard tongue for weeks and weeks."

Oh yeah? That was enough of a compliment to spur him into action. The first lick exploded across his taste buds, earthy and so thick with her desire. For him. This was his wife, who was wet and slick *for him*. It was nearly spiritual. Why didn't they tell you the mere act of signing a piece of paper had so much significance?

That was a discovery best explored further through hands-on experience. Her juices flowed over his tongue as he drove deeper, added a finger to the party, swirled along her crease until she started bucking against his face and still she seemed to crave more.

He gave it to her, sliding a wet finger between her cheeks to toy with her while simultaneously working the nub at her pleasure center with his teeth. Her thighs clenched, and she rocked against his fingers, pushing them deeper, and then she came with a cry that vibrated through his gut.

That was not something he could possibly hear enough.

She sat up far before he would have said she'd had time to recover, pushed him free of her body and rolled him until she was on top. Looked like they were moving on. Noted. But he couldn't find a thing to complain about as she straddled his hips. She'd never taken off her white strappy stilettos and she parked one on each side of his thighs, easing her center into a place just south of where he really wanted it, but that fit with his need to go slow, so he let her.

He'd teased up a flush along her cheeks and her beautiful peaked nipples rode high on her breasts. As she stared down at him from her perch, she was the most gorgeous thing he'd ever seen, with those pursed lips and a sated sheen in her eyes that he'd been personally responsible for putting there.

He wanted to do it again. And again.

And finally, he could. He reached for her, but she shook her head, clamping her thighs tight against him as she laced his fingers with hers to draw his hands away from her body. She weighed practically nothing and it would be an easy matter to break free, but he was kind of curious what she had in mind that required him to stay still.

He found out when she released his fingers to trail her own down his torso until she reached his groin. All the breath whooshed from his lungs as she palmed him to stroke downward with one hard thrust.

Fire tore through his body in a maelstrom of need.

His eyelids flew shut as he struggled to breathe, to hold it together, to keep from exploding right there in her hand. She wasn't in a merciful mood obviously because she crawled backward to kneel over him, captured his gaze in her hot one, and licked him.

The sight of her pink tongue laving across his flesh nearly undid him. Then she sucked him fully into her mouth and he pulsed against her tongue and it was almost too much to hold back. He clawed back the release with some kind of superpower he had no idea he possessed.

Anti-Orgasm Man. He should get a T-shirt for his effort.

Except his wife had some powers of her own and worked him back into a frenzy in under a minute flat. This was going to be a very short honeymoon indeed if she didn't stop *this instant*.

"Whoa, sweetheart," he bit out hoarsely and tried to ease out from her mouth without catching his sensitized flesh on her teeth. She pushed him deeper into her throat in response, melting his bones in the process so it was really difficult to get his arms to work.

"Please," he begged as she swirled her tongue counterclockwise so fast that he felt the answering lick of heat explode outward clear to his toes. His head fell backward against the bed as his legs tensed and he genuinely had no clue what he was begging her to do—stop or keep going.

She took the decision out of his hands by purring with him deep in her mouth and the vibration was the tipping point. The release rushed through his veins, gathered at the base of his spine and pushed from his body like a tsunami, eating everything in its path. She took it all and more, massaging him to a brilliant finish that wrung him out. Spent, he collapsed back on the mattress, too drained to move.

"That was for following the rules," she told him with a smug laugh. "You deserve about ten more."

If he'd known that was the prize for proving to himself and everyone else that he could go without sex, it might have made the whole moratorium a lot easier. Without opening his eyes, he nodded. "You have my permission to proceed."

"Ha, I didn't mean right this minute."

She fell silent and the pause was so heavy that he opened his eyes. Roz was lounging on the bed between his thighs, decked out like a naked offering with one leg draped over his calf and an elbow crooked on the far side of his hip. It was the most erotic pose he'd ever seen in his life. And that was saying something considering the sizzle factor of the photograph she'd starred in.

"Thank you," she said. "For what you said to my father."

Her expression was so enigmatic, he couldn't do anything but let his own gaze travel over it in search of clues for what he should say next. *You're welcome* seemed highly lacking in weight given the catch he'd noted in her voice. Neither was this a conversation he wanted to have while in bed with a naked woman.

Except she wasn't any garden-variety naked woman that he had no plans to see again.

It was Roz. And he most definitely would be waking up with her in the morning. So many mornings that he was at a loss how to avoid the significant overtones of this kind of sex, where they were apparently going to talk about stuff between rounds of pleasure.

Maybe that was the key. He just had to move them along until they were back in a place where there was nothing but heat between them. Clearly he hadn't gotten her hot enough yet if she could still think about things outside of this room.

"Let's talk about that later, shall we?" he murmured.

The tendrils of hair around her face had increased exponentially and he itched to pull the entire mass free of its confines. So he indulged himself. Leaning up, he plucked pins from her dark hair. Slowly, he let chunks of hair fall to her shoulders, and the enigmatic, slightly guarded expression melted away.

Better. She deserved about ten more orgasms, too. Enough that she could only focus on how good he could make her feel and not the crappy stuff about her life that he had an inexplicable drive to fix for her.

"Tonight is about making up for lost time," he told her as the last pin fell free. "I thought I'd never see you again after Vegas. I can't lie. I wanted to."

Why had he blurted that out? They were supposed to be reeling back the true confessions, not throwing down more.

She blinked and let the tiniest lift of her lips register. "I'd like to say I forgot about you. I tried. Never happened."

And here they were. Married. It was something he was having difficulty reconciling in his mind when Roz fit so easily into the "hot fling" box in his head. Surely there had been a woman at some point in the past whom he'd seen more than once, but he couldn't recall the face of anyone but this one. She'd filled his thoughts so much over the past month or so that he suddenly feared he'd have a hard time getting her out when they divorced.

More sex needed, stat. Obviously. They were doing far too much chitchatting.

Reaching for her, he snagged her shoulders and hauled her up the length of his body, which went a long way toward reviving him for round two. She met him in a fiery kiss that shot sensation down his throat. Roz spread her legs to straddle him, this time hitting the exact spot he wanted her to be in, apparently on board with no more talking.

The heat built on itself instantly, putting urgency into their kisses, and the thrust of her tongue against his had sweet fire laced through it that he welcomed. This time, there was no need to go slow and he didn't waste the opportunity. Taking a half second to pull out the box of condoms he'd stashed in his bedside table in anticipation of their wedding night, he dove back onto her, rolling to put her under him so he could focus.

She needed oblivion. He could give her that. Taking her mouth in a fierce kiss, he let his hands roam over her amazing body, caressing whatever he could reach until she was moaning deep in her chest. Her blistering fingers closed around his erection, priming it, and then she reached for the condoms before he could. In what might be the hottest thing she'd done thus far, she rolled it on him, squeezing and teasing as she went, then notching him at her entrance.

He caught her gaze as he paused, savoring this moment before he plunged because it was his favorite. The anticipation built and she flexed her hips, eager for him but not taking the initiative, apparently content to let him go at his own pace.

Roz was his match in every way. The reality seeped through him as they stared at each other, their chests heaving with the exertion of holding back. And then he pushed inside and not even the feel of her mouth could match the exquisiteness of the way her silk caressed every millimeter. He sucked in a breath as she took him deeper, wrapping her legs around him to hold him inside.

The pressure and tension climbed until he had to move, to feel. Gasping, she arched against him, grazing her breasts against his torso, and that felt unbelievable, too. Sensation swirled, driving him faster and faster and she closed around him again and again, squeezing until she was crying out her pleasure. His second release built and she was still watching him, her eyes dark and sensual and so open that he fell into them, hopefully never to surface.

They exploded together and it was only as they came down, wrapped in each other's arms, that he realized that they'd done it missionary style, like a real couple. A first. He'd have said he hated that position but it had felt so right with Roz. Something warm lingered in his chest as he pushed hair out of her face. She kissed his temple and snuggled deeper into his embrace.

This was maybe the most sated he'd ever been in his life. And they hadn't even had sex that many times. Quantity had always been his goal in the past, but apparently quality trumped that. Because they'd gotten married? Because he knew they had tomorrow night and the next and the next, so he didn't have to cram all his appetites into a few hours?

Whatever it was, it felt different. He liked it. Who knew?

This was uncharted territory and he didn't quite know what to do with it. Sex hadn't decreased the intimacy quotient after all. But he'd always shied away from that because rejection wasn't something he dealt with well, or rather, more to the point, he'd never felt like finding out how well he'd deal with it.

His father had done such a thorough job of rejecting him that he'd lived most of his life with total hatred of a man he'd never met. That was what had made the pact with Jonas and Warren so easy. He had no interest in learning how much more it would hurt to be rejected by someone he'd fallen in love with. Obviously it had driven Marcus to a permanent solution. What made Hendrix so much more capable of handling the same?

The rational part of his brain kicked in. Honestly, he'd have to give a woman a chance to reject him in order to fully test that.

Had he been given an opportunity to do exactly that? Roz had been great so far in their relationship. Maybe she was the exception to the rule. Maybe he could test out having a little more with her...

He settled her a little closer, letting her warm him thoroughly, and snagged the sheet to cover them. They hadn't slept at all that night in Vegas, so this would be a first, too. Waking up with a woman had also been something he studiously avoided, but waking up with Roz held enormous appeal.

If "more" didn't work out, then they could get a divorce like they'd always planned. It was practically a foolproof experiment in something that he'd never have said he'd want but couldn't seem to stop himself from exploring.

Eight

Hendrix and Roz had opted not to go away for their honeymoon, largely because that was something real couples did. But also because Helene had already scheduled a splashy fundraiser, the biggest one of the summer, for four days after the wedding. The event was supposed to generate the majority of the money needed to push her campaign through to the election. In other words, it was a big deal.

Helene had specifically asked them to make an appearance so it didn't seem like they were hiding. *Go big or go home,* she'd said with a smile and Roz hadn't really been able to find a good argument against attending. Though she'd racked her brain for one because a big social event with plenty of opportunity for her to feel like she still wasn't good enough to be associated with the Harris name didn't sound like fun.

The afternoon of, Hendrix came home from work

early carrying a bag emblazoned with the name of an exclusive store that Roz knew only carried women's clothing. Intrigued, she eyed the bag.

"You entering a drag queen revue that I don't know about?" she asked from her perch on the lounger near the window of their bedroom. It was an enormous room in an even more enormous house that felt genuinely empty when her husband wasn't in it. Probably because it was his, not hers.

Or at least that was the excuse she kept telling herself so she didn't have to think about what it meant that she sometimes missed him. That she thought about him all day long and only some of it was sexual.

"Maybe." He waggled his brows. "Let's see if it fits."

He pulled the dress from a layer of tissue paper and held it up to his chest as she giggled over his antics. But then the dress fully unfurled, revealing what he'd picked out. Oh, God, it was gorgeous. Red, with a gold clasp at the waist that gathered the material close.

"I think it would fit me better than you," she said wryly. "Is this your subtle way of getting me excited about the idea of hanging out with North Carolina's movers and shakers?"

"Depends." He shot her an adorable smile that made her pulse beat a little strangely as the dress became the second-most-beautiful thing in the room. "Did it work?"

Oh, it worked all right, but not even close to the way he meant.

"Only if it goes with the gold shoes I have in my closet." She held out a hand for the gown because the whole thing felt inevitable. "I'll try it on. But I'm only wearing it because you picked it out."

The silk slid through her hands like water as she laid it on the couch, then stood to wiggle out of her pants and shirt. The dress was strapless on one side and came up into an elegant over-the-shoulder style on the other. It settled against her curves like it had been made for her and fell to the ground in a waterfall of red. A high slit revealed enough leg to raise some eyebrows, which she sincerely hoped Hendrix would use as a convenient way to get his hands on her during dinner.

"You look amazing," he said quietly and when she glanced at him, pride glinted from his eyes.

"You have good taste," she shot back, mystified why the compliment pleased her so much. The gift as a whole pleased her in ways she'd never have expected. No man had ever bought her clothes before. She'd never had a need for one to, nor would she have accepted such a gift from anyone else.

Sure, there was an agenda buried in the middle of his gesture. He needed her by his side at his mother's thing and now she couldn't use *I have nothing to wear* as an excuse to weasel out of it. But she didn't care. The dress fit like a dream, clearly indicating her husband paid attention to details, and the way he was looking at her made her feel desired more sharply than anything he'd done in their entire history. That was saying something.

She half expected him to reach for her, but he started chattering about something that had happened at work earlier as he stripped out of his suit, then went to take a shower. Too bad. She'd be happy to show up late but he wasn't on board with that.

The limo ride was uneventful and she started to get antsy. The wedding hadn't been too bad in terms of dirty looks and noses in the air. But she'd been the bride and it was practically a requirement that people treat her nicely on her wedding day. This fundraiser was a whole different ball game and she didn't often do this kind of society thing. For a reason.

Only for Helene would she brave it. And because Hendrix had done something so unexpected as buy her a dress.

"Nervous?" Hendrix murmured as they exited the limo. "I'll hold your hand."

"You're supposed to," she reminded him blithely. "Because we're married and making sure people are fully aware of that fact."

When he clasped her fingers in his, though, it didn't feel utilitarian. Especially when he glanced down at her and smiled like they shared a secret. "I'm also doing it because I want to."

That warmed her enormously. For about two minutes. Because that's when she saw her father. Whom she had not realized would be in attendance. Of course he'd wrangled an invitation to the premiere Helene Harris for Governor event of the season. Maybe Helene had even invited him of her own free will.

Roz's chest turned to ice.

"I wonder if there's a closet in this place," she said into Hendrix's ear with a little nuzzle. If she could entice him into a back hall, they could spend an hour there before anyone even noticed they'd arrived. Then there wouldn't be a big to-do about them disappearing, and she could get good and relaxed before braving the hypercritical looks and comments.

Hendrix smiled at a few people and snaked an arm around Roz, pulling her close. But instead of copping a feel, like she'd have laid odds on, he held her waist in a perfectly respectable fashion. "Maybe we'll look later."

"Maybe we should look now." She slid her own arm around his waist in kind, but let her hand drift south with a caress designed to remind him they were at their best when they were burning up with need for each other. Though why she had to be the aggressor in this situation, she wasn't quite sure.

Instead of shooting her a salacious grin that communicated all the naughty thoughts in his mind, he pulled her into a shadowy alcove away from the crush. Oh, this had possibilities. The area wasn't enclosed, but could be considered private. Emboldened, she slipped the button free on his tux jacket, gauging exactly how much cover it might provide if he had a mind to get handsy.

That got her a smile, but without much carnal heat laced through it. No worries. She could get him hot and bothered pretty quickly and let her fingers do some walking. But he just laced his fingers with hers and pulled them free of his body.

"Roz, come on."

That didn't sound like the precursor to a hot round of mutual orgasmic delight. "I'm trying to, but you're not helping any."

"Why do we always have to have sex in public?"

Agape, she stared at him. "I must not be doing it right if you have to ask that question."

"I'm being serious." Their fingers were still entwined and he brought one to his mouth to kiss the back of her hand tenderly. "There's no one on earth who gets me more excited than you. We're not talking about whether or not you have the ability to get me off, but why you're trying to do it in the middle of my mother's fundraiser."

Guilt put her back up. "I guess the thrill is gone. And so early in our marriage, too. I thought that didn't wear off until at least after the first year."

He rolled his eyes. "I literally just told you this is not a conversation about how much I desire you. I'm trying to figure out why you have a seemingly self-destructive need to have sex in public. That's what got us into this marriage in the first place."

So now all this was her fault? "There were two people in that hot tub, Hendrix."

"Willingly," he threw in far too fast and that pissed her off, too. "I'm not pushing blame onto you. I wasn't saying no as you pulled me into that closet at the wedding. But I am right now. Wait."

He tightened his grip on her fingers as he correctly guessed she was about to storm off to…somewhere that she hadn't quite worked out yet.

"Sweetheart, listen to me."

And she was so out of sorts that she did, despite knowing in her marrow she wasn't going to like what he had to say.

"You want me so badly that you can't wait?" he asked. "That's great. I want you like that, too. The problem is that we both use that heat as a distraction. From life, from…I don't know. Crap going on inside. Whatever it is, I don't want to do that anymore."

The earnestness in his expression, his tone, in the very stroke of his fingers over hers bled through her, catching on something so deep inside that it hurt. "I don't do that."

He didn't even have the grace to go along with the

lie. "You do. We're cut from the same cloth. Why do you think we were both so willing to go through with this marriage? We understand each other."

Oh, God. That was so true it nearly wrenched her heart from its mooring. If he made her cry, she was never going to forgive him. She'd spent *thirty minutes* on her makeup. "What are you saying?"

His smile did nothing to fix the stuff raging through her chest. "I'm saying let's take our sex life behind closed doors. Permanently. Let's make it about us. About discovering what we can be to each other besides a distraction."

"So there's no more chance of public humiliation, you mean?"

He shook his head, dashing the out she'd handed him. "No. Well, I mean, yes, of course that is a very good side benefit. But I'm talking about removing the reasons why we're both so good at creating scandals. Stop avoiding intimacy and get real with me. At home."

That was the worst idea she'd ever heard in her life. "You first."

He nodded. "I'm at the head of the line, sweetheart. Get in the queue behind me and let's do this ride the way it was intended."

Her lungs hitched. "You're not just talking about laying down a new no-sex-in-public rule. Are you?"

"I don't know what I'm talking about." He laughed self-consciously, finally releasing her fingers to run a hand through his hair. "All I know is that my mom asked me to get married so her campaign wouldn't take a hit and all I could think about was getting you into bed again. Then we made a mutual decision that sex was off the table until after the ceremony. It really made me think about who I want to be when I grow up. An oversexed player who can't control himself? I don't want to be that guy. Not with you."

Stunned, she blinked up at him but his expression didn't waver. He was serious about making changes and somehow, she was wrapped in the middle of all of it. Like maybe he wanted to be a better person because of her. That was… She didn't know what that was, had no experience with this kind of truth.

"So where does that leave us?" she whispered.

He tilted his head until their foreheads touched. "A married couple who's expected at a fundraiser. Can we get through that and then we'll talk?"

She nodded and the motion brought his head up just at the right angle to join their lips. The kiss had nothing to do with sex, nothing to do with heat. It was a sweet encapsulation of the entire conversation. A little tender, a little confused and so much better than she'd have ever dreamed.

Somehow, she floated along behind him as he led her back into the fray and the fact that they hadn't gotten naked meant something significant. Hell if she knew what. Later tonight, maybe she'd get a chance to find out.

Turned out that Roz hadn't actually needed the orgasm to relax after all. Hendrix held her hand like he'd promised and generally stuck by her side through the whole of the fundraiser. The evening wound to a close without one snide comment being wafted in her direction. Whether that was because Hendrix had studiously kept her far away from her father—a fact she couldn't help but notice and appreciate—or because the marriage had really worked to soften society's opinion toward them, she couldn't say.

Ultimately, the only thing that mattered was that she ended the evening on a high she hadn't felt in a long time. Not even sex could compete with the burst of pure gratitude racing through her veins as the limo wheeled them toward Hendrix's house. Their house. It was technically theirs, for now, as he was sharing it with her. No harm in claiming it as such, right?

"I think that was a success, don't you, Mr. Harris?" she commented as he held the door open for her to precede him.

He shut it with a resounding click. "I'm sorry, I missed everything you just said outside of 'Mr. Harris,'" he murmured and propelled her up the stairs with insistent hands on her hips.

She let him because it suited her to get to a place where they could pick up their discussion from earlier. "You like it when I call you Mr. Harris? I can do that a whole bunch more."

"I insist that you do."

Once in the bedroom he sat her down on the bed, knelt at her feet and took enormous care with removing her shoes, unbuckling the straps with painstakingly slow pulls, watching her as he did it. His gaze flickered as he finally slipped off one shoe and then the other. He lifted her arch to his mouth, kissing it sensuously.

It was such an unexpected move that something akin to nerves popped up, brewing inside until she had to say something to break the weird tension.

"We got through the fundraiser," she said. "Is this the part where we're going to talk?"

"Uh-huh," he purred against her foot and dragged his lips up her leg.

It happened to the be the one revealed by the slit that opened almost all the way to her hipbone, so he had a lot of real estate to cover. Her flesh heated under his mouth, sending an arrow of desire through her core.

"First," he said. "I'm going to tell you how absolutely wild you drive me. Are you listening?"

He nibbled at the skin of her thigh and slid a hand up the inside of her dress, exactly as she'd imagined he would—at the table while they were eating dinner. She'd envisioned it being a huge turn-on to have his hands under her dress while they were sitting there with members of high society, especially given how sanctimonious they'd all been about the photograph. And Hendrix had taken that possibility off the table and opened up a whole different world at the same time.

This wasn't a turn-on because she was putting one over on the high and mighty. It was a turn-on because of the man doing the caressing. Exactly as he'd suggested, taking their sex life behind closed doors put a sheen on the encounter that she couldn't recall ever having felt before.

"I hear you," she whispered. "Tell me more."

His fingers slid higher, slowly working their way toward the edge of her panties and then dipping underneath the hem to knuckle across her sex. She gasped as the contact sang through her, automatically widening her legs to give him plenty of access.

"Wild." He gathered her dress in one hand as he slid up the other leg to bunch the red silk at her thighs. "Do you have any concept of how difficult it was to tell you no at the fundraiser?"

"Seemed pretty easy to me," she mumbled and immediately felt like a selfish shrew. "But I'm sure it wasn't."

"No," he agreed far too graciously instead of calling her on her cattiness like he should have. "I carried around a boner for at least half the time. This dress…" He heaved a lusty sigh as he trailed a finger from the fabric gathered over her shoulder down over her breasts, which tightened deliciously from no more than that light touch. "I'm going to have to do this the right way."

"Because you have such a habit of doing it wrong?" she suggested sarcastically.

"I mean, I can't take it off. Not yet." He speared her with a glance so laden with heat and implications that her core went slick and achy instantly, even before he put his hands under the skirt and hooked her underwear, drawing off the damp scrap to toss it over his shoulder.

Pulling her to the edge of the bed, he spread her thighs and treated her to the deepest, wettest French kiss imaginable. A moan escaped her throat as he lit her up from the inside out, heat exploding along her skin as Hendrix set fire to every inch of her body. He closed his eyes as he pleasured her and she could scarcely look away from the raw need plastered all over his face.

It should be the other way around. He had his mouth on her in the most intimate of kisses, and she felt herself coming apart as she watched his tongue swirl through her folds. His fingers twined through the silk of her dress, the one he'd given her as a sweet, unexpected gift, and that gave everything a significance she scarcely understood.

The release rolled through her, made so much more powerful by the fact that he was letting her see how much she affected him. He was still telling her how wild he was over her, and she was still listening. When she came, she cried out his name, hands to his jaw because she couldn't stand not touching him as her flesh separated from her bones, breaking her into a million unrecoverable pieces.

His eyes blinked open, allowing him to witness it as she slid into oblivion and it was a horrible shame that he wasn't right there with her. She wanted that, wanted to watch him come apart with abandon.

"Make love to me," she murmured and guided his lips to hers for a kiss that tasted like earth and fire. It was elemental in all its glory and she wanted more.

He got out of his clothes fast enough to communicate how much he liked that suggestion but when he reached for her, she pulled him onto the bed in the same position she'd just been in and straddled him, still wearing the dress.

"I might never take it off again," she informed him as she settled against his groin, teasing him with her still-damp core. Hard, thick flesh met hers and she wanted him with a fierceness she could hardly contain.

He groaned as she arched her back, thrusting her covered breasts against his chest. "It feels divine."

And that was enough of a recommendation for her to keep going, exactly like this. She pulled a condom from the gathered place at her waist, which she'd stashed there earlier in hopes of finding a closet at the fundraiser, but this was far better.

His gaze reflected his agreement, going hot with understanding as he spied the package in her fingers.

"I see you attended the fundraiser fully prepared to go the distance."

"Yeah. But it's okay. This is exactly the way our evening was supposed to go." How he'd converted her, she still didn't know. But it sure felt like how this ride should be experienced. If it wasn't, she didn't want to know about it.

Condom in place, she slid down until they were joined and he was so deep inside that there was no room for anything else. He captured her gaze and held it for an eternity, even as he slid his arms around her to hold her tight. It was the most intimate position she'd ever been in with another human being and it was so beautiful her heart ached.

And then it got even better as they moved in tandem in a sensuous rolling rhythm unlike anything she'd ever felt. Her head tipped back as she rode the wave of sensation and Hendrix fused his mouth to her throat, suckling at her skin. He murmured things against it, telling her how much he liked the way she felt, how sexy she was. The pretty words infused her blood, heightening the experience.

The release split through her body almost before she'd realized it was imminent. It was quieter, deeper than the first one. More encompassing. She let it expand, grabbing on to the sensation because it was something she wanted to savor. Hendrix's expression went tense with his own release and he drew it out with a long kiss, perfectly in sync with her in a way she knew in her bones would never have happened if they'd banged each other in a closet.

This was something else, taking their relationship to the next level.

He picked her up and set her on her feet so he could finally remove the dress and then gathered her into his arms to lay spoon style under the covers. She didn't resist, couldn't have. She wanted all of this to be as real as it felt, but as she lay there in the dark listening to her husband breathe, her eyes refused to stay closed.

None of this was going to last. She'd forgotten that in the midst of letting Hendrix prove they could have a closed-door relationship. She'd forgotten that their marriage had become intimate long before they'd signed any papers and she'd let herself get swept away in the beauty he'd shown her.

She did use sex as a distraction, as an avoidance tactic. Because she hadn't wanted to be in this position. Ever. But she'd let him change the dynamic between them.

They were still getting a divorce. She *couldn't* forget that part because it was the theme of her life.

She lost everything important to her eventually and Hendrix fell into that category just as much as anything else. This wasn't the start of a new trend. Just the continuation of an old one that was destined to break her heart.

Nine

Helene made a rare appearance at the office, bringing a huge catered lunch with her that the employees all appreciated. Hendrix let her have her fun as the company still had her name on it even though she'd transitioned the CEO job to him long ago. As the last of the potato salad disappeared from the break room and the employees drifted back to their desks, Hendrix crossed his arms and leaned back on the counter to contemplate his mom.

"What gives?" he asked with a chin jerk at the mostly decimated spread. "You get a large donation or something?"

Her lips curved into the smile that never failed to make him feel like they were a team. At last, it seemed like they were back on solid ground again.

Sure, she smiled at everyone, because she had the sunniest personality of anyone he'd ever known, but she was still his mom no matter what and he valued their bond more than he could explain.

"Paul Carpenter dumped five million in my lap. You didn't have anything to do with that, did you?"

He shrugged, wishing he could say it was an act of generosity and that she shouldn't read anything into it, but odds were good the donation came with strings. Carpenter had another think coming, if so. Having the billionaire as a father-in-law hadn't checked out like he'd expected. It chafed something fierce to have his hopes realized of being aligned with a powerful old money family, only to find out the patriarch was an ass.

"Not even close. I don't like how he treats Roz. If you recall, I might have given him that impression the last time we spoke at the wedding."

"Well, he's not the only one with a giving soul. The fundraiser was a huge success. I came by to thank you for hanging out with us old people."

Hendrix snorted. The day Helene could be described as old had yet to come. She had boundless energy, a magnanimous spirit and could still give women half her age a run for their money. "You're only seventeen years older than me, so you can stop with the old business. And you're welcome."

"You know what this means, right?" Helene eyed him curiously. "Your marriage to Roz worked to smooth over the scandal. My approval ratings are high. Seems like you did it. I don't know how to say thank you for this enormous sacrifice you made for me."

He grinned to cover the slight pulse bobble at what his mother was really saying—he and Roz had

reached their goal much faster than originally anticipated. Her speech had all the hallmarks of what you
said as something was winding down. And he did not
want to think of his marriage that way. "It was really
my pleasure."

His mom stuck her fingers in her ears in mock exasperation. "I don't want to know. This time, keep your
sex life to yourself."

"I'm trying." And it was working well. So well, he
could scarcely believe how easily he'd slid deeper into
his relationship with Roz. They fit together seamlessly
and it was nearly too good to be true. Far too good to
be talking about ending it already. "I really like her."

God, was he fourteen again? He was an adult who
could surely find a better way to describe how his insides got a little brighter at the mere thought of his wife.
But what was he supposed to say about the woman he
woke up to every morning? Or about how he hadn't
yet figured out why his marriage *wasn't* making him
run screaming for the hills?

"I can tell," his mom said lightly. "I'm headed to see
her next. You wanna come with me?"

His eyebrows shot up automatically. "You're going
to see Roz?"

Helene and his wife weren't having lunch any longer
even though he'd told Roz repeatedly that it was fine
if she built a friendship with Helene. He still felt like
he'd nipped that relationship in the bud prematurely.
It didn't sit well and if they were mending the fences
he'd knocked down, he definitely didn't want to get
between them again.

"I am," she confirmed. "I can't put off my promise

to her any longer and still sleep at night. So I'm doing the clown thing. Full makeup and all."

"The press will eat it up," he promised and she nodded her agreement.

"Yes, I'm counting on it. It should be quite a circus, no pun intended."

He laughed, glad that despite the many other changes that had been forced on them over the years, they could still hang out and crack jokes with each other. He'd never censored one word to his mother and she was the one person he could be completely real with.

Well, not the only one. He could be real with Roz. He'd never censored anything he'd said to her either, a first. Usually he watched what he said to women because who wanted to give false expectations? But his relationship with Roz required absolute honesty from the get-go and it was a facet of their relationship he hadn't fully appreciated until now.

Tomorrow if he woke up and knew with certainty that he was done, he just had to announce it was time to file for divorce and she'd say okay. It was freeing to know he never had to pull punches with the woman he was sleeping with.

Not so freeing to be contemplating the fact that he'd practically been handed permission to bring up that divorce. He wasn't ready to think about that. They hadn't been married that long and surely Helene would want them to see this thing through a little while longer. Just to be absolutely certain that a divorce wouldn't undo all the good they'd done already.

"I have to admit, I'm intrigued by the whole clown idea," he told her. "But I have that presentation on restructuring the supply chain and I need to do a thorough sweep of the warehouse like I've been threatening to do for weeks."

Helene wrinkled her nose. "That sounds boring."

"Because it is. Being the CEO isn't all curly wigs and water-squirting flowers." Neither was being a political candidate, but she knew he was kidding.

"That's the benefit of being the boss," she reminded him and pushed him ahead of her out of the break room where his admin had started cleaning up the leftover boxes. "You can leave the boring stuff for another day and come watch me be a clown. It's for a good cause. And it's an opportunity to be seen with your lovely bride in a stellar photo op where everyone will not only be dressed but overdressed."

Seeing Roz in the middle of the day for no other reason than because he wanted to held enormous appeal that he chose not to examine too closely. And it was coupled with an opportunity to see what she did on a daily basis unobtrusively. He did have a certain curiosity about her charity. Because…*clowns*. It was such a strange thing to be passionate about.

"Sold." He buttoned his suit jacket. "Let me—"

"Not one foot in your office or you'll never emerge." Helene looped an arm through the crook of his elbow and tugged. "Ride with me in my car. We'll drop you off back here to get your car later."

And that was how he found himself at Carolina Presbyterian Hospital with his mother in clown makeup. The children's ward was a lively place, if not a little depressing. Easy to see why clowns might make the whole thing a tiny bit less awful. God willing, he'd never have to personally empathize with what these families were going through. He made a mental note to write Roz a check, which he should have done a long time ago.

He snuck a glance at Roz from the corner of his eye as he lounged in the spot he'd reserved for himself, which was well out of the way, yet afforded him a front-row seat for the show. His wife was gorgeous, focused and quite possibly the tensest he'd ever seen her, including the time they'd braved the florist, their wedding reception and, his least favorite, the encounter with her father in the hall after nearly being caught with their pants down.

Either she didn't like that he'd accompanied his mother or she was worried that something was going to go wrong with this once-in-a-lifetime opportunity to get buzz for her charity.

While Helene entertained the kids with stuffed animals she'd carried into the hospital in a big bag, Hendrix edged toward Roz, who had yet to acknowledge his existence. Not that he was nursing a teeny bit of hurt over that or anything.

"Hey," he murmured, mindful of the two separate news crews that were covering the gubernatorial candidate's foray into the world of therapy clowning, a thing he'd had no idea had a name, but apparently did.

"Hey." Her mouth pinched back into a straight line that he immediately wanted to kiss away.

Definitely tense and dang it if it wasn't on the tip of his tongue to suggest they find a closet somewhere because she was wound tight. But they weren't *that couple* any longer. For a reason. So he'd have to handle his wife's tension verbally. "You have a problem with me being here?"

KAT CANTRELL   151

"What?" She glanced at him and then immediately flicked her gaze back to Helene. "No. I don't care. It's a free country."

Which was the kind of thing you said when you *did* care but hadn't planned on letting anyone else in on the secret.

"Your shoes are too tight?" he guessed but she didn't smile at the joke.

"This is a big deal, Hendrix. I'm allowed to be nervous."

The sarcasm lacing the edge of her words was pure Roz, but he'd spent far too much time in her company to accept her comment as pure truth. She wasn't nervous. Tense, yes. But it wasn't nerves.

And like what had happened at their engagement party, he was nothing if not painfully aware that he could read her so easily because he was paying attention to *her*, not how best to get under that severe suit she'd donned like armor.

"She's doing fine," he told her with a nod toward his mom. "Come get some coffee with me."

Roz shot him another side-eyed glance, as if afraid to take her gaze off Helene for one second. "I can't leave. This is my charity on the line."

"On the line?" he repeated. "Like if Mom does the wrong thing, it's all going to collapse? You know no one is going to stop letting you do clowns just because she fails to make one of the kids smile, right?"

Her shoulders rolled back a couple of times as if she couldn't find a comfortable stance. "Maybe not. But maybe it's all going to collapse for other reasons."

That wasn't the fierce Rosalind Carpenter he knew. "If it does, that's not on you."

"It is," she hissed back under her breath. "Why do you think I needed your mother in the first place? Not because I thought kids would like to meet the woman who may be the governor by January."

"Will be," he corrected automatically because there was no way Helene was going to fail to reach her goal, not if he had anything to say about it. After all, he'd signed a marriage license to ensure that his mom got to move into the Governor's Mansion. The fact that his marriage had become so much more still wasn't something he had a handle on. "Why don't you clue me in on why Helene is really here if it's not to bring joy to some sick kids?"

Roz's eyes snapped shut and her chest heaved a couple of times through some deep breaths. "Actually, coffee would be good."

Despite being certain she'd found yet another avoidance tactic since she couldn't use sex, he nodded once and put a hand to her waist to guide her out of the room. After all, coffee had been his suggestion, but not because he'd intended to give her an out. It was a little uncomfortable to realize that while he might not be censoring his words with her, that didn't mean she was returning the favor.

And he wanted to know what was swirling beneath her skin. He wanted to know *her*. They might be on the downslide, but he couldn't contemplate letting her go, not right now. There was still too much to explore here.

Instead of taking her to the cafeteria where the coffee would be weak and tepid, he texted his driver to hit the Starbucks on the corner, then found the most private corner in the surprisingly busy children's ward.

He let Roz choose her seat and then took the opposite one.

She stared out the window, and he stared at her. The severe hairstyle she'd chosen pulled at her lush features, but nothing could change the radiance that gave her such a traffic-stopping face. When he'd left her this morning, she'd still been in bed, her long dark hair tumbling over her shoulders the way he liked it.

But he didn't think she'd appreciate it if he pulled the pins free right here in the middle of the hospital. "Coffee's on its way."

She nodded. "Thanks. I need it."

"This is the conversation you want to have?"

Her mouth tightened. "I didn't want to have a conversation at all."

"But you needed the air," he guessed and her wince said he'd called it in one. "Roz, I'm not going to bite. If you want to talk to me, I'm not going anywhere. But if you don't, then let's sit here while you collect yourself. Then we'll go back and do clowns with no one the wiser that you had an anxiety attack or whatever."

Her double take was so sharp, it should have knocked her off the chair. "Anxiety attack? Is that what it looked like? Could you tell I was mid-freak-out? Oh, God. Did any of the cameras pick it up? They did. Of course they did. They're all over the place and—"

"Sweetheart, you need to breathe now." He gathered up both her hands in his and held them in his lap, rubbing at her wrists as he racked his brain for information about what he'd accidentally triggered with his random comment. "Breathe. Again. Roz. Look at me."

She did and no, he hadn't imagined the wild flare of her irises a moment ago. Something had her spooked.

But she was breathing as instructed, though the death grip she had on his hands would leave a mark, particularly where her wedding rings bit into his index finger. Didn't matter. He didn't have any intention of letting her go.

His driver appeared with two lattes, set them on the table and vanished quickly. Hendrix ignored the white-and-green cups in favor of his alternately white-and-green wife, who, if he didn't miss his guess, might actually be about to lose her lunch.

"Um…" How did you go about delicately asking your wife if she had a positive test result to discuss? "Are you feeling faint? Do I need to call a doctor?"

What if she *was* pregnant? A thousand different things flashed through his head in an instant. But only some of them were of the panicked variety. Some weren't that unpleasant. Some were maybe even a little bit awed and hopeful.

"Oh, God, no!" she burst out. "Please don't bother anyone. I'm fine."

"Of course you are," he murmured and rubbed at her wrists again. "But maybe you could give me a little more to go on as to why we're sitting here in the corner not drinking the hot coffee that I got for us?"

She slipped a hand from his before he was ready to lose the contact and palmed her cup, sipped at the contents and shot him a fake smile. "See? Drinking."

"See?" He waved a hand in front of his face. "Still sitting here in the dark about what's going on with you. Roz, we're married. I've touched you in the most intimate places. I've done more illicit, dirty, sinful things with you than with anyone else in my life. You fell asleep in my arms last night. What is all of that but a demonstration of trust? There is nothing you can say to me that would change—"

"I'm afraid of clowns."

Oh, God. Now it was out there and Roz had nowhere to hide. She'd blurted out her deepest secret and even worse, she'd done it in the middle of Helene's shot in the arm for Clown-Around.

Hendrix wasn't laughing. He should be. There was nothing scary about clowns. Especially not when it was her mother-in-law underneath the makeup. Geez, she'd half thought seeing Helene all dressed up would be the magic bullet to fix all of the crazy going on inside that had only gotten worse the more Roz forced herself to be around the source of her fear.

"Okay." Hendrix's beautiful eyes flashed as he removed the coffee from her grip and recaptured her hand. As if he knew that holding her in place was something she desperately needed but didn't know how to ask for. "That's not what I thought you were going to say."

"No, probably not." Her mouth twisted into a wry smile designed to disguise the fact that she wished she could cry. "I wasn't expecting me to say it, either. It's dumb, I know."

He shook his head fiercely. "No. What's dumb is that you're holding all of it inside when I'm here. Tell me what I can do, sweetheart."

That's when her heart fluttered so hard that there was no way it could possibly stay behind her rib cage. *Now* she was feeling light-headed and like she might need a doctor to fix whatever he'd just broken inside her.

"Hold my hand," she mumbled because what else was she supposed to say when his impassioned statements might loosen her tear ducts after all?

"I am. I'm not going to stop."

He wouldn't, either. Because he was Hendrix Harris, the hero of her story, who stood up to her father and had such a good relationship with his mother that he'd willingly marry the wild Carpenter daughter with seemingly nothing to personally gain from it. In bed, he worshipped Roz. Out of it, he talked her down. He was everything she'd never have said she wanted—but did—and that was pushing buttons inside that weren't meshing well with clowns.

But at least she didn't feel like she was standing on the edge of a mile-high cliff any longer, legs about to give out as the darkness yawned at her feet. She could breathe. Thanks to Hendrix.

"I started Clown-Around because I needed to stop being afraid." He didn't blink as she blurted out her second-biggest secret, and he didn't interrupt with a bunch of advice on how to fix it. "I really thought it was going to work."

"Facing your fears is a good step," he agreed and shut his mouth expectantly, as if to indicate this was still a conversation and it was her turn again. He was good at that and she didn't mistake it as anything other than a skill.

That or he was just good at being with *her*, and she might appreciate that even more.

It was the thing she clung to as she spilled out the story of her eight-year-old self missing an entire semester of school because no one could figure out how to tell her she wasn't allowed to sit at the bedside of her dying mother.

At first, they'd tried. Her nanny would drive her to school, only to get a call from the headmistress that Roz had snuck out again. Fortunately, her father had found her at the hospital before the police had gotten involved, but his mandate that she not try that trick again had only fueled her need to both defy him and spend time with her mother. Sneaking out of school became great practice for later, when she did it to hang out with boys nearly twice her age.

As she recalled all of it for Hendrix, she didn't leave any of it out, especially not the ugly parts because he deserved to know what was going on with her, as he'd asked to.

"She was so sick," Roz recalled, not bothering to wipe the stream of tears that finally flowed. They'd just be followed by more. "The chemo was almost worse than the cancer and they'd come to get her for the treatments. I wouldn't let her go. There were these clowns."

She shuddered involuntarily, but Hendrix didn't say anything, just kept rubbing a thumb over the pulse point of her wrist, which was oddly comforting.

"Every day, I imagined that I was helping draw all the poison from her body when I sat by her bedside and held her hand. But they wouldn't let me go with her to the treatments and when she came back, it was like they'd sucked a little more of her life away."

Verbalizing all of this was not helping. If anything, the absolute terror of it became that much fresher as she relived how the two clowns wrenched her hand out of her mother's, with their big fake smiles and balloon animal distractions. They'd been employed by the hospital administration to keep her out of the way as the staff tried to care for her mother. She knew that as a rational adult. But the associations in her head with clowns and the way her mother slipped away more and more each day—that association wasn't fading like the psychologists had said it would.

"And now you know the worst about me," she informed him blithely.

Instead of responding, he dashed away the tears from her cheeks with one thumb, still clinging to her other hand as promised. His strength was amazing, and definitely not a quality she'd have put on her top twenty when it came to men. It was a bonus, particularly since he had twenty out of twenty on the list of what she'd have said would embody her perfect man.

What was she going to do with him?

Divorce him, most likely. Her heart lurched as she forced herself to accept the reality that all of his solid, quiet strength, the strength that was currently holding her together, wasn't permanent. She didn't get to keep things. The clowns were a great big reminder of that, one she needed to heed well.

"So what you're telling me is," he drawled, "that the worst thing about you is that you went through an incredibly traumatic series of events as a child and clowns were in the middle of it. And now they freak you out. Stop me when I get to the part where I'm supposed to cast the first stone."

She rolled her eyes. Miraculously, the fact that he was cracking jokes allowed her to reel back the emotion and take a deep breath. "Yeah, okay. It's not on the same level as adultery. But it's still real and scary and—"

"Something we need to deal with," he cut in, his

gaze heavy on her with sympathy and tenderness. "And we will. You know what most people do with fears? They run really fast in the other direction. You started an extremely worthwhile charity while trying to deal with *your* fear. I don't think I've ever been more impressed with a human being in my life than I am with you right now."

Okay, not so much with reeling back the emotions then. The tears started up again as she stared at him. "It's not working, though, in case you missed that part."

He shook his head. "Doesn't matter. We'll try something else. What matters is that you're amazing and you can't erase that by throwing down your failures."

She hadn't done anything special. But he had. She felt hollowed out and refilled all at the same time, and Hendrix was the reason. That scared her more than anything else that had happened today. "I don't think I can go back in there."

Which wasn't the biggest issue but the only one that she could reasonably be expected to address at this point. It was also the most critical.

Nodding, he squeezed her hand. "That makes sense. The problem is that you want to."

How did he see the things inside her so clearly? It was as frustrating as it was extraordinary. It meant that she needed to watch herself around him. If she wasn't careful, he'd pick up on the way her insides were going mushy as he sat with her in the corner of the children's ward holding her hand when he had a multimillion-dollar business to run.

"The problem is that I need to," she corrected. "This is my charity. Your mother is helping me enormously by bringing credibility to my organization."

And it was doubtful she needed to explain that her credibility was lacking. He understood how scandals affected everything—regardless of whether you deserved it—far better than anyone else in her life.

"Here's an idea," he said casually. "Why don't you be a clown?"

"Say what?" But she'd heard him and the concept filtered through all the angst and fear and found a small snippet of reason, latching onto it with teeth. "You mean with makeup and everything?"

"Sure." He shrugged. "Maybe you haven't been able to fix your fear because you're too far away. You can't just get near your fears. You need to be inside them, ripping the things to shreds, blasting them apart internally."

"Oh, sure, because that's what you do?"

The sarcasm didn't even faze him. He cocked his head and stared straight down into her soul. "Married you, didn't I?"

Before she could get the first of many questions out around the lump in her throat, one of Helene's staffers interrupted them, shattering the intensely intimate moment. Good. They'd gotten way too deep when what she should be doing is creating distance. The last thing she wanted to hear was how freaked he'd been to lose his independence and how great it was that he had an imminent divorce to keep his fears of commitment at bay. It wasn't hard to imagine a player like Hendrix Harris with a little calendar in his head where he ticked off the days until he could shed his marriage.

It was *very* hard, however, to imagine how she'd handle it when that day came. Because losing him was a given and the longer this dragged on, the harder it was going to be to keep pretending she wasn't falling for him—which meant she should do herself a favor and cauterize the wound now.

Ten

Hendrix didn't get a chance to finish his conversation with Roz. Helene's stint as a clown ended faster than anyone would have liked when one of the patients took a scary turn for the worse. Hospital personnel cleared the area and a calm but firm nurse assured Helene that someone would update her on the little boy's status as soon as they knew something.

A somber note to end the day. Hendrix couldn't stop thinking about how short life was, the revelations Roz had made about her childhood and how to pick up their conversation without seeming insensitive. But his own fears that he'd mentioned were as relevant now as they had been before he'd agreed to this marriage.

Even so, he wanted to take a chance. With Roz. And he wanted to talk about how rejection wasn't something he handled well, air his fears the same way she had.

But she insisted that he go back to the office with his mom so she could take her car to Clown-Around's tiny storefront and finish some paperwork. He wasn't dense. He'd given her a lot to think about and she wanted to be alone. What kind of potential start to a real marriage would it give them if he pushed her into a discussion before she was ready?

Distracted, he went back to work but he couldn't concentrate, so he drove home early. The expressway was a mess. Bumper-to-bumper traffic greeted him with nothing but red taillights. Of course. Probably because he wasn't supposed to go home.

It didn't matter anyway. By the time he got there, Roz wasn't home yet. He prowled around at loose ends, wondering when the hell his house had turned into such a mausoleum that he couldn't be there by himself. He'd lived here alone for years and years. In fact, it was extremely rare for him to bring a woman home in the first place. Roz had been unique in more ways than one.

By the time Roz finally graced him with her presence, he'd eaten a bowl of cereal standing up in the kitchen, chewed the head off of his housekeeper because she'd dared suggest that he should sit at the empty dining room table, and rearranged the furniture in the living room that he'd used one time in the past year—at his engagement party.

In other words, nothing constructive. He had it bad and he wasn't happy about it.

Her key rattled in the lock and he pounced, swinging the door wide before she could get it open herself. Cleary startled, she stood on the doorstep clutching the key, hand still extended.

"I was waiting for you," he explained. Likely she'd

figured that out given his obvious eagerness. "You didn't say you'd be late."

A wariness snapped over her expression that wasn't typically part of her demeanor. "Was I supposed to?"

"No. I mean, we don't have that kind of deal, where you have to check in." Frustrated all at once for no reason, he stepped back to let her into the house. "You weren't late because of me, were you?"

She shook her head. "You mean because of our earlier conversation? No. You gave me advice that I appreciated. I appreciate a lot of things about you."

Well, if that didn't sound like a good segue, he didn't know what would. "I appreciate a lot of things about you, too. On that note, my mother told me earlier today that things are looking really good for her campaign. She thinks the marriage did exactly what it was supposed to."

Roz swept past him to head for the stairs, scarcely even pausing as she called over her shoulder, "That's great."

A prickle of unease moved down his spine as he followed her, even though he probably shouldn't. She'd come home late and didn't seem to be in a chatty mood. He needed to back off, but he couldn't help himself. This conversation was too important to wait.

"It is. It means that everything we hoped this marriage would do is happening. Has happened. Her donations are pouring in. She helped your charity, and while I guess we don't know the results of that yet—"

"It was amazing," she said flatly and blew through the door of the bedroom to sink onto the bed, where she removed her shoes with a completely blank expression on her face. "I had calls from three different hospitals looking to form long-term partnerships. Helene's already agreed to do a couple more go-rounds for me."

"Wow, that sounds…good?" Her tone had all the inflection of a wet noodle, so he was flying blind.

"Yeah, it's good." She shut her eyes for a beat, pointedly not looking at him. "Things are going well for her. She told me that too when I called her. So we should probably talk about our exit strategy. It may be a little premature, but it's coming faster than I'd assumed and I'd really like to get started on it."

Exit strategy? "You mean the divorce?"

The word tasted nasty in his mouth as he spit it out. It reverberated through his chest, and he didn't like the feeling of emptiness that it caused. A divorce was not what he wanted. Not yet. Not before he'd figured out how to step through the minefield his marriage had become. He couldn't fathom giving up Roz but neither did he want to come right out and say that. For a lot of reasons.

The pact being first and foremost. It weighed so heavy on his mind that it was a wonder his brain wasn't sliding out through his nose.

She glanced up at him for the first time since walking through the door. "I was thinking it might be safe for me to move back to my loft. I miss it. This house is nice but it's not mine, you know?"

He nodded even though he didn't know. Hell, if she'd wanted to live at her loft while they were married, he would have accommodated that. They'd chosen his house for their marital experiment because it had historical significance and there was a possibility they'd do a lot of entertaining.

That possibility still existed. This conversation was

extremely premature, in fact. They couldn't get a divorce tonight.

But all at once, he wasn't sure that was his biggest problem. The divorce was merely symbolic of what was happening faster than he could wrap his hands around—the end of his marriage. "You're thinking of moving back to your loft soon?"

She shrugged. "Maybe tomorrow. No one is really paying attention to us anymore now that we're a respectable married couple. It would hardly raise eyebrows if anyone realized I didn't live here anymore."

"It might." The first tendrils of panic started winding through his chest. Roz was already halfway out the door and he hadn't had one second to sort through what he hoped to say in order to get her to stay. "I think it would be a mistake to split up too early. We might still be called on to attend one of my mother's functions. It would look weird if we weren't there as a couple."

"I don't know." Roz rubbed at her forehead again as if this whole conversation was giving her a headache. "I got the impression from your mother everything was fine. Maybe I don't need to be there."

Maybe I need you there.

But he couldn't force his tongue to form the words. What if she said too bad or laughed? If she really cared about him the way he cared about her, she wouldn't have even brought up the divorce. She'd have left that conspicuously out of the conversation. For the first time, she wasn't so easy to read and he was definitely paying attention to *her*, not her panties.

He'd had enough practice at it over the course of their engagement and marriage that it was second nature now to shove any physical needs to the back-

ground while he focused on what was happening between them. He didn't need the ache in his chest to
remind him that what was happening had all the hallmarks of the end.

Because he'd taken public sex off the menu of their
marriage? Surely not. The ache in his chest intensified
as he contemplated her. What a not-so-funny paradox
that would be if he'd ruined their relationship by at-
tempting to remove all possibility of scandal. Actually,
that was irony at its finest if so. They had a marriage
built on sex. Only. Just like he would have sworn up
and down was perfect for him. Who wouldn't want
that? He was married to a hot woman that he got to
sleep with at night. But apparently that wasn't enough
for her to stick around.

What would be? The continued irony was that he
wasn't even talking to her about that. Couldn't even
open his mouth and say *I'm falling for you.*

If he didn't use the word *love* in that sentence, he
wasn't breaking the pact, right?

He was skating a fine line between a mutual agreement to end an amicable fixer marriage and laying his
heart on the line for her to stomp all over it—and the
way this was going, the latter felt like more and more
of a possibility.

That couldn't happen if he didn't let on how this
conversation had the potential to rip him to shreds.

"We don't have to get divorced right away. What's
the hurry? Why not let it ride for a while longer," he
said casually as if his entire body wasn't frozen.

She blinked at him. "What would be the point?"

What indeed? All at once, the ache in his chest grew
way too strong to bear. Wasn't she the slightest bit sad

at the thought of losing what was great about them? The parts that were great were really great. The parts that were bad were…what? There *were* no bad parts. So what was her hurry?

"Because we enjoy each other's company and like the idea of being married?"

She recoiled. "You mean sex."

"Well, sure." Too late, he realized that was probably not the smartest thing to say as her expression closed in. "Not solely that."

But of course she knew as well as he did that sex was what they were both good at. What they'd started their relationship with. What else was there?

The black swirl in his gut answered that statement. There was a lot more here—on his side. But she didn't seem overly interested in hearing about that, nor did she jump up in a big hurry to reciprocate with declarations of her own about what elements of their marriage she might wish could continue.

"I can't, Hendrix," she said simply.

And without any elaboration on her part, his world fell apart.

It was every bit the rejection he'd been so careful to guard against. The only saving grace being that she didn't know how much those three words had sliced through all of his internal organs.

It wasn't Roz's fault that he'd hoped for something legit to come out of this marriage and ended up disillusioned. It was his. And he had to step into the role she'd cast for him whether he liked the idea of being Rosalind Carpenter's ex-husband or not.

It was fine. He still had a decade-long friendship with Jonas and Warren that wasn't in any danger. That was the place he truly belonged and it was enough. His ridiculous need for something real and legitimate with Roz was nothing but a pipe dream.

They didn't talk about it again, and neither did they settle back into the relationship they'd had for that brief period after the wedding. Hendrix hated the distance, he hated that he was such a chicken, hated that Roz didn't seem overly upset about any of it. He moped around until the weekend, when it all got very real.

While Roz packed up her clothes and personal items, Hendrix elected to be somewhere other than the house. He drove around Raleigh aimlessly and somehow ended up at his mother's curb on Cowper Drive, where she lived in a gorgeous house that he'd helped her select. It was Saturday, so odds were good that she was at some event cutting a ribbon or kissing some babies as she rallied the voters. But he texted her just in case and for the first time in what felt like a long while, fate smiled on him. She was home.

He rang the doorbell. Brookes, the head of his mother's security, answered the door. Hendrix nodded at the man whom he'd personally vetted before allowing him anywhere near Helene. Brookes had checked out in every way. On more than one occasion, Hendrix had wondered if there was something a little more than security going on between Brookes and his mom, but she'd denied it.

Given his reaction when Helene and Roz had lunch, he wouldn't have handled sharing his mother in that respect very well, either. He made a mental note to mention to his mother that he'd recently become aware that he was a selfish crybaby when it came to anyone intruding on his territory, and that maybe she should think about dating anyway despite her son's shortcomings.

"Hey, you," his mother called as she came out of her study wearing a crisp summer suit that had no wrinkles, a feat only someone as stylish as Helene could pull off. "I've got thirty minutes before I have to leave for brunch. Unless you want to be my plus one?"

He shrugged. What else did have to do besides watch the best thing that had ever happened to him walk out of his life? "I could do worse."

Her brows drew together as she contemplated him. "What's wrong, sweetie?"

"Why does something have to be wrong?"

She flicked a subtle hand at Brookes, who vanished into the other room. "Not that I don't enjoy seeing you, but when you come by on a Saturday and start talking about a date with your mother like it's a good thing, I'm concerned. Spill it. Did you have a fight with Roz?"

"No fight." There would have to be a difference of opinion for there to be a fight and he'd agreed with every word she'd said. There was no point to continuing this farce of a marriage. "You said yourself that things were fine with your campaign. You even went out of your way to tell us both that. So what else would be the natural conclusion to a fixer marriage but a fast, no-fault divorce once the problem is fixed?"

Besides, he was pretty sure the black swirl in his gut that wouldn't ease meant he'd been right all along to never have a woman in his bed twice. Better all the way around not to fight Roz on her insistence that it was over. What was he supposed to do, open himself up for exactly the same kind of rejection that had devastated Marcus?

His friends wouldn't have an ounce of sympathy for him either, not after he'd violated the pact. Jonas at least might have had some understanding if Hendrix had managed to find someone who loved him back like Jonas had. Warren wouldn't even let him get the first sentence out and would get started on his own brand of rejection. Hendrix would be dealing with Roz's evisceration *and* lose his friends.

Thankfully, he hadn't even tried.

His mother cocked her head. "So, what? You're done with Roz and thought you'd hang out with your mom for the rest of your life?"

"Sure. What's wrong with that?"

He and his mother were a unit. The real kind. Maybe not peanut butter and jelly, but better because they'd been there for each other over the years when neither of them had anyone else. His mom would never reject him.

Nor did she have a life of her own with someone great who took care of her. Guilt swamped him as he wondered if he had something to do with that.

"For a Harris, you're being a moron," she said coolly. "I told you and Roz that my campaign was fine because I wanted to take that out of the equation."

"Well, congrats. You did and now we have no reason to be married. What else would you have expected to be the outcome of that?"

"A marriage, Hendrix. A real one. I didn't come up with the idea of you marrying Roz *solely* to save my campaign. It was a great benefit and I genuinely appreciate it. But I want to see you happy. She's it for you, honey. I could see it in the photograph."

"What you saw was chemistry," he countered flatly before the hopeful part inside could latch onto the idea that he'd missed something crucial in this whole messy scenario. "We have it. In spades. But there's nothing else there."

"That's ridiculous. You might have figured out a way to lie to yourself, but I have thirty years of practice in reading you. I saw you two together. I listened to Roz talk about you. There's more."

On *his* side. Sure. Not hers.

"Doesn't matter," he growled. "She's out. She told me straight to my face that it was over. Unless you're suggesting that I should resort to chaining her up in the basement, I have to accept that it's indeed over. I wasn't given a choice."

Clearly exasperated, Helene fisted her hands on her hips and despite the fact that he'd been taller than her since he'd turned seventeen, she managed to tower over him. "So, let me get this straight. You told her that you were in love with her and that you might have married her to fix the scandal, but now you'd like to see what it looks like if you stay married because you want to. And she said 'forget it, I'm out'?"

He shifted uncomfortably. How had his mother conjured up the perfect speech to describe the things in his heart when he couldn't have spit out those words at gunpoint? "Yeah. Basically. Except not quite like that."

Or at all like that. He hadn't given her the opportunity to hear those things because it was better not to lay it all out. Saying that stuff out loud meant Roz could counter it easily. Who wanted that kind of out-right rejection?

"You didn't tell her, did you?" His mother's gentle tone still had plenty of censure in it.

"I don't deal well with rejection," he mumbled.

"Call Channel Five. There's a newsflash for you."

Her sarcasm wasn't lost on him. The fact that he hadn't told Roz meant he *never* had to deal with it. Instead, he was hiding at his mother's house.

He didn't deal well with relationships, either. He'd spent the whole of his life yearning to belong and holding on with a death grip where he did eke out a place. Neither had led to a healthy balance.

"You don't deal well with it because you have no experience with it. Plus it sucks," she told him. "No one wants to stand in line to let another person hand out pain and misery. But sweetie, Roz makes you happy, not miserable. Why don't you want to fight for that?"

"My father…" He swallowed. He hadn't mentioned the bastard in probably fifteen years and he didn't like doing it now, especially as his mother's mouth tightened. "He didn't even know me and he rejected me. How much worse would it be if I told Roz that I wanted to stay married and she said no anyway?"

"Let me ask you this. How bad does it hurt now?"

Horrifically bad. Worse than he'd allowed himself to admit. Talking about it wasn't helping. "Pretty much like a constant stomach ache."

She rubbed at his arm in that comforting way that only moms knew how to do. "That's also what it will feel like if she says no. So you'd be no worse off. But if you tell her and she says yes, how much better will that feel? Also, you should remember that your father didn't reject you. He rejected me. You didn't even exist yet, not as a real live person he could look in the face and then say he didn't want. You can't let someone else's mistakes cause you to make mistakes of your own."

"You think letting Roz go is a mistake?" His gut was screaming *yes* at a million and five decibels, drowning out the very excellent points his mother was making.

"The important question is whether you think that. But I wouldn't have encouraged you to marry her if I didn't think she could be much more than a mechanism to fix a problem. I'm shocked you didn't realize that already." His mother's voice broke unexpectedly and he glanced at her to see tears gathering in the corners of her eyes. "Just when you think your kid can't surprise you… You really were doing this whole thing for me, weren't you?"

He scowled. "Of course. Well, at first. You're the only mom I have and you're the greatest. Why wouldn't I do anything you needed from me?"

It hadn't hurt that marrying Roz on a temporary basis gave him the perfect excuse to avoid rejection. Too bad it hadn't worked out that way.

"Good answer." She grinned through her tears and then turned him toward the door with a little push. "Now I need you to go home and tell Roz to stop packing because you have important stuff to tell her. Do that for me and at some point in the future we'll laugh about how you almost really screwed this up."

His spirit lightened so fast that it made his head spin. She made something hard sound so easy. Hendrix took two steps toward the door and then stopped. "What if—"

"What-ifs are for losers who can't carry the name

Harris, sweetie. In other words, not you." She hustled him toward the door in an almost comical one-two shuffle. "I didn't raise a coward and I'm not going to be satisfied until I have grandbabies. So just keep that in mind."

Babies. The same emotions reappeared that had flooded him back at the hospital when he'd had a small suspicion Roz might be sick for reasons that had nothing to do with clowns. That might have been the clincher. He was too far gone to do anything other than take his mother's advice. "More favors? Marriage wasn't enough for you?"

"That's right. And more important, it's not enough for you, either. Chop, chop. I have a brunch to get to."

His mother closed the door behind him and he got all the way to his car before letting loose with the smile he'd been fighting. Helene Harris was one-of-a-kind. And so was his wife. He had to take a chance and tell her how he felt about her, or he'd never forgive himself. This was his best shot at being a part of something that made him happy and he'd given it a pass instead of fighting for it.

Hopefully, Roz was still at home so he could convince her to stay for reasons that had nothing to do with sex and everything to do with a promise of forever.

The moving company Roz had called made short work of transporting the boxes of clothes, shoes and other personal items she'd taken to Hendrix's house. Good thing. She wasn't in any mood to handle logistics right now.

Hendrix had left earlier, probably to go celebrate his forthcoming independence, and the fact that he was gone was good, too. She could leave without an extended goodbye that would likely yank more tears from her depths that she didn't want to lose. The first and second crying jags of the morning had already depleted what small amount of energy she still had after packing the boxes.

What was wrong with her? There had never been a scenario where she wasn't going to lose this marriage. Why was it hitting her so hard? Because she hadn't prepared properly for it to end? Maybe because it had ended so quickly, with almost no protest from the man she'd married, never mind that she'd stupidly begun to hope things might turn out differently.

That was the problem. She'd fallen into this bit of wonderful she'd found with Hendrix and forgotten it would soon vanish like so many other things in her life.

The moving truck pulled away from the front of Hendrix's Oakwood home and there was nothing left for Roz to do except follow it to her loft. Except she couldn't force herself to pull into the parking garage. She kept driving. The moving company had preauthorization with her building security and they were professionals who didn't need a neurotic, weepy woman supervising them.

Clown-Around could always use more attention. The boost Helene had given the organization surpassed Roz's wildest dreams. Becoming a Harris had launched her into a place that being a Carpenter had never touched. In more ways than one. The thought of how often she'd been *touched* as a Harris depressed her thoroughly.

The paperwork on her desk held zero appeal. She scouted around her tiny office for something else to do, finally landing in the supply closet. It could use organizing. All of the clown makeup and props had fallen into disarray after Helene had stopped by, and frankly, the last thing Roz had wanted to do was surround herself with the trappings that still held so many horrible memories.

But she was already so out of sorts that for once, the wigs lining overhead shelves and the multicolored outfits on hangers at her back didn't bother her. They were just costumes. Easily donned and easily taken off. She grabbed one of the wigs and stuck it on her head.

See? Easy. Not scary. Just some fake curly hair in an outrageous color.

All at once, she sank to the ground and put her face in her hands as the sheer weight of everything overwhelmed her.

Clowns hadn't taken her mother from her. Cancer had. For that matter, no one in a red nose had forced her father to stop caring about her—unless she was doing something he disapproved of, which he cared about plenty. Floppy shoes had done nothing to get her in trouble or bring down society's censure over a racy photograph. She'd done all of that on her own.

Clowns weren't the problem. She was. She'd assigned so much blame to the crappy hand fate had dealt her as a child that she'd practically let it ruin her life. It was only because luck had handed her Hendrix Harris on a silver platter that anything good had happened.

She didn't want that to be over. She didn't want to live each day scared to death to assign importance to the man she'd married. Most of all, she wanted to know what it felt like to know she could wake up each day next to someone who got her. Someone who loved her.

She'd been so busy looking for the hammer about to drop on her happiness that she hadn't considered the possibility that there was no hammer. Hendrix had even said they could put off the divorce, yet she'd let herself become convinced it was better to get it over with rather than see what might happen if she stopped assuming the worst. Maybe they could have tried being married for a few more weeks and let things develop. Go a little deeper.

If only Hendrix was here, she'd tell him that's what she wanted before she lost her nerve.

A chime sounded at the front door as someone pushed it open. Great. She'd forgotten to lock it again. She had to get better at remembering that or else move her offices to a more secure location. Anyone could wander in off the street.

But when she popped out of the closet, cell phone in hand in case she needed to dial 911, the nerves in her fingers went completely numb. The phone slipped from her grip and clattered to the parquet flooring.

As if she'd conjured him, Hendrix stood just inside the door, as gorgeous in a pair of jeans and a T-shirt as he was out of them. Because he had the same smile on his face regardless, the one that he was aiming at her now. The same one that had flushed through her on that dance floor at the Calypso Room a million years ago when she'd first caught sight of him.

"Hendrix Harris," she'd murmured then. And now apparently, as she realized she'd spoken out loud.

"Rosalind Harris," he returned easily, which was not even close to what he'd said to her that night in Vegas but almost made her swoon in a similar fashion. "I like what you've done with your hair."

Her fingers flew to her head and met the clown wig. Oh, God. She started to pull it off and then defiantly dropped her hand. "I'm practicing."

"To be a clown?"

She shook her head. "Facing down my shortcomings. How did you know I was here?"

Which was only the first of a whole slew of other questions, ones that she couldn't seem to get out around the lump in her throat. Hendrix was so close that she could reach out and touch him. She almost did. But she'd given up that right because she was an idiot, clearly.

"I didn't. I went to your loft first but the moving guys said they hadn't seen you. So it was worth a shot to come here. I saw your car outside."

"You were looking for me? That's funny. I…" *Need to tell you some things.* But she had no idea how to take the first step. When she'd wished he was here so she could say what was in her heart, she hadn't actually thought that would happen. He was so beautiful and smelled so delicious and familiar that her muscles had frozen. "You could have called."

"I wasn't sure what I was going to say. I, um, drove around a lot so I could practice." His smile reappeared. "I guess we're both doing that today."

Oddly, the fact that he seemed nervous and unable to figure out how to navigate either melted her heart. And gave her the slimmest glimmer of insight that maybe she'd been completely wrong about everything. "Were you practicing something like, 'watching my mom at the hospital made me realize I have a lifelong dream to be a clown'? Because that can be arranged."

Instead of laughing or throwing out a joke of his

own, he feathered a thumb across her cheek. "More like I messed up and let you pack all your stuff so you could leave me, when that's not what I want."

Her whole body froze. Except for her heart. That was beating a mile a minute as something bright fluttered through it. "It's not?"

He shook his head once, never letting go of her gaze. "You're my peanut butter *and* my jelly. Without you, I've got two useless pieces of bread that taste like sawdust. I want a chance to see what kind of marriage we can have without all the extra baggage. I mean, not to put too much pressure on you all at once." He hesitated, looking so miserable that she feared he would stop saying these beautiful things. "I'm trying to say that I want—"

"I love you," she blurted out. Oh, God. What was wrong with her that she couldn't stop behaving like a dimwit when it came to this man? "Not that *I'm* trying to put pressure on *you*—"

"I love you, too," he broke in and she was pretty sure the dazed look on his face was reflected on her own. "I'm changing my answer."

"Because you're a dimwit, too?" Maybe she should stop talking. "I mean, I'm a dimwit. Not you. I was scared that I was going to lose you—"

"No, you're right," he agreed readily. "I'm a complete and total dimwit. I have a problem with rejection so I try really hard to avoid it."

"I wasn't— I mean, I would never reject…" Except for when she'd told him she couldn't stay. She should have stayed. What if he'd never come looking for her? She would have missed out on the best thing that had ever happened to her. "I messed up, too. A lot. I should have told you I was falling for you and that I didn't want a divorce."

Something tender filtered through his gaze. "Funny, that's exactly what I practiced saying to you in the car as I drove around the whole of Raleigh. You stole my line."

"So that's it then? I don't want a divorce, you don't want a divorce. We love each other and we're staying married?" It sounded too good to be true, like a situation ripe for being ripped from her hands. Her pulse wobbled. This was the part where she had to calm down and face her fears like an adult who could handle her life. "I have a hard time trusting that all good things aren't about to come to an instant end."

She swallowed the rest, wishing he'd run true to form and interrupt her with his own revelations. But that didn't happen. He did hold out his hand and when she clasped it, the way he squeezed back was better than any time he'd ever touched her, bar none. Because it was encouraging, accepting. A show of solidarity. *I'm here and I'm not going anywhere*, he said without saying a word.

That loosened her tongue fast. A multitude of emotions poured out as she explained how clowns and cancer and rebellion and marriage had all tumbled together in her head. How she wasn't afraid any longer. She wrapped it up by pointing to the wig. "I'm inside my fears. Blasting them apart where they live. You gave me that. That, along with about a million other reasons, is why I can tell you I love you."

Sure, she still didn't want to lose him but she had absolute faith that if that ever did happen—regardless of the reason—she'd find a way to be okay.

"My turn." Hendrix reached up and plucked the wig off of her head, then plopped it onto his own. "This is the approved method to work through all this stuff, right?"

She nodded as the tears spilled over. "You look like a dork."

He just grinned and patted his red curly hair. "I look like a man who has finally figured out the key to dealing with the idiotic crap running through his head. I almost gave you up without a fight because I was convinced you were going to say thanks but no thanks if I brought up the things I was feeling. Color me shocked that you beat me to it."

"Not sorry."

"I'm just going to insist that you let me say 'I love you' first from now on."

"That's a much better marriage deal than the first one you offered me. I accept." Roz fished her wedding rings from her pocket and handed them to him solemnly. "As long as we both shall live?"

He better. She wasn't a serial wife. This was forever and she knew beyond a shadow of a doubt that she'd love him until the day she died.

He slid the cool bands onto her third finger and it was a thousand times more meaningful than the actual wedding ceremony. "I do."

Epilogue

Jonas and Warren were already seated in the corner booth when Hendrix arrived—late, because his wife had been very unwilling to let him out of the shower.

"This seems familiar," he joked as he slid into the seat next to Jonas and raised his brows at Warren. "Down to you being buried in your phone."

Warren glanced up from the lit screen and then immediately back down. "I like my job. I won't apologize for it."

"I like my job too but I like conversing with real people, as well," Hendrix shot back mildly, well aware that he was stalling. "Maybe you could try it?"

With a sigh, Warren laid his precious link to Flying Squirrel, his energy drink company, facedown on the table. "I'm dealing with a crap-ton of issues that have no solution, but okay. Let's talk about the Blue Devils why don't we? Or maybe the Hornets? What's the topic du jour, guys?"

Hendrix picked up his beer and set it back down again. There was no easy way to do this, so he just ripped the Band-Aid off. "I'm not divorcing Roz."

A thundercloud drifted over Warren's face as Jonas started laughing.

"I knew it." Warren put his head in his hands with a moan. "You fell in love with her, didn't you?"

"It's not that big of a deal." Hendrix scowled at his friend, knowing full well that it was a big deal to him. "Jonas did it, too."

Warren drained his beer, his mouth tight against the glass as his throat worked. He put the glass down with a *thunk*. "And both of you are really stretching my forgiveness gene."

"It was a shock to me too, if that helps."

"It doesn't."

Jonas put a comforting hand on Warren's arm. "It's okay, you'll find yourself in this same situation and see how hard it is to fight what you're feeling."

"I'll never go against the pact," Warren countered fiercely, his voice rising above the thumping music and happy hour crowd. "There were—are—reasons we made that pact. You guys are completely dishonoring Marcus's memory."

Marcus had been a coward. Hendrix had only recently begun to reframe his thoughts on the matter, but after seeing a coward's face in the mirror for the length of time it had taken for him to figure out that love wasn't the problem, he knew a little better what cowardice looked like. "Maybe we should talk about those reasons."

Instead of agreeing like a rational person might, Warren slid from the booth and dropped his phone into his pocket. "I can't do this now."

Hendrix and Jonas watched him stride from the bar like the hounds of hell were nipping at his heels. Dealing with rejection did suck, no two ways about it. But he was getting better at it because he wasn't a coward, not any longer. He was a Harris through and through, every bit his mother's child. Helene had raised him with her own special blend of Southern grit and he'd turned out okay despite never knowing his father. He was done letting that disappointment drive him to make mistakes.

"Welcome to the club." Solemnly, Jonas clinked his glass to Hendrix's and they drank to their respective marriages that had both turned out to be love matches in spite of their bone-headedness.

"Thanks. I hate to say it, but being a member of that club means I really don't want to sit around in a bar with you when I could be at home with my wife."

Jonas grinned. "As I agree with the sentiment, you can say it twice."

Hendrix made it to his house in Oakwood in record time. Their house. His and Roz's. She'd moved back in and put her loft up for sale even though he'd told her at least four times that he'd move in with her. His Oakwood place was a legitimate house but wherever Roz was made it home.

He found her in the bedroom, spread across the bed. Naked.

"Thought you'd never get here," she murmured throatily. "I was about to send you a selfie to hurry you along."

"So our next scandal can be a phone-hack leak of our personal photo album?" His clothes hit the floor in under thirty seconds.

"No more scandals. We're a respectable married couple, remember?" Roz squealed as he flipped her over on the bed and crawled up the length of her back.

"Only in public. Behind closed doors, all bets are off."

She shuddered under his tongue and arched in pleasure. "See what you've done to me? I'm a total sex addict, thanks to you. Before we got married, I was in the running for most pious fiancée alive."

"Not sorry." As much as he enjoyed Roz's back, he liked her front a lot better. That's where her eyes were and he'd discovered a wealth of intimacy in them when they made love, an act which he planned to repeat a million more times. He rolled her in his arms and sank into her.

She was his favorite part of being married.

* * * * *

THE GIRL HE NEVER NOTICED

LINDSAY ARMSTRONG

CHAPTER ONE

'MISS MONTROSE,' Cameron Hillier said, 'where the hell is my date?'

Liz Montrose raised her eyebrows. 'I have no idea, Mr Hillier. How should I?'

'Because it's your job—you're my diary secretary, aren't you?'

Liz stared at Cam Hillier, as he was known, with her nostrils slightly pinched. She didn't know him well. She'd only been in this position for a week and a half, and only because an agency had supplied her to fill the gap created by his regular diary secretary's illness. But even that short time had been long enough to discover that he could be difficult, demanding and arrogant.

What was she supposed to do about the apparent non-appearance of his date, though?

She looked around a little wildly. They were in the outer office—his secretary Molly Swanson's domain—and Molly, heaven bless her, Liz thought, was holding a phone receiver out to her and making gestures behind his back.

'Uh, I'll just check,' Liz said to her boss.

He shrugged and walked back into his office.

'What's her name?' Liz whispered to Molly as she took the phone.

'Portia Pengelly.'

Liz grimaced, then frowned. 'Not the model and TV star?'

Molly nodded at the same time as someone answered the phone.

'Uh—Miss Pengelly?' Liz said down the line and, on receiving confirmation, went on, 'Miss Pengelly, I'm calling on behalf of Mr Hillier, Mr Cameron Hillier...'

Two minutes later she handed the receiver back to Molly, her face a study of someone caught between laughter and disaster.

'What?' Molly queried.

'She'd rather go out with a two-timing snake! How can I tell him that?'

Cam Hillier's office was minimalist: a thick green carpet, ivory slatted blinds at the windows, a broad oak desk with a green leather chair behind it and two smaller ones in front of it. Liz thought it was uncluttered and restful, although the art on the walls reflected two of the very different and not necessarily restful enterprises that had made him a multi-millionaire—horses and a fishing fleet.

There were silver-framed paintings of stallions, mares and foals. There were seascapes with trawlers in them—trawlers with their nets out and flocks of seagulls around them.

Liz had studied these pictures in her boss's absence and

discovered a curious and common theme: Shakespeare.
The three stallions portrayed were called Hamlet,
Prospero and Othello. The trawlers were named *Miss
Miranda*, *Juliet's Joy*, *As You Like It*, *Cordelia's Catch*
and so on.

She would, she felt, like to know where the
Shakespeare theme came from. But the thing was you
did not take Cam Hillier lightly or engage in idle chit-
chat with him. She'd been made aware of this before
she'd laid eyes on him. The employment agency she
worked for had warned her that he was an extremely
high-powered businessman and not easy to handle, so
if she had any reservations about how to cope with a
man like that she should not even consider the position. They'd also warned her that 'diary secretary' could
cover a multitude of sins.

But she'd coped with a variety of high-powered businessmen before; in fact she seemed to have a gift for
it. Though, it crossed her mind that she'd never had to
tell any of those men that the woman in their life would
rather consort with a snake...

And there was another difference with Cam Hillier.
He was young—early thirties at the most—he was extremely fit, and he was—well, she'd heard it said by his
female accountant: 'In an indefinable way he's as sexy
as hell.'

What was so indefinable about it? she'd wondered at
the time. He was tall, lean and rangy, with broad shoulders. He had thick dark hair, and deep, brooding blue
eyes in not a precisely handsome face, true, but those

eyes alone could send a shiver down your spine as they summed you up.

In fact, to her annoyance, Liz had to admit that she was not immune to Cam Hillier's powerfully masculine presence. Nor could she persuade her mind to discard the cameo-like memory that had brought this home to her…

It was a hot Sydney day as they walked side by side down a crowded pavement to a meeting. They were walking because it was only two blocks from his offices to their destination. The traffic was roaring past, the tall buildings of the CBD were creating a canyon-like effect and the sidewalk was crowded when Liz caught her heel on an uneven paver.

She staggered, and would have fallen, but he grabbed her and held her with his hands on her shoulders until she regained her balance.

'Th-thanks,' she stammered.

'OK?' He looked down at her with an eyebrow lifted.

'Fine,' she lied. Because she was anything but fine. Out of nowhere she was deeply affected by the feel of his hands on her, deeply affected by his closeness, by how tall he was, how wide his shoulders were, how thick his dark hair was.

Above all, she was stunned by the unfurling sensations that ran through her body under the impact of being so close to Cam Hillier.

She did have the presence of mind to lower her lashes swiftly so he couldn't read her eyes; she would have

been mortified if she'd blushed or given any other in-
dication of her disarray.

He dropped his hands and they walked on.

Since that day Liz had been particularly careful in her
boss's presence not to trip or do anything that could trigger those sensations again. If Cam Hillier had noticed
anything he'd given no sign of it—which, of course, had
been helpful. Not so helpful was the tiny voice from
somewhere inside her that didn't appreciate her having
the status of a robot where he was concerned.

She'd been shocked when that thought had surfaced.
She'd told herself she'd have hated him if he'd acted
in any way outside the employer/employee range; she
couldn't believe she was even thinking it!

And finally she'd filed the incident away under
the label of 'momentary aberration', even though she
couldn't quite command herself to banish it entirely.

But somewhat to her surprise—considering the conflicting emotions she was subject to, considering the fact
that although Cam Hillier could be a maddening boss
he had a crooked grin that was quite a revelation—she'd
managed to cope with the job with her usual savoir-faire
for the most part.

He wasn't smiling now as he looked up from the
papers he was studying and raised an eyebrow at her.

'Miss Pengelly…' Liz began, and swallowed. *Miss
Pengelly regrets?* In all honesty she couldn't say that.
Miss Pengelly sends her regards? Portia certainly hadn't
done that! 'Uh—she's not coming. Miss Pengelly isn't,'
she added, in case there was any misunderstanding.

Cam Hillier twitched his eyebrows together and swore under his breath. 'Just like that?' he shot at Liz.

'Er—more or less.' Liz felt her cheeks warm a little.

Cam studied her keenly, then that crooked grin played across his lips and was gone almost before it had begun. 'I see,' he said gravely. 'I'm sorry if you were embarrassed, but the thing is—you'll have to come in her place.'

'I certainly will not!' It was out before Liz could stop herself.

'Why not? It's only a cocktail party.'

Liz breathed unevenly. 'Precisely. Why can't you go on your own?'

'I don't like going to parties on my own. I tend to get mobbed. Portia,' he said with some exasperation, 'was brilliant at deflecting unwanted advances. They took one look at her and I guess—' he shrugged '—felt the competition was just too great.'

Liz blinked. 'Is that all she was…?' She tailed off and gestured, as if to say *strike that*… 'Look here, Mr Hillier,' she said instead, 'if your diary secretary—the one I'm replacing—were here, you wouldn't be able to take *him* along to ward off the…unwanted advances.'

'True,' he agreed. 'But Roger would have been able to find me someone.'

Liz compressed her lips as she thought with distaste, *rent-an-escort*? 'Well, I can't do that either,' she said tartly, and was struck by another line of defence. 'And I certainly don't have Portia Pengelly's…er…powers of repelling boarders.'

Cam Hillier got up and strolled round his desk. 'Oh, I

don't know about that.' He sat on the corner of the desk and studied her—particularly her scraped-back hair and her horn-rimmed glasses. 'You're very fair, aren't you?' he murmured.

'What's that got to do with it?' Liz enquired tartly, and added as she looked down at her elegant but essentially plain ivory linen dress, 'Anyway, I'm not dressed for a party!'

He shrugged. 'You'll do. In fact, those light blue eyes, that fair hair and the severe outfit give you quite an "Ice Queen" aura. Just as effective in its own way as Portia, I'd say.'

Liz felt herself literally swell with anger, and had to take some deep breaths. But almost immediately her desire to slap his face and walk out was tempered by the thought that she was to be very well paid for the month she'd agreed to work for him. And also tempered by the thought that walking out—not to mention striking him—would place a question mark if not a huge black mark against her record with the employment agency...

He watched and waited attentively.

She muttered something under her breath and said audibly, but coolly, 'I'll come. But purely on an employer/employee basis—and I'll need a few minutes to freshen up.'

What she saw in his eyes then—a wicked little glint of amusement—did not improve her mood, but he stood up and said only, 'Thank you, Miss Montrose. I appreciate this gesture. I'll meet you in the foyer in fifteen minutes.'

* * *

Liz washed her face and hands in the staff bathroom—a symphony of mottled black marble and wide, well-lit mirrors. She was still simmering with annoyance, and not only that. She was seriously offended, she discovered—and dying to bite back!

She stared at herself in the mirror. It was on purpose that she dressed formally but plainly for work, but it was not how she always dressed. She happened to have a mother who was a brilliant dressmaker. And the little ivory dress she wore happened to have a silk jacket that went with it. Moreover, she'd picked up the jacket from the dry cleaner's during her lunch hour, and it had been hanging since then, in its plastic shroud, on the back of her office door. It was now hanging on the back of the bathroom door.

She stared at it, then lifted it down, pulled off the plastic and slipped it on. It had wide shoulders, a round neck, a narrow waist and flared slightly over her hips. She pushed the long fitted sleeves up, as the fashion of the moment dictated, but the impact of it came as much from the material as the style—a shadowy leopard skin pattern in blue, black and silver. It was unusual and stunning.

She smiled faintly at the difference it made to her—a bit like Joseph's amazing coloured coat, she thought wryly. Because her image now was much closer to that of a cocktail-party-goer rather than an office girl. Well, almost, she temporised, and slipped the jacket off—only to hesitate for another moment as she hung it up carefully.

Then she made up her mind.

She reached up and pulled the pins out of hair. It tumbled to just above her shoulders in a fair, blunt-cut curtain. She took off her glasses and reached into her purse for her contact lenses. She applied them delicately from the pad of her forefinger. Then she got out her little make-up purse and inspected the contents—she only used the minimum during the day, so she didn't have a lot to work with, but there was eyeshadow and mascara and some lip gloss.

She went to work on her eyes and again, as she stood back to study her image, the difference was quite startling. She sprayed on some perfume, brushed her hair, then tossed her head to give it a slightly tousled look and slipped the jacket on again, doing it up with its concealed hooks and eyes. Her shoes, fortunately, were pewter-grey suede and went with the jacket perfectly.

She stood back one last time and was pleased with what she saw. But she stopped and frowned suddenly.

Did she look like an ice queen? If only he knew…

Cam Hillier was in the foyer talking to Molly when Liz walked in. He had his back to her, but he saw Molly's eyes widen as she looked past him and he swung round.

For a moment he didn't recognise Liz. Then she saw him do a double-take and he whistled softly. It was something she would have found extremely satisfying except for one thing. He also allowed his blue gaze to drift down her body, to linger on her legs, and then he looked back into her eyes in the way that men let women know they were being summed up as bed partners.

To her annoyance that pointed, slow drift of assessment up and down her body reignited those sensations she'd experienced when she'd tripped on the pavement: accelerated breathing, a rush through her senses, an awareness of how tall and beautifully made he was.

Only thanks to her lingering resentment did she manage not to blush. She even tilted her chin at him instead.

'I see,' he said gravely. He shoved his hands in his trouser pockets before adding equally gravely, although she didn't for a moment imagine it was genuine. 'I'm sorry if I offended you, Miss Montrose. I was not to know you could look like this—stunning, in other words. Nor was I to know that you could conjure *haute couture* clothes out of thin air.' He studied her jacket for a moment, then looked into her eyes. 'OK. Let's go.'

They reached the cocktail party venue in record time. This was partly due to the power and manoeuvrability of his car, a graphite-blue Aston Martin, and partly due to his skill as a driver and his knowledge of the back streets so he'd been able to avoid the after-work Sydney traffic.

Liz had refused to clutch the armrest, or demonstrate any form of nerves, but she did say when they pulled up and he killed the motor, 'I think you missed your calling, Mr Hillier. You should be driving Formula One cars.'

'I did. In my misspent youth,' he replied easily. 'It got a bit boring.'

'Well, I couldn't call that drive boring. But you can't park here, can you?'

He'd pulled up in the driveway of the house next door to what she could see was a mansion behind a high wall that was lit up like a birthday cake and obviously the party venue.

'It's not a problem,' he murmured.

'But what if the owner wants to get in or out?' she queried.

'The owner is out,' he replied.

Liz shrugged and surveyed the scene again.

She knew they were in Bellevue Hill, one of Sydney's classiest suburbs, and she knew she was in for a classy event. None of it appealed to her in the slightest.

'All right.' She reached for the door handle. 'Shall we get this over and done with?'

'Just a moment,' Cam Hillier said dryly. 'I've acknowledged that I may have offended you—I've apologised. And you, with this stunning metamorphosis, have clearly had the last laugh. Is there any reason, therefore, for you to look so disapproving? Like a minder—or a governess.'

Liz flushed faintly and was struck speechless.

'What exactly do you disapprove of?' he queried.

Liz found her tongue. 'If you really want to know—'

'I do,' he broke in to assure her.

She opened her mouth, then bit her lip. 'Nothing. It's not my place to approve or otherwise. There.' She widened her eyes, straightened her spine and squared her shoulders, slipping her hair delicately behind her ears. Lastly she did some facial gymnastics, and then turned to him. 'How's that?'

Cam Hillier stared at her expressionlessly for a long moment and a curious thing happened. In the close confines of the car it wasn't disapproval that threaded through the air between them, but an awareness of each other.

Liz found herself conscious again of the width of his shoulders beneath the jacket of his charcoal suit, worn with a green shirt and a darker green tie. She was aware of the little lines beside his mouth and that clever, brooding dark blue gaze.

Not only that, but she seemed to be more sensitive to textures—such as the beautiful quality fabric of his suit and the rich leather of the car's upholstery.

And she was very aware of the way he was watching her… A physical summing up again, that brought her out in little goosebumps—because they were so close it was impossible, she suddenly found, not to imagine his arms around her, his hand in her hair, his mouth on hers.

She turned away abruptly.

He said nothing but opened his door. Liz did the same and got out without his assistance.

Although Liz had been fully aware she was in for a classy event, what she saw as she stepped through the front door of the Bellevue Hill home almost took her breath away. A broad stone-flagged passage led to the first of three descending terraces and a magnificent view of Sydney Harbour in the last of the daylight. Flaming braziers lit the terraces, pottery urns were laden with exotic flowering shrubs, and on the third and lowest terrace an aquamarine pool appeared to flow over the edge.

There were a lot of guests already assembled—an animated throng—the women making a bouquet of colours as well. In a corner of the middle terrace an energetic band was making African music with a mesmerising rhythm and the soft but fascinating throb of drums.

A dinner-suited waiter wearing white gloves was at their side immediately, offering champagne.

Liz was about to decline, but Cam simply put a glass in her hand. No sooner had he done so than their hostess descended on them.

She was a tall, striking woman, wearing a rose-pink caftan and a quantity of gold and diamond jewellery. Her silver hair was streaked with pink.

'My dear Cam,' she enthused as she came up to them, 'I thought you weren't coming!' She turned to Liz and her eyebrows shot up. 'But who is this?'

'This, Narelle, is Liz Montrose. Liz, may I introduce you to Narelle Hastings?'

Liz extended her hand and murmured, 'How do you do?'

'Very well, my dear, very well,' Narelle Hastings replied as she summed Liz up speedily and expertly, taking in not only her fair looks but her stylish outfit. 'So you've supplanted Portia?'

'Not at all,' Cam Hillier responded. 'Portia has had second thoughts about me, and since Liz is replacing

Roger who is off sick at the moment, I press-ganged her into coming rather than being partnerless. That's all.'

'Darling,' Narelle said fondly to him, 'call it what you will, but don't expect me to believe it gospel and verse.' She turned to Liz. 'You're far too lovely to be just a sec-retary, my dear, and in his own way Cam's not bad either. It is what makes the world go round. But anyway—' she turned back to Cam '—how's Archie?'

'A nervous wreck. Wenonah's puppies are due any day.'

Narelle Hastings chuckled. 'Give him my love. Oh! Excuse me! Some more latecomers. And don't forget,' she said to Liz, 'life wasn't meant to be all work and no play, so enjoy yourself with Cam while you can!' And she wandered off.

'Don't tell me how to look,' Liz warned him.

'Wouldn't dream of it. Uh—Narelle can be a little eccentric.'

'Even so, I knew this wasn't a good idea,' she added darkly.

He studied her, then shrugged. 'I don't see it as a matter of great importance.'

Liz glanced sideways at him, as if to say *you wouldn't*! But that was a mistake, because she was suddenly con-scious again of just how dangerously attractive Cameron Hillier was. Tall and dark, with that fine-tuned physique, he effortlessly drew the eyes of many of the women around them. Was it so far off the mark to imagine him being mobbed? No, that was ridiculous…

'It's not your reputation that's at stake,' she retorted finally. 'That was probably…' She paused.

'Ruined years ago?' he suggested.

Liz grimaced and looked away, thinking again, belatedly, of black marks on her record. *Did not actually come to blows with temporary employer, but did insult him by suggesting he had a questionable reputation...*

'This place is quite amazing,' she said, switching to a conversational tone, and she took a sip of champagne. 'Is the party in aid of any special event?'

Cam Hillier raised his eyebrows in some surprise at this change of pace on her part, then looked amused. 'Uh—probably not. Narelle never needs an excuse to throw a party. She's a pillar of the social scene.'

'How...interesting,' Liz said politely.

'You don't agree with holding a party just for the sake of it?' he queried.

'Did I say that? If you can afford it—' She broke off and shrugged.

'You didn't say it, but I got the feeling you were thinking it. By the way, she happens to be my great-aunt.'

Liz looked rueful and took another sip of champagne. 'Thanks.'

He looked a question at her.

'For telling me that. I...sometimes I have a problem with...with speaking my mind,' she admitted. 'But I would never say anything less than complimentary about someone's great-aunt.'

This time Cam Hillier did more than flash that crooked grin; he laughed.

'What's funny about that?'

'I'm not sure,' he returned, still looking amused. 'Confirmation of what I suspected? That you can be outspoken to a fault. Or the fact that you regard great-aunts as somehow sacred?'

Liz grimaced. 'I guess it did sound a bit odd, but you know what I mean. In general I don't like to get personal.'

He looked sceptical, but chose not to explain why. He said, 'Narelle can look after herself better than most. But how come you appear to handle a position that requires great diplomacy with ease when you have a problem with outspokenness?'

'Yes, well, it's been a bit of a mystery to me at times,' she conceded. 'Although I have been told it can be quite refreshing. But of course I do try to rein it in.'

'Not with me, though?' he suggested.

Liz studied her glass and took another sip. 'To be honest, Mr Hillier, I've never before been told to pass on the message that my employer's…um…date would rather consort with a two-timing snake than go to a party with him.'

Cam Hillier whistled softly. 'She must have been steamed up about something!'

'Yes—*you*. Then there was your own assertion that to go to a party alone would leave you open to being mobbed by women—I had a bit of difficulty with that—'

'It's my money,' he broke in.

'Uh-huh? Like your great-aunt, I won't take that one as gospel and verse either,' Liz said with considerable irony, and flinched as a flashlight went off. 'Add to that the distinct possibility that we could be now tagged as an item, and throw into the mix that death-defying drive through the back streets of Sydney, is it any wonder I'm having trouble holding my tongue?'

'Probably not,' he conceded. 'Would you like to leave the job forthwith?'

'Ah,' Liz said, and studied her glass, a little surprised to see that it was half empty, before raising her blue eyes to his. 'Actually, no. I need the money. So if we could just get back to office hours, and the more usual kind of insanity that goes with a diary secretary's position, I'd appreciate it.'

He considered for a moment. 'How old are you, and how did you get this job—with the agency, I mean?'

'I'm twenty-four, and I have a degree in Business Management. I topped the class, which you may find hard to believe—but it's true.'

He narrowed his gaze. 'I don't. I realised you were as bright as a tack from the way you handled yourself in the first few hours of our relationship—our *working* relationship,' he said as she looked set to take issue with him.

'Oh?' Liz looked surprised. 'How so?'

'Remember the Fortune proposal—the seafood marketing one? I virtually tossed it in your lap the first day, because it was incomplete, and told you to fix it?'

Liz nodded. 'I do,' she said dryly.

He smiled. 'Throwing you in at the deep end and not what you were employed for anyway? Possibly. But I saw you study it, and then I happened to hear you on the phone to Fortune with your summation of it and what needed to be done to fix it. I was impressed.'

Liz took another sip of champagne. 'Well, thanks.'

'And Molly tells me you're a bit of an IT whiz.'

'Not really—but I do like computers and software,' she responded.

'It does lead me to wonder why you're temping rather than carving out a career for yourself,' he said meditatively.

Liz looked around.

A few couples had started to dance, and she was suddenly consumed by a desire to be free to do what she liked—which at this moment was to surrender herself to the African beat, the call of the drums and the wild. To be free of problems… To have a partner to dance with, to talk to, to share things with. Someone to help her lighten the load she was carrying.

Someone to help her live a bit. It was so long since she'd danced—so long since she'd let her hair down, so to speak—she'd forgotten what it was like…

As if drawn by a magnet her gaze came back to her escort, to find him looking down at her with a faint frown in his eyes and also an unspoken question. For one amazed moment she thought he was going to ask her to dance with him. That was followed by another amazed moment as she pictured herself moving into his arms and letting her body sway to the music.

Had he guessed which way her thoughts were heading? And if so, how? she wondered. Had there been a link forged between them now that he'd noticed her as a woman and not a robot—a mental link as well as a physical one?

She looked away as a tremor of alarm ran through her. She didn't want to be linked to a man, did she? She

didn't want to go through that again. She was mad to
have allowed Cam Hillier to taunt her into showing him
she wasn't just a stick of office furniture…

She said the first thing that came to mind to break
any mental link… 'Who's Archie?'

'My nephew.'

'He sounds like an animal lover.'

'He is.'

Liz waited for a moment, but it became obvious Cam
Hillier was not prepared to be more forthcoming on the
subject of his nephew.

Liz lifted her shoulders and looked out over the
crowd.

Then her gaze sharpened, and widened, as she focused on a tall figure across the terrace. A man—a man
who had once meant the world to her.

She turned away abruptly and handed her glass to her
boss. 'Forgive me,' she said hurriedly, 'but I need—I
need to find the powder room.' And she turned on her
heel and walked inside.

How she came to get lost in Narelle Hastings' mansion
she was never quite sure. She did find a powder room,
and spent a useless ten minutes trying to calm herself
down, but for the rest of it her inner turmoil must have
been so great she'd been unable to think straight.

She came out of the powder room determined to make
a discreet exit from the house, the party, Cam Hillier,
the lot—only to see Narelle farewelling several guests.
She did a quick about-turn and went through several
doorways to find herself in the kitchen. Fortunately it

was empty of staff, but she knew that could only be a very temporary state of affairs.

Never mind, she told herself. She'd leave by the back door!

The back door at first yielded a promising prospect—a service courtyard, a high wall with a gate in it.

Excellent! Except when she got to it, it was to find the gate locked.

She drew a frustrated, trembling breath as it occurred to her how acutely embarrassing this could turn out to be. How on earth would she explain it to Cameron Hillier—not to mention his great-aunt, whose house she appeared to be wandering through at will?

She gazed at the back door, and as she did so she heard voices coming from within. She doubted she had the nerve to brave the kitchen again. She turned away and studied her options. No good trying to get over the wall that fronted the street—she'd be bound to bump into someone. But the house next door, also behind the wall, was the one whose driveway Cam had parked in—the one whose owner was out, according to him. He must know them and know they were away to make that assertion, she reasoned. It certainly made that wall a better bet.

She dredged her memory and recalled that the driveway had gates that could possibly be locked too—and this adjacent wall was inside those gates. But hang on! Further along the pavement, hadn't there been a pedestrian gate? No—just a gateway. Yes! So all she had to do was climb over the wall…How the hell was she going to do that, though?

She tensed as the back door opened, and slipped into some shadows as a kitchen hand emerged and deposited a load of garbage into a green wheelie bin and slammed it shut. He didn't see her and went back inside, closing the door, but his use of the wheelie bin gave her an idea. She could push it against the wall, hoist herself onto it and slip over it to the house next door.

As with just about everything that had happened to her on this never-ending day, it wasn't a perfect plan.

Firstly, just as she was about to emerge from the shadows and move the bin to the wall, more kitchen hands emerged with loads of garbage. This led her to reconsider things.

What if she did manage to get over the wall and someone came out to find the bin in a different position? But she couldn't skulk around this service courtyard for much longer. A glance at her watch told her she'd already been there for twenty minutes.

She was biting her lip and clenching her fists in a bid to keep calm, almost certain she would have to go through the kitchen again, when something decided the matter for her.

She heard a male voice from the kitchen, calling out that he was locking the back door. She even heard the key turn.

She closed her eyes briefly, then sprinted to the bin, shoved it up against the wall, took her shoes off and threw them over. She looped her purse over her shoulder and, hitching up her dress, climbed onto the bin. Going over from Narelle's side was easy, thanks to the height of the wheelie bin. Getting down the other side was not so easy. She had to hang onto the coping and try to guess what the shortfall was.

It was only about a foot, but she lost her balance as she dropped to the ground, and fell over. She was picking herself up and examining her torn tights and a graze on her knee when the driveway gates, with the sound of a car motor behind them, began to open inwards.

She straightened up and stared with fatal fascination at a pair of headlights as a long, low, sleek car nosed through the gates and stopped abreast of her.

The driver's window was on her side, and it lowered soundlessly. She bent her head, and as her gaze clashed with the man behind the wheel things clicked into place for her...

'Oh, I see,' she said bitterly. '*You* own this place. That's how you knew it was safe to park in the driveway!'

'Got it in two, Liz,' Cam Hillier agreed from inside his graphite-blue Aston Martin. 'But what the devil *you* think you're doing is a mystery to me.'

opened the top buttons of his shirt. He'd

them each a brandy.

As for Liz, she'd cleaned herself

in a guest bathroom. She'd r

bathed her knee and hands bu

her face and hands seemed

had hardly seemed

dress, a streak o

She'd bee

until the

was

'W

30

velvet-covered se

table with a

a fire

Above the fireplace

original Heidelberg School painting, a lovely impressionist pictoral scene that was unmistakably Australian. Tom Roberts? she wondered.

There were two matching armchairs, and some lovely pieces of furniture scattered on the polished wooden floors. The windows looked out over a floodlit scene—an elegant pool with a fountain, tall cypress pines, and beyond the lights of Sydney Harbour.

Not as spectacular as his great-aunt's residence, Cam Hillier's house was nevertheless stylish and very expensive—worth how many millions Liz couldn't even begin to think.

Its owner was seated in an armchair across from her.

He'd shrugged off his jacket, pulled off his tie and

also poured

up as best she could
removed her torn tights,
a plaster to it. She'd washed
not reapplied any make-up. It
appropriate when she had a rip in her
of dirt on her jacket and was shoeless.
unable to find one shoe in the driveway—
'd discovered it in a tub of water the gardener
apparently soaking a root-bound plant in.

So far, the only explanation she'd offered was that she'd seen someone at the party she'd had no desire to meet, so she'd tried to make a quick getaway that had gone horribly wrong.

She took a sip of her brandy, and felt a little better as its warmth slipped down.

She eyed Cameron Hillier and had to acknowledge that he was equally impressive lying back in an armchair, in his shirtsleeves and with his thick dark hair ruffled, as he'd been at his great-aunt's party. On top of that those fascinating, brooding blue eyes appeared to be looking right through her…

'He?' she answered at last. 'What makes you think—?'

'Come on, Liz,' he said roughly. 'If this story is true at all, I can't imagine a woman provoking that kind of reaction! Anyway, I saw you fix your gaze on some guy, then go quite pale and still before you…decamped. Causing *me* no little discomfort, incidentally,' he added dryly.

Her eyes widened. 'Did you get mobbed?'

He looked daggers at her for a moment. 'No. But I did get Narelle to search the powder rooms when I realised how long you'd been gone. She was,' he said bitterly, 'riveted.'

'And then?'

He shrugged. 'There seemed to be no sign of you, so we finally assumed you'd called a taxi and left.'

'Meanwhile I was lurking around in the service courtyard,' Liz said with a sigh. 'All right, it *was* a he. We…we were an item once, but it didn't work out and I just—I just didn't want to have to—to face him,' she said rather jaggedly.

Cam Hillier frowned. 'Fair enough,' he said slowly. 'But why not tell me and simply walk out through the front door?'

Liz bit her lip and took another sip of brandy. 'I got a bit of a shock—I felt a little overwrought,' she confessed.

'A little?' he marvelled. 'I would say more like hysterical—and that doesn't make sense. You laid yourself open to Narelle suspecting you of casing the joint. So could I, come to that. One or the other or both of us might have called the police. Plus,' he added pithily, 'I wouldn't have taken you for a hysterical type.'

Ah, but you don't know the circumstances, Liz thought, and took another fortifying sip of brandy.

'Affairs of the heart are…can be different,' she said quietly. 'You can be the essence of calm at other times, but—' She stopped and gestured, but she didn't look at him because she sounded lame even to her own ears.

He surprised her. 'So,' he said slowly, and with a considering look, 'not such an Ice Queen after all, Ms Montrose?'

Liz didn't reply.

He frowned. 'I've just remembered something. You're a single mother, aren't you?'

Liz looked up at that, her eyes suddenly as cool as ice.

He waved an impatient hand. 'I'm not being critical, but it's just occurred to me that's why you're temping.'

'Yes,' she said, and relaxed a little.

'Tell me about it.'

She cradled her glass in both hands for a moment, and, as always happened to her when she thought of the miracle in her life, some warmth flowed through her. 'She's nearly four, her name's Scout, and she's a—a living doll.' She couldn't help the smile in her voice.

'Who looks after her when you're working?'

'My mother. We live together. My father's dead.'

'It works well?' He raised an eyebrow.

'It works well,' Liz agreed. 'Scout loves my mother, and Mum…' She looked rueful. 'Well, she sometimes needs looking after, too. She can be a touch eccentric.' She sobered. 'It can be a bit of a battle at times, but we get by.'

'And Scout's father?'

Liz was jolted out of her warm place. Her expression tightened as she swallowed and took hold of herself. 'Mr Hillier, that's really none of your business.'

He studied her thoughtfully, thinking that the change

in her was quite remarkable. Obviously Scout's father was a sore point.

He grimaced, but said, 'Miss Montrose, the way you were climbing over my wall, the way you apparently roamed around my great-aunt's house *is* my business. There are a lot of valuables in both.' His blue eyes were narrowed and sharp as he stared at her. 'And I don't think I'm getting a good enough explanation for it.'

'I—I don't understand what you mean. I had no idea this was your house. I had no idea I'd be going to your great-aunt's house this evening,' she said with growing passion. 'Only an idiot would on the spur of the moment decide to rob you both!'

'Or a single mother in financial difficulties?'

He waited, then said when she didn't seem able to frame a response, 'A single mother with a very expensive taste in clothes, by the look of it.'

Liz closed her eyes and berated herself inwardly for having been such a fool. 'They aren't expensive. My mother makes them. All right!' she said suddenly, and tossed her head as she saw the disbelief in his eyes. 'It was Scout's father I saw at the party. That's what threw me into such a state. I haven't spoken to him or laid eyes on him for years.'

'Have you tried to?'

She shook her head. 'I knew it was well and truly finished between us. I came to see he'd been on the rebound and—' her voice shook a little '—it was only a fling for him. I had no choice but to—' She broke off to smile bleakly. 'No choice but take it on the chin and retire. The only thing was—'

'You didn't know you were pregnant?' Cam Hillier said with some cynicism.

She ignored the cynicism. 'Oh, yes, I did.' She took a sip of brandy and prayed she wouldn't cry. She sniffed and patted her face to deflect any tears.

'You didn't tell him?' Cam queried with a frown.

'I did tell him. He said the only thing to do in the circumstances was have an abortion. He—he did offer to help me through it, but he also revealed that he was not only making a fresh start with this other woman, he was moving interstate and taking up a new position. He—I got the impression he even thought I may have tried to trap him into marriage. So…' She shrugged. 'I refused. I said, Don't worry! I can cope! And I walked out. That was the last time I saw him.'

Cam Hillier was silent.

'Although,' Liz said, 'I did go away for a month, and then I changed campuses and became an external student, so I have no idea if he tried to contact me again before he moved.'

'He still doesn't know you had the baby?'

'No.'

'Do you want to keep it from him for ever?'

'Yes!' Liz moved restlessly and stared down at her glass, then put it on the coffee table. 'When Scout was born all I could think was that she was *mine*. He'd never even wanted her to see the light of day, so why should he share her?' She gestured. 'I still feel that way, but…' She paused painfully. 'One day I'm going to have to think of it from Scout's point of view. When she's older and can understand things, she may want to know about her father.'

'But you don't want him to know in the meantime? That's why you took such astonishingly evasive measures tonight.' Cam Hillier rested his jaw on his fist. 'Do you think he'd react any differently?'

Liz heaved a sigh. 'I don't know, but it's hard to imagine anyone resisting Scout. She—she looks like him sometimes. And I did read an article about him fairly recently. He's beginning to make a name for himself in his chosen field. He and his wife have been married for four years. They have no children. There may be a dozen reasons for that, and I may be paranoid, but I can't help it—I'm scared stiff they'll somehow lure Scout away from me.'

'Liz.' He sat forward. 'You're her mother. They can't—unless you can't provide for her.'

'Maybe not legally, but there could be other ways. As she grows up she might find she prefers what they have to offer. They have a settled home. He has growing prestige. Whereas I am…I'm just getting by.' The raw, stark emotion was plain to see in her eyes.

'Have you got over him, Liz?'

A complete silence blanketed the room until the hoot from a harbour ferry broke it.

'I haven't forgotten or forgiven.' She stared out at the pool. 'Not that I was—not that I *wasn't* incredibly naïve and foolish. I haven't forgiven myself for that.'

'You should. These things happen. Not always with such consequences, but life has its lessons along the way.'

And, to her surprise, there was something like understanding in his eyes.

She moistened her lips and took several breaths to steady herself, because his lack of judgement of her was nearly her undoing. She gazed down at her bare feet and fought to control her tears.

Then she bit her lip as where she was, who *he* was, and how she'd poured all her troubles out to a virtual stranger with the added complication of him being her employer hit her.

Her eyes dilated and she took a ragged breath and straightened. 'I'm sorry,' she said huskily. 'If you want to sack me I'd understand, but do you believe me now?'

'Yes.' Cam Hillier didn't hesitate. 'Uh—no, I don't want to sack you. But I'll take you home now.' He drained the last of his brandy and stood up.

'Oh, I can get a taxi,' she assured him hastily, and followed suit.

He raised an eyebrow. 'With only one shoe? Your other one is ruined.'

'I—'

'Don't argue,' he recommended. He shrugged into his jacket, but didn't bother with his tie. Then he glanced at his watch. At the same time his mobile rang. He got it out of his pocket and looked at the screen.

'Ah, Portia,' he murmured. 'Wanting to berate me or make disparaging comparisons, do you think?' He clicked the phone off and shoved it into his pocket.

Liz took a guilty breath. 'I shouldn't have told you that. And—and she might want to explain. I think you should talk to her.'

He looked down at her, his deep blue eyes alight with mocking amusement. 'Your concern for my love-life is touching, Miss Montrose, but Portia and I have come to the end of the road. After you.' He gestured for her to precede him.

Liz clicked her tongue exasperatedly and tried to walk out as regally as was possible with no shoes on.

Cam Hillier dropped her off at her apartment building, and waited and watched as she crossed the pavement towards the entrance.

She'd insisted on putting on both shoes, although one still squelched a bit. He drummed his fingers on the steering wheel as it occurred to him that her long legs were just as good as Portia's. In fact, he thought, her figure might not be as voluptuous as Portia's but she was quite tall, with straight shoulders, a long, narrow waist. And the whole was slim and elegant—how had he not noticed it before?

Because he'd been put off by her glasses, her scraped-back hair, an unspoken but slightly militant air—or all three?

He grimaced, because he couldn't doubt now that under that composed, touch-me-not Ice Queen there existed real heartbreak. He'd seen that kind of heart-break before. The other thing he couldn't doubt was that she'd sparked his interest. Was it the challenge, though? Of breaking through the ice until he created a warm, loving woman? Was it because he sensed a response in her whether she liked it or not?

Whatever, he reflected, in a little over two weeks she was destined to walk out of his life. Unless…

He didn't articulate the thought as he finally drove off.

The next morning Liz placed a boiled egg with a face drawn on it in front of her daughter. Scout clapped her hands delightedly.

At the same time Mary Montrose said, 'You must have been late last night, Liz? I didn't even hear you come in.'

Yes, thank heavens, Liz thought. She'd been curiously unwilling to share the events of the evening with her mother—not to mention to expose the mess she'd been in, ripped, torn and with one soaked shoe.

Now, though, she gave Mary a much abridged version of the evening.

Mary sat up excitedly. 'I once designed an outfit for Narelle Hastings. Did you say she's Cameron Hillier's great-aunt?'

'So he said.' Liz smiled inwardly as she decapitated Scout's egg and spread the contents on toast soldiers. Her mother was an avid follower of the social scene.

'Let's see…' Mary meditated for a moment. 'I believe Narelle was his mother's aunt—that *would* make her his great-aunt. Well! There you go! Of course there've been a couple of tragedies for the Hastings/Hillier clan.'

Liz wiped some egg from Scout's little face and dropped a kiss on her nose. 'Good girl, you made short work of that! Like what?' she asked her mother.

'Cameron's parents were killed in an aircraft accident,

and his sister in an avalanche of all things. What's he like?'

Liz hesitated as she realised she wasn't at all sure what to make of Cameron Hillier. 'He's OK,' she said slowly, and looked at her watch. 'I'll have to make tracks shortly. So! What have you two girls got on today?'

'Koalas,' Scout said. She was as fair as Liz, with round blue eyes. Her hair was a cloud of curls and she glowed with health.

Liz pretended surprise. 'You're going to buy a koala?'

'No, Mummy,' Scout corrected lovingly. 'We're going to see them at the zoo! Aren't we, Nanna?'

'As well as all sorts of other animals, sweetheart,' her grandmother confirmed fondly. 'I'm looking forward to it myself!'

Liz took a breath as she thought of the sunny day outside, the ferry-ride across the harbour to Taronga Zoo, and how she'd love to be going with them. She bit her lip, then glanced gratefully at her mother. 'There are times when I don't know how to thank you,' she murmured.

'You don't have to,' Mary answered. 'You know that.'

Liz blinked, then got up to get ready for work.

The flat she and Scout shared with her mother was in an inner Sydney suburb. It was comfortable—her mother had seen to that—but the neighbourhood couldn't be described as classy...something Mary often lamented. But it was handy for the suburb of Paddington, for Oxford

Street and its trendy shopping and vibrant cafés. There were also markets, and history that included the Victoria Army Barracks and fine old terrace houses. If you were a sports fan, the iconic Sydney Cricket Ground was handy, as well as Centennial and Moore Parks. They often took picnics to the park.

The flat had three bedrooms and a small study. They'd converted the study into a bedroom for Scout, and the third bedroom into a workroom for Mary. It resembled an Aladdin's cave, Liz sometimes thought. There were racks of clothes in a mouth-watering selection of colours and fabrics. There was a rainbow selection of buttons, beads, sequins, the feathers Mary fashioned into fascinators, ribbons and motifs.

Mary had a small band of customers she 'created' for, as she preferred to put it. Gone were the heady days after Liz's father's death, when Mary had followed a life-long dream and invested in her own boutique. It hadn't prospered—not because the clothes weren't exquisite, but because, as her father had known, Mary had no business sense at all. Not only hadn't it prospered, it had all but destroyed Mary's resources.

But the two people Mary Montrose loved creating for above all were her daughter and granddaughter.

So it was that, although Liz operated on a fairly tight budget, no one would have guessed it from her clothes. And she went to work the day after the distressing scenario that had played out between two harbourside mansions looking the essence of chic, having decided it was a bit foolish to play down the originality of her clothes now.

She wore slim black pants to hide the graze on her knee, and a black and white blouson top with three-quarter sleeves, belted at the waist. Her shoes were black patent wedges with high cork soles—shoes she adored—and she wore a black and white, silver and bead Pandora-style bracelet.

As she finished dressing, she went to pin back her hair—then thought better of that too. There seemed to be no point now. She also put in her contact lenses.

But as she rode the bus to work she was thinking not of how she looked but other things. Cam Hillier in particular.

She'd tossed and turned quite a lot last night, as her overburdened mind had replayed the whole dismal event several times.

She had to acknowledge that he'd been... He hadn't been critical, had he? She couldn't deny she'd got herself into a mess—not only last night, of course, but in her life, and Scout's—which could easily invite criticism...

What did he really think? she wondered, and immediately wondered why it should concern her. After her disastrous liaison with Scout's father she'd not only been too preoccupied with her first priority—Scout, and building a life for both of them—but she'd had no interest in men. Once bitten twice shy, had been her motto. She'd even perfected a technique that had become, without her realising it until yesterday, she thought ironically, patently successful—Ice Queen armour.

It had all taken its toll, however, despite her joy in Scout. Not only in the battle to keep afloat economically, but also with her guilt at having to rely on her mother for help, therefore restricting her mother's life too. She had the feeling that she was growing old before her time, that she would never be able to let her hair down and enjoy herself in mixed company because of the cloud of bitterness that lay on her soul towards men.

So why was she now thinking about a man as she hadn't for years?

Why was she now suddenly physically vulnerable to a man she didn't really approve of, to make matters worse?

She paused her thoughts as a mental image of Cam Hillier came to her, and she had to acknowledge on a suddenly indrawn breath that he fascinated her in a curious sort of love/hate way—although of course it couldn't be love... But just when she wanted to hurl a brick at him for his sheer bloody-minded arrogance he did something, as he had last night, that changed a person's opinion of him. He hadn't been judgemental. He'd even made it possible for her spill her heart to him.

It was more too, she reflected. Not only his compelling looks and physique, but a vigorous mind that worked at the speed of lightning, an intellect you longed to have the freedom to match. Something about him that made you feel alive even if you were furious.

She gazed unseeingly out of the window and thought, what did it matter? She'd shortly be gone from his life. And even if she stayed within his orbit there was always the thorny question of Portia Pengelly—or if not Portia whoever her replacement would be.

She smiled a wintry little smile and shrugged, with not the slightest inkling of what awaited her shortly.

Ten minutes later she buzzed for a lift on the ground floor of the tower that contained the offices of the Hillier Corporation. One came almost immediately from the basement car park, and she stepped into it to find herself alone with her boss as the doors closed smoothly.

'Miss Montrose,' he said.

'Mr Hillier,' she responded.

He looked her up and down, taking in her stylish outfit, the sheen of her hair and her glossy mouth. And his lips quirked as he said, 'Hard to connect you with the wall-climbing cat burglar of last night.'

Liz directed him a tart little look before lowering her carefully darkened lashes, and said nothing.

'So I take it you're quite restored, Liz?'

'Yes,' she said coolly, and wasn't going to elaborate, but then thought better of it. 'Thank you. You were...' She couldn't think of the right word. 'Thank you.'

'That's all right.'

The lift slid to a stop and the doors opened, revealing the Hillier foyer, but for some strange reason neither of them made a move immediately. Not so strange, though, Liz thought suddenly. In the sense that it had happened to her before, in his car last evening, when she'd been trapped in a bubble of acute awareness of Cameron Hillier.

His suit was different today—slate-grey, worn with a pale blue shirt and a navy and silver tie—but it was just as beautifully tailored and moulded his broad shoulders just as effectively. There was a narrow black leather belt around his lean waist, and his black shoes shone and looked to be handmade.

But it wasn't a case of clothes making the man, Liz thought. It was the other way around. Add to that the tingling fresh aura of a man who'd showered and shaved recently, the comb lines in his thick hair, those intriguing blue eyes and his long-fingered hands… Her eyes widened as she realised even his hands impressed her. All of him stirred her senses in a way that made her long to have some physical contact with him—a touch, a mingling of their breath as they kissed…

Then their gazes lifted to each other's and she could see a nerve flickering in his jaw—a nerve that told her he was battling a similar compulsion. She'd known from the way he'd looked at her last night that he was no longer seeing her as a stick of furniture, but to think that he wanted her as she seemed to want him was electrifying.

It was as the lift doors started to close that they came out of their long moment of immobility. He pressed a button and the doors reversed their motion. He gestured for her to step out ahead of him.

She did so with a murmured thank-you, and headed for her small office. They both greeted Molly Swanson.

'Uh—give me ten minutes, then bring the diary in, Liz. And coffee, please, Molly.' He strode through into his office.

'How did it go? Last night?' Molly enquired. 'By the way, I've already had three calls from Miss Pengelly!'

'Oh, dear.' Liz grimaced. 'I'm afraid it might be over.'

'Probably just as well,' Molly said with a wise little look in her eyes. 'What he needs is a proper wife, not these film star types—I never thought she could act her way out of a paper bag, anyway!'

Liz blinked, but fortunately Molly was diverted by the discreet buzzing of her phone.

Eight minutes later, Liz gathered herself in readiness to present herself to her employer with the diary.

She'd poured herself a cup of cold water from the cooler, but instead of drinking it she'd dipped her hanky into it and splashed her wrists and patted her forehead.

I must be mad, she'd thought. *He* must be mad even to contemplate getting involved with me. Or is all he has in mind a replacement for Portia? Someone to deflect all the women he attracts—and I refuse to believe it's only because of his money.

Things were back to thoroughly businesslike as they went through his engagements for the day one by one, and he sipped strong black aromatic coffee from a Lalique glass in a silver holder.

'All right,' he said. 'Have you got the briefs for the Fortune conference?'

She nodded.

'I'll want you there. There's quite a bit of paperwork to be passed around and collected, et cetera. And I'll need you to drive me to and pick me up from the

Bromwich lunch. There's no damn parking to be found for miles.'

'Fine,' she murmured, then hesitated.

He looked up. 'A problem?'

'You want me to drive your car?'

'Why not?'

'To be honest—' Liz bit her lip '—I'd be petrified of putting a scratch on it.'

He sat back. 'Hadn't thought of that. So would I—to be honest.' He looked wry. 'Uh—get a car from the car pool.'

Liz relaxed. 'I think that's a much better idea.'

His lips twitched, and she thought he was going to say something humorous, but the moment passed and he looked at her in the completely deadpan way he had that had a built-in annoyance factor for anyone on the receiving end of it.

Liz was not immune to the annoyance as she found herself reduced to the status of a slightly troublesome employee. Then, if anything, she got more annoyed— but with herself. She had been distinctly frosty in the lift before they'd found themselves trapped in that curious moment of physical awareness, hadn't she?

She had told herself they would both be mad even to contemplate anything like a relationship—and she believed that. But some little part of her was obviously hankering to be treated… How? As a friend?

If I were out on a beach I'd believe I'd got a touch of the sun, she thought grimly. This man doesn't work that way, and there's no reason why he should.

She cleared her throat and said politely, 'What time would you like to leave?'

'Twelve-thirty.' He turned away.

The Fortune conference was scheduled for nine-thirty, and Liz and Molly worked together to prepare the conference room.

It got underway on time and went relatively smoothly. Liz did her bit, distributing and retrieving documents, providing water and coffee—and coping with the over-effusive thanks she got from the short, dumpy, middle-aged vice-President of the Fortune Seafood Group.

She only smiled coolly in return, but something—some prickling of her nervous system—caused her to look in Cam Hillier's direction, to find his gaze on her, steadfast and disapproving. Until a faint tide of colour rose in her cheeks, and he looked away at last.

Surely he couldn't think she was courting masculine approval or something stupid like that?

On the other hand, she reminded herself, she might find it stupid, but it could be an occupational hazard of being a single mother—men wondering if you were promiscuous...

It became further apparent that her boss was not in a good mood when she drove him to the Bromwich lunch in a company Mercedes. The reasons for this were two-fold.

'Hmm...' he said. 'You're a very cautious driver, Ms Montrose.'

Liz looked left and right and left again, and drove

across an intersection. 'It's not my car, your life is in my hands, Mr Hillier, and I have a certain respect for my own.'

'Undue caution can be its own hazard,' he commented. 'Roger is a better driver.'

Liz could feel her temper rising, but she held on to it. She said nothing.

He went on, 'Come to think of it, I don't have to worry about Roger receiving indecent proposals from visiting old-enough-to-know-better seafood purveyors either. Uh—you could have driven a bus through that gap, Liz.'

She lost it without any outward sign. She nosed the Mercedes carefully into the kerb, reversed it to a better angle, then switched off and handed him the keys.

She didn't shout, she didn't bang anything, but she did say, 'If you want to get to the Bromwich lunch in one piece, *you* drive. And don't ever ask me to drive you anywhere again. Furthermore, I can handle indecent proposals—any kind of proposals!—so you don't have a thing to worry about. As for the aspersions you cast on my driving, I happen to think *you're* a menace on the road.'

'Liz—'

But she ignored him as she opened her door and stepped out of the car.

CHAPTER THREE

TWO MINUTES LATER he was in the driver's seat, she was in the passenger seat, and she had no idea if he was fighting mad or laughing at her—although she suspected the latter.

'Right,' he said as he eased the car back into the traffic. 'Get onto Bromwich and tell them I'm not coming.'

Liz gasped. 'Why not? You can't—'

'I can. I never did want to go to their damn lunch anyway.'

'But you agreed!' she reminded him.

'All the same, they'll be fine without me. It is a lunch for two hundred people. I could quite easily have got lost in the crowd,' he said broodingly.

Liz thought, with irony, that it was highly unlikely, but she said tautly, 'And what will I tell them?'

'Tell them…' he paused, 'I've had a row with my diary secretary, during which she not only threatened to take me apart but I got told I was a *menace*, and that I'm feeling somewhat diminished and unable to contemplate socialising on a large scale as a result.'

Liz looked at him with extreme frustration. 'Apart

from anything else, that has *got* to be so untrue!' she said through her teeth.

He grimaced. 'You could also tell them,' he added, 'that since it's a nice day I've decided the beach is a better place for lunch. We'll go and have some fish and chips. Like fish and chips?'

She lifted her hands in a gesture of despair. 'I suppose nothing will persuade you this is a very bad idea?'

'Nothing,' he agreed, then grinned that lightning crooked grin. 'Maybe you should have thought of that before you had a hissy fit and handed over the car.'

'You were being enough to—you were impossible!'

'Mmm…' He said it meditatively, and with a faint frown. 'I seem to be slightly off-key today. Do you have the same problem? After what happened in the lift?' he added softly.

Liz studied the road ahead, and wondered what would happen if she admitted to him that she had no idea how to cope with the attraction that had sprung up between them. Yes, it might have happened to her for the first time in a long time, but did that mean she wasn't scared stiff of it? Of course she was. She knew it. She clenched her hands briefly in her lap. Besides, what could come of it?

An affair at the most, she reasoned. Cameron Hillier was not going to marry a single mother who sometimes struggled to pay her bills. Marry! Dear heaven, what was she thinking? Even with the best intentions and no impediments they had to be a long way from *that*.

And, having thought of her bills, she couldn't stop

herself from thinking of them again—that and the fact that she had no other job lined up yet.

Just get yourself out of this without losing your job if you can, Liz, she recommended to herself.

'I apologise for losing my temper,' she said at last. 'I—I'm probably not a very good driver. I haven't had a lot of experience, but I was doing my best.' She looked ruefully heavenwards.

Cam Hillier cast her a swift glance that was laced with mockery. 'That's all?'

She swallowed, fully understanding the mockery— she was dodging the issue of what had happened between them in the lift and he knew it.

She twisted her hands together, but said quite evenly, 'I'm afraid so.'

There was silence in the car until he said, 'That has a ring of finality to it. In other words we're never destined to be more than we are, Ms Montrose?'

Liz pushed her hair behind her ears. 'We're not,' she agreed barely audibly. 'Oh.' She reached for her purse— anything to break the tension of the moment. 'I'll ring Bromwich—although I may not get anyone at this late stage.'

'So be it,' he said, and she knew he wasn't talking about the lunch he was going to miss.

She hesitated, but decided she might as well cement her stance on the matter—in a manner of speaking... 'You don't have to take me to lunch, Mr Hillier. I'd quite understand.'

'Not at all, Ms Montrose,' he drawled. 'For one thing, I'm starving. And, since Roger and I often have lunch when we're on the road together, you don't need to view it with any suspicion.'

'Suspicion?'

This time he looked at her with satirical amusement glinting in his blue eyes. 'Suspicion that I might try to chat you up or—break down your icy ramparts.'

Liz knew—she could feel what was happening to her—and this time nothing in the world could have stopped her from blushing brightly. She took refuge from the embarrassment of it by contacting the Bromwich lunch venue.

The restaurant he took her to had an open area on a boardwalk above the beach. They found a table shaded by a canvas umbrella, ordered, and looked out over the sparkling waters of Sydney Harbour. They could see the Opera House and the Harbour Bridge.

And he was as good as his word. He didn't try to chat her up or break her down, but somehow made it possible for them to be companionable as they ate their fish and chips.

He was so different, Liz thought, from how he could be at other times. Not only had he left the arrogant multi-millionaire of the office behind, but also the moody persona he'd been in the car. He even looked younger, and she found herself catching her breath once or twice—once when an errant breeze lifted his dark hair, and once when he played absently with the salt cellar in his long fingers.

'Well…' He consulted his watch finally. 'Let's get back to work.'

'Thanks for that.' She stood up.

He followed suit, and for one brief moment they looked into each other's eyes—a searching, perfectly sober exchange—before they both looked away again, and started to walk to the car.

Liz knew she was to suffer the consequences of that pleasant lunch in the form of a yet another restless night.

Not so Scout, though. She was still bubbling with excitement at what she'd seen at the zoo, and she fell asleep almost as soon as her head touched the pillow.

Liz dropped a kiss on her curls and tiptoed out. But when she went to bed she tossed and turned for ages as flashes of what had been an extraordinary day came back to haunt her.

Such as when that light breeze had ruffled his hair and it had affected her so curiously—given her goose-bumps, to be precise. Such as when he'd played absently with the salt cellar and she'd suffered a mental flash of having his hands on her naked body.

I've got to deal with this, she told herself, going hot and cold again. I don't think I can get out of this job without affecting my rating with the agency, and without having to take less money—which would play havoc with my budget. I've got to think of Scout and what's best for her. A brief affair with a man who, if you go on his present track record, doesn't appear to be able to commit? Not to Portia Pengelly, anyway, and that means he was using her—he more or less admitted that.

I've got to remember what it felt like to find out

I'd been used, and to be told an abortion was the only course of action in the circumstances...

She stared into the darkness, then closed her eyes on the tears that came.

She resumed her monologue when her tears subsided. So, Liz, even if you are no longer the Ice Queen you were, you've got to get through this. Don't let another man bring you down.

She was helped by the fact that Cam Hillier was away for the next couple of days, but when he came back she still had two weeks left to work for him.

He seemed to be in a different mood, though. Less abrasive—with her, anyway—and there were no *double entendres*, no signs that they'd ever stood in a lift absolutely mesmerised by each other.

Had he made it up with Portia? she wondered. Did that account for his better mood? Or had he found a replacement for Portia?

Whatever it was, Liz relaxed a bit, and she did not take exception when they got caught in a traffic jam on the way to a meeting, and to kill the time he asked her about her earlier life.

It was a dull day and had rained overnight. There was an accident up ahead and the traffic was hopelessly gridlocked. There was a helicopter flying overhead.

'It must be a serious accident,' Liz murmured. 'We could be late.'

He switched off the motor and shrugged. 'Nothing we can do,' he said, with uncharacteristic patience. 'Tell me how you grew up?'

Liz pleated the skirt of the red dress she wore with a light black jacket, and thought, Why not?

'Uh…let's see,' she said reflectively. 'My father was a teacher and very academic, whilst my mother…' She paused, because sometimes it was hard to sum up her mother. 'She's this intensely creative person—*so* good with her hands but not terribly practical.'

She smiled. 'You wouldn't have thought it could work between them, but it did. She could always liven him up, and he could always deflect her from her madder schemes. As a teacher, of course, he was really keen on education, and he coached me a lot. That's how I came to go to a private school on a scholarship. I also went to uni on scholarships. He—' She stopped.

'Go on,' Cam murmured after a few moments.

She cast him an oblique little glance, wondering at the same time why he was interested in this—why she was even humouring him…

'I used to think I took more after him—we read together and studied things together—but lately some of Mum has started to shine through. She's an inspired cook, and I'm interested in it now—although I'll never be the seamstress she is.'

'So how did you cope with getting your degree and being a single mum?' he queried. 'Simple arithmetic suggests Scout must have intervened somewhere along the line.'

Liz looked at his hands on the steering wheel and switched her gaze away immediately. Was this just plain curiosity, or…? But was there any reason not to give him the bare bones of it anyway?

'It was hard work, but in some ways it kept me sane. It was a goal I could still achieve, I guess—although I had to work part-time.' She paused and looked rueful. 'At all sorts of crazy jobs at the same time.'

'Such as?'

'I was a receptionist in a tattoo parlour once.' She looked nostalgic for a moment. 'I actually got a bunch of flowers from a group of bikies I came to know there when Scout was born. Uh—I worked in a bottle shop, a supermarket. I did some nanny work, house cleaning.'

She stopped and gestured. 'My father had died by then—he never knew Scout—but I was determined to get my degree because I knew how disappointed he would have been if I hadn't.'

'How did you get into this kind of work?'

Liz smiled. 'I had a lucky break. One of my lecturers had contacts with the agency, and a good idea of the kind of replacement staff they supplied. She schooled me on most aspects of a diary secretary's duties, my mother set me up with a suitable wardrobe, and *voilà*!—as they say.'

'Helped along by being as bright as a tack.' He said it almost to himself. 'I gather you take time off between assignments?'

She nodded. 'I always try for a couple of weeks—not only to give my mother a break, but to be able to spend more time with Scout myself.'

'So she still makes your clothes? Your mother?'

'Yes. She made that jacket.' Liz explained how she'd come to have it with her on the day of the cocktail party. 'She actually made it for the part-time weekend job I have as cashier at a very upmarket restaurant.'

'Your father would be proud of you.'

'I don't know about that.'

'And Scout's father? Any more sightings?'

Liz shook her head but looked uneasy. 'I'm wondering if he's moved back to Sydney and that's why he was at your great-aunt's party.'

'I can find out, if you like. But even if he has Sydney's a big city.' He flicked her an interrogative look.

'No. No, thanks. I think I'll just let sleeping dogs lie. Oh, look—they're diverting the traffic. We could be just in time.'

He seemed about to say something, then he shrugged and switched on the motor.

As often happened when something came up out of the blue, things came in pairs, Liz discovered that same evening. She heard a radio interview with Scout's father in which he talked mainly about the economy—he was an economist—but also about his move back to his hometown from Perth. And the fact that he had no children as yet, but he and his wife were still hoping for some.

She'd flicked the radio off and tried to concentrate on the fact that her only emotion towards Scout's father was now distaste—tried to concentrate on it in order to disguise the cold little bubble of fear the rest of it had brought her.

The next morning her boss made an unusual request.

She was tidying away the clutter on his desk, prior to a meeting with his chief of Human Resources, when he took a phone call that didn't seem to be business-orientated.

'Broke the window?' he said down the line, with a surprised lift of his eyebrows. 'I wouldn't have thought he was strong enough to— Well, never mind. Tell him not to try it again until I'm there.' He put down the phone and watched Liz abstractedly for a few minutes, and then with a frown of concentration.

Liz, becoming aware of this, looked down at her exemplary outfit—a summer suit. Matching jacket and A-line skirt. There didn't seem to be anything wrong with it—no buttons undone, no bra strap showing or anything like that. So she looked back at him with a query in her eyes.

He drummed his fingers on the desk. 'Do you remember a song about a boomerang that wouldn't come back?'

She blinked and thought for a moment, then shook her head. 'No.'

'I seem to,' he said slowly. 'See if you can find it, please.'

Liz opened her mouth, but she was forestalled by the arrival of his chief of Human Resources.

Later that day she was able to tell him she'd found the boomerang song, and was rather charmed by it. 'It's a golden oldie. Charlie Drake was the artist,' she said. 'Not only wouldn't his boomerang come back, but he hit the Flying Doctor.'

'Excellent,' Cam Hillier said. But that was all he said, leaving Liz completely mystified.

* * *

Some days later he surprised her again.

She was a bit preoccupied, because just before she'd left for work and had been checking her purse she'd found she'd inadvertently picked up a note meant for her mother. It was from an old friend of her mother's who ran a dancing school, and it concerned the school's annual concert. Would Mary be interested in designing the costumes for the concert? It would mean about three months' work, it said.

But Mary Montrose had penned a reply on the back of it.

So sorry. Would have loved to but I just don't have the time these days. All good wishes...

She hadn't posted it yet.

Only because of looking after Scout could she not do it, Liz thought to herself, and flinched. But what to do? Scout spent two mornings a week at a daycare centre; more Liz could not afford. And those two free mornings a week would not be enough to allow Mary to take on a job she would have loved.

Liz had replaced the note on the hall table, feeling jolted and miserable, and came to work.

It was after she'd gone through the day's schedule with her boss that he asked to see the next day's schedule.

Liz handed the diary over.

He scanned it in silence for a minute or two, then said decisively, 'Reschedule the lot.' He handed the book back to her.

Liz actually felt herself go pale. 'The lot?'

'That's what I said.' He sat back in his chair.

'But...' Liz stopped and bit her lip. There were at least ten appointments in one form or another to be re-scheduled. There were at least five major appointments amongst them, involving third, fourth and even fifth parties, so cancellation would produce a ripple effect of chaos down the line.

She swallowed. 'All right. Uh—what will you being doing tomorrow? I mean, what would you like me to say? Mr Hillier has been called away urgently? Or...' She paused and gazed at him.

That crooked grin chased across Cam Hillier's lips, but he said gravely, 'Yep. Especially said in those cool, well-bred tones. It should do the trick admirably.'

Liz frowned. 'I don't sound—are you saying I sound snooty?'

'Yes, you do.' He raised an eyebrow at her. 'Probably your private school.'

She grimaced, and after a moment deliberately changed the subject. 'Should I know what you *are* doing tomorrow, Mr Hillier, or would you rather I remained in ignorance?'

He noted the change of subject with a twist of his lips. 'That would be hard, because you'll be with me. I'm going up to Yewarra and I need your help, I'll be engaging staff.'

'Yewarra?' she repeated, somewhat dazedly.

'It's an estate I have in the Blue Mountains.'

'The Blue...' Liz caught herself sounding like a parrot and changed tack. 'I mean—how long will it take?'

'Just a day—just working hours,' he replied smoothly, and shrugged. 'Let's leave here at eight a.m.—then we *will* be back in working hours. And come casual.'

'You're planning to drive up there?' she queried.

'Uh-huh. Why not?'

Liz moved uneasily. 'I prefer not to feel as if I'm low-flying when I'm in a car.'

He grinned. 'I promise to obey the speed limits tomorrow. Anyway, it's a very good car and I'm a very good driver.'

Liz opened her mouth to say his modesty was amazing but she changed her mind. As she knew to her cost, you could never quite tell how Cam Hillier was going to react in a confrontation...

'So,' he said, lying back in his chair with his hands behind his head, 'only three more days before Roger is restored to our midst—completely recovered from his glandular fever, so he assures me.'

'Yes,' she said quietly.

'And you head off into the sunset, Liz.'

'That too,' she agreed.

'But we've worked well together. Oh—' he sat up and gestured widely '—apart from the couple of times you've narrowly restrained yourself from slapping my face, and the day you threatened me with worse.' His blue eyes were alive with satanic amusement.

'I get the feeling you're never going to let me forget that, so it's just as well I *am* riding off into the sunset or something like that.'

She was destined not to know what his response

would have been, because the door of his office burst
open and Portia Pengelly swept in.

'Cam, I have to speak to you—*oh*!' Portia stopped
dead, then advanced slowly and ominously with that
knee-in-front-of-knee model's walk. She wore a simple
black silk shift dress splashed with vibrant colours. She
had a bright watermelon cardigan draped over her shoulders, and carried a large tote in the same colour. Her
famous straw-coloured locks were gorgeously dishev-
elled and her long legs were bare.

'Who is *this*?' she demanded as she gazed at Liz.

Liz got up and took up the diary. 'I work here. Uh—if
that'll be all, Mr Hillier, I'll get back to work. Excuse
me,' she said to Portia, and left the room—but not quite
quickly enough to miss Portia Pengelly uttering Cam
Hillier's Christian name in what sounded like an impassioned plea.

They set off on the dot of eight the next morning.

Liz had taken her boss's advice to 'come casual'
to heart. She wore a short-sleeved pale grey jumper
with a black and white bow pattern on the front, and
slimline jeans with a broad cuff that came, fashionably,
to just above her ankles. She had a cardigan to match
the jumper, a black leather bag, and pale grey leather
flatties.

He also wore jeans, with a denim shirt, and he slung
a leather jacket into the back of the Aston Martin.

They didn't say much as he negotiated the traffic out
of Sydney—with decorum, she noted, and relaxed somewhat—and headed west. Once they were beyond Penrith

the road started to climb—and the Blue Mountains started to live up to their name.

Liz had read somewhere that their distinctive blue haze was the result of the release of oils into the air from the forests of eucalypts that cloaked their slopes. She'd further read, though, that they were not so much mountains but the rugged ramparts, scored and slashed with gullies and ravines, of a vast plateau.

Whatever, she thought, as the powerful vehicle chewed up the kilometres effortlessly and the road got steeper, they were awe-inspiring and yet somehow secretive at the same time, cloaked in their blue haze. And indeed they had proved to be. Until 1994 they'd kept in their remote and isolated valleys the secret of the Wollemi pine—a living fossil said to date back to Gondwana and the time of the dinosaur.

It was when they'd almost reached their destination that he said out of the blue, 'What's your next assignment, Liz?'

She grimaced. 'I don't have one yet. But I'm sure something will come up,' she added. 'It's just hard to predict at times.'

'How will you manage if something doesn't come up for some time?'

Liz moved restlessly. 'I'll be fine.' She paused, then cast him a cool little look. 'Please, I do appreciate your concern, but I think it's best left alone. I'll be gone in a couple of days and it's difficult for me—for both of us, probably—to remain professional if this keeps cropping up between us.'

'Professional?' He drove for a mile or so. 'That flew

out of the window, in a manner of speaking, before any of *this* "cropped up".'

Liz frowned. 'What do you mean?'

He took his eyes off the road to look at her just long enough for her to see the irony in his eyes. 'Narelle was right. We're not cut out to be only employer and employee. There is, Ms Montrose, not to put too fine a point on it, a kind of electricity between us that started to sizzle right here in this car outside my house almost two weeks ago. Or perhaps even earlier—that day in the office when you put on your magic coat and let down your hair.'

CHAPTER FOUR

LIZ'S MOUTH fell open.

'And it continued the next morning in the lift,' he added, as he changed gear and they swept round a corner. 'In fact it's never gone away—despite your best efforts to kill it stone-dead.'

It struck Liz that they had driven through the pretty village of Leura with her barely noticing it, and were now on a country road. It also struck her that it was impossible to refute his claim.

She stared down at her hands. 'Look,' she said, barely audibly, 'you'd be mad to want to get involved with me. And vice versa.'

Out of the corner of her eye she saw that crooked grin come and go before he said, 'It doesn't work that way.'

'If we're two sane adults, it should,' she replied coolly. 'You can make choices, can't you?'

He changed gear again and slowed down. 'On the virtually nothing we have to go on? It'd be like a stab in the dark.' He turned the wheel and they coasted into a driveway barred by a pair of tall wrought-iron gates.

'Is this it?' Liz asked.

'This is it.' He pressed a buzzer mounted on the dashboard and the gates started to open. 'Welcome to Yewarra, Liz.'

For a moment Liz felt like escaping—escaping his car, his estate and Cam Hillier himself. She fleetingly felt overburdened, and as if she were entering a zone she had no control over.

Moments later, however, she was enchanted as he drove slowly up the gravelled driveway.

Beneath majestic trees there were beds of white and blue agapanthus. There was flowering jasmine and honeysuckle climbing up jacarandas bursting into pale violet bloom. There were gardenias and roses. It was a glorious riot of colour and perfume.

She turned to him, her face alight with appreciation. 'This is just—beautiful.'

He grimaced. 'Thanks. In a way it's a tribute to my mother. A tribute to her love of gardens and her innate sense of refined living that somehow survived the often harsh life she shared with my father.'

He pulled up beside a fountain. The house beyond it was two-storeyed and built of warm, earthy stone with a shingle roof. The windows were framed in timber and had wrought-iron security grids. The front door—a double door—was beautifully carved with a dolphin motif and had curved brass handles.

'The house isn't bad either,' she commented with a wry little smile. 'Did you build it?'

'No. And I've hardly done anything to it. Well, I changed that,' he amended, and gestured to the fountain.

'It was this rather nauseating circle of coy naked ladies clutching plump cherubs.'

What stood there now couldn't have been more different. A bronze dolphin leapt out of the water, cascading sparkling droplets.

Liz stared at it. 'Do dolphins have any special significance?'

He considered. 'It's not inappropriate for someone whose roots go back to a seafaring life, I guess.'

Liz thought of the paintings in his office in Sydney. 'But you've come a long way since then,' she offered quietly.

'A long way,' he agreed. But, although he said it easily enough, she thought she detected the faintest echo of a grim undertone.

At that moment the front doors flew open and a small boy of about five stood on the doorstep, waving excitedly at the same time as he was restrained by a nanny.

Liz's eyes widened. 'Who…?' she began, and bit her lip, not wanting to sound nosy.

'That's Archie,' Cam Hillier said. 'He's my sister's orphaned son. I've adopted him.'

He opened his door and got out, and Archie escaped his nanny's restraining hand and flew over the gravel, calling, 'Cam! Cam—am I glad to see you! Wenonah has had *six* puppies but they only want to let me keep one!'

Cam Hillier picked his nephew up and hugged him. 'But just think,' he said, 'of the five other kids who'd love to have a puppy but couldn't if you kept them all.'

Liz blinked. She'd assumed his nephew Archie would

be older. She certainly hadn't expected to see Cameron
Hillier so at home with a five-year-old…

'I suppose that's true,' Archie said slowly. 'Oh, well,
maybe I won't mind.' He hugged Cam. 'Are you staying?'

'Not tonight,' Cam said, but added as Archie's face
fell, 'I'll be up for the weekend.' He put the little boy
down. 'Archie, meet Liz—she works for me.'

'How do you do, Liz?' Archie said with impeccable
manners. 'Would you like to see my menagerie?'

Both Cam and the nanny, still standing on the doorstep, opened their mouths to intervene, but Liz got in
first. 'How do you do, Archie? I would indeed.'

Archie slid his hand into hers. 'It's down this path.
I'll show you.'

'Not too long, Archie,' Cam said. 'Liz and I have
work to do.'

Archie's menagerie was in a fenced-off compound not
far from the house. There was netting stretched over the
top, and there were shrubs growing within and without
to shade it. Old hollow tree trunks lay inside. The paths
were gravel. He had rabbits in hutches, and a family
of guinea pigs in a marvellous cage fashioned like a
castle, with climbing wheels and slides and bells. He
had a white cockatoo with a sulphur crest and a limited
vocabulary— 'Hello, cocky!' and 'Oh, golly gosh!' He
had a pond with a small waterfall and slippery stones,
with greenery growing through it all and six frogs enjoying it. In another pond he had goldfish.

'Did you do all this?' Liz asked, rather enchanted,

surveying the menagerie and thinking how much Scout would love it.

'No, silly. I'm only five,' Archie replied. 'Cam did most if it. But I helped. Here.' He handed Liz a guinea pig. 'That's Golly, and this one—' he drew another one out of the castle-like cage '—is Ginny. She's his wife and they're all the kids.' Archie pointed into the cage.

'I see,' Liz replied gravely as she stroked Golly. 'So where is Wenonah? And her puppies?'

'Down at the stables. Wenonah can be a bit naughty about rabbits and things. She likes to chase them. But I'm going to train the puppy I get not to. Thing is—' his brow creased '—I don't know whether to get a boy or a girl.'

'Perhaps Cam can help you there? He might have an idea on the subject.'

Archie brightened. 'He usually does. Now, this is something special—my blue-tongue lizard!'

'Oh, wow!' Liz carefully put Golly back and sank down on her knees. 'Oh, my!'

That was how Cam found them some time later, both Liz and Archie on their knees and laughing together as they tried to entice Wally the blue-tongue lizard out of his cave.

Liz looked up and got up, brushing her knees. 'Sorry, but this is fascinating. I was just thinking how much Scout would enjoy it.'

'Who's Scout?' Archie enquired. 'Does he like animals?'

'*She*—she's my little girl, and she adores animals at the moment.'

'You should bring her over to play with me,' Archie said.

'Oh—'

Cam intervened. 'We'll see, Archie. Can I have Liz now?'

Archie agreed, but grudgingly.

'You made a hit there,' Cam commented as they walked back to the house.

'You get into "little kid mode" if you're around them long enough,' Liz said humorously, and stepped through the dolphin doors—only to stop with a gasp.

The entrance hall was a gallery that led to a lounge below. It had a vast stone fireplace and some priceless-looking rugs scattered about the stone-flagged floor. It was furnished with sumptuously comfortable settees and just a few equally priceless-looking ornaments and paintings. The overall colour scheme was warm and inviting—cream and terracotta with dashes of mint-green. But it was the wall of ceiling-high windows overlooking the most stunning view that had made Liz gasp.

A valley dropped precipitously below that wall of windows and fled away into the morning sunlight in all its wild splendour.

'It's—amazing. Do you ever get used to it?' she asked.

'Not really. It changes—different lights, different times of day, different weather. Uh—the study is down those stairs.'

The study came as another surprise to Liz. It presented

quite a different view—a sunlit, peaceful view—across a formal garden to grassy paddocks with wooden fences and horses grazing, lazily switching their tails. Beyond the paddocks she could see a shingle-roofed building with two wings and a clock tower in the middle—obviously the stables.

She turned back from the windows and surveyed the study. It was wood-panelled and lined with books on two sides. On the other walls there were very similar paintings to those in his office in Sydney: horses and trawlers. Her lips twitched.

The carpet was Ming blue, and the chairs on either side of the desk were covered in navy leather.

She sat down as directed, and he took his place behind the desk.

'I don't know how you manage to tear yourself away from the place,' she commented, as he poured coffee from a pewter flask. She cocked her head to one side as she accepted her cup. 'Was the menagerie your idea?'

'More or less.' He stirred his coffee. 'Archie's always been interested in animals, so I thought instead of mice in shoeboxes we might as well do it properly.' He looked down at his mug, 'It has also, I think, helped him get over the loss of his mother.'

Liz hesitated, then decided not to pursue that. 'Well, I *am* here to work, so—' She broke off when she noticed an ironic little glint in his eye as he crossed his arms and simply watched her.

And it all came flooding back—what had been said in the car before her enchantment with his gardens and his nephew's menagerie had claimed her.

She closed her eyes as she felt the colour that flooded her cheeks. As her lashes fluttered up, she said with effort, 'Let's not go there, Mr Hillier. In fact I refuse to discuss it.'

He lay back in his chair, dangling a silver pen in his long fingers. 'Why? It *did* happen.'

'It was an aberration,' Liz said coolly, reverting to her Ice Queen role.

He grinned—a full version of that crooked but utterly charismatic smile this time. 'Just a bit of naughtiness between two people for reasons unknown?'

'Well,' Liz said, thinking fast, 'you *had* been stood up out of the blue. Could that have been at the back of your mind?'

'Portia couldn't have been further from my mind.' He drummed his fingers on the desk and shrugged. 'That may sound—'

'It sounds pretty cold-blooded,' she broke in.

He looked at her. 'Portia thought that in exchange for her—charms—she could persuade me to back a clothing range. Swimsuits, in fact. She had her heart set on designing and no doubt modelling them,' he said dryly. 'When I looked into it I found it was an overcrowded market and a poor investment. Despite the fact that I'd never made any promises of any kind, she took the view that I had—uh—two-timed her.'

Liz blinked. 'Oh?'

He raised an eyebrow at her. 'You sound surprised.'

'I am,' Liz confessed.

'You assumed it was all over another woman?'

he suggested, with a glint of wicked amusement in his eyes.

Liz bit her lip and looked annoyed, because she knew she was being mocked. All the same it *was* what she'd automatically assumed. 'Well…yes. But did you honestly expect her still to want to go out with you?' she added. 'I would have thought not.'

Cam Hillier dragged his hand through his hair with a rueful look. 'Yep—got that bit wrong,' he confessed. 'I thought she'd at least trust my judgement.' He shrugged. 'Where money's concerned anyway.'

'I see,' Liz said—quite inadequately, she felt. But what else could she say?

He sat back with a faint smile. 'And it is over between us.'

'But only yesterday it didn't sound as if it was over for her!' Liz protested.

'Look, it is now,' he said dryly. 'Believe me.'

Liz shivered suddenly as she watched his mouth set, and knew she couldn't disbelieve him.

'But don't for one minute imagine that Portia won't find someone else.' He paused and looked at her penetratingly. 'Probably a lot sooner than I will, since you're so hell-bent on being the Ice Queen.'

Liz's lips parted in sheer shock. 'How did you…?'

He shrugged. 'We've known each other for nearly a month now. Quite long enough for me to detect when you're in chilly mode.'

Liz blinked helplessly several times and opened her mouth—but he spoke first. 'Never mind, we'll leave all that aside. How are you with horses?'

She opened her mouth again—to repeat bewilderedly *Horses?*—but just stopped herself in time. 'I have no idea why you want to know,' she said, 'but I like horses. I rode as a kid. If, though, you're going to ask me about trawlers, I've never been on one and have no desire to do so!'

His eyebrows shot up. 'Why would I?'

Liz gestured to the walls. 'They seem to go together for you. Horses and trawlers. And, probably because I don't understand any of this, in a fog of bewilderment I thought they might come next.'

He looked quizzical. 'No, but I suppose they *do* go together for me. I inherited a trawler fleet from my father, which eventually made the horses possible.'

Liz gazed at him. 'Why Shakespeare, though?'

He looked surprised. 'You noticed?'

She nodded.

'My mother again,' he said. 'She was hot on Shakespeare.'

'I see.' Liz was silent for a moment, then, 'Do you want to tell me why it matters whether I like horses? Come to that, why you've pretty thoroughly gone through my background with a toothcomb—and why I have the feeling I'm up here under false pretences?' she added, as she was gripped by the sensation that all was not what it seemed.

'Well, it *is* about engaging staff, Liz. I'd like to offer you the position of managing this place.'

This time Liz was struck seriously speechless.

'It's not a domestic position, it's a logistic one,' he went on. 'I do quite a lot of entertaining up here, and we often have house parties. I have good household staff, but I need someone to co-ordinate things both here and in the stables.'

'How…how so?' she asked, her voice breaking and husky with surprise. 'I'm not that good with horses.'

'It's not to do with the horses *per se*. We stand three stallions, we have twenty of our own mares, and we agist outside mares in foal and with foals at foot. The paperwork to keep track of it all alone is a big job. Checking the pedigrees of prospective mares for our stallions—it goes on. I need someone who can organise all that on a computer program.'

Liz breathed deeply but said nothing.

'I need to free up my stud master and the people who actually work with the horses from the paperwork—and incidentally free them up from all the people who stream in and out of the place.'

'Ah.' It was all Liz could think of to say.

He cast her an ironic little look, but continued. 'There's a comfortable staff cottage that would go with the position—big enough for you and Scout, as well as your mother. There's even a ready-made friend for Scout in Archie,' he said, and gazed at her steadily.

'But—' She stopped to clear her throat. 'Why me?'

'You've impressed me,' he said, and shrugged. 'You're as good as Roger—if not better in some areas. I think you're wasted as a diary secretary. I think you have the organisational skills as well as the people skills to do the job justice.'

'I…' Liz pressed her hands together and took another

deep breath. 'I don't know what to say,' she confessed. 'It's the last thing I was expecting.'

'Let's talk remuneration, then.' And for the next few minutes he outlined a package that was generous. So much so that to knock it back would be not so much looking a gift horse in the mouth but kicking it in the teeth...

'We'd have a three-month trial period,' he said, and grinned. 'Just in case you hanker for the bright lights or whatever.'

'If I didn't bring my mother—' Liz heard herself say cautiously, then couldn't go on.

He eyed her narrowly. 'Why wouldn't you?'

She gestured, then told him about the note she'd intercepted. 'She's been so wonderful, but I know it's something she'd love to do—I just haven't been able to work out how.' She shook her head. 'It wouldn't work up here, either.'

'You could share Archie's nanny for the times when you couldn't be with Scout.'

Liz stared at him, her eyes suddenly dark and uncertain. 'Why are you doing this—really? Are there any strings attached?'

'Such as?' He said it barely audibly.

'Such as going down a slippery slope into your bed?'

They stared at each other and she saw his eyes harden, but he answered in a drawl, 'My dear Liz, if you imagine I'd need to go to all these lengths to do that, you're wrong.'

'What's that supposed to mean?'

'You know as well as I do that if we gave each other just the smallest leeway we wouldn't be able to help ourselves. *But*—and I emphasise this—' his voice hardened this time '—if you prefer to go on your solitary way, so be it.'

'You were the one who brought it up,' Liz said hotly, then looked uncomfortable.

'At least I'm honest,' he countered.

'I haven't been dishonest.'

'Not precisely,' he agreed, and simply waited for her reply.

Liz ground her teeth. 'What you may not know is that being a single mother lays you open to…to certain men thinking you're…promiscuous.'

She wasn't expecting any more surprises at this point, but she got one when Cameron Hillier leant forward suddenly, his blue eyes intent. 'I know quite a bit about single mothers. My sister was one—and that, I guess, even while I'm not prepared to be dishonest, is why I have some sympathy for you, Liz Montrose.'

Her mouth fell open. She snapped it shut. So that explained the understanding she thought she'd seen in his eyes when she'd told him her story!

'And, further towards complete honesty,' he went on, 'I need the right influence in Archie's life at the moment—which I think you could be. I can't be with him nearly as much as I should. He starts school next year, so that will distance us even more. I want this last year of his before school to be memorable for him. And safe. And happy.'

'You don't know—how do you know I could do that?'

He sat back. 'I saw you with him just now. I've seen, from the moment you first mentioned her, how much your daughter means to you. How it lights you up just to say her name.'

'I still…' She paused helplessly. 'It's come up so fast!'

'It's part of my success—the ability to sum things up and make quick decisions.'

Liz looked at him askance. 'Your modesty is amazing at times.'

'I know,' he agreed seriously, but she could suddenly see the glimmer of laughter in his eyes.

'Well—'

'Er…excuse me?' a strange voice said, and they both swung round to see a woman standing in the doorway. 'Lunch is ready, Mr Hillier. I've served it in the kitchen if that's all right with you?'

Cam Hillier rose. 'That's fine, Mrs Preston. Thank you.'

It was a huge kitchen—brick-walled, with a tiled floor and rich woodwork. Herbs grew in pots along the windowsills, a vast antique dresser displayed a lovely array of china, but all the appliances were modern and stainless steel.

There was a long refectory table at one end that seated six in ladder-back chairs with raffia seats.

The lady who answered to 'Mrs Preston', grey-haired, pink-cheeked and of comfortable girth, was dishing up steaks, Liz saw, and baked Idaho potatoes topped with sour cream and chives. A bowl brimming with salad—cos lettuce, tomatoes, cucumber, capsicum and shallots—was also set out, and there was a bread basket laden with fresh warm rolls.

The steaks, she realised from their tantalising aroma, had been marinated and grilled along with button mushrooms.

A bottle of red wine was breathing in a pottery container.

'Hungry?' Cam asked as they sat down.

'I've suddenly realised I'm starving,' she confessed and looked around. 'Where's Archie?'

'At the dentist in Leura—just for a check-up. Mrs Preston,' Cam added, 'may I tell Miss Montrose what you told me on the phone a couple of days ago?'

Mrs Preston blinked at Liz, then said, 'Of course.'

Cam reached for the bottle of wine and poured them each a glass. 'For quite some years now Mrs Preston has been housekeeper and most inspired chef all rolled into one.' He lifted his glass in a silent toast and went on, 'Well, maybe *you'd* like to tell it, Mrs Preston?'

The housekeeper clasped her hands together and faced Liz. 'I did ring Mr Hillier a couple of days ago because I knew he'd understand.' She stopped to cast her boss an affectionate glance. 'I'm getting on a bit now,' she went on to Liz, 'and I'd really like to concentrate on my cooking. I've always liked to choose my own fresh ingredients, but for the rest of the provisioning of a household this size, and with the amount of entertaining we do, I'd like just to be able to write a list and hand it over to someone.'

She paused to draw several breaths and then continued, 'I don't want to have to worry any more about the state of the linen closet or whether we need new napkins. I don't want to have to worry about the hiring and firing of the cleaning staff, or counting the silver in case any of them are light-fingered, or wondering if I gave the same set of guests the same meals the last time they were here because I forgot to make a note of it. I'd rather there was someone who could co-ordinate it all,' she said a little wistfully.

Cam looked at Liz with a question in his eyes, and she registered the fleeting thought that he hadn't conjured up this job he'd offered her out of the blue—for whatever reason. It *did* exist. What also existed, she found herself thinking, was the fact that Cameron Hillier was well-loved by his staff. Not only Mrs Preston but Molly Swanson—and a few others she had met…

She swallowed a piece of melt-in-the-mouth steak and said, 'I think, whatever the outcome—my outcome, I mean—it would be criminal to burden you with all those other things any longer, Mrs Preston. This meal is one of the most delicious I've ever had.'

'Thank you, Miss Montrose.' Mrs Preston looked set to turn away, but she hesitated and added, 'Archie really took to you. He said you've got a little girl?'

'I do,' Liz confirmed. 'She's nearly four.'

'It's a wonderful place for kids up here.'

* * *

'So far, what do you think?' Cam Hillier queried as they walked side-by-side down to the stables after lunch.

There was a light breeze to temper the bite of the sun and to stir her hair, and the summery smell of grass and horses was all around as the path wound through the paddocks.

'I—I still don't know what to say,' Liz confessed.

He looked down at her. 'In case you're worried it's a glorified housekeeper position, I can tell you that you'd not only be in charge of the inner workings of the house but also the gardens—the whole damn lot,' he said, with a wave of his hand.

'Surely you'd be better off with a man?' she countered. 'I mean a man who could...well...' She looked around a little helplessly. 'Mend fences and so on.'

'A man who could mend fences in all likelihood couldn't run the house. A woman, on the other hand, with a sharp eye and the ability to hire the help she needs when she needs it, should be able to do both.' He paused and looked down at her. 'A woman, furthermore, who stands no nonsense from anyone has to be an asset.'

Liz released a long slow breath. 'You make me feel like a sergeant-major. I'm sorry I once threatened you, but you did ask for it.'

'Apology accepted,' he said gravely. 'Where were we? Yes. The house does need some upgrading. I've noticed it lately. Also there's the stable computer program.'

Liz was silent.

'It would look good on your résumé,' he said.

'Manager of the Yewarra Estate. It would look better than Temporary Diary Secretary.'

'Assuming I agreed, when would you expect me to start?'

He looked down at her wryly. 'Not before Roger comes back and you hand over to him. And you might need a few days off to get organised. Here we are.'

The stables were picturesque, with tubs of petunias dotted about, swept walkways and the earthy smell of manure combined with the sweet smell of hay on the air. They were also a hive of activity—and Liz saw what Cam Hillier had meant when he'd mentioned all the people who streamed in and out of the place. The stables had a separate entrance from the house.

The office yielded another scene. A giant of a man in his forties, with sandy hair and freckles, and 'outdoor type' written all over him, was sitting in front of a computer almost literally tearing his hair out.

He was Bob Collins, stud master, and he greeted Cam and Liz distractedly. 'I've lost it again,' he divulged as the cause of his distraction. 'The whole darn program seems to have disappeared down some bloody cyber black hole!'

Cam glanced at Liz. She grimaced, but pulled up a chair next to Bob and, after a few questions, began tapping the computer keys. Within a few minutes she'd restored his program.

Bob looked at her properly for the first time, clapped her on the back, and swung round to Cam. 'I don't know where you got her from, but can I have her? Please?'

Cam grinned. 'Maybe. She has to make up her mind.'

* * *

They were walking back to the house, not talking, both lost in their own thoughts, when his phone rang.

'Yep. Uh-huh… This afternoon? Well, OK, but tell Jim he'll have to fly straight back to Sydney.'

He clicked the phone off and turned to Liz. 'Change of plan. Our legal adviser needs to see me urgently. He's flying up in the company helicopter and staying the night. I—'

'How will I get home?' Liz interrupted with some agitation.

'I wasn't planning to keep you here against your will,' he said dryly. 'You're going back to Sydney on the chopper.'

Liz went red. 'Sorry,' she mumbled.

He stopped and rested his hand on her shoulder, swinging her round to face him. 'If,' he said, 'you really don't trust me, Liz, we might as well call the whole thing off here and now.'

She drew a deep breath and called on all her composure. 'I haven't had time to wonder about that—whether I trust you or not,' she said. 'I was thinking of Scout and my mother. I've never been away from them overnight before.'

His hand on her shoulder fell away, and she thought he was going to say something more, but he started to walk towards the house.

She hesitated, then followed suit.

The helicopter was blue and white, and the legal adviser looked harassed as he climbed out of it. The helicopter pad was on the other side of the house from the menagerie.

Liz felt harassed as she waited to board, but hoped she didn't look it. It was now late afternoon. She'd spent the rest of the afternoon in Mrs Preston's company, being shown over the house. It was impossible not to be impressed—especially with the nursery wing. There was a playroom that would be any kid's dream. All sorts of wonderful characters in large cut-outs lined the walls—characters out of *Peter Pan*, *Alice in Wonderland* and more—and many toys. There was a small kitchenette and three bedrooms…

On the other hand Cam Hillier, waiting with her beside the helipad, looked casual and relaxed. He had Archie with him, and it was obvious the little boy was delighted at this unscheduled change of plan.

'Can I think this over?' Liz said.

'Sure,' he agreed easily, and advanced towards the legal adviser. 'Good day, Pete. This is Liz, but she's on her way out. In you get, Liz.'

Is that all? Liz found herself wondering as she climbed into the chopper and started to belt herself up. Then she stopped abruptly.

'Uh—hang on a moment,' she said to the pilot. 'I forgot to ask him—can we just hang on a moment?'

The pilot shrugged rather boredly. 'Whatever you like.'

So Liz unbuckled herself and climbed out, and the two men on the pad turned back to her, looking surprised.

'Uh—Mr Hillier, I forgot to ask you if you'll be in the office tomorrow and at what time?'

'Not sure at this stage, Liz.'

Liz paled. 'But I've rescheduled some of today's appointments for tomorrow!'

'Then you may have to reschedule them again.'

She planted her hands on her hips. 'And what will I tell them this time?'

He shrugged. 'It's up to you.'

Liz took an angry breath, but forced herself to calm down. 'OK,' she said with an airy shrug. 'I'll tell them you've *gone fishing*!'

And with that she swung on her heel and climbed back into the chopper. 'You can go now,' she informed the pilot, her eyes the only giveaway of her true mental state. They were sparkling with anger.

He looked at her, this time with a grin tugging at his lips. 'That was telling him—good on you!'

'You—you find him hard to work for?'

The pilot inclined his head as he fired up the motor and the rotors started to turn. 'At times. But on the whole he's best bloke I've ever worked for. I guess we all think the same.'

'And that,' Liz said to her mother later that evening, having summed up the salient points of her day, 'is a sentiment shared by I would say his housekeeper, his stud master, and his secretary Molly Swanson. He can be difficult, but they really admire and respect him. His nephew adores him.' She shook her head in some confusion. 'I really didn't believe he had that side to him. Not that I'd actually thought about it.'

'Take it,' Mary said impulsively. 'Take the job. I say that because I see it as a career move for you. I see it as a way that may open all sorts of opportunities for you. If it doesn't, you can always come back to this. Anyway, the money alone will take a lot of the stress and strain from you. And I'll come with you!'

'Mum, no,' Liz said, and explained about the note she'd read. 'If I take it, one of the reasons I'll do it is so that you can have more of a life of your own, doing what you love and are so good at.'

Mary looked stubborn, and the argument went backwards and forwards until Liz said frustratedly, 'He may even have changed his mind by tomorrow—he can be annoying at times, and I more or less told him so today. He can certainly be an arrogant multi-millionaire.'

But when she went to bed she was thinking of Archie, and that brought his uncle into a different light for her. Arrogant Cam Hillier could certainly be—but when you saw him with his nephew he was a different man. Different and appealing…

Unaware that he'd just been categorised as an arrogant multi-millionaire, Cam Hillier nevertheless found himself thinking of Liz as he poured himself a nightcap and took it to his study. His legal adviser had gone to bed and so had Archie—a lot earlier.

She was a strange mixture, he decided, and grinned suddenly as he recalled her parting jibe on the helipad. So bright and capable, so attractive… He thought of her slim, elegant figure today, beneath her jumper and jeans, and the easy, fluid way she walked. He thought of the way she could look right through you out of those chilly blue eyes, but on the other hand how she could light up as she had over his gardens and with Archie.

He sobered, though, as he thought that there was no doubt she had a tortured soul.

No wonder, he reflected as he stared into the amber depths of his drink, and remembered with the stabbing sense of loss it always brought his sister Amelia, Archie's mother, and what single motherhood had done to her...

He sighed and transferred his attention to the paintings on his study walls—horses and trawlers and Shakespeare. And one trawler in particular, *Miss Miranda*, because it had been the first trawler his parents had bought. There was a new Miranda now, *Miss Miranda II*, much larger than her predecessor, and yet to be immortalised in paint.

He shrugged as he strolled back to his desk and sank down into his swivel chair. He found himself thinking back to his parents' early days.

They must have made an unlikely couple when they'd first married: the girl from an impoverished but blue-blooded background, and the tall, laconic bushman who'd grown up in Cooktown in Far North Queensland on a cattle station, with the sea in his veins and a dream of owning a prawning fleet.

In fact they'd made such an unlikely couple to his mother's family, the Hastings clan, they'd virtually cast her off—apart from Narelle, his great-aunt. Yet his parents had been deeply in love until the day they'd died—together. It had been a love that had carried them through all their trials and tribulations—all their hard days at sea on boats that smelt of fish and diesel and often broke down. Through days of tropical heat in Cooktown, when the boats had been laid up in the off-season, and through nights when the catch had been small enough to break your heart.

Somehow, though, his mother had managed to make wherever they were a home—even if only via a hibiscus bloom in a glass, or a little decoupage of shells, and her warm smile. And she'd been able to do that even when she must have been longing for more temperate climates, a gracious home and great gardens such as she'd known as a child. And his father, even when he'd been bone-tired and looking every year of his age and more, had always seemed to know when that shadow was not far from his mother. He'd always been able to make the sun shine for her again—sometimes just with a touch of a hand on her hair.

Cam drained his glass and twirled it in his fingers.

Why did thinking of his parents so often make him feel—what? As if he was playing his life like a discordant piece of music?

Was it because, although he'd taken the strands of all their hard work and pulled them together, and gone on to make a huge fortune from them, he didn't have what they'd had?

On the other side of the scale, though, was the memory of his sister Amelia, who'd loved unwisely and been dumped, never to be the same girl again. And now there was Archie—both motherless and fatherless because Amelia had taken the secret of who his father was to her grave.

If that wasn't enough to make one cynical about love and its disastrous consequences, what was?

He grimaced. Hot on the heels of that had to come all the women who pursued him for his money.

Funny, really, he mused, but in his heart of hearts was he as cynical about love as Liz Montrose?

He stretched and linked his hands behind his head, and wondered if the fault was with him—this feeling of discord with his life. Were his expectations of women way too high? Was that why he'd stopped even looking for his ideal woman? Was it all underpinned by the tragedy of his sister?

And in a more general sense was he frustrated because he felt he wasn't doing the right thing by Archie? Yes, he could give him everything that opened and shut—yes, he could come up with ideas like the menagerie—but his time was another matter.

He unlinked his hands and sat up abruptly as it came to him that it wasn't only Archie who needed more of his time. He himself had got onto a treadmill of work and the acquisition of more power that at times felt like a strait-jacket, but he didn't seem to be able to get himself off it.

He took up his glass and stared unseeingly across the room.

Was it all bound up with not having a permanent woman in his life or a proper family? he wondered. He set his glass down with a sudden thump at the thought.

Was that why he was making sure Liz Montrose couldn't ride off into the sunset? Because of more than a physical attraction he couldn't seem to eradicate? Did he have at the back of his mind the prospect of creating a family unit with her and her daughter and Archie? Was that why he'd broken the unspoken truce between them just before offering her a job?

He hadn't planned to do that. He'd been needled into doing it because she could be so damn cool—and he not only wanted her body, he wanted *her*.

But what if a tortured Ice Queen turned out to be the one he really wanted and couldn't have? he asked himself.

CHAPTER FIVE

LIZ WAS LATE for work the next morning—thanks to an uncharacteristic tantrum from Scout. She hadn't wanted to get dressed, she hadn't wanted breakfast, she hadn't wanted to do anything she usually did.

Since she wasn't running a temperature, and had no other symptoms, Liz had concluded that her daughter had picked up her own uneasy vibes after another restless night.

'Go,' Mary had said. 'Well, finish getting dressed first. She'll be fine with me. And remember what I said,' she'd added pointedly.

So Liz had hurriedly finished dressing, thanking heaven she'd chosen a simple outfit—the ultimate little black dress, with a square neck, cap sleeves, a belted waistline and a short skirt. She'd slipped on high-heeled taupe shoes, dragged on two broad colourful bangles, grabbed her purse and run for the bus.

She was only fifteen minutes late now, after a lightning call into the staff powder room to put on some make-up and check her hair. Therefore it was a rather nasty surprise to be told as she greeted Molly that her boss was waiting for her.

'W-waiting?' she stammered. 'I didn't think he'd be in today—well, not this morning anyway.'

'He's been here over an hour. Grab the diary,' Molly recommended.

Liz did as she was told, and, after taking several deep breaths, knocked and let herself into Cam Hillier's office.

He was on the phone and gestured for her to sit down.

She put the diary on the desk and not only sat down but tried to regroup as best she could, while he talked on the phone, lying back in his chair, half turned away from her.

She pushed her hair behind her ears, smoothed her skirt and crossed her ankles. She did some discreet facial exercises, then squared her shoulders and folded her hands in her lap and studied them.

'Ready?'

Her lashes flew up and to her consternation she realised that she hadn't noticed him finish his call. 'Uh—yes. I'm sorry I'm late.'

'But you weren't expecting me to be in?' he suggested.

'It wasn't that. Scout was a little off-colour. Mind you,' she added honestly, 'I *wasn't* expecting you to be in.'

He watched her for a long moment, his dense blue eyes entirely enigmatic. 'I decided,' he said at last, 'that my reputation might not stand a "gone fishing" tag.'

Liz coloured faintly. 'I wouldn't have done that,' she murmured.

'Yesterday afternoon you would have,' he countered gravely.

Liz moved a little uneasily and said nothing.

He got up and walked over to the wide windows that overlooked the city. Gone was the informality, clothes-wise, of yesterday. Today he wore a navy suit, with a grey and white pinstriped shirt and a midnight-blue tie. Today he looked every inch the successful businessman who'd diversified from a fishing fleet into many other enterprises.

He turned to look at her. 'So? Any decision?'

Liz licked her lips. 'Well, I've discussed it with my mother, and she—' She broke off and cleared her throat. 'No,' she amended. '*I'd* like to take the position—if you haven't changed your mind?'

He shoved his hands into his pockets. 'Why would I?'

Liz grimaced. 'Because of the "gone fishing" tag?'

He smiled briefly. 'I was being bloody-minded. I probably deserved it. No, I haven't changed my mind. Go on? I take it you'd like me to believe you and not your mother made the decision?'

'Yes,' she admitted, and smoothed her skirt again. 'To be honest, I couldn't in all conscience turn it down. Financially it would put me in a much better place. It would be like working from home, and it would mean I don't have to take part-time weekend work. Career-wise—as you said—it would look much better on my résumé. It would give me so much more time with Scout, and...' She paused and swallowed. 'Overall, I think it would make me look like a much more suitable mother—able to offer Scout much more, sort of thing.'

'If Scout's father decided to contest your suitability, do you mean?'

She nodded.

'So you're going to tell him?'

'No. But…' Liz hesitated. 'He has moved back to Sydney.' She explained how she'd come to know this. 'So that's another reason I'd be happier somewhere else.'

'You can't keep running away from him, Liz.'

She spread her hands. 'I know that. Still, I would be happier. And I think a better job like this would make me feel I had more…stature—would make me feel a lot better about myself, my life, et cetera.'

He brooded over this for a moment, then, 'And your mother? What's her opinion?'

'She's all for it—although it took a bit of persuading to get her to agree to stay in Sydney and take up the costume design job. But I pointed out that she's only fifty and she needs a life of her own. Of course she'll come up and spend time with us—if that's OK?'

'Fine.' His lips twisted. 'Are you looking forward to it, though? All the pragmatism in the world isn't going be much good to you if you hate it up there. If you feel it's beneath your skills or whatever.'

'*Hate* it up there?' Liz repeated wryly. 'That would be hard to do.'

'Or if you feel lonely.'

Their gazes caught as he said it, and Liz found she

couldn't look away. Something in the way he said it, and the way he was looking at her, held her trapped.

She moistened her lips. 'I plan to be too busy to feel lonely.'

But she knew immediately this wasn't the right response. It didn't answer the unasked question he was posing—the question of, as he had put it, the electricity that sometimes sizzled between them. Even now it was there between them as he stood watching her, so tall, so— She sought for the right expression. So dynamic that she couldn't help being physically moved by him—moved and made to wonder what it would be like to be in his arms.

She actually felt all the little hairs on her body stand up as she wondered this, and realised to her amazement that she'd given herself goosebumps again.

But there was more.

Lonely, she thought on a sudden indrawn breath.

She'd been lonely for years. Lonely for that special companionship with a man who was your lover. And she had no doubt that Cameron Hillier would meld those two roles brilliantly. For how long, though, before another Portia crossed his path? Well, maybe not a Portia, but— Stop it! she told herself. Don't go there…

'Liz? Are we going to play games about this?'

She trembled inwardly, but it struck her that she'd only ever been honest with this man, and she'd continue to be so.

'If you mean am I going to deny that an attraction exists for me? No, I'm not. But…' She paused and rubbed her palms together, then laced her fingers. 'I can't let it affect me. I made one terrible mistake in the name of what I thought was love, but it turned out to be only a passing attraction. I'm still trying to pick up the pieces—the pieces not only of my life but of my—my morale, maybe.'

She stopped, and didn't know that a terrible tension was visible in her expression. She did try to lighten her tone. 'You'd think five years would be enough to get over it.' She smiled briefly. 'But not so. And then, if you'll forgive me, Mr Hillier, there's you.'

'Go on,' he invited dryly. 'Or can I guess? You don't know whether my intentions are honourable or the opposite?' He paused, then said deliberately, 'I certainly wouldn't be so heartless as to leave you pregnant and alone.'

'I did…walk out on him,' she whispered.

'Liz, you're twenty-four now. That means you would have only been *nineteen* when it happened. Right?' he said interrogatively.

'Well, yes. But—'

'How old was he?' he continued. 'Older, I gather?'

'He—he was thirty-five.'

'And who was he? I don't want names,' he added as she took a quick, tempestuous breath. 'What was he in your life?'

Her shoulders slumped. 'One of my tutors.'

He studied her for a long moment. 'That's an old, old story, Liz,' he said. 'An older man in some sort of authority. A young, possibly naïve, starstruck girl. He shouldn't have walked out of your life without a backward glance when things came right for him with another woman. He should have known better *right from the start.'*

Liz fiddled with her bangles for a long moment and found that breathing was difficult. Why? she questioned herself. Because those had been her own bitter sentiments even while she'd changed courses and campuses and finally finished her degree as an external student?

'Look,' she said in a strained voice to match the expression in her eyes, 'for whatever reason—I mean legitimate or otherwise—I'm not ready to go down that road again.'

'Why are you taking the job, then?'

She gestured. 'It's the only opportunity that's come my way so far to climb out of the hole Scout and I are stuck in. And…' She stopped.

'Go on?' he prompted.

She moistened her lips. 'This may sound strange, but seeing you with Archie sort of—made up my mind. But if it's going to…' She hesitated.

'Going to what? Make my life uncomfortable?' he suggested.

Liz coloured. 'I don't— I mean I—' She bit her lip.

He crossed to the desk and dropped into his chair. 'Perhaps I should take up wood-chopping?' His lips twitched.

'Seriously,' Liz said quietly, 'perhaps we should forget all about it?'

He swung his chair round so he was facing her, and she could see suddenly that he was stone-cold sober. 'No. You seem convinced you can handle it, so I'll do the same.'

'I still don't quite understand why you've offered me the position if—' She stopped a little helplessly.

'If I'm not going to get you down the slippery slope into my bed?' He looked coolly amused. 'I think it's because of my sister,' he went on. 'One reason, anyway. Hers was a similar story to yours, but we never got to know who Archie's father was. She refused to say, but she was obviously traumatized. She was bitter, and she felt she'd been betrayed. I sometimes wonder if she thought I would—' he gestured '—take matters into my own hands if she told me who he was. Then she was killed on a skiing holiday in an avalanche when Archie was three, and the secret died with her.'

'Would you have?' Liz asked round-eyed. 'Taken matters…?'

Cam Hillier looked away, his mouth set in a hard line. 'I don't know what I might have done. I hated seeing her so distressed.'

'So you had absolutely no idea who he was?'

'No. She was overseas at the time.'

'Oh. I'm sorry.'

He stared past her, his eyes bleak, then he shrugged. 'So we're on, Miss Montrose?'

Liz hesitated.

'Don't worry. I won't impose on you.'

He was not to know that his promise not to impose on her had sent an irrational—*highly* irrational—shiver down her spine, although she ignored it.

'Yes,' she said at last.

'OK. I'll get things underway. Now, let's see what the diary holds for today.'

Liz hesitated, then reached for the diary and went through his appointments one by one.

At the end of it he told her what he wanted her to arrange for him in the next few days, and it was all normal and businesslike as Liz made notes. Finally she stood up, saying, 'I'll get on to it.' She turned away.

It was as she was almost at the door that he said her name.

She turned back with her eyebrows raised.

He paused, then said quietly, 'You can always talk to me, you know. If you need to—or want to.'

Liz stared at him, and to her horror felt tears rising to the surface. She blinked several times and cleared her throat. 'Thanks,' she said huskily. 'Thank you.' And she turned away quickly, praying he would not notice how she'd been affected by a few simple words of kindness...

Lying in bed that night, though, she wondered if it was that unexpected streak of kindness in him that she— loved? No—not that, surely? But it was something that drew her to him.

CHAPTER SIX

A MONTH after she'd started work at Yewarra, Liz had to concede that Cam Hillier had kept his promise.

It had been a hard-working but satisfying month. She'd settled into the cottage, which wasn't far from the house and, although small, was comfortable, with its own fenced garden. It was not only comfortable but picturesque, with some lovely creepers smothering its white walls. There was also a double swing seat with a canopy in the garden that just invited you to relax on it.

Probably because of having lived in an apartment all her life Scout loved the garden, and Liz loved the fact that when she could work from the cottage, in an inglenook converted to a small office, she could keep an eye on Scout through the window.

It also gave Liz her own freedom. Although she sometimes accepted Mrs Preston's invitation to eat up at the house, she more often cooked for herself and Scout. And when Cam was in residence and entertaining she had a place to retreat to.

At the same time—and she hadn't thought it possible—Scout was weaving her way more and more into her heart. She tried to analyse why, and decided it had something to do with she herself being under much less stress and being able to spend much more time with Scout.

They'd got into the habit of Scout coming into her bed every morning, bringing her favourite doll, Jenny Penny.

One morning Scout said to Liz, 'You've got me and I've got Jenny Penny. We're lucky, Mummy!'

'Sweetheart,' Liz responded, giving her blue-eyed, curly-haired daughter half a hundred kisses—a game they played— 'I am so lucky to have you I can't believe it sometimes!'

She *had* been aware that she'd been under discreet surveillance as she'd fitted into the job. Mrs Preston might be a motherly soul, and Bob might be a friendly bear of a man, but that hadn't stopped them from monitoring her progress—especially where Archie was concerned.

It hadn't annoyed her. It had made sense.

Mary had come up for a couple of weekends, and appeared satisfied that her daughter and granddaughter were in a good place. At the same time Liz had been happy to see that her mother was in high spirits—excited, and full of ideas for the costumes she was designing. Plus, Liz thought she'd detected that Mary might have a man in her life, from the odd things she'd let drop about how this or that had appealed to Martin.

But Liz's enquiries had only sent her mother faintly pink at the same time as she shrugged noncommittally.

Mary had also met Cam a couple of times and been visibly impressed. Not that that was so surprising, Liz acknowledged. What *was* surprising—although Mary had always been intuitive—was her mother's discreet summing up of the situation between her daughter and her daughter's employer.

She knows, Liz thought with an inward tremor. Somehow she's divined that things aren't quite as they seem between Cam and me.

Mary had said nothing, however, and Liz was more than happy to allow it to lie unspoken between them and, hopefully, to sink away into oblivion.

As for the work side of Liz's life—she'd gone through the big house and identified what needed repairing, replacing or upgrading, and she'd set it all in motion. She'd had a section of the stable driveway repaved where it had badly needed it, and she'd personally checked all the fence lines on Yewarra.

She'd done this on a quiet mare Bob had told her she could ride whenever she wanted to. She'd thoroughly enjoyed getting back into the saddle, and she loved the country air and the scenery.

Setting up a computer program for the stables had come easily to her, and had provided a source of great pleasure for Scout and Archie as she often took them with her to check out the foals born on Yewarra. They made up names for them as they watched them progress from stiff-legged newborns to frisky and confident in an amazingly short time.

There had been some moments of unease for her,

however, during the month. Faint shadows that had darkened her enjoyment and sense of fulfilment...

Don't get too used to this, she'd warned herself. Whatever you do, don't get a feeling of *mistress of all she surveys*. Don't let yourself feel too much at home because sooner or later you'll have to move on.

She'd reiterated those warnings to herself a couple of times, when Cam had been home with a party of guests, but from a slightly different angle. It was one thing to work with Mrs Preston and the household staff to make sure everything went like clockwork. It was another to watch from the sidelines and feel a bit like Cinderella.

And it was yet another again to find herself keeping tabs on her employer—no, not that, she thought with impatience. Surely not that! So what? To have a sixth sense whenever he was home as to his whereabouts? To feel her skin prickling in a way that told her he was nearby?

To—go on: admit it—feel needled by the way he kept his distance from her? How ridiculous is that? she asked herself more than once.

Then there was Archie.

A serious, sensitive little boy, with grey eyes and brown hair that stuck up stubbornly from his crown, he worried about all sorts of things—when five of Wenonah's puppies were sent to their new homes he hardly ate all day and couldn't sleep that night. And he pulled at her heartstrings at times when she thought about him being motherless and fatherless. When she could see how he hero-worshipped Cam, who tried to temper the little time he could spend with the boy by sending him postcards and books and weird and wonderful things from different parts of the country and overseas—things that Archie took inordinate pride in and kept in a special cabinet in his room.

'Of course they're not all suitable for a five-year-old,' Archie's nanny said to her once, when they were looking through them. 'Take this.' She pulled down a full-size boomerang from a shelf Archie couldn't reach. 'Archie didn't realise he shouldn't experiment with it inside and he threw it through a window, breaking the glass. He was really upset—until Mr Hillier found him a song about a man whose boomerang wouldn't come back. Archie loves it. It really cracks him up and it made him feel much better.'

'I—I know it,' Liz said with a smile in her voice, and she thought, so that explains *that*!

She couldn't deny that she was getting very fond of Archie.

As for Scout, although she'd missed Mary for a time, she'd taken to Daisy Kerr, Archie's nanny, and so had Liz. Daisy was a practical girl, very mindful of her responsibilities, but with a streak of romance and nonsense in her that lent itself to the magical world kids loved.

And, between them, Liz and Daisy had soon joined forces to occupy the children with all sorts of games.

One memorable one had been the baby elephant walk. When a real baby elephant had been born at Taronga Zoo, they'd watched its progress avidly on the internet, and Liz had found a recording of Henry Mancini's "Baby Elephant Walk" from the movie *Hatari*.

She and Daisy had mimicked elephants, and with one

arm outstretched for the trunk and one held behind the back they'd paced around the playroom to the music. Scout and Archie had quickly caught on, and it had become a favourite game.

None of them had realised that Cam was watching one day, unseen from the doorway, as they shuffled their way around and then all fell in a heap, the kids screaming with laughter. Liz had coloured at the indignity of it as she'd hastily got to her feet and patted herself down, but her boss had been laughing and she'd caught a glint of approval in his blue gaze.

Scout had been a little wary of Archie to begin with. It was plain Archie saw himself as the senior child on Yewarra, not to mention owner and architect of the menagerie. As such he dictated what they should do and what they should play.

Scout bore it with equanimity until one day, almost a month on, when Archie removed a toy from her. She screamed blue murder as she wrested it back, and then she pushed him over.

'Scout!' Liz scolded as she picked up the astonished Archie and gave him a hug.

'Mine!' Scout declared as she clasped the toy to her chest and stamped her foot.

'Well…' Liz said a little helplessly

'Like mother like daughter,' Cam Hillier murmured, causing Liz to swing round in surprise.

'I didn't know you were here!'

He straightened from where he'd propped his wide shoulders against the playroom doorframe. 'Just arrived.

I drove up. So she's got a temper and a mind of her own, young Scout?'

Liz grimaced. 'Apparently. I've never seen her react like that before.' She turned back. 'Scout, you mustn't do that. Archie, are you all right?'

Daisy took over at this point. 'You'll be fine, won't you, Archie? And we'll all be friends now. I know—let's go and see Wenonah and her puppy.'

Liz and Cam watched the three of them head off towards the stables, peace and contentment restored, although Liz felt somewhat guilty.

'Thank heavens for Wenonah and her puppy—look, I'm sorry,' she said. 'They usually get along like a house on fire.'

He shrugged. 'It probably won't do Archie any harm to learn from an early age that the female sex can be unpredictable.'

Liz opened her mouth, closed it, then chuckled. 'But you must admit I don't go around pushing people over. Or screaming at them,' she said humorously.

He glanced down at her quizzically as they walked side by side into the kitchen.

Liz clicked her tongue. 'Well, maybe I *did* threaten you once—but under extreme provocation, and I would never have carried it out! I didn't scream either.' She stopped and had to laugh. 'I would have loved to, though.'

'Oh, good. There are some things I did want to speak to you about. When would you like to have a tour?'

'I think I'm going to hit the sack after this. How about tomorrow morning?'

'Fine.' But she said it slowly and looked at him rather narrowly.

'What?' he queried.

'Are you feeling OK? I only ask,' she added hastily, 'because I've never seen you less than…well, full of energy.'

Cam Hillier drummed his fingers on the table, then raked a hand through his hair and rubbed the blue shadows on his jaw. He wondered what she would say if he told her the truth.

That he was growingly plagued by thoughts of her. That when he allowed himself to step into his imagination he could picture himself exploring the pale, satiny, secret places of her slim elegant body. He could visualise himself, with the lightest touch, bringing her to the incandescence he'd seen in her once or twice—but much more than that, more personal, more physical, more joyful.

He could see her, in his mind's eye, breathless, beaded with sweat, and achingly beautiful as she responded to his ardour with her own…

How would she react if she knew that to see her apparently blooming when he was going through all this was actually annoying the hell out of him?

That, and something else. He was the one who had visualised a family unit. He was the one who'd dug into his subconscious and realised his business life had taken over his whole life—to its detriment—but he didn't seem to be able to change gears and slow down. It had been *his* somewhat shadowy intention to see how

Liz fitted into Yewarra, and therefore by extension his life, to make it work better for him—for both of them.

Yes, he'd kept his distance for the last month, to give her time to settle in and because he'd made her a promise, but it had become an increasing hardship. What he hadn't expected was to find that the family circle had been well and truly forged—Liz, Scout and Archie— and *he* now felt like an outsider in his own home.

Was there any softening in her attitude towards men, and towards him in particular? he wondered, and was on the point of simply asking her outright. Take it easy, he advised himself instead. Don't go crashing around like a bull in a china shop. But he grimaced. He knew himself well enough to know that he would bring the subject up sooner or later…

'I'm OK,' he said at length. 'Thank you for your concern,' he added formally, although he couldn't prevent the faintest hint of irony as well. 'I should be back to fighting fit by tomorrow.' And the sooner I get out of here the better, he added, but this time to himself.

Liz might not have been privy to her employer's thoughts, but she found she was curiously restless after their encounter.

Restless and uneasy, but not able to say why.

The next morning she told herself she'd been imagining things as they toured the house and she pointed out to Cam what she'd organised for it.

He appeared to be back to normal. He looked refreshed, and his manner was easy. He also looked quintessentially at home on his country estate, in jeans and a khaki bush shirt. And he'd already—with Archie and Scout's assistance—been on a tadpole-gathering exercise in a creek not far from the house, to add to the menagerie's frog population.

Scout, who'd been a bit awestruck when she'd first met Cam Hillier, had completely lost her reserve now, Liz noted. And that led her to think, still with some amazement, about the two sides that made up her employer: the dictatorial, high-flying businessman, and the man who was surprisingly good with little kids.

'This is the only room where it seemed like a good idea to start from scratch,' she said as they stood in the doorway of the veranda lounge, which was glassed in conservatory-style, with a paved area outside and views of the valley. It was the focal point for guests for morning and afternoon tea. As such, it got a lot of use—and was showing it.

Cam had already approved the upgrading of two guest bedrooms, the new plumbing she'd ordered for some of the bathrooms, the new range she'd ordered for Mrs Preston, and he'd waved a hand when she told him about the linen, crockery and kitchenware she'd ordered.

'I got a quote and some sketches and samples from an interior decorating firm,' she told him, 'but I thought you'd like the final say.'

'Show me.'

So she displayed the sketches, the pictures of furniture and the fabric samples.

Cam studied them. 'Got a pin?'

She frowned. 'A pin?'

'Do you always repeat what people say to you?' he enquired.

'No,' she retorted.

'You seem to do it a lot with me.'

'That's because you consistently take me by surprise!' she countered. 'What on earth—?' She paused and stared at him. 'Don't tell me you're going to choose one with a pin?'

He laughed at her expression. 'It's not sacrilege, and since I don't have a wife to do it for me, what's left? Or why don't you choose?'

'Because I don't have to live with it. Because I'm not…' She stopped and stared at him as a vision she'd warned herself so often against entertaining raced through her mind.

'Because you're not my wife? Of course I know that, dear Liz,' he drawled, and once again couldn't help a certain tinge of irony.

She might have missed it yesterday, but Liz didn't miss it now. She blinked as she became aware of a need to proceed with caution, of dangerous undercurrents between them that she didn't fully understand—or was that being naïve?

Of course it was, she chastised herself. She could feel the physical tension between them. She could feel the heat…

They were standing facing each other, separated by no more than a foot. His shirt was open at the neck and she could see the curly black hair in the vee of it. She took an unexpected breath as she visualised him without his shirt, with all the muscles of his powerful, sleek torso exposed. She felt her fingertips tingle, as if they were passing over his skin, tracing a path through those springy black curls downwards…

She felt her nipples tingle and she had a sudden, mind-blowing vision of his hand on her, tracing a similar path downwards from her breasts.

Worse, she was unable to tear her gaze from his— and she had no doubt he'd be able to read what was going through her mind as colour mounted in her cheeks and her breathing accelerated. She was not to know he could also see a pulse fluttering at the base of her throat, but she did see a nerve suddenly beating in his jaw—something she'd seen before.

She swallowed desperately and opened her mouth to say she knew not what—anything to defuse the situation—but he got in first.

'You are a woman of taste and discrimination, wouldn't you say?' His gaze wandered up and down her in a way that she thought might be slightly insolent—why?

But it did help her regain some composure. 'I guess that's for others to decide,' she said tartly, and for good measure added, 'If you really want to know, I don't like any of these ideas.'

She turned to look around at the veranda room. 'It's a room to be comfortable in—not stiff and formal, as these sketches are.' She gestured to the drawings. 'It's not a room for pastel colours and spindly furniture. You need vibrant colours and comfortable chairs. You need some indoor plants. You need—' She broke off and put her fingers to her lips, realising that in her confusion and everything else she'd got quite carried away. 'Sorry. That's only my—thinking.'

He watched her with a glint of amusement. 'Do it,' he said simply.

'What?' She raised an eyebrow at him. 'Do what?'

'Liz, you're doing it again,' he remonstrated. 'Decorate it yourself, along the lines you've just described to me. I like the sound of it. I won't,' he added deliberately, 'confuse you with a wife.'

Liz opened her mouth, but Mrs Preston intervened as she came into the room.

'Liz—excuse me, Mr Hillier—I just wanted to check with you whether the barbecue is going ahead this afternoon?'

'Oh!' Liz hesitated, then turned to Cam. 'I was going to have an early barbecue for the kids—round about five this afternoon, in my garden. We've done that a couple of times lately and they both really enjoy it. But you might like to have Archie to yourself?'

'What I'd like is to be invited to the barbecue,' Cam Hillier said blandly.

'So I don't need to cater for you this evening, Mr Hillier?' Mrs Preston put in—a little hastily, Liz thought with an inward frown.

Cam raised his eyebrows at Liz.

'Uh—no. I mean, yes. I mean...' Liz stopped on an edge of frustration. 'No, you don't, Mrs Preston. Please do come to the barbecue, Mr Hillier.'

'If you're sure it's not too much trouble, Miss Montrose?' he replied formally.

'Not at all,' she said, with the slightest edge that she

hoped wasn't apparent to Mrs Preston. But she knew she was being laughed at and couldn't help herself. 'We specialise in sausages on bread.'

'Oh!' Mrs Preston had turned away, but now she turned back, her face a study of consternation. 'Oh, look—I can help out, Liz. You can't give Mr Hillier kids' food.'

'I was only joking, Mrs Preston,' Liz said contritely, and she put her arms around that troubled lady. 'I've got—let me see...' She paused to do a mental run-through of her fridge and pantry. 'Some prime T-bones, and I can whip up a potato gnocchi with bacon and some pecorino cheese, and a green salad. How does that sound?'

Mrs Preston relaxed and patted Liz's cheek. 'I should have known you were teasing me.'

'But were you?' Cam Hillier murmured when his housekeeper was out of earshot.

'What do you mean?' Liz queried.

'*Were* you teasing her? I can actually see you deliberately condemning me to sausages on bread,' he elucidated.

Liz gathered all her sketches and samples before gainsaying a reply. 'Have you got nothing else to do but torment me?'

'*You*—' he pointed his forefingers at her pistol-wise '—are supposed to be giving *me*—' he reversed his hands '—a tour of all the great things you've done or plan to do for Yewarra.'

Liz caught her breath. 'If—' she said icily.

'Hang on—let me rephrase,' he interrupted humorously.

'Don't bother,' she flashed.

'Liz!' He was openly laughing now. 'Where's your sense of humour?'

'To quote you—flown out of the window.' She stopped and bit her lip frustratedly, because the conversation where he'd used that phrase was the last thing she wanted to bring to mind. The day he'd told her that professionalism between them had flown out of the window...

She was saved by his mobile phone.

He pulled it out of his pocket impatiently, and spoke into it equally impatiently. 'Roger, didn't I tell you not to bother me? What? All right. Hang on—no, I'll ring you back.' He flicked the phone off.

'You'll be happy to know you're released for the rest of the day, Miss Montrose,' he said dryly. 'Something has come up, as they say.'

'Oh? Not bad news?' she heard herself ask.

'If you call the potential acquisition of another company via some delicate negotiations that require my expert touch bad news, no.'

Liz blinked confusedly. 'You don't sound too happy about it, though.'

He moved his shoulders and grimaced. 'It's more work.'

'Surely—surely you could cut back?' she suggested. And with inner surprise heard herself add, 'Do you *need* another company?'

'No. But it gets to be a habit. I'll see you at five.'

Liz stared after him as he strode out of the veranda room and found herself prey to some conflicting emotions. Surely Cameron Hillier didn't deserve her sympathy for any reason? But *was* it sympathy? Or a sort of admiration tinged with—? Don't tell me, she reprimanded herself.

Surely I'm not joining the ranks of his devoted staff?

She sat down suddenly with a frown as it occurred to her that the frenetic pace her boss worked at might be a two-edged sword for him. He hadn't sounded enthusiastic at the prospect of another take-over. He'd admitted it was habit-forming in a dry way, as if to say he did it but he didn't exactly approve.

Did he have trouble relaxing? Was he unable to unwind? And if so why?

She blinked several times as it crossed her mind that she was not the only one with burdens of one sort or another. She blinked again as this revelation that Cam Hillier might need help made him suddenly more accessible to her—closer. As if she wanted to be closer, even able to help.

But what about what had gone—before she'd felt this streak of sympathy for him? What about the simmering sensual tension that had surrounded them? Where had it exploded from? In the month she'd been at Yewarra he'd given no sign of it during his visits, and she'd been highly successful at clamping down on her feelings. Or so she'd thought…

So how, and why, had it escaped from the box today, over an interior decorating issue?

Not that at all. It had been the mention of not being his wife, she suddenly realised. It was the thought of *being* his wife that had raced through her mind and opened up that flood of pure sensuality for her.

She looked around, looked at the samples and sketches she'd folded up neatly, and thought of her brief to redecorate the room. But none of those thoughts could chase away the one that underlined them. Why did she feel like a giddy schoolgirl with an adolescent crush?

The barbecue, although Liz had been dreading another encounter with Cam Hillier, and was feeling tense and uneasy in consequence, was going smoothly—at first.

She'd loaded the brick barbecue with paper and wood, and ensured the cooking grid was clean. She'd put a colourful cloth on the veranda table, along with a bunch of flowers she'd picked, and she'd lit some candles in glasses even though the sun hadn't set, to add a festive note to an occasion that the kids loved.

She'd showered, and changed into a grey short-sleeved jumper and jeans, and—as she usually did on these occasions—she'd devised a treasure hunt through the garden for Scout and Archie. Something they also loved.

As promised, she'd produced steaks, potato gnocchi and a salad, as well as sausages on bread. There was also a chocolate ice cream log waiting in the freezer.

Although all set to do the cooking on the barbecue herself, when Cam arrived with Archie Liz found herself manipulated by her boss into releasing the reins after he'd taken one shrewd glance at her. He'd brought a bottle of wine and he poured her a glass and told her to relax.

She sat down in two minds at first, but the lengthening shadows as the lovely afternoon slid towards evening, the perfume from the garden and the birdsong got to her, and she found herself feeling a little better.

He was a good cook, and he handled the fire well, she had to acknowledge when the steaks and sausages were ready. Nothing was burnt, and nothing was rare to dripping blood. It was all just right. And not only Scout and Archie, sitting on a rug on the lawn, tucked in with gusto, so did she.

Then came the chocolate ice cream log, and with it an extra surprise. Liz had stuck some sparklers into it, causing round-eyed wonder in to the kids when she lit them.

'Wow! Now it's a real party,' Archie enthused. 'Don't be scared, Scout,' he added, as Scout stuck her thumb in her mouth. 'They won't hurt you—promise. Yippee!' And, grabbing Scout by the hand, he danced around the garden with her until she forgot to be nervous.

But that wasn't the end of the surprises—although the next one was for Liz. When the kids had finished their ice cream and quietened down, could even be seen to be yawning, although they tried valiantly to hide it, Mrs Preston and Daisy appeared, with the suggestion that Scout might like to spend the night in the nursery up at the big house tonight.

Scout said, 'Yes, please—pretty please, Mummy,' before Liz had a chance to get a word in, and Archie added his own impassioned plea.

So she agreed ruefully.

It was after she'd collected Scout's pyjamas and was about to head up to the big house that Mrs Preston said, 'You two relax, now. Oh, look—you haven't finished the wine!'

Thus it was that peace and quiet descended on the garden, and Liz found herself alone with Cam and with a second glass of wine in her hand. A silver sickle moon was rising, and there was a pale plume of smoke coming from the barbecue as it sank to a bed of ashes. There were fireflies hovering above the flowerbeds, fluttering their delicate wings.

She frowned, however. 'They didn't have to do that.'

He grimaced, and went to say something in reply, she thought. But all he said in the end was, 'They do get on well, the kids.'

'I guess they have quite a bit in common. They're pretty articulate for their ages—probably because they're single kids, so they get a lot of adult attention. They have that in common. I think Archie is particularly bright, actually. And quite sensitive.'

'I think he's certainly appreciated having you and Scout around. He seems…' Cam paused, then grimaced. 'I know it sounds strange for a five-year-old, but he seems more relaxed.'

'Except when he gets shoved around—but it hasn't happened again. I've asked Daisy to watch out for it.'

'They've probably established their parameters. Their no-go zones.' He glanced at her. 'As we have.'

Liz looked down at her wine and sipped it.

'What would you say if I suggested we move our parameters, Liz?'

She opened her mouth to ask him what he meant, but that would be unworthy, she knew. In fact it would be fair to say their parameters had moved themselves of their own accord, only hours ago.

'I—I thought it was going so well,' she said desolately at last.

CHAPTER SEVEN

'It is going well, Liz,' he said dryly.

'Not if we keep—' She broke off, floundering.

'Finding ourselves wanting each other? So I wasn't imagining it earlier?'

She glinted an ironic little glance at him.

'Dear Liz,' he drawled as he interpreted the glance, 'you're not always that easy to read. For example, I arrived in your garden tonight to find you in chilly mode—prepared to hold me not so much at arm's length but at one hundred feet down a hole. Or—' he paused and inspected his glass '—prepared to scratch my eyes out if I so much as put a foot wrong.'

Liz sat up with a gasp. 'That's not true!'

He shrugged. 'Uptight, then. Which made me wonder.'

She subsided.

He watched her thoughtfully. 'Don't you think it's about time you admitted you're human? That you may have had good cause to freeze off any attraction under the weight of the betrayal you suffered but you can't go through the rest of your life like that?'

'So…so…' Her voice shook a little. 'You think I'm being melodramatic and ridiculous?'

'I didn't say that, but it is a proposition I'm putting to you. Take courage is what I'm really trying to say.'

'By having an affair with you?' She said it out of a tight throat. 'I—'

'Liz, I'm not going to get you pregnant and desert you,' he said deliberately. 'But we can't go on like this. *I* can't go on like this. I want you. I know I said I wouldn't but—' He stopped frustratedly.

'It will spoil everything, though.'

'Why?'

She licked her lips. 'Well, it would have to be sort of clandestine, and…'

'Why the hell should it be? You're probably the only one around here who doesn't believe it might be on the cards.' He lifted an ironic eyebrow at her. 'Why do you think we've been left alone in a romantically moonlit garden?'

Liz's eyes widened. 'You mean Mrs Preston and Daisy…?'

He nodded. 'They've both given me to understand you and I would be well-suited.'

'In so many words?' Liz was stunned.

He shook his head and looked amused. 'But they never lose an opportunity to sing your praises. Bob's the same. Even Hamish.' Hamish was the crusty head gardener. 'He has allowed it to pass his lips that you're "not bad for a lass". Now, that's a *real* compliment.'

Liz compressed her lips as she thought of the gossip that must have been going on behind her back.

'And Scout and Archie are too young to be affected,' he went on. 'If you're happy to go on in your job there's no reason why you shouldn't.'

Liz got up and paced across the lawn, with her arms folded, her glass in her hand.

He watched her in silence.

She turned to him at last, her eyes dark with the effort to concentrate.

'Liz,' he said barely audibly, 'let go. For once, just let go. The last thing I want to do is hurt you.' He put his glass down on the lawn and got up. 'Give me that.' He took her glass from her and put it down too. Then he put his hands around her waist loosely, and drew her slowly towards him.

Liz stiffened, but as she looked up into his face in the moonlight she suddenly knew she couldn't resist him. She raised her hand tentatively and touched her fingertips to the little lines beside his mouth—something she realised she'd wanted to do for ever, it seemed. Just as she'd wanted to be drawn to the flame of this tall, dangerously alive, incredibly exciting and tempting man for ever…

He turned his head and kissed her fingers, ran his hands up and down her back, then down to the flare of her hips. She breathed raggedly as her whole body came alive with delicious tremors.

He bent his head and started to kiss her.

Some minutes later, he picked her up and carried her to the swing seat, sat down with her across his lap.

'Forgive me,' he said then, 'but I've been wanting to do this for some time. And so have you, I can't help feeling. Maybe that's all we should think of?' And he cupped her cheek lightly.

Liz was arrested, with her lips parted, her eyes huge. And if she thought she'd been affected by him on a hot Sydney pavement, in his car, in his office, in his veranda room it was nothing to the mounting sensations she was experiencing now, in his arms.

She could literally feel her body come alight where it was in contact with his. She felt, to her astonishment, a primitive urge to throw her arms round his neck and surrender her mouth, her breasts, her whole body to him, to be played in whatever key he liked. But what she would really like, she knew, would be for him to mix his keys. To be gentle, although a little teasing, to be strong when she needed it, to be in charge when she was about to explode with desire—because she just knew he could do that to her...make her ignite.

She groaned and closed her eyes, and when she felt his mouth on hers she did put her arms around his neck and draw him closer.

He did just as she'd wished, as if he'd read her mind. He ran his fingers through her hair, then down her neck and round her throat, and that was nice. It made her skin feel like silk. But when he slipped his hand beneath her jumper and beneath her bra strap it was more than nice. It was exquisite. And tremors ran up and down her because it was almost too much to bear.

As if he sensed it, he removed his hand and stopped kissing her briefly to say, 'This can be a two-way street.'

A smile curved her lips, and she freed her hands and slid them beneath his shirt.

It was glorious, she found. A glorious warmth that came to her as she held him close. It was a kinship that banished the lonely years—but a kinship with an exciting, dangerous edge to it, she thought. A blending of their bodies—a transference, as his hands moved on her and hers moved on him, of lovely sensations and rhythms that had to lead to the final act they both not only sought but needed desperately.

But that was where the danger lay, she knew. Not only because of the consequences that could arise— she would never allow that to happen to her again—but could she afford the less tangible consequences? The giving of her soul into a man's keeping with this act, only to have it brutally returned to her?

She faltered in his arms.

He raised his head. 'Liz?' Then he smiled down at her. 'Not an Ice Queen at all. The opposite, if anything. I—'

But he never did get to say it, because she freed herself and fell off his lap.

'Liz!' He reached for her. 'What's wrong?'

She scrambled up, evading his hands and smoothing her clothes. 'You make it sound as if I'm in the habit of doing this.'

'I didn't say that.'

'You didn't have to.' She dragged her fingers through her hair.

'Liz.' He pushed himself off the swing seat and towered over her. 'You are being ridiculous now. Look, I know you might have cause to be sensitive about what men think of you, but—'

'Oh, I *am*.' She retreated a few steps. 'Sorry, but that's me!'

'Despite the fact you light up like a firecracker in my arms? No,' he said as she gasped, 'I'm *not* going to sugar-coat things between us just because you had one lousy experience.'

'Sugar-coating or not, you'll be talking to yourself. I'm going in!' And she ran across the dew-spangled lawn and into the house.

He made no attempt to follow her.

The next morning she studied herself in the bathroom mirror and flinched.

There were dark shadows under her eyes, she was pale, and she looked—not to put too fine a point on it—tormented.

She took a hot shower and dressed in navy shorts and a white T-shirt. She didn't even have Scout to distract her, she thought dismally, as she made coffee and poured herself a mug. But coffee would help, she assured herself as she picked up the phone that had a direct line to the house. Help her to do what she knew she had to do.

Two minutes later she waited for Mrs Preston to put the house phone down, then she slammed hers into its cradle and wouldn't have given a damn if it never worked again.

She took her coffee to the kitchen table, and to her horror found herself crying again. She licked the salty tears from her lips and forced herself to sip her coffee as she wondered what to do.

Her plan had been to offer her resignation to Cameron Hillier via the telephone, and not take no for an answer. That was not possible, however, because according to Mrs Preston he'd driven away from Yewarra last night.

Had he left any messages? Any instructions? Had he said when he'd be back? No, no and no, had been Mrs Preston's response. All he'd left was a note, telling her what he'd done. There'd been a puzzled note in Mrs Preston's voice—puzzled and questioning at the same time. Liz had understood, but had had no answer for her.

Typical of the arrogant man she knew him to be, she thought bitterly. How could he not know that with one short observation he'd made her feel cheap last night? How could he not know that, for her, when she gave herself to a man it could never be just sex? It was a head over heels, all bells and whistles affair for her. It was the way she was made and it had taken one awful lesson to teach her that.

On the other hand, was he entitled to be angry with her? Had she overreacted?

She paused her thoughts and got up to look out of the kitchen window. It was an overcast morning, as grey as she felt. Not only grey, but down in the dumps and… hopeless.

What if she'd said yes? Would she have spent her life feeling as if she was treading on eggshells in case it didn't last and he turned to some other woman? After all, despite his explanation of the situation that had developed between him and Portia Pengelly, she couldn't help feeling a streak of sympathy for Portia.

She also flinched inwardly because she knew herself well enough to know that she might *never* feel safe with a man again, despite the irrationality of it. It too was the way she was made. No half-measures for Liz Montrose, she thought grimly. Could she change?

But even if she did there was something holding her back—something she couldn't quite pin down in her mind. Unless…?

She stared unseeingly out of the window and thought suddenly, *Of course!* It was her reputation that was troubling her so deeply. Living with a man in an informal relationship, as opposed to Scout's father who was solidly married—could she ever feel right about that? Not so much not right, but secure in her position as the most suitable parent for Scout?

She folded her arms around her, trying desperately to find some comfort and some solution.

If she didn't agree to move in with Cam Hillier, what on earth was she going to do? Walk away? Uproot Scout? Leave Archie? Go back to living with her mother—who definitely had a man in her life and was loving every minute of it, as well as her costume-designing project?

But how could she stay…?

She reached for the other phone, the one with an outside line, and rang Cam Hillier's mobile. She couldn't allow things to simply hang, but perhaps she could offer him a week's notice so as not to destabilise his household completely?

What she got was a recorded message advising callers that he was unavailable and they should contact Roger Woodward if the matter was urgent. It wasn't even his own voice. It was Roger's.

She pressed her lips together as she put the phone down, and thought, *All right!* She had no choice but to go on as usual—for the time being.

Several days later Cam stared around his office in the Hillier Corporation's premises and knew he was in deep trouble.

He'd just signed the final document that had acquired him another company and he couldn't give a damn. Worse than that, he hated the drive within him that had seen him add another burden to his life—a life that was already overburdened and completely unsatisfactory.

He'd been more right than he knew when he'd posed that question to himself—what if a tortured Ice Queen was the one woman he really wanted and couldn't have?

What if?

He'd turn into a more demented workaholic than ever. He'd turn into a monster to work for. He'd…

He threw his pen down on the desk and ground his teeth. There had to be a way to get through to Liz. He knew now they set each other alight physically—it certainly wasn't one-sided—but how to make her see there was so much more they could share? How to make her see he needed her?

He shrugged and thought with amazement that Liz Montrose had planted herself in his heart probably from the moment he'd caught her climbing over his wall. That was the way it had happened, and he was helpless to change it.

And the irony was she loved Yewarra and Archie, and Scout loved...

He sat up suddenly. Archie and Scout—would they get through to Liz where he had failed?

He came back with a house party.

It was an impromptu party in that it had somehow been missed in both his office and the Yewarra diary until it was too late cancel. And Liz and Mrs Preston had only had a couple of hours and their work cut out to have everything ready for six overnight guests.

As for her own *contretemps*—how she was going to face Cam Hillier—Liz had no idea. But she comforted herself with the thought that at least she could stay very much in the background, as she usually did when there were guests.

An hour before dinner was due to be served she learnt that she was to be denied even that respite.

She got an urgent call from Mrs Preston with the news that her offsider, Rose, who acted as a waitress, had cut her hand and wouldn't be able to work. Could Liz hand Scout over to Daisy for the night and take her place?

Liz breathed heavily, but she could tell from Mrs Preston's voice that the housekeeper was under a lot of pressure. 'Sure,' she said. 'Give me half an hour.'

* * *

She showered, and changed hastily into a little black dress and flat shoes.

She hesitated briefly in front of the bathroom mirror, then swept her hair back into a neat, severe pleat and applied no make-up. She thought of replacing her contact lenses with her glasses, but decided she didn't need to go to extremes.

Then she gathered up Scout, and everything she needed, and ran over to the big house. Archie was delighted with the unexpected change of plan, and proudly displayed the latest curiosity Cam had brought home for him: a didgeridoo that was taller than Archie himself.

Liz glanced at Daisy, who raised her eyes heavenwards.

'Problem is I can't play it—and girls aren't allowed to, Cam said.' Archie suddenly looked as troubled as only he could at times.

Liz squatted down in front of him and put an arm round him. Scout came and snuggled into her other side. She dropped light kisses on their heads. 'It's very hard,' she said seriously, 'to play a didgeridoo. You need to learn a special kind of breathing, and you need to be a bit bigger and older. So until that happens, Archie, what say we find out all about them? How they're made, where this one may have come from, and so on.'

Archie considered the matter. 'OK,' he said at last. 'Will you help me, Liz?'

'Sure,' Liz promised. 'In the meantime, goodnight to both of you. Sleep tight!' She hugged them both, and to

Daisy added, 'I took them for a run through the paddock this afternoon to check out the new foals, so they should be happy to go to bed PDQ!'

Mrs Preston was standing in the middle of the kitchen still as a statue, with her fists clenched and her eyes closed, when Liz got there.

'Mrs P! What's wrong?' Liz flew across the tiled floor. 'Are you all right?'

Mrs Preston opened her eyes and unclenched her fists. 'I'm all right, dear,' she said. 'It must be the late notice we got that's making me feel a bit flustered. And, of course, Rose cutting her hand like that.'

'Just tell me what to do. Between us we can cope!' Although she sounded bright and breezy, Liz swallowed suddenly, but told herself it was no good both she *and* Mrs Preston going to water. 'What delicious dishes have you concocted tonight?'

Mrs Preston visibly took hold of herself. 'Leek soup with croutons, roast duck with maraschino cherries, and my hot chocolate pudding for dessert. The table is set. I'll carve the duck and we'll serve it with the vegetables buffet-style on the sideboard, so they can help themselves. Could you be a love and check the table, Liz? Oh, and put out the canapés?'

'Roger wilco!'

The dining room looked lovely. The long table was clothed in cream damask with matching napkins, and a centrepiece of massed blue agapanthus stood between two silver-branched candlesticks.

Liz did a quick check of the cutlery, the crystal and

the china and found it all present and correct, then carried the canapé platters through to the veranda room. There were delicate bites of caviar—red and black—on toast, and anchovies on biscuits. There were olives and small meatballs on toothpicks, with a savoury sauce in a fluted silver dipping dish. A hot pepperoni sausage had been cut into circles and was accompanied by squares of cool Edam. There were tiny butterfly prawns with their tail shells still attached, so they could be dipped into the thousand island sauce in a crystal bowl.

It was the prawns that reminded Liz of the need for napkins for the canapés. She found them, and jogged back to the veranda room—not that they were running late, but she had the feeling that the less time Mrs Preston was left alone tonight, the better.

She deployed the napkins and swung round—to run straight into Cam Hillier.

'Whoa!' he said, and steadied her with his hands on her shoulders, as he'd done once before on a hot Sydney pavement—an encounter that seemed like a lifetime away as it flashed through Liz's mind.

'Oh!' she breathed, and then to all intents and purposes was struck dumb, as the familiar sensations her boss could inflict on her ran in a clamouring tremor through her body.

'Liz?' He frowned, giving no indication that he was at all affected as she was. 'What are you doing?'

'Uh…' She took some quick breaths. 'Hello! I'm filling in for Rose. She had an accident—she cut her hand.'

His gaze took in her pinned-back hair and moved

down her body to her flat shoes. 'You're going to waitress?'

She nodded. 'Don't worry,' she assured him, 'I don't mind! Mrs Preston really needs a hand and—'

'No,' he interrupted.

Liz blinked. 'No? But—'

'No,' he repeated.

'Why not?' She stared up at him, utterly confused. He was wearing a crisp check shirt open at the throat, and pressed khaki trousers. She could smell his faint lemony aftershave, and his hair was tidy and slightly damp.

'Because,' he said, 'you're coming to this dinner as a guest.'

He removed his hands from her shoulders and with calm authority reached round her head to release her hair from its pins, which he then ceremoniously presented to her.

Liz gasped. 'How…? Why…? You can't… I can't do that! I'm not dressed or anything.' She stopped abruptly with extreme frustration. What she wore could be the least of her problems!

'You *are* dressed.' He inspected the little black dress. 'Perhaps not Joseph's amazing coat of many colours, but it'll do.'

Her mouth fell open—and Daisy walked into the veranda room, calling her name.

'There you are, Liz! Oh, sorry, Mr Hillier—I was looking for Liz to tell her that she was right. Both Archie and Scout are fast asleep!'

'That's great news, Daisy,' Cam said. 'Daisy, I have

a huge favour to ask of you,' he added. 'We seem to be short-staffed—would you mind helping Mrs Preston out with dinner tonight? Liz was going to, but I'd like her to be a guest.'

Daisy's eyes nearly fell out on stalks, but she rallied immediately. 'Of course I wouldn't mind. But…' She trailed off and looked a little anxiously at Liz.

'I look a mess?' Liz said dryly.

'No, you don't!' Daisy said loyally. 'You always look wonderful. It's just that your hair needs a brush! I'll get one.' And she twirled on her heels and ran out.

Leaving Liz confronting her employer with a mixture of sheer bewilderment and disbelief in her eyes.

'Why are you doing this?' she asked, her voice husky with surprise and uncertainty.

'Because if you ever do agree to live with me, Liz Montrose, I'd rather not have it bandied about that you were once one of my kitchen staff. For your sake, that is. *I* don't give a damn.'

Five minutes later, with her hair brushed but still no reply formulated to what her boss had said to her, Liz was being introduced to the house guests as his estate manager.

Half an hour later she was seated on his right hand, with her spoon poised to partake of Mrs Preston's pale green leek soup that was artistically swirled with cream.

It was going amazingly well, this dinner party that she had gatecrashed.

The guest party comprised two middle-aged couples,

a vibrant woman in her early thirties, and Cam's legal adviser in an unofficial capacity. The talk was wide-ranging as the duck with its lovely accompaniment of glowing maraschino cherries was served, and Liz was gradually able to lose her slightly frozen air.

And then the talk became localised—on horses. On breeding, racing, and buying and selling horses.

Thanks to the computer program Liz had set up for Bob, and her involvement in the stables, it wasn't all double Dutch to her. She was even able to describe several of the latest foals that had been born in the past few weeks.

That was when she realised that all the guests had come to view the latest crop of yearlings Yewarra had bred.

It grew on Liz that the vibrant woman—her name was Vanessa—with her golden pageboy hair, her scarlet lips and nails, her trim figure and toffee-coloured eyes, was a little curious about her. Twice she had surprised those unusual eyes resting on her speculatively.

And twice Liz had found herself thinking, *If you're wondering about me in the context of Cam Hillier, Vanessa, that's nothing to my utter confusion on the subject! But what are you doing here? A new girlfriend? No, that doesn't make sense. But…*

Finally the evening came to an end, and all the guests went to bed.

Liz retreated to the kitchen, to find it empty and gleaming. She breathed a sigh of relief and poured herself a glass of water. Daisy had obviously been a tower of strength in the kitchen tonight.

Something prompted her to go out through the kitchen door and wander through the herb garden that was Mrs Preston's pride and joy until she came to the lip of the valley.

It was only a gradual decline at that point, but it was protected by a low hedge and was an amazing spot to star-gaze. There was even a bench, and she sank down onto it and stared upwards, with her lips parted in amazement at the heavenly firmament above her.

That was how Cam Hillier found her.

'One of my favourite spots, too,' he murmured as he sat down beside her. 'I was looking for you. Put your glass down,' he instructed.

Liz opened her mouth to question this, but did as she was told instead, and he handed her a glass of champagne.

'You hardly had a mouthful of wine at dinner, and there's a refreshing quality to a glass of bubbly at the end of the day. Cheers!' He touched his glass to hers.

'Cheers,' Liz repeated, but sounded notably subdued—which she was. Subdued, tired, and entirely unsure how to cope with Cam Hillier.

'What's up?' he queried.

Liz took a large sip. 'Brrr…' She shook her head, but found her tongue suddenly loosened. 'Up? I don't know. I have no idea. If you were to ask me what's going on I wouldn't be able to tell you. I'm mystified. I'm bothered and bewildered. That's what's up,' she finished.

He laughed softly. 'OK, I'll tell you. We got into a verbal stoush the last time we met.'

She made a slight strangled sound.

He stopped, but she said nothing so he went on. 'Yes, a war of words after a rather lovely interlude, when I made an unfortunate remark which incensed you and you slammed your way inside, whilst I slammed my way back to Sydney in the dead of night, where I remained, incensed, for some days.'

He paused and went on with an entirely unexpected tinge of remorse, 'I don't very often get said no to—which may account for my lack of graciousness or my pure bloody-mindedness when it does happen. What do you think?'

'I…' Liz paused, then found she couldn't go on as a lone tear traced down her cheek. She licked the saltiness off her upper lip.

'I mean,' he went on after a long moment, 'would I be able to mend some fences between us?'

'I can't…I can't move in with you,' she said, her voice husky with emotion. 'Surely you must see that?'

'No, I don't. Why not?'

'I'd…' She hesitated, and breathed in the scent of mint from the herb garden, 'I wouldn't feel right. Anyway—' She stopped helplessly.

'Liz, surely by now you must appreciate that you have a rather amazing effect on me?'

'You don't show it.' It was out before she could help herself.

'When?'

'Earlier. When we first met.' She clicked her tongue, because that wasn't what she'd meant or wanted to say, and moved restlessly. 'I even wondered if you'd brought Vanessa up here to…to taunt me.'

'Much as I don't mind the thought of you being jealous of Vanessa,' he said dryly, 'she's happily married to a champion jockey who rarely socialises on account of his weight battles.'

Liz flinched. 'Sorry,' she murmured.

'Have another sip,' he advised. 'What would you do if I told you that, along with wanting to stick pins into an Ice Queen effigy, I haven't been able to sleep. I've been a monster to work with. I kept thinking of how good you felt in my arms. I kept undressing you in my mind. Incidentally, how have *your* few days been?'

Liz swallowed as she recalled her days—as she thought of how she'd exchanged the swings for the roundabouts in her emotions. Round and round, up and down she'd been, as she'd alternated between maintaining her anger and wondering if he was right. Was it time to let go of her past and try to live again? Was she being unnecessarily melodramatic and tragic? But of course that hadn't been all she'd grappled with over the week.

There'd been memories of the pleasure he'd brought to her, memories of the man himself and how he could be funny and outrageously immodest when he wasn't being an arrogant multi-millionaire. How he was so good with kids—the last thing she'd have suspected of him when she'd gone to work for him. All the little things she couldn't banish that made up Cam Hillier.

'I was…a little uneven myself,' she admitted, barely audibly.

'Good.'

She looked askance at him. *'Good?'*

'I'd hate to think I was suffering alone.'

For some reason this caused Liz to chuckle—a watery little sound, but nonetheless a sound of amusement. 'You're incorrigible,' she murmured, and with a sigh of something like resignation she laid her head on his shoulder.

But she raised it immediately to look into his eyes. 'Where do we go from here, though?' There was real perturbation in her voice. 'I still can't move in with you.'

'There is another option.' He picked up her free hand and threaded his fingers through hers. 'You could marry me.'

Liz stiffened in disbelief. 'I can't just *marry* you!'

'There seems to be a hell of a lot you can't do,' he said dryly. 'What *can* you do?'

She went to get up and run as far away from him as she could, but he caught her around the waist and sat her down. He kept his hands on her waist.

'Let's not fight about this, Liz,' he recommended coolly. 'You said something to me once about two sane adults. Perhaps that's what we need now—some sanity. Let's get to the basics.'

He watched the way her mouth worked for a moment, but no sound came and he went on. 'I need a mother for Archie. You need a father for Scout and a settled background.' He raised his eyebrows. 'You couldn't find a much more solid background than this.'

Liz stared at him with her lips parted, her eyes stunned.

'Then there's you.' He tightened his hands on her

waist as she moved convulsively. 'Just listen to me,' he warned. 'You've settled into Yewarra and the life here as if you were born to it. If you don't love it, you've given a very good imitation of it. Has it been an act?' he queried curtly.

'No,' she whispered.

'And Archie?'

'I *love* Archie,' she said torturedly. 'But—'

'What about us?' His gaze raked her face, and his eyes were as brooding as she'd ever seen them. 'Let's be brutally honest for once, Liz. We're not going to be a one-night wonder. We wouldn't have felt this way for two crazy months if we were.'

She licked her lips.

'And they *have* been two crazy months, haven't they? Like a slow form of torture.'

She released a long, slow breath. 'Yes,' she said at last. 'Oh, yes.'

His hands relaxed at last on her waist. He took them away and drew her into his arms. 'Maybe we need a couple of days on our own—to get used to this idea. Would you come away with me for a while?'

'What about the kids?'

'I only meant a few days, and Archie is used to that. Perhaps your mother would come up to be with Scout?'

She took a breath. 'Well…'

'Well?' he repeated after a long moment.

It occurred to Liz that one of her hurdles in this matter was getting to the core of Cam Hillier. Discovering whether she could trust him or not. Finding out what was really behind this amazing offer of marriage.

'I—if I did it,' she said hesitantly, 'I couldn't make any promises. But you've been very good to me,' she heard herself say, 'so—'

'Liz.' His voice was suddenly rough. 'Do it or don't do it—but not out of gratitude.'

She sat up abruptly. 'I *am* grateful!'

'Then the offer's withdrawn.'

She sucked in a large amount of air. 'You're not only incorrigible, you're impossible, Cam Hillier,' she told him roundly.

'No, I'm not. Be honest, Liz. We want each other, and gratitude's got nothing to do with it.'

She opened and closed her mouth several times as her mind whirled like a Catherine wheel, seeking excuses, twirling round and round in search of escape avenues. But of course he was right. There were none.

'True,' she breathed at last. 'You're right.'

His clasp on her hand tightened almost unbearably. 'Then the offer's open again.'

'Thanks. I'll—I'll come.'

He released her hand and put his arm round her shoulders.

Liz closed her eyes and surrendered herself to the warmth that passed between them. At the same time she was conscious that she'd put her foot on an unknown path—but she just didn't seem to have the strength of mind to resist Cam Hillier.

She took refuge in the mundane, because the enormity of it all was threatening to overwhelm her.

'I'm a bit worried about Mrs Preston. She got herself into quite a state tonight.'

'I'll get her some help before we go. Don't worry. You're worse than Archie.' He slipped his fingers beneath her chin and looked down into her eyes. 'In fact,' he murmured, 'don't worry about a thing. I'll take care of it all.' And he started to kiss her.

CHAPTER EIGHT

HE TOOK HER to the Great Barrier Reef three days later. He'd told her that much, but said the rest would be a surprise.

They flew to Hamilton Island, just off Queensland's Whitsunday coast, on a commercial flight. She was quiet at first—until he put his hand over hers.

'They'll be fine—the kids.'

She looked quickly at him. 'How did you know I was thinking about them?'

'It was a safe bet,' he said wryly. 'Unless you're re-gretting coming away with me?'

'No…'

He narrowed his eyes at her slight hesitation, but didn't take issue with it.

She marvelled as the jet floated over the sparkling waters, the reefs, the islands of the Whitsunday Passage and right over the marina, with its masts and colourful surrounds, to land. Then she discovered they were not staying on Hamilton, although they walked around the busy harbour with its shops and art galleries, its cafés. Their luggage—not that there was a lot—seemed to have been mysteriously taken care of.

Her discovery that they weren't staying on Hamilton came in the form of a question.

'Have you got a hat?' he asked, as they stopped in front of a shop with a divine selection of hats. 'You need a hat out on the water.'

'Out on the… No, I don't have one I can squash into a suitcase. Out on the water?' she repeated.

'You'll see. Let's choose.' So they spent half an hour with Liz trying on sunhats—half an hour during which the two young, pretty shop assistants got all blushing and giggly beneath the charm and presence of Cameron Hillier.

But it was light-hearted and fun, and Liz found herself feeling light-hearted too. It was as if, she thought, all the pressure from all the difficult decisions was flowing out of her system under the influence of the holiday spirit of the island.

She chose a straw hat with a wide brim, and wore it out of the shop. They stopped at a café and had iced coffees, and shared a sinfully delicious pastry. Then, swinging her hand in his, he led down to the marina to a catamaran tied up to a jetty.

Its name was *Leilani*, and she was the last word in luxury: a blend of glossy woodwork, thick carpets, beautiful fabrics, bright brass work and sparkling white paint. The main saloon was huge, with a shipshape built-in galley. The staterooms—there were three—were wood-panelled and had sumptuous bed clothing.

There were two decks—one that led off the saloon, and an upper deck behind the fly-bridge controls.

Liz was wide-eyed even before she got to see *Leilani*'s interior. A young man in whites named Rob welcomed them aboard with a salute, and showed her to her state-room. He returned upstairs and she heard him talking to Cam, but not what was said. When she got back on the upper deck the conference was over, and to her surprise the young man whom she'd assumed was the skipper hopped off onto the jetty as Cam started the engines and untied the lines.

'He isn't coming?' she queried.

Cam looked over his shoulder as the cat started to reverse out of the berth. 'Nope.'

She blinked. 'Do you know how to handle a boat this size?'

'Liz, I virtually grew up on boats.' He cast her a laughing look. 'Of course I do.'

She chewed her lip.

This time he laughed at her openly. 'You're getting more and more like Archie,' he teased, as he turned *Leilani* neatly on her own length and headed her for the harbour mouth. 'I'll show you how to do it—but maybe not today.'

'Do you own her—is she yours or have you borrowed her?'

'I own her.'

'I'm surprised she hasn't got a Shakespearean name!'

He said wryly, 'She was already named when I got her. It's supposed to be unlucky to change a boat's name. But funnily enough Leilani was a famous racehorse. OK. I'll need to concentrate for a few minutes,' he added as they cleared the harbour entrance.

'Where are we going?'

'Whitehaven,' he said. 'We should be there in time to see the sun set. There's nothing like it.'

He was right.

By the time the sun started to drop below the horizon they'd anchored off Whitehaven Beach, Liz had unpacked, and she was starting to feel more at home.

She'd been helped in this by the fact that once Cam was satisfied the anchor was set, and he'd turned off the motors and various other systems, he'd followed her down to the lower deck and taken her into his arms.

'A difficult few days,' he said wryly.

She could only nod in agreement. They'd decided to maintain a businesslike stance at Yewarra in front of staff and children alike—even Liz's mother, when she arrived. 'It's nothing to do with anyone but us,' he'd said. 'And we'll tell them it's a business trip to do with real estate.'

'But they'll probably be dying of curiosity,' she'd responded. 'Not the children, but...'

'Would you rather I kissed you every time I felt like it?' he'd countered.

Liz had blushed brightly and shaken her head.

'Thought not,' he'd said, with a glint of sheer devilry.

In the event he'd spent quite a bit of those three days in Sydney tidying up loose ends before going away. And Liz had spent the time he was away feeling like pinching herself—because, hard as it was to remain unaffected in his presence, it was harder to feel she'd made a rational decision when he wasn't around.

The one argument she'd bolstered herself with was that she owed it to Cam Hillier to at least try to understand him. It might be close to gratitude, but she couldn't help it; she certainly wouldn't be telling him that, though.

Now, anchored off Whitehaven Beach on his beautiful boat, he put his hand on her waist from behind and swung her round. 'I'm sorely in need of this,' he said huskily.

Liz smiled up at him and relaxed against him. 'You and me both.'

He released her waist and gathered her into his arms, making her feel slim and willowy, and said against the corner of her mouth, 'No desire to fight me or call me a menace?'

Liz suffered a jolt of laughter, but said ruefully, 'I don't know where it all went.'

'All the hostility?' He nuzzled the top of her head and moved his hands on her hips.

'Mmm… Could be something to do with—I mean it's very hard to say no to a guy with a boat like this!'

He laughed down at her and she caught her breath, because in all his dark glory he was devastatingly attractive and he made her heart beat faster and her pulses race.

'Tell you what.' He kissed her lightly. 'Why don't you change into something more comfortable whilst I whip up the sundowners that are traditional in this part of the world?'

She drew away and looked down at her clothes. She

was still wearing the jeans and top she'd travelled in. 'I guess I could. It *is* warm. How about you?'

'I'm going to sling on some shorts—but don't be long. The sun goes fast when it makes up its mind to retire.'

'Just going!' She clasped his fingers, then went inside and down to her stateroom.

'A maxi-dress! You *must* have a maxi-dress,' had been her mother's emphatic response upon learning her daughter was going to Hamilton Island in the Whitsundays, even if it was on business. 'They're all the rage. I'll bring you one!'

And despite the short notice she'd done just that—a lovely long floaty creation in white, with a wide band of tangerine swirls round the hem. It was strapless, with a built-in bra, and had a matching tangerine and white scarf to drape elegantly around her neck.

Liz slipped it on and discovered the lovely dress had a strange effect on her. It made her feel as light as a feather. It made her feel flirty and young and desirable.

In fact she stretched out her arms and did a dancing circle in front of the mirror. Then, mindful of the sun's downward path, she brushed her hair, shook her head to tousle it, put on some lipgloss and, barefoot—because that seemed to fit the scene—moved lightly up to the saloon and out on to the back deck.

Cam was already there, changed into navy shorts and a white T-shirt. He was sitting with his long legs propped up on the side of the boat. On the table beside him stood two creamy white cocktails, complete with paper parasols. There was also a pewter tray of smoked salmon canapés, topped with cream cheese and capers.

'You're a marvel, Mr Hillier!' She laughed at him with her hands on her hips. 'I had no idea you were so domesticated.'

He turned to look at her, and it was his turn to catch his breath—although she didn't know it.

Nor could she know that it crossed his mind that she'd never looked so lovely—slender, sparkling with vitality, and absolutely gorgeous...

He stood up. 'I cannot tell a lie. I did make the cocktails, but Rob organised the canapés along with a catering package. You—' he held out his hand to her '—are stunning.'

She laughed up at him as he drew her towards him. 'I also cannot tell a lie. I *feel* stunning. I mean, not that I look stunning, but I feel—'

'I know what you mean.' He bent his head and kissed her. 'OK.' He released her. 'Sit down. Cheers!' He handed her the cocktail. 'To the sunset.'

'To the sunset!' she echoed, and stared entranced at the white beach so well named and the colours in the sky as the sun sank below the tree-lined horizon.

That wasn't all there was to the sunset, though. The sky got even more colourful after the sun had disappeared, with streaks of gold cloud against a violet background that was reflected in the water, and a liquid orange horizon.

There were several other boats at anchor, and as the sunset finally withdrew its amazing colours from the sky they lit their anchor lights. Cam did the same, and then went to pour them another Mai Tai cocktail.

Liz stayed out on the deck, enjoying the warm, tropical air and the peace and serenity. It was a calm night, with just the soft lap of water against the hull.

'You could get addicted to this lifestyle,' she said with a grin when he brought their drinks out, then she sat up, looking electrified, as soft but lively music piped out onto the deck. 'How did you know?'

'Know what?'

She cocked her head to listen. 'That I was a frustrated disco dancer as a kid? I haven't danced for years. Except with Scout. She loves dancing too.' She smiled and sat back. 'I feel young all of a sudden.'

'You *are* young.' He pulled up his chair so that they were sitting knee to knee, and leant forward to fiddle with the end of her scarf. 'Actually, you make *me* feel young.'

Liz looked surprised. 'You're not old. How old are you?'

He grimaced. 'Thirty-three. Today.'

Liz sat forward in surprise. 'Why didn't you tell me?'

He lifted his shoulders. 'Birthdays come and go. They don't mean much when you start to get on. What would you have done, anyway?'

She thought for a moment. 'You seem to have everything that opens and shuts—so a present might have been difficult. But at least a card.'

'To put on my mantelpiece?' He looked amused.

'No,' she agreed ruefully. 'OK, here's my last offer.'

She leant right forward and kissed him lightly. 'Happy Birthday, Mr Hillier!'

'Miss Montrose—thank you. But I hope that was only an appetiser,' he replied wryly.

Liz trembled as she saw a nerve beat in his jaw—she'd seen it before, and she knew that under the light-hearted fun there lurked a rising tide of desire. It caused her nerves to tighten a fraction—not that she was feeling like a block of wood herself, she thought dryly, but was she ready for the inevitable?

He didn't press the matter. Whether he sensed that slight nervous reaction or not, she didn't know, but he merely kissed her back lightly and handed her a cocktail."

'Finish that. Then we have a veritable feast to get through.

A feast it was: a seafood platter heaped with prawns, crab, calamari and two lobster tails. There was also a side salad, and there was white wine to go with it. It was the kind of meal to eat slowly, often using fingers and not being too self-conscious about the smears left on your glass, despite the fingerbowl and linen napkins.

It was the perfect feast to eat on the back deck of a boat surrounded by midnight-blue sea and sky—although she could just make out the amazing sands of Whitehaven Beach.

It was a meal that lent itself to talking when the mood took them, about nothing very much, and to not feeling awkward when a silence grew. Because—and Liz grew more aware of it—there seemed to be a mental unity between them.

'That was lovely,' she said as he gathered up their plates and consigned their food scraps overboard. She got up and helped him carry the plates and accoutrements back into the galley, then washed her hands.

He did the same. 'Coffee?'

'Yes, please—I don't believe it!'

He raised an eyebrow at her.

'It's eleven o'clock.'

He grinned. 'Almost Cinderella time. Sit down. It's getting a bit cool outside. I'll make the coffee.'

Liz sank down on to the built-in settee that curved around an oval polished table. The settee was covered in mushroom-pink velour that teamed well with the cinnamon-coloured carpet, and there were jewel-bright scatter cushions in topaz, hyacinth and bronze.

She looked around. There were two lamps, shedding soft light from behind their cream shades, and beyond the saloon up a couple of steps was the wheelhouse, almost in darkness, but with a formidable array of instruments and pinpricks of light. A faint hum echoed throughout the boat.

Where she sat was superbly comfortable, and she could see across to the galley where her boss—she amended that. Her lover-to-be?—was making coffee.

'I could have done that,' she said.

'I can make decent coffee.' He reached for a plunger pot from the cabinet, then a container of coffee from the freezer. 'I have it down to a fine art,' he continued. 'Same coffee, same size measuring spoon and I can't go wrong.' He took down two Wedgwood mugs, spooned the coffee into the pot, poured boiling water on and balanced the plunger on top. 'Four minutes, then plunge.'

Liz couldn't help herself. She started to laugh softly. 'So you have an identical set-up in all your houses?'

'Yep. But I only have two houses.'

'And a boat?'

'And a boat. Actually...' He assembled cream, sugar and spoons on a tray with the mugs and pot, and brought it over to the table. 'I wasn't prevaricating about the real estate aspect of this trip. I'm looking at a house on Hamilton.'

'Oh, so you're combining pleasure with a bit of business?' she teased. 'Or maybe a bit of pleasure with a lot of business?'

'Not at all,' he denied. 'I'm relying on your judgement in the matter.'

Liz sobered. 'Really? I mean—do you *need* another house?'

'Really?' He sat down and plunged the coffee, and a lovely aroma rose from the pot. He poured it and moved her mug towards her. 'Help yourself. Do I need another house? No. But at least it's not another company.'

Liz digested this with a frown. 'Are you—do you— are you happy? With your life, I mean?'

He studied his coffee, then stirred some sugar in. 'I have a few regrets. Apart from Archie and Narelle I have no close relatives left. No one to benefit from the fruits of my labours, you might say.' He shrugged. 'No one to wish me happy birthday.' He looked humorous and held up a hand. 'I don't really care about that. But

I do sometimes care—greatly—that my parents didn't live to see all this.' He looked around. 'And Amelia, my sister.'

'So…' Liz hazarded. 'Are you saying…?' She paused to gather her thoughts better.

'Do I sometimes feel like saying stop the world I want to get off? Substitute the Hillier Corporation for the world? Yes.' He shrugged.

'Why—why don't you?' she breathed.

'Liz.' He looked across at her. 'It's not that easy. I employ a lot of people. And I don't know what I'd do with my time, anyway.'

He looked across at her and she could suddenly see something different about him. She could see the stamp of inner tension on the lines of his face and in his eyes.

Then he shrugged and added, 'Perhaps there's a side of me that could never sit and twiddle its thumbs? Perhaps it's the way I'm made?'

'Perhaps not,' she said huskily at length. 'Maybe it's the way things have happened for you.' She grimaced. 'Like me.'

He opened his mouth to say something, but there was a whir as an unseen machine in the wheelhouse came alive.

She looked a question at him.

'It's the weather fax,' he said with a faint frown. 'Any change in the forecast comes through automatically.'

A smile curved Liz's lips. 'Go and have a look. I know you won't rest easy until you do.'

He raked a hand through his hair and got up. 'I will.

Contrary to what you may believe about me in a car, I'm a very cautious seaman. I'll only be a moment.'

But he was a bit longer than that, and Liz leant back in a corner and curled her legs up beside her. She fell asleep without even realising it.

Cam came back with a piece of paper in his hands and the news that they'd need to change their anchorage tomorrow because of a strong wind warning.

He stopped as he realised she was asleep, and let the sheet of paper flutter to the table as he stared down at her.

He looked at the grace of her body beneath the long dress, her hand beneath her cheek, and thought that she must be really tired. Perhaps two Mai Tais and a couple of glasses of wine had contributed? Perhaps the trauma of it all…?

His lips twisted as he pulled the table away and bent to pick her up in his arms. She made a tiny murmur, but didn't wake as he carried her to her stateroom.

He put her down carefully on one side of the double bed and rolled a light-as-air eiderdown over her.

He stood looking down at her for a minute or so. Then he said, 'Goodnight, Cinderella.'

Liz slept for a few hours, then a nightmare gripped her and she woke with no idea where she was. There were different unaccountable sounds to be heard, and the terrifying conviction that she'd lost Scout.

She thrashed around on a bed she didn't know, grappling with an eiderdown she didn't remember, and was drenched in ice-cold sweat as she called Scout's name…

'Liz? Liz!' A lamp flicked on and Cam stood over her, wearing only sleep shorts. 'What's wrong?'

'I've lost Scout,' she gasped. 'Where am I?'

He sat down on the bed and pulled her up into his arms. 'You haven't lost Scout, and you're safe and sound on my boat. Remember? *Leilani* and Whitehaven Beach? Remember the sunset?'

Shudders racked her and her mouth worked.

'Scout is safe at home with Daisy and Archie and your mother at Yewarra.'

Very slowly the look of terror left her eyes and she closed them. 'Oh, thank heavens,' she breathed. Her lashes flew up. 'Are you sure?'

'Quite sure.' He said it into her hair. 'Quite sure.'

'Hold me—please hold me,' she whispered. 'I couldn't bear it if I lost Scout.'

'You're not going to lose her,' he promised. 'Hang on.' He unwound the eiderdown and lay down with her in his arms, pulling it over them. 'There. How's that?'

Liz moved against him and found the last remnants of the nightmare and her sense of dislocation leave against the security of the warmth and bulk of his body, the strength of his arms around her.

'That's wonderful.' She laid her cheek on his shoulder. 'Do you still want to marry me?'

'Liz…?' He lifted his head to look into her eyes. 'Yes. But—'

'Then do it—please. Don't take any nonsense from

me. I can be stubborn for stubborn's sake sometimes. Don't let me go—oh! I'm still dressed!'

'Liz, stop.'

He held her close, staring into her eyes with his mouth set firmly until she subsided somewhat, although she was still shivering every now and then.

'Yes, you *are* still dressed,' he said quietly. 'I don't take advantage of sleeping girls. And I don't think we should make any earth-shattering decisions right now, either. You were over-tired, overwrought, and you got a fright. So let's just take things slowly,' he said dryly, and moved away slightly.

She flinched inwardly, because whatever she might have been one thing had become crystal-clear to her through it all. Cam Hillier was her answer. Not for Scout's sake—for her sake. He not only made her feel safe, he attracted her like no other man ever had...

'Do you mean share this bed chastely?' she said huskily. 'I don't think I can. I think I've gone beyond that. You can always claim I seduced you if—if it's not what you want, too.'

He took a ragged breath. 'Not what I *want*?' he repeated through his teeth. 'If you had any idea, Cinderella...'

'Cinderella?' Her eyes widened.

He shrugged. 'It wasn't so far from midnight when I put you to bed.'

'Damn,' she said.

He lifted a surprised eyebrow at her.

'I was planning—well, I was thinking along the lines of being a birthday surprise for you. If things fell out that way. I mean, it wasn't a set-in-concrete kind of plan—more just a thought.' She trailed off, thinking that—heaven help her!—it was true.

He was silent for so long she looked away and bit her lip.

Then he said, 'Liz, I'm not made of steel.'

She looked back. 'Neither am I,' she said, barely audibly, and laid her hand on his cheek. 'I want to be held and kissed. I want to be wanted. I want to be able to show you how much I want you. Do you know when you first brought me out in goosebumps? A few days after I started working for you, when I tripped on the pavement and you caught me. Remember?'

She waited as his eyes narrowed and she saw recognition come to them.

'So I've actually been battling this thing between us longer than you have. Think of that.'

He groaned and pulled her very close. 'Don't say I didn't put up a fight,' he warned, and buried his face in her hair.

'I knew it would be like this,' Cam said.

'Like what?'

They were lying facing each other. The eiderdown had hit the carpet, along with Liz's maxi-dress and her bikini briefs—all she'd worn under it.

Her hair was spread on the pillow and looked almost ethereally fair in the lamplight.

He drew his fingers down between her breasts. 'That you'd be pale and satiny, as well as slim and elegant and achingly beautiful.'

She caught his hand and raised it to her lips. 'I sort of suspected you'd be the stuff a girl's dreams are made of. As for these—' she kissed his hand again '—I love them. They've played havoc with my equilibrium at times. They are now.'

'Like this?' He took his hand back and traced the outline of her flank down to the curve of her hip.

She caught her bottom lip between her teeth as his hand strayed to her thigh. 'Yes, like that,' she said, as those exploring fingers slid to an even more intimate position on her body. She gasped and wound her arms round his neck as all sorts of lovely sensations ran through her.

'Cam...' she said on a breath, and all playfulness left her—because she was body and soul in thrall to what he was doing to her, and because she knew he wanted her as much as she wanted him.

She could feel them moving to the same drumbeat as their bodies blended together. She could feel the powerful chemistry between them. She could glory in all the fineness of Cam's sleek powerful body, and she did. She traced the line of that dark springy hair down his torso, as she'd pictured herself doing not many days ago. She pressed her breasts against the wall of his chest and slid her leg between his.

She was overtaken by a feeling of joy as they touched, tasted and held each other. She felt like a flame in his arms—hot and desirable, then light as quicksilver. She felt wanton in one breath and irresistible to him in the next—incandescent, and totally abandoned to the pleasure he was bringing her.

Their final union brought her close to tears as the pleasure mounted to a star-shot pitch, but he held her and guided her with all the finesse and strength and control she'd probably always known Cameron Hillier would bring to this act. So that even while she was helpless with pleasure she knew she wasn't alone. She felt cherished at the same time…

'Mmmm,' he said when they were still at last. 'That was worth the wait.'

Liz put her hand on his shoulder and kissed the long, strong column of his throat. 'That was… I can't tell you… It was too wonderful to put into words.'

He traced the outline of her mouth with one long finger and looked consideringly into her eyes. 'I could try. You, my sweet, prickly, gorgeous-all-rolled-into-one Liz, created a bit of heaven on earth for me.'

She smiled and smoothed her palm on his shoulder. 'Thank you.' A tiny glint of laughter lurked in her eyes. 'But I couldn't have done it without you.'

She felt the jolt of laughter that shook him. 'No?'

'No. And you do know I'm teasing you, don't you? Because I was utterly at your mercy, Mr Hillier.'

'Not so, Miss Montrose. Well,' he amended, 'let's split the credit.'

'Sounds fair enough,' she said gravely, but all of a sudden she sobered as it came back to her—what she'd said about marrying him.

'Liz?'

She looked up into his eyes to see that he too had sobered, and that there was a question mark in their blue depths. For a moment it trembled on her lips to tell him that she'd fallen deeply in love with him—that she probably had way back, despite everything to the contrary she'd told herself.

But a remnant of fear generated from her past held her silent. Just take it slowly, she thought. Yes, she'd done it again—given herself to a man. And it was so much more than sex for her, but—for the time being anyway—should she protect herself by being the sole possessor of that knowledge?

'Nothing,' she breathed, and buried her face in his shoulder.

They had two more days on *Leilani*.

They moved the next morning to an anchorage protected from the strong winds predicted—this time to a rocky bay with turquoise waters and its own reef.

They swam and fished. They went ashore in the rubber dinghy and climbed to a saddle between the hills, from where they could see a panoramic view of the Whitsundays. They snorkelled over the coral. They paddled the light portable canoes *Leilani* carried.

Liz almost lived in her ice-blue bikini. She wore a borrowed baseball cap when they streaked across the water in the dinghy. She donned a long-sleeved white blouse as protection against the sun, and wore her sunhat on the boat. She reserved her maxi-dress for the evening.

The one thing they didn't do was discuss marriage again.

It puzzled Liz—from both their points of view. Her

unwitting reluctance to bring the subject up, and whatever reason Cam had for not doing so either. In fact a couple of times she caught him watching her with a faint frown in his eyes, as if he couldn't quite make her out. On both occasions she felt a little tremor of unease. But then he'd be such a charismatic companion she'd forget the unease and simply enjoy being with him on his beautiful boat.

One thing she particularly enjoyed was seeing him relax, and the feeling that had already occurred to her came alive in her again—Cam Hillier needed rescuing from himself. Could she do it on a permanent basis? Could she find the key to making a life with him that would be satisfying enough to ease him from the stratosphere he inhabited and which she had the strong feeling he was growing to hate?

She had to smile dryly at the thought, however. Who was to say her demons would ever let her go enough to be able to share *any* kind of a life with him?

And then it all came apart at the seams…

He said to her, apropos of nothing, 'There's no one else anchored here today.'

They were lying on loungers on the back deck. Liz looked around. 'So there isn't.' Then she sat up with a faint frown. 'You said that with a peculiar sort of significance.'

He moved his sunglasses to the top of his head. 'I have this fantasy.' He shrugged. 'I suppose you could say it involves mermaids.'

Liz studied him, but he was looking out over the

water. 'Go on. What has that to do with no one else being here?'

'We could skinny-dip.'

She took a breath. 'But we're not mermaids—or mermen,' she pointed out.

'All the better, really.'

'Cam—' She didn't go on.

'Liz?' He waited a moment. 'The problem is—my problem is—I'd love to see your naked body in the water.'

Liz looked down at herself. 'It's not a hugely camouflaging bikini.'

'Still…'

She looked out over the water. It looked incredibly inviting as it sparkled under a clear sky and a hot sun. Why not?

She rose noiselessly, stepped out of her bikini, and climbed down to the duckboard where she dived into the water before Cam had a chance even to get to his feet.

'Come in,' she called when she surfaced. 'It feels wonderful.'

It did, she thought as she floated on her back, but not as wonderful as when he dived in beside her and took her in his arms.

'Good thinking?' he asked, all sleek and wet and tanned, and strong and quite naked.

'Brilliant thinking,' she conceded. 'I feel like a siren,' she confessed as she lay back in the water across his arm.

'You look like one.' He drew his free hand across

the tips of her breasts, then put his hands around her waist and lifted her up. She laughed down at him with her hands on his shoulders as she dripped all over him. Then she broke free and swam away from him.

'You swim like a fish,' he called when he caught up with her. 'And you make love like a siren—come back to the boat.'

'Now?'

'Yes, now,' he said definitely.

Liz laughed, but she changed direction obediently and swam for the boat.

He followed her up the ladder, and when they reached the deck he picked her up and carried her, dripping wet, down to his stateroom, where he laid her on the bed.

'Cam,' she protested, 'we're making a mess.'

'Doesn't matter,' he growled as he lay down beside her and took her in his arms. 'This—what I desperately want to do with you—is not for public consumption.'

'There was no one there—and it was your idea anyway.'

'Perhaps—but not this. There. Comfortable?' he asked as he rolled her on top of him.

Liz took several urgent breaths, and her voice wasn't quite steady as he cradled her hips and moved against her. 'I don't know if that's the right word for it. It's…' She paused and bit her bottom lip. 'Sensational,' she breathed.

He withdrew his hands from her hips and ran them through her hair, causing a shower of droplets. They both laughed, then sobered abruptly as they began to kiss each other and writhe against each other with desperate need.

It was a swift release, that brought them back to earth gasping. Liz, at least, was stunned at the force of the need that had overtaken them. She was still breathing raggedly as they lay side by side, holding each other close.

'Where did th-that come from?' she asked unsteadily as she pulled up the sheet.

He smoothed her hair. 'You. Being a siren.'

'Not you? Being a merman?'

'I don't think there is such a thing.'

'All the same, do you really mean that? About me being a siren? It's the second time you've—well, not *accused* me of it, but something—' she hesitated '—something similar.'

She felt the movement as he shrugged, but he said nothing. In fact she got the feeling he was somewhat preoccupied. She got the feeling from the way he was watching her that he was waiting for something…

She pushed herself up and rested her elbow on the pillow, her head on her hand. 'Is something wrong?' She slipped her fingertips over the smooth skin of his shoulder.

He stared expressionlessly into her eyes, then he said, 'You're right. We have made a mess. Let's strip the bed and remake it. But have a shower first.' He threw back the sheet and got up.

Liz hesitated, feeling as if she'd stepped into a minefield. She studied his long, strong back for a moment as he reached into a cupboard for clothes. Then, with a mental shake of her head, she got up in a few quick movements and slipped past him into her stateroom, with its *en-suite* shower. She closed the door—something she wouldn't usually have done.

He didn't take issue with it.

They remade the bed in silence.

Liz had put on a pair of yellow shorts with a cream blouse and tied her hair back. He'd also donned shorts, and a black T-shirt. The tension that lay between them was palpable.

How? Why? Liz wondered.

She didn't get the opportunity to answer either of those questions as his phone rang—it was never far away from him. It was Roger, and when Cam clicked it off she knew from his expression and the few terse questions he'd posed that it was something serious.

She clutched her throat. 'Scout?' she whispered.

'Liz, *no*. She's fine. So is Archie. But Mrs Preston had been hospitalised with heart problems. I made her promise to get a check-up when you said you were worried about her.'

Liz's hand fell away. 'Oh,' she breathed, in a mixture of intense relief and concern.

'There's more. Daisy's got the flu.'

'Oh, no! So who…?'

'Your mother has taken command, with the help of Bob's wife, but I think we should go back as soon as we can.'

'Of course.' Liz looked around a little helplessly. 'But how soon can that be?'

He was already on his mobile. 'Roger's organising a flight from Hamilton. Hello, Rob?' he said into the phone. 'Listen, mate, I need to get home ASAP. Organise a chopper to pick us up off Whitehaven Beach. Come on it yourself, and you can sail *Leilani* back to Hamilton.'

Liz's mouth had fallen open at these instructions. She closed it but got no chance to comment.

'OK,' Cam said, 'let's up anchor. It'll take us about half an hour to get to Whitehaven.'

'What if there are no helicopters available?'

He looked at her, as if to say, *You didn't really say that, did you?* 'Then he'll buy one.'

'Oh, come on!' Liz clicked her tongue. 'You don't expect me to believe that?'

'Believe it or not, Ms Montrose, it's something I have done before.' He paused and looked around. 'Would you mind packing for both of us?'

Liz stared at him, but she recognised this Cam Hillier, and she turned away, saying very quietly, 'Not at all.'

She didn't see him hesitate, his gaze on her back, or see his mouth harden just before he left the stateroom.

Liz stood in the same spot for several minutes.

She heard the powerful motors fire up. She heard above that the whine of the electric winch and the rattle of the anchor chain as it came up. All sounds she knew now.

She felt the vibration beneath her feet change slightly as he engaged the gears and the boat got underway...

She licked a couple of tears from her upper lip—because something had gone terribly wrong and she had no idea what it was. *Ms Montrose*, she thought. Had she gone back to that? *Why* had she gone back to that?

Why this almost insane rush to get home? Yes, when he made up his mind to do something he often did it at a hundred miles an hour—and it wasn't that she didn't want to get home as soon as possible—but *this*?

Wouldn't they be alone together any more? What about that fierce lovemaking? Where did that fit in?

She buried her face in her hands.

They got back to Yewarra after dark that same evening.

Roger had organised a flight for them on a private jet from Hamilton Island with a business associate of Cam's. The associate was on the flight, so there'd been no chance of any personal conversation. And they'd flown from Sydney to Yewarra on the company helicopter—ditto no personal conversation.

Liz was unsure whether it had been fortuitous or otherwise.

Both Scout and Archie were already in bed and asleep, but Mary Montrose was there to greet them. And she had assurances that Daisy was resting comfortably and so was Mrs Preston, although she was still in hospital.

Liz hugged her mother and Cam shook her hand.

'Thanks so much for stepping into the breach, Mrs Montrose,' he said to her, and Liz could see her mother blossoming beneath his sheer charm. 'I hope you've moved into the house?'

'Yes,' Mary said, 'along with Scout. Although only

into the nursery wing. I guess you'll stay there too?' she said to Liz.

'Uh—actually,' Cam said, 'Liz and I have some news for you. We've agreed to get married.'

CHAPTER NINE

'HOW COULD YOU?'

They were in his study with the door closed. It was a windy night, and she could hear trees tossing their branches and leaves outside, as well as occasional rumbles of distant thunder

Liz was stormy-eyed and incredulous, despite the fact that her mother had greeted Cam's news with effusive enthusiasm before faltering to an anxious silence as she'd taken in her daughter's expression.

Then she'd said, 'I'll leave you two alone,' and gone away towards the nursery wing.

'It's what you told me to do,' he countered, lying back in his chair behind the desk. *'"Don't take any nonsense from me,"'* he quoted. *'"I can be stubborn for stubborn's sake."* Remember, Liz?' He raised a sardonic eyebrow at her and picked up his drink—he'd stopped to pour them both a brandy on their way down to the study.

Despite the drink, Liz couldn't help feeling that to be back in his study, on the opposite side of his desk from him, was taking them straight back to an employer/employee relationship, and it hurt her dreadfully.

'There's nothing wrong with my memory,' she said

helplessly, then took a breath to compose herself. 'I also remember—not that many hours ago—being all of a sudden being frozen out after we'd slept together as if we'd never get enough of each other. The last thing I expected after that was to be told I planned to marry you.'

'But you do, don't you, Liz? Because of Scout.'

Liz paled. 'But you knew,' she whispered. 'You yourself told me that you needed a mother for Archie and I needed security for Scout.'

He got up abruptly and carried his glass over to the paintings on the wall. He stared at one in particular—the painting of a trawler with the name of *Miss Miranda*. 'I didn't know I was going to feel like this.'

She stared at him. He was gazing at the picture with one hand shoved in his pocket and tension stamped into every line of his body. Even his expression was drawn with new lines she'd never seen before.

'Like what?' she queried huskily.

He turned to her at last. 'As if I've got my just desserts. As if after playing the field—' his lips twisted with self-directed mockery '—after having a charmed life where women were concerned, being able to enjoy them without any deep commitment, I've finally fallen for one I can't have.'

Her eyes grew huge and her lips parted in astonishment. 'C-can't have?' she stammered.

He smiled briefly, and it didn't reach his eyes. 'You're doing it again, Liz. Repeating things.'

'Only because I can't believe you said that. You have—we have—I don't know how much more you could want.' Tears of confusion and desperation beaded her lashes.

He came back and sat down opposite her. 'I thought it would be enough to have you on any terms, Liz. That's why I lured you into the job up here at Yewarra. That's why—' he gestured '—I played on your insecurity over Scout. Only to discover that when you agreed to marry me you had Scout on your mind, not me. I didn't want that.'

She gasped, and her mind flew back to the first time they'd made love—to their first night on the boat and the nightmare she'd had. Flew back to his initial resistance that she, in her unwisdom, had not given enough thought to.

'You should have told me this then.'

'I nearly did. I *did* tell you I wasn't made of steel,' he said dryly. 'I didn't seem able to also admit that I was a fool—an incredible fool—not to know what had happened to me.'

'What about this morning? Was it only this morning?' she breathed. 'It seems like an eon ago.'

'This morning?' he repeated. 'What I really wanted this morning was to hear you say you loved me madly, in a way that I could believe it.'

Liz let out a long, slow breath. 'What I don't understand now is why you told my mother we were planning to marry.'

He drummed his fingers on the desk. 'That was a devil riding me. But I am prepared to give you the protection of my name if you feel it will safeguard Scout from her father. It'll be a marriage of convenience, though.' He shrugged.

'Is that what you think I want?' she whispered, paper-pale now.

He raised an eyebrow. 'Isn't it?'

Her lips trembled, and she got slowly to her feet as every fibre of her being shouted at her to deny the charge. Why couldn't she say no? It's *not* what I want. Why couldn't she tell him she'd fallen deeply and ir-revocably in love with him?

Because she had no proof? Because she saw now in hindsight that the way things had played out it *did* look as if she'd been angling for marriage because of Scout?

Because she was still unable to bare her soul to any man?

'No, it's not what I want,' she said, barely audibly. 'Cam.' She swallowed. 'It's over. We'll leave first thing tomorrow morning. It—it could never have worked be-tween us. Too many issues.' She shook her head as a couple of tears coursed down her cheeks. 'I told you once you'd be mad to want to get involved with me. I was right. Not that I blame you for the mess I...I am.' She turned away, then turned back. *'Please,'* she begged, 'just let me go.'

'Liz—' he said harshly, but she fled out of the study.

CHAPTER TEN

'WHERE'S ARCHIE?' Scout said plaintively. 'And where's 'Nonah's puppy? Why can't I play with them any more?' She looked around her grandmother's flat discontent-edly. 'I don't like this place.'

Liz sighed inwardly.

It was three weeks since they'd left Yewarra—a heart-wrenching move if ever there'd been one, as she'd thought at the time.

She could still see in her mind's eye Archie, stand-ing at the dolphin fountain waving goodbye, looking pale and confused. She could still see Cam, standing beside him but not waving, as she'd driven Scout and her mother away.

She could still remember every word of the stilted last interview she'd had with Cam, during which he'd insisted on paying her three-month contract out.

She could particularly recall the almost irresistible urge she'd had to throw herself into his arms and beg him to take her on any terms, even if she were unable to tell him what he wanted to hear. She closed her eyes in pain every time she thought of it...

She couldn't get out of her mind the thought of Cam

Hillier needing help to stabilise his life and how she was too emotionally crippled to give it to him.

In the three weeks since that parting she'd lost weight, she'd slept little, and she'd done battle with herself over and over. Had she walked away from a man who loved her for no good reason? On the other hand, would he ever trust her?

Her mother had been an absolute stalwart, doing her very best to make the dislocation more bearable for both her and Scout, but Liz knew she would have to make some changes. She couldn't go on living with her mother in the way she had. Mary was obviously very close to her new beau, Martin. She was also knee-deep in concert costumes.

But it had been a week before Liz had even been able to pull herself together and start looking for an alternative life and a job.

She'd got in touch with the agency she'd worked for and put herself back on their books. So far nothing had come up, but she had got her old weekend job as a restaurant receptionist back. Next thing on her list was a flat of her own.

It was not long after Scout had made her displeasure with their new life known that the phone rang. It was the agency, with an offer of a diary secretary position for two weeks starting the next day.

Liz accepted it after consulting her mother, although she was dreading getting back on the old treadmill. And the next morning she presented herself at a suite of offices in the city, the home of Wakefield Inc—a company that operated a cargo shipping line.

She was, she'd been told, replacing the president's diary secretary, who had fallen and broken a leg. That was all she knew.

As always for work, she'd dressed carefully in a fresh suit with a pretty top. But her hair was tied back and she wore her glasses.

She was greeted by a receptionist, whose name-plate labelled her as Gwendolyn, as she stepped out of the lift, and was ushered immediately towards the president's office when she'd explained who she was.

'In you go,' Gwendolyn said cheerfully. 'He's asked to see you immediately.'

Liz took a deep breath and hesitated. She could partly see into the office, and it looked quite different from the last office she'd worked in. No pictures of horses and trawlers that she could see, and a completely different colour scheme—beige carpet, beige walls and a brown leather buttoned settee. The desk was hidden from her, and she took another deep breath and walked through the door—only to find herself almost fainting from sheer shock.

Because it was Cam Hillier who sat behind the desk belonging to the president of Wakefield Inc—a company she'd never heard of before yesterday.

She stopped as if shot.

He got up and came round the desk towards her. 'Liz,' he said quietly. 'Come in.'

'Y-you?' she stammered. 'I don't understand.'

He smiled briefly. 'It's the company I bought while you were up at Yewarra. Remember?'

Her eyes were huge and her face was pale as her lips

worked but no sound came. She stared at him. He was formally dressed, in a navy suit she recognised. He was as dynamic and attractive as he'd ever been—although she thought he looked pale too.

'I—I don't understand,' she repeated. 'I'm supposed to be temping for someone who's broken a leg.'

'I made that up. I also asked for you personally.'

She blinked. 'You…you got me here deliberately? Why?' she asked hoarsely.

'Because I can't live without you. I need you desperately, Liz.' He put a hand out as she rocked on her feet, and closed it around her arm to steady her. 'Archie can't live without you. None of us can. So we'd be grateful for anything you can give us, but you have to come back.'

'Anything?' she whispered.

And whether it was the shock of seeing him again when she'd never expected to, or the shock of discovering he'd sought her out, it was as if some unseen hand had turned a key in her heart and everything she'd longed to say but been unable to came pouring out…

'Don't you understand? I would never have slept with you if I didn't love you. That's the way I'm made. I know—I know it looked as if it was all about Scout, but it wasn't. It was *you*. It was you from way back.'

Tears were pouring down her cheeks and she was shaking.

'Liz.' He put his arms around her, and despite her tears she could see that he was visibly shaken too, 'Liz, my darling…'

'I don't know why I couldn't say this before,' she wept. 'I *wanted* to, but—' She couldn't go on.

'I understand. I always understood,' he said softly. 'I just couldn't help myself from rushing my fences at times.'

'I'm surprised you don't hate me,' she said, distraught.

His lips twisted. 'Maybe this will reassure you more than any words,' he murmured, and took off her glasses. He started to kiss her—her tear-drenched cheeks, her brow and her mouth.

When they finally drew apart Liz was breathless, but her tears had stopped and she looked up at him in wonderment. 'It—it *is* real,' she said tentatively.

'I really love you,' he said. 'I've never felt this way before. As if I'm finally making the right music. As if the rest of the world can go to hell so long as I have you.'

He traced the outline of her swollen mouth with his forefinger. 'I never told you this—I've never told anyone this—but my parents were soul mates, and I've been looking for my soul mate for a long time. So long I didn't think it was going to happen. Until I met you.'

Liz moved in his arms. 'I had no idea.'

'Remember when you offered to take me apart?' he asked, with a wryly lifted eyebrow.

'I didn't! Well—' she shook her head '—if you say so.'

He grinned. 'That was when the danger bells started to ring for me. Although, to be honest—' he looked rueful '—when you climbed over my wall I had an inkling there could be something special about you.'

Liz gasped. 'But...'

He shrugged. 'Don't ask me why. I guess it's the way these things happen. But by the time I got you to Yewarra it was more than danger bells. It was the growing conviction that you and you alone were going to be that special one for me—if only I could get you to see it—if only I could get you to trust me.'

Liz closed her eyes and rested her head on his shoulder. 'I'm sorry.'

He kissed her lightly, then took her hand and drew her over to the buttoned settee, where they sat down with their arms around each other.

'Don't be sorry,' he said. 'Marry me instead.'

Liz laid her cheek on his shoulder. 'I can't think of anything I would rather do, but—' she sat up suddenly, and looked into his eyes with a tinge of concern in her own '—I do know I can be difficult—'

'So do I,' he interrupted. 'I've seen it. Outspoken, for example. Fighting mad at times. However, since I'm such a model of patience, so easy-going, so tolerant, so predictable, et cetera, we should complement each other.'

'Patient? Tolerant? Predictable?' Liz stared at him in disbelief, then she started to laugh. 'For a moment I thought you actually believed that,' she gurgled. 'Oh, Cam, you can be totally unpredictable, intolerant and impatient, but you can also be—in lots of ways—my hero, and I love you so very much!'

He held her as if he'd never let her go. And the magic started to course through her—the assault on her senses, the thrilling, magnetic effect he'd had on her almost from the beginning claimed her.

They could have been on the moon, she thought, as they revelled in each other. It was as if the world had melted away and all that mattered was that they'd found each other.

It was when they finally drew apart that Cam said, 'We need to get out of here.'

'Yes.' Liz pushed her hair back—he'd taken it down, and there were clips scattered she knew not where. 'Yes. But it might look—funny.'

'No, it won't.' He helped her to her feet and patted her collar down. 'Well, you did come in looking all Ice Queen, but now you look gorgeous so I don't suppose anyone will mind.'

'Cam,' she breathed, as colour came into her cheeks, but said no more as he kissed her, then took her hand and led her to the door—and once more demonstrated how unpredictable Cameron Hillier could be.

There were several people in the reception area, grouped around the reception desk. They all greeted Cam with the deference that told Liz they were employees.

He returned the greetings and rang for the lift then said to Gwendolyn, 'Gwen, may I introduce you to my future wife? This is Liz. Oh, and by the way, I won't be in for a couple of weeks, maybe even months. If anything seems desperate get hold of Roger Woodward at Hilliers, he'll sort it out.'

There was dead silence and several mouths hanging open for a couple of seconds then Gwen shot up and scooted round her desk to shake Liz's hand as well as Cam's. 'I'm so happy for you both!' she enthused. 'Not that I realized—or knew anything about it—still, all the very best wishes!' And she pumped Cam's hand again.

Another devoted employee in the making, Liz thought wryly but she was warmed as everyone else shook hands and they finally stepped into the lift.

'Poor Roger,' she said as they descended to the car park.

Cam looked surprised.

'He'll probably be tearing his hair out soon. I know the feeling,' she explained.

He took her hands. 'I apologize for all my former sins,' he said gravely. 'But there was one thing I nearly did that I narrowly, very narrowly, restrained myself from doing.'

She looked up at him expectantly.

'This.' He took her in his arms then buried a hand in her hair and started to kiss her.

They didn't notice the lift stop or the doors open, they noticed nothing until someone clearing their throat got through to them.

They broke apart to discover they had an audience of four highly interested spectators, one of them with his finger on the open button.

'Different lift but that's exactly what I wanted to do,' Cam said to her then taking her hand again led her out into the car park, adding to the small crowd, 'Forgive us but we've just agreed to get married.'

And their little crowd of spectators burst into spontaneous applause.

Liz was pink-cheeked but laughing as they made their way to the Aston Martin. Laughing and full of loving.

They flew up to Yewarra the next morning. Mrs Preston and Daisy were there to greet them, both with tears in their eyes. Bob and his wife were at the helipad—even Hamish the head gardener was there. But it was Archie who really wrung Liz's heartstrings.

He hugged Cam first, then he hugged Scout but he stood in front of Liz looking up at her with all the considerable concern he was capable of and said, 'You won't go away again, will you, Liz? You won't take Scout away again, will you? 'Cause nothing feels the same when you're not here.'

Liz sank down on her knees and put her arms around Archie and Scout. 'No. We won't go away again, I promise.'

Archie stared into her eyes for a long moment and then, as if he'd really received the reassurance he wanted, he turned to Scout. 'Guess what, Golly and Ginny have had more kids! Want to see them?'

Scout nodded and they raced off together towards the menagerie.

Liz rose to her feet and Cam took her hand. 'Thanks,' he said huskily. 'Thanks.'

They were married on Whitehaven Beach several weeks later.

Liz and Cam, with Archie and Scout and the marriage celebrant, arrived by helicopter. The guests had set out on *Leilani* and another boat from Hamilton Island earlier and were ferried to the beach by tender.

The bride wore a dress her mother had made, a glorious strapless gown of ivory lace and tulle and she had flowers woven into her hair. The bridegroom wore a cream suit. Scout and Archie both wore sailor suits. Everyone was shoeless.

Mary Montrose couldn't have looked happier. Narelle Hastings with bronze streaks in her hair to match her outfit looked faintly smug and she mntioned several times to anyone who'd listen that she'd known this was on the cards right from the beginning. Daisy and Mrs Preston were tearful again but joyfully so. So was Molly Swanson. Even Roger Woodward upon whose shoulders the organization of this unusual wedding had fallen looked happy and uplifted.

Although, he still had to get everyone safely back to Hamilton apart from the wedding party, he reminded himself, and who would have thought Cameron Hillier and Lizbeth Montrose would be so unconventional?

He clicked his tongue then had to smile as he recalled their faces when they'd told him what they wanted. They'd both been alight with love and laughter.

And now, as the sun sank, they were pronounced man and wife and as a hush fell over the guests, they stared into each other's eyes and it was plain to see that at that moment they only existed for each other as the sky turned to liquid gold and so did the water.

Then the spell was broken and the business of ferrying everyone back to *Leilani*, where a feast awaited them, began.

* * *

Several hours later, Cam and Liz farewelled their guests, who were returning to Hamilton Island on the second boat, all but two that was. Archie and Scout, both asleep now, would stay with them as they cruised the Whitsundays for the next couple of weeks.

They stood side by side as the second boat identifiable by its running lights negotiated the Solway Passage and disappeared from sight. All the guests were to spend two nights at the resort on Hamilton.

'So,' Cam put an arm around her, 'it went well. Even Roger managed to enjoy himself.'

Liz gurgled with laughter. 'Poor Roger! Yes, it went well.' She leant against him. 'Do you feel married?'

He looked down at her somewhat alarmed. 'Don't you?'

'I do.' She turned her face up to him. 'I really do.'

He cupped her cheeks, kissed her lightly, then swept her into his arms.

Twelve months later Yewarra was looking its best after good rain that had given all the gardens a boost for their final late summer flowerings.

Liz was wandering through the beds of massed roses, inhaling their delicate perfume when Cam came looking for her and he found her leaning against a tree trunk, day-dreaming.

He'd been away for a few days, and he'd just driven in. He'd discarded his suit jacket and loosened his tie and the sight of him, so tall and beautifully made, still, twelve months on, had the power to send her pulses racing.

'You're back,' she said and lifted her face for his kiss. She wore a floral summer dress that skimmed her figure, and sandals.

'You look good enough to eat,' he murmured. 'I'm not only back, I'm back where I belong.' He kissed her thoroughly then he linked his arm through hers and they started to stroll through the gardens. 'Missed me?'

She nodded but her lips curved into a smile as she thought about the changes in him. How he'd cut his work load down and what he couldn't he did mostly from home so that he was rarely gone from her, and then only for short stretches.

How he was so much more relaxed and able to enjoy their lifestyle. Not, she knew, that he wouldn't need different challenges from time to time but the frenetic pace of his previous life was a thing of the past.

As for herself, she couldn't be happier...

'How come you're so alone?' he queried as they strolled along. 'Not a kid in sight.'

'They were invited to a birthday party down the road. Daisy took them and stayed on to give a hand.'

He stopped and swung her round to face him, and frowned. 'Why do you look—I don't know—secretive?'

'Ah,' Liz said, 'so you noticed?'

His lips twisted. 'I notice everything about you, Liz Hillier. I always did. Hang on, let me guess.' He scanned her from head to toe but his gaze came back to rest on her face, her eyes particularly. 'It's a baby, isn't it?'

'It's a baby,' she agreed gravely.

He paused. 'How do you feel about that?' he asked slowly then.

'I'm over the moon.' She slipped her arms around his neck. 'Can I tell you why?'

'Of course…'

'I used to worry,' she said barely audibly, 'that I could never prove to you how much I loved you, I could only say it. But this is my proof. I want your baby with all my being.'

'Oh, Liz,' was all he said but she could see his heart in his eyes, and she knew that he really believed her.

He caught his breath as he saw the joy in her. 'Come,' he said, and she knew exactly what he had in mind.

They turned and walked away through the gardens to towards the house, hand in hand again.

MILLS & BOON

THE HEART OF ROMANCE

A ROMANCE FOR EVERY READER

ODERN

Prepare to be swept off your feet by sophisticated, sexy and seductive heroes, in some of the world's most glamourous and romantic locations, where power and passion collide.

STORICAL

Escape with historical heroes from time gone by. Whether your passion is for wicked Regency Rakes, muscled Vikings or rugged Highlanders, awaken the romance of the past.

EDICAL

Set your pulse racing with dedicated, delectable doctors in the high-pressure world of medicine, where emotions run high and passion, comfort and love are the best medicine.

ue Love

Celebrate true love with tender stories of heartfelt romance, from the rush of falling in love to the joy a new baby can bring, and a focus on the emotional heart of a relationship.

Desire

Indulge in secrets and scandal, intense drama and plenty of sizzling hot action with powerful and passionate heroes who have it all: wealth, status, good looks,…everything but the right woman.

EROES

Experience all the excitement of a gripping thriller, with an intense romance at its heart. Resourceful, true-to-life women and strong, fearless men face danger and desire - a killer combination!

To see which titles are coming soon, please visit

millsandboon.co.uk/nextmonth

JOIN US ON SOCIAL MEDIA!

Stay up to date with our latest releases, author news and gossip, special offers and discounts, and all the behind-the-scenes action from Mills & Boon...

 @millsandboon

 @millsandboonuk

 facebook.com/millsandboon

 @millsandboonuk

It might just be true love...

MILLS & BOON

MODERN

Power and Passion

Prepare to be swept off your feet by sophisticated, sexy and seductive heroes, in some of the world's most glamourous and romantic locations, where power and passion collide.

MILLS & BOON
Desire

Indulge in secrets and scandal, intense drama and plenty of sizzling hot action with powerful and passionate heroes who have it all: wealth, status, good looks…everything but the right woman.

LET'S TALK

Romance

For exclusive extracts, competitions
and special offers, find us online:

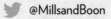

f facebook.com/millsandboon

🐦 @MillsandBoon

📷 @MillsandBoonUK

Get in touch on 01413 063232

For all the latest titles coming soon, visit
millsandboon.co.uk/nextmonth